Bright Lights for the West End Nannies

Pam Weaver has written more than fifteen books and is a Sunday Times bestselling author. Her new series, The West End Nannies, is based on her own experience in the 1960s, working in children's residential care, day nurseries and as a Hyde Park nanny. She began writing in the 1990s and likes to say that it only took her sixteen years to become an overnight success. She lives in Worthing and apart from writing, enjoys recycling gifted material into bags that are sold for charity.

Also by Pam Weaver

The West End Nannies

The West End Nannies
Bright Lights for the West End Nannies

Pam Weaver
Bright Lights for the *West End* Nannies

canelo
HERA

First published in the United Kingdom in 2026 by

Hera Books, an imprint of
Canelo Digital Publishing Limited,
20 Vauxhall Bridge Road,
London SW1V 2SA
United Kingdom

A Penguin Random House Company
The authorised representative in the EEA is Dorling Kindersley Verlag GmbH. Arnulfstr. 124,
80636 Munich, Germany

Copyright © Pam Weaver 2026

The moral right of Pam Weaver to be identified as the creator of this work has been asserted in
accordance with the Copyright, Designs and Patents Act, 1988.
All rights reserved. No part of this publication may be reproduced or transmitted in any form or
by any means, electronic or mechanical, including photocopy, recording, or any information
storage and retrieval system, without permission in writing from the publisher.
No part of this book may be used or reproduced in any manner for the purpose of training
artificial intelligence technologies or systems. In accordance with Article 4(3) of the DSM
Directive 2019/790, Canelo expressly reserves this work from the text and data mining exception.

A CIP catalogue record for this book is available from the British Library.

ISBN 9 781 83598 224 2

This book is a work of fiction. Names, characters, businesses, organizations, places and events are
either the product of the author's imagination or are used fictitiously. Any resemblance to actual
persons, living or dead, events or locales is entirely coincidental.

Cover design by Diane Meacham

Cover images © Alamy Stock Photo, Getty Images / iStock, Shutterstock.com

Printed and bound in Great Britain by Clays Ltd, Elcograf S.p.A.

Look for more great books at
www.herabooks.com | www.dk.com

I dedicate this book to three lovely brothers, Leon, Levi and Rocco who each had a life limiting disease and to their amazingly courageous mother, Charlotte, also to G-Ma, my friend Rosie, who wanted their names to be in a book.

Chapter 1

August 1964

'The Teddy Bear's Picnic'
Henry Hall & The BBC Dance Orchestra

Eighteen-year-old Rita Brownlow stepped back to survey the toddlers' dining room. It was perfect. The top table was covered in a bright yellow crepe paper tablecloth with beautifully scalloped edges and a line of confetti right down the middle. In front of every chair there was a paper plate and a party hat. The birthday girl, however, had a super-duper party crown and a special chair; to give it a more regal appearance, Rita had draped the chair with an old purple curtain and sprinkled a little confetti on the seat. Behind the birthday girl's chair, she had placed two adult-sized chairs.

The door opened and Christine, one of the newer student nursery nurses, came in. 'Wowzer,' she breathed. 'You've made this look really special.'

'It's meant to be special,' Rita said stoutly. 'It's not every day you turn five years old.'

Christine chuckled. 'Or that your new mummy and daddy are allowed to come to your birthday party.'

Rita nodded. 'I only wish that Jenny was here to see it,' she said. 'She did so much to help that child, giving her confidence, making her relax, helping her to move on.'

I

'And Jenny was…?'

'She was my old room-mate,' said Rita. 'She passed her National Nursery Exam Board qualification last summer. She's in private now. Some swanky place just off Park Lane.'

'Wowzer,' Christine said again. 'That's what I want to be – a private nanny.'

'You've got a way to go yet,' Rita cautioned as she readjusted a paper plate that had gone skew-whiff, while in her head she was thinking, *you and me both!*

Christine Andrews, a slender girl with a mop of unruly black hair, was less than six months into her two-year training course. She seemed a capable girl, thoroughly modern, who enjoyed dancing and going to the pictures. Christine was reliable and did her work well, and as far as Rita could recall, she hadn't yet fallen foul of Matron's temper.

As for Rita, she only had a couple more weeks in Harefield House before she finished her training altogether. She had taken her exam in May and passed with flying colours. Matron had given her a glowing reference which, on a recommendation from Jenny Lamar, her old room-mate, she had taken to the West End Nannies agency on her last day off. Rubbing shoulders with people who worked in fabulously upmarket places for titled, fabulously rich or famous people and listening to their stories was so inspiring that Rita was determined to do the same. How else could someone like her get to live in a large house or travel abroad? It was the stuff of dreams. Mrs Hunter, the proprietor, had subjected her to an hour-long interview, after which Rita had been accepted by the agency and she was now awaiting her first post. It felt as if she was in a kind of limbo – neither a nursery student not yet a fully-fledged nursery nurse, but by the middle of next week, she would be on her way.

There was a tradition that every child in Harefield House had a birthday party, the one day in the year when he or she was made to feel very special. For most of their time in the nursery, the children were seen as either one of the babies, a tweenie (aged between one year and three years old) or a toddler – just another child, who, having been placed in the care of the local council, had been admitted because their mother was sick, or the family was homeless, or perhaps they'd been neglected or abandoned.

On that special day, he or she wore a party hat far superior to everyone else's, they sat on the birthday chair at the top table and everybody sang 'Happy Birthday'. Cook would bake a birthday cake, with candles, and Surrey County Council funds would have bought them a birthday present. Usually it was something like a cuddly toy, or a game, maybe a football or occasionally a dolly. Today was no exception, apart from the fact that Maisie Thompson was up for adoption and her soon-to-be parents had been invited to the party as well.

All at once, they could hear the children coming back into the nursery after their run-around in the garden. 'You'd better give them a hand in the cloakroom while I go to the kitchen for the tea trolley.' Rita said.

The two girls parted.

Dora, the girl from the estate who worked in the kitchen, had loaded the tea trolley with the most amazing party food.

'Is it all ready?' Rita asked.

'I've put the cake under the upside down cake tin so she won't see it until the last minute,' said Dora. 'You can take the trolley now and I'll give you five minutes to settle everybody down, then I'll bring in the adults' tea. Is that all right?'

'Perfect,' said Rita. Taking the candles and the box of matches off the trolley and handing them back to Dora, she added apologetically, 'We'd better not do that.'

Dora gave her a puzzled frown but slowly the reasons why dawned on her, and her hand flew to her mouth. 'Oh crumbs, I'm sorry. I never gave it a thought.'

'It's okay,' Rita said quickly.

Maisie had come to the nursery about eighteen months ago. As a two-year-old she had suffered severe burns on her leg when a log fell out of an unguarded fire. She had been entirely alone in the flat where she lived when the accident happened. Her mother was nowhere to be seen but, thankfully, Maisie's screams as her nightdress caught fire were answered by concerned neighbours. An ambulance and the police were called and Maisie was rushed to hospital. After that, the poor child had spent months and months in hospital having treatments and skin grafts. It took a while to find her mother, and it turned out that she had a serious drinking problem. Eventually Mrs Thompson was prosecuted for child neglect and Maisie came into care.

Although there were no coal fires in the nursery because it had central heating, Maisie was understandably nervous around flames. If Mr Dacombe, the gardener, burned some rubbish at the bottom of the garden or if some other child had birthday candles on their cake, the girls made sure that Maisie was either nowhere near it or else they blocked her view.

Rita pushed the trolley towards the children's dining room where she was met by a rush of noisy and excited children scrambling for a place at the table. Maisie followed them, holding her prospective mother's hand as she guided her into the room. Maisie's soon-to-be father, Mr Osborne, who was grinning like a Cheshire cat, stepped aside to let Rita pass.

Rosemary Sherman, the new nursery warden who had replaced the formidable Miss Collins, clapped her hands and the children quietened down. Rita parked the trolley, then, after they had all said grace, she and the other nursery nurses, Christine, Julie, who was a year into her training, Bernice, Rita's room-mate, and Sister Morton, passed the plates of food around and everyone tucked in.

Rita had never seen Maisie looking so happy. When everyone had had their fill of peanut butter, egg and cress and honey sandwiches, cakes, chocolate fingers and jelly and ice cream, it was time to open her presents. Maisie received an Etch A Sketch board from Harefield House and Mr and Mrs

Osborne had bought her a Chatty Cathy doll in a pink and white striped dress. Once Mr Osborne had removed the doll from her box, he showed Maisie a small ring on her back. He encouraged Maisie to pull it and the doll said, 'Please take me with you.'

At first Maisie was startled and pushed it away but once she was convinced the doll wasn't alive, she pulled the ring a second time. 'I love you,' said the doll and Maisie was thrilled.

A couple of seconds later, Matron came into the room. An overweight woman, Matron Evans didn't spend a lot of time with the children, but she usually turned up for a special occasion. She spent some time talking to Mr and Mrs Osborne before looking across to Rita, and saying, 'Time for the birthday cake, I think.'

Rita uncovered the cake and set it down in front of Maisie. It was an amazing creation. Cook had made it look like an open Jack in the Box with a colourful cartoon character bursting from under the lid. There was an audible gasp from everyone in the room followed by enthusiastic applause. Maisie was delighted and so were her parents.

'That's amazing,' Mrs Osborne remarked.

'We have a very talented cook,' Matron said, her chest expanding as she took in a smug breath.

'It certainly looks better than one from Woolworth's,' a voice boomed out.

The clapping died down and everyone froze. The room went silent as Matron turned around slowly to face her staff. 'Who said that?'

Christine Andrews made an awkward acknowledgement with her hand half raised.

Matron frowned. 'That's quite enough of that, thank you very much,' she snapped. 'And I'll thank you to keep your opinions to yourself.'

Christine's face was scarlet as she hung her head.

Matron came to the table with five cake candles and a box of matches. Rita, who had bent down to tie young Peter's shoelace, glanced up to see all the staff looking from one to another. Everyone knew what would happen if she struck that match. Maise would most likely burst into tears or even worse be thrown into an absolute panic. What on earth was Matron thinking of? Had she really forgotten Maisie's history?

A voice in Rita's head was saying, *Do something, somebody do something...* But nobody moved. Closing her eyes for a split second, Rita knew there was only one course of action. *She* would have to be the one to stop Matron. She would have to be the one to say something.

'Excuse me, Matron,' Rita began quietly.

She was ignored. Matron fumbled with the match box.

'Matron,' she said, her voice a little louder. 'This is Maisie's cake, Maisie Thompson.'

Matron turned her head crossly. 'I'm perfectly aware of that!'

Rita positioned her arm between the cake and Matron's matches as she mouthed, '*The matches. She doesn't like fire.*'

'Get out of the way you stupid girl!' Matron snapped.

Rita glanced behind her at the birthday girl. Thank God Maisie hadn't yet noticed what Matron was doing. She turned and, putting her hand on top of the matchbox, she said, 'Maisie is afraid of fire.'

Rita saw the split second in Matron's eyes when the penny dropped, but then she saw something else. Naked anger. She had been made to look a fool in front of Mr and Mrs Osborne. One member of staff had made a flippant remark and another had questioned her authority. How would that look in front of Maise's new parents? They'd think she didn't know about the children in her care.

'Stuff and nonsense,' she said. 'She's well over that now and we can't have a birthday cake without candles.'

With that, she struck the match. Maisie heard the sound and a second later the room was filled with a plaintive cry. 'I don't like it! I don't like it!'

Mrs Osborne pulled the little girl into her arms. 'It's all right, darling. It won't come near you, Mummy's here.'

Blowing the match out and throwing the open box onto the trolley in a fit of temper, Matron turned on her heel and lumbered out of the room.

—

The next day was Rita's day off, the last she would have before she left the nursery for good. When the night nurse came in with a cup of tea to wake her room-mate Bernie, Rita got up too because she had to catch the train. That would be the last time too – not going to see Gran, she would still do that, but it was time to end their annual pilgrimage.

'Have a good day,' Bernie said as she headed for the nursery. 'Want me to save you some supper?'

'I think I'll be okay, thanks.'

Bernie nodded. 'Enjoy,' she called as she closed the door.

Rita smiled to herself. When nineteen-year-old Bernie had arrived in the nursery, even though her parents were posh, she looked as if she'd stepped out of a 1930s black and white film with her old fashioned 'frock' and ghastly permed hair. Bernie looked very different now. She wasn't exactly a beauty, but with her fair hair in a fabulous style cut by Dick from the Baker Street training school she was becoming a modern girl.

Apart from the slight incident with the birthday cake, Maisie's party had been a resounding success and for Rita, it felt good to end her time in Harefield House on a positive note. Nursery nurse training was not easy. She and her fellow students worked a ten-hour day, six days a week with two weeks holiday a year. For that she was paid the princely sum of £197, less £101 board and lodging a year. Rita was luckier than some. She had a small amount of money of her own so she could live a little less frugally than the others, except that she was a saver and had ambition.

It had been an awkward moment when Matron was about to light the birthday candles on Maisie's cake and because Rita knew she had embarrassed her, she had expected to be summoned to the office for a dressing down. Surprisingly, that didn't happen, but rather than feeling a sense of relief it left her with apprehension and anxiety. Matron didn't suffer fools gladly and she could be vindictive. Rita reassured herself though that she had already passed her exam so Matron couldn't do anything which would make a radical difference to her chances in life, and quite frankly, Rita had little respect for the woman.

Making sure her room was perfectly tidy and her bed well made, Rita went downstairs just before eight o'clock. First, she collected a dishcloth from under the sink in the kitchen and filled a screw top bottle with some water. She packed both into her bag and then she ate breakfast with some of the girls who told her that Matron was in a bit of a mood this morning. As soon as she'd finished, Rita made a quick getaway.

The train arrived on time, and from Worthing station she caught the Southdown bus to Offington Corner. It was a beautiful day but already she had a tightness in her chest and the beginning of a headache. There was no sign of Gran, so with a heavy heart she turned towards the entrance and made her way in.

Chapter 2

'It's Over'

Roy Orbison

It was nice here. The sun was warm and she could hear the sound of buzzing bees. It felt a bit like she was deep in the countryside, but she wasn't. She was in Durrington Cemetery.

When Rita had disembarked the train, she left her suitcase and a holdall in the left luggage department. It might have been simpler to go straight home and dump them there, but Rita had wanted a moment or two on her own up here before she and Gran met up for their annual pilgrimage.

The entrance was next to the chapel and archway. Rita gazed up at it with new eyes ever since someone told her they had been designed by Sir Giles Gilbert Scott, the same man who designed the iconic red telephone boxes which were dotted all over the country. From there she had walked up the hill towards her mother's grave. It wasn't far and she had spent the first few minutes cleaning her mother's headstone with the dishcloth using the water from the bottle. Now that was done and a few weeds disposed of, she sat on the bench to wait for her grandmother. There wasn't much birdsong, but she watched a large tortoiseshell butterfly settle on a field scabious flower nearby and in the distance, further up the hill, she thought she saw a rabbit lopping around the gravestones.

Rita leaned back and closed her eyes. This had to be the last time she came back like this, she really couldn't keep doing it. It took too much out of her. She'd loved her mother, of course she had, but she didn't want to keep coming back every July, year after year. It was far too painful and it was beginning to feel too much like an obligation for both of them. There were times when Rita wondered if her grandmother thought she would forget Mum if they didn't come up to her grave on the anniversary of her mother's death but Rita preferred to remember the good times rather than that awful day. They would lay flowers and then her Gran would say, 'she was took too soon' and Rita would struggle to swallow the tightness in her own throat.

Rita opened her eyes and even though she knew the words off by heart, she looked again at the inscription on her mother's head stone.

In loving memory of Valerie Anne Brownlow...

Rita had only been a child at the time; eleven years old and just a few weeks before had taken her 11-plus exam. She'd done her best but her examination mark was what they called a borderline pass, so the authorities had written to her mother saying they wanted her to go in for an interview. Her teacher had taken her into Worthing Town Hall where they'd sat with six other children and their teachers in the same predicament. Somewhere along the line, Rita had been told that there were only three places left in the grammar school so she knew that passing this interview was imperative. 'Just do your best,' Mum had said as she kissed her goodbye that morning. 'That'll be good enough for me.'

Rita had done her best and her headmistress had given out the results on that particular morning assembly. She had passed! She was going to Gaisford Girl's school on South Farm Road in the autumn. Rita was thrilled and couldn't wait to tell her mother when she got home from school. Mum may not have pressured her, but Rita knew it would mean the world to her and Gran if she made it into grammar school.

It had been an odd day, that day... It began well, with her favourite subjects; composition followed by music and movement, but as time went on things took a much darker turn. As she'd played in the school playground during the afternoon break, everybody became aware of a lot of police activity in the area. They had all gathered at the school fence as police cars, their bells clanging, raced along the road past the school. The teachers were talking among themselves about a robbery at the local shop. Rita's mum worked in a bank so she would be safely ensconced inside behind closed doors. Mum would be back home by four thirty so, excited to share her own news and dying to hear if her mum knew more about the robbery, Rita ran all the way home.

As she turned onto Tarring Road, there was a crowd of people outside her house. Some were her neighbours, but others were complete strangers. Rita began to feel nervous but she didn't know why. As she drew closer, people began whispering behind their hands and it seemed that everyone was looking at her.

When she pushed open the gate, a press cameraman leaned forward and took her picture. The bright flash startled her and made her jump. Rita heard Mrs Humphries, her friend Nat's mum, snap, 'There's no need for that young man!'

Rita and Nat used to play together but even though his mum was by the gate, there was no sign of Nat. Several other neighbours and the strangers remonstrated with the man who, it had to be said, looked a little sheepish by now. Who were these people? And why were they waiting outside her gate? Rita's heart began to thump. Biting back her tears, she ran up the path and into the house.

As she burst through the front door, there was a policeman standing in the kitchen. 'Oh!'

'Are you Rita?' he said gruffly.

By now Rita's heart was banging so hard in her chest she thought it would pop out, but she managed to give him a shy nod of her head.

'Your gran's in the dining room.'

When Rita walked in, several other people, mostly men in gabardine macs were standing around the room. Her gran was sitting at the table and as Rita came into the room she stood up.

'Oh Rita... Love,' she began. She looked a wreck. It was obvious she'd been crying which was very unnerving because Gran never cried – not ever.

'Where's Mummy?'

The men began to leave the room and Rita stared in horror and disbelief as her grandmother covered her face with her handkerchief and wailed out loud.

Recalling the moment now, Rita sighed deeply. This was why she had to stop this ritual. It was too painful and it brought back such tender memories. She willed herself not to start crying or she would be a complete mess by the time she returned to the nursery.

Shaking away the memory, Rita turned to look down the hill and saw Gran coming towards her; walking a little slower these days, perhaps, but still hale and hearty. Rita stood and waved.

As she waited for her grandmother, Rita looked back at her mother's head stone.

In loving memory of Valerie Anne Brownlow

20 April 1918 – 17 July 1956

Brutally murdered during a robbery in National
Provincial Bank, Goring.

R.I.P.

After they'd laid their flowers and her grandmother had said a few bleak words from some obscure poem over the grave (where on earth did she find them?), they both walked back down the hill to catch the bus home.

'Just before you came, I was thinking about Nat Humphries,' Rita said. 'Whatever happened to him?'

'No idea,' said Gran. 'Why do you ask?'

Rita shrugged. 'Just curious.'

Twenty minutes later they were sitting in the kitchen of the small two-up two-down cottage in Goring-by-Sea where Rita had spent the rest of her childhood after Mum died. Nothing had changed. The same old wallpaper (posies of flowers and teacups) and the same oil cloth on the table. The tired armchairs sported new cushion covers but everything else was stuck in a time warp.

Her grandmother had already prepared their meal and covered the bread and butter and cake with a damp tea towel. As soon as they got in, she turned on the oven and switched on the gas under the chip pan. Within minutes the home-made meat pie was heating up and the potato chips were bubbling away nicely. All her gran had left to do was make the tea.

'What will you do now you've finished your training?' Gran asked.

'I've applied to a nannies agency,' Rita explained. 'They're checking my references and then they'll recommend me to some clients.'

'What sort of people will you be working for?'

'Ideally somebody rich and famous,' Rita said with a chuckle. 'I'd like the opportunity to travel as well; to see other countries.'

'Go abroad?' Gran gasped. 'What, on your own? Are you sure you'll be safe? I mean you read such awful things in the *News of the World*.'

'Of course I will,' said Rita. 'Girls can do anything now, Gran. And besides, I won't be alone, will I? I'll be with the family I'm working for and looking after their children.'

Her grandmother put the full tea pot onto the stand with a flourish. 'Take a tip from me,' she said gravely. 'Always make sure you've got enough money to get yourself back home if you have to. Girls get taken advantage of, taken off as white slaves and all sorts. Make sure you can get away.'

Rita suppressed a smile as she covered her hand with hers. 'Gran, I'll be fine. I'll be fine.'

As they ate their meal, they talked of her mother again. 'Do you remember when…?' 'I still think about the day when we…' 'Whatever happened to that old chicken that used to try and follow her to work?'

When Rita brought that one up, her grandmother gave her an old-fashioned look. 'What do you *think* happened to it?'

'You didn't.'

'No, I didn't,' said Gran, 'but the fox did.'

They chuckled for a moment or two then Rita took a deep breath and told her gran she wanted to make this the last time she came back to the cemetery on the anniversary of the day mum died.

'I need to draw a line under it all, Gran,' she said apologetically. 'It's not that I want to forget Mum, of course I don't, but from now on I think I'd prefer to remember the good things about her. Is that all right?'

Rita held her breath. The last thing she wanted to do was upset her. Had she seemed callous or uncaring?

'I think you're quite right, love,' said Gran. 'It's time for us both to move on.'

'That doesn't mean I won't want to go up there sometimes,' Rita added hastily.

'I know, I know,' said Gran.

'I promise I won't forget her.'

'Neither will I, love. She was my daughter as well as your mum.'

As they hugged each other, Rita could feel her grandmother's tears on her own cheek. 'You're a good girl,' Gran whispered.

They finished their meal and had a cup of tea and then it was time to say goodbye.

'I've put my case in the left luggage office at Worthing station,' Rita said fishing in her handbag. The last time they had written to each other they had arranged that most of Rita's stuff should come back home until she was settled in her new post. 'Where shall I put the ticket?'

'Put in on the dubree,' said Gran. Rita smiled. Her grandmother always had weird names for things she'd temporarily forgotten. Thing-a-mee, whatsit, ooh-jar-capivit, they were all made up names, yet funnily enough, Rita always seemed to know what she meant. This time, the dubree was probably the mantelpiece. 'I'll ask Eddie to pick it up in his car.' Eddie was her gran's next-door neighbour.

'You will keep in touch,' said Gran as Rita put the ticket behind the clock.

'Of course I will! You're not getting rid of me that easily Granny,' she teased. 'I love you to bits.'

Placated, her grandmother nodded and smiled.

Just as she was leaving for the station, her grandmother pushed a brown paper parcel into her hands. 'I want you to have this,' she said.

Rita turned it over. 'What is it?'

'Open it when you get back.'

—

When Rita got back to the nursery, for the first time ever, she felt a tad uncomfortable in her bedroom. Something wasn't quite right, but it was something she couldn't quite put her finger on. Her dressing table, her bed and her chest of drawers looked much the same as she'd left them, but her hair brush was the wrong way round… and her hand cream was lying on top of the bed. Matron was a stickler for a tidy room, so everyone kept their things shipshape and Bristol fashion. If they didn't, she had the habit of stripping the bed and dumping everything on the floor. After that she would empty every drawer and put it on the top of the bedding and if you had really annoyed her, the things from the wardrobe would be on top of that! Rita knew to her cost that it took ages to put everything back in its place and then she would have to go and find Matron to ask her to come and inspect the room again. That was why she would never have left her hand cream on the bed like that. Somebody had obviously been in here rummaging through her things – but who would have done such a thing and what were they looking for? Could it be one of her room-mates? She'd shared a room with Bernie for almost a year and she couldn't imagine for one minute that she would touch anything that didn't belong to her without permission. Christine, the new girl, was an unknown quantity but she didn't seem to be the type of person to do that either.

Rita soon pinpointed what had been moved. She was left-handed but her brush was on the right side of the dressing table and some of her jumpers had been disturbed in her drawer. The book she was reading last night was on top of her pillow when she knew that for the sake of tidiness, she had slipped it *under* the pillow. The bookmark she'd used to keep her place was on the sheet below the pillow. Maybe someone had shaken the book to see if something was hidden inside?

It was a real puzzle, but nothing appeared to be missing.

A little later she was sitting on her bed, tearing the paper off the parcel her grandmother had given her. It turned out to be a framed photograph of her mother with a soldier. They were out in the country somewhere, standing together on a flat rock with what seemed to be a meadow all around them. Her mother looked about eighteen and beautiful. Even though the picture was in black and white, Rita could see in her mind's eye that her mother's chestnut hair, caught up at the sides with combs, gleamed in the sunlight. Shapely and attractive, her mother wore a floral dress with a swallow brooch on the collar, but much more importantly, she looked so, so happy. The soldier had his arm around her mum's slim waist and he had thrown his head, laughing. Tall and athletic-looking, he was deliciously handsome. His hair was cut very short but even so, he had a film star look about him. And he wasn't just any soldier – he was an American GI.

Rita had never really asked her mother about her father. Somehow, when she was only a child, it didn't seem that important. She just accepted the way things were. A couple of her friends at school had lost their fathers in the war and Rita just presumed the same thing had happened to her. One of her friends said her mum didn't like talking about her dad because it upset her, so, not wanting to upset her own mother, Rita never asked questions. As long as she could remember, it had always been just her and Mum and Gran.

Searching the folds of the wrapping paper she found a small piece of card. The writing on it was Gran's.

This is your mum when she was nineteen. She had just got engaged.

Rita picked up the picture again and looked carefully at her mother's left hand. She could just make out the shape of a ring on her finger. Or was it a ring? It looked a little odd. She returned to the card.

They didn't have a ring, so he made one of grass.

Yes, she could see it now. Just a slightly darker shade than her mum's finger; a small piece of grass. He must have carefully woven it together.

His name was Dexter and he was your dad.

Rita ran her finger over the glass. So that's what he looked like. *My dad*, she thought to herself. *Dexter. I wonder what happened to him?*

Rita looked at the card for a third and last time. Her grandmother had written,

When you want to know more just tell me.

Chapter 3

'I'm Into Something Good'

Herman's Hermits

Rita hadn't put the photograph of her parents on display because she couldn't face the inevitable questions from her room-mates Bernie and Christine, but that didn't stop her looking at it every now and then. Life was about to change anyway; she had less than a week left in Harefield House. Her NNEB was in the bag, and she would soon be living the life of Riley in some posh house in Mayfair or some such place.

Matron seemed particularly tight-lipped and grumpy but nobody knew why. It crossed Rita's mind that it might be because Miss Grimwold, the nursery supervisor, was coming on a visit. Matron always did get a little tense when she turned up, and the girls found her visits difficult as well. Miss Grimwold, famed for her magnificent hats, was quite an agreeable person but Matron always wanted to create a good impression. As a result, the whole nursery had to be perfect, so floors were scrubbed and polished to a mirror shine, the children's beds were lined up with a ruler, all the toys had to be thoroughly washed even though it may have only been done the day before and the children themselves had to wear their best clothes. It put an unnecessary strain on everyone that even the children themselves picked up on.

'I don't think Matron's in a bad mood because of Miss Grimwold. I think it's probably still because you pointed out that

Maisie didn't like candles in front of her new parents,' Bernie reminded her as they made the beds in the tweenie room.

'I'd forgotten about that,' said Rita. 'I don't understand why she would be so knocky about it. I didn't do it to embarrass her, I was thinking of poor Maisie.' She paused as a sudden thought came to mind. 'What about Christine? Matron was in a bad mood with her that day, too. Is she all right?'

'Matron took her into the office and gave her a dressing down,' said Bernie, 'then she stopped her two hours off duty.'

'So the poor girl had to work a twelve-hour shift with no break?'

Bernie nodded.

'Just for saying the cake was better than one from Woolworth's?' Rita snatched the dirty sheets from a bed and threw them to the floor in an angry gesture.

'You know what Matron's like,' said Bernie. 'She doesn't like anyone making comments, good or bad. We should all be seen and not heard.'

'That's illegal, you know, stopping our off-duty.'

'I know,' said Bernie, 'but who's going to say anything?'

They both knew Bernie was right. Matron was a bully, but nobody ever answered back because she could be so vindictive. If someone crossed her, she could make their lives a misery – perhaps even threaten them with the sack. It meant that every girl was at her mercy because Matron played on the fact that every single student in Harefield House wanted nothing more than to be a fully qualified nursery nurse. Rita tutted crossly to herself. That woman had too much power, which was another reason why she wanted to move on. Matron's pettiness was enough to get anyone down and Rita wanted to work where she would be treated with more respect.

Bernie pulled back the sheets on Billy's bed. 'Oh dear. He wet himself again.'

'I think he's having a rough time,' said Rita. 'He keeps asking for his gampy.'

'Whatever's that?'

Rita shrugged. 'No idea. His favourite toy perhaps?'

Bernie frowned crossly. 'So the poor little lamb has lost his mummy and his gampy.' She wiped the rubber sheet which protected the mattress with a Dettol-soaked cleaning cloth and dried it vigorously with a piece of towelling. 'Why don't social workers think of these things when they bring the children into care?'

'Probably because they've got a thousand and one other things to think about,' said Rita shaking her head.

'That's all very well,' Bernie went on, 'but I think people in that role should behave more professionally. Don't they understand the effect being separated from their mother has on a child?'

Rita was a little surprised by her passion on the subject. 'I'm sure they do. And Billy is usually calm and settled.'

'Well I'm not so sure,' Bernie said stoutly. 'I've been reading up about child psychology and just because a child is quiet and compliant that doesn't mean he's unaffected by his abandonment and loss.'

Rita didn't know what to say. Everyone knew the children in the nursery were often withdrawn and upset when they first came in but they soon settled down. She was putting on a clean pillowcase on Lisa's pillow after she had found tiny specks on blood on it, knowing that when Lisa was in bed she picked the skin around her finger nails. Rita became thoughtful. Maybe Bernie was right. Maybe children like Lisa and Billy didn't 'settle down'. Maybe they just suffered in silence, and wet the bed or picked the skin around their nails until they bled…

Bernie looked a little sheepish. 'I'm sorry to go on about it but I feel for the poor kid. He's had a double whammy. Cuddling gampy, whatever that is, might have given him a little comfort at night and then he might not have wet the bed.'

'You could be right,' said Rita, 'and you've certainly given me food for thought.'

The weather was warm and sunny, so the girls made the most of the opportunity to take the children out each day. Rosebery Park was close to the nursery and it didn't take long to walk there. It had a lake and plenty of room to run around as well as a children's area with swings and a slide. Of course the students still had to do their chores first, but with everybody pulling out the stops they soon finished.

Rita had four children from tweenies (tweenies were the little ones aged from one year up to three) in a coach built quad pram. Although roughly the same age, they all looked very different. Tony was a chubby little boy with white-blonde hair, Cory was West African, Ling's parents were Chinese and Patrick had a heavily freckled face and flaming red hair. It seemed that bad luck, parental illness or homelessness could happen to anyone wherever they came from. Rita strapped them in to keep them safe and followed Bernie and Sylvie who were each walking in between two toddlers on reins.

The older children were excited when they saw the swings and couldn't wait to run over to them. Patrick had fallen asleep and Tony was hardly walking yet but Cory and Ling held their arms up and bounced up and down on their bottoms to be let out of the quad pram. It was a challenge keeping a weather eye on all of them, but Rita enjoyed 'chasing' Cory and Ling around. The sound of their giggles told her that they loved it and when she put the pair of them together in the swing boat they enjoyed that too.

'Did you get a nannies post yet?' Sylvie asked.

Rita shook her head.

'I would have thought you'd be all fixed up by now,' Bernie remarked. 'It's getting a bit close to your leaving day isn't it?'

'Tell me about it,' said Rita. By now Cory and Ling were happily crawling around on the grass and she had noticed that Tony was grizzling in the pram. 'I honestly thought Mrs Hunter would contact me as soon as she got my final reference from Matron.'

'Was it okay?' said Bernie. 'I mean, she didn't say anything horrible?'

'No,' said Rita going to the pram to fetch Tony. 'It wasn't too bad at all. I was a bit surprised but she was quite complimentary and said I was kind to the children, all that sort of stuff.' She paused. 'Of course she took all the credit. Apparently it was because of her tutorage that I'm conscientious, trustworthy and all that.'

Sylvie laughed aloud. 'She did the same sort of thing with Connie when she left. We laughed like drains because according to Matron, Connie was shy and withdrawn but Matron had managed to encourage her to come out of her shell to connect more with the children.'

'Connie!' Rita exclaimed, and the three of them laughed.

Connie was the last person to be called shy and withdrawn. Loud and brash, Connie was the life and soul of any party. She had men tripping over themselves to take her out and the kids in the nursery adored her.

Bernie had to fetch one of her children from the nether reaches of the playground but when she got back she asked Rita, 'What will you do if the agency doesn't get in touch?'

'I guess I'll have to go back home again,' said Rita cuddling Tony.

'You wouldn't like to stay on?' said Sylvie.

Rita knew she was teasing but her reply was robust. 'No, I flippin' well wouldn't. I'm sick of scrubbing floors and late passes. I want a bit more out of life.'

'Like what?' said Sylvie doing her best to sound innocent.

Rita sat on a swing with Tony on her lap and pushed her legs so that they swung gently. 'What would I like is a cushy job with a big fat wage packet, holidays abroad, and a gorgeous looking fella with a red sports car.'

'You don't want much then,' Bernie laughed.

A little girl in a pink dress was trying to give Ling a hug. 'Be careful darling,' her mother called. 'Don't be rough with the little baby.'

Rita could see that Ling was loving every minute of her new friend's clumsy cuddles so she called out, 'Don't worry. I'm sure she's fine.'

Bernie glanced at her watch. 'We'd better get back. It's almost eleven thirty.'

Sylvie called her children over and grabbed the ends of the reins which she had tucked into their pockets while they ran around. Bernie was already holding hands with her two.

As Rita leaned over the pram to place Tony back in, the woman smiled. 'I've never seen a pram for four babies before.'

Rita strapped Tony inside and reached for Cory. The woman watched as she sat him next to Patrick and gave him some toys that she'd hidden under the fold of the hood. With three children in the pram, she only had Ling to collect, and her new friend seemed disappointed as Rita came to fetch her.

'Oh...'

'Sorry sweetheart,' Rita said gently, 'but we have to go now. It'll soon be Ling's dinner time.'

The little girl's mother came to pick her daughter up and swung her onto her hip. As she watched Rita strapping the last of her charges into the quad pram the woman gave her a puzzled frown. 'Are they all yours?'

—

When she went into the staff room for dinner on her very last day, Rita looked on the top of the cupboard to see if she had any mail. There was usually a small pile of letters next to the water jug and glasses but today there was nothing. The dinner was her favourite – shepherd's pie – but she had suddenly lost her appetite. Why hadn't the agency replied?

It was Jenny Lamar who had told her about the West End Nannies Agency. She and Jenny had shared a room with another girl, Carole, for some time before Bernie came to the nursery. Carole had left to get married and have a baby then soon after, Jenny had landed herself a cushy job just off Park Lane. Rita had been really impressed so she'd asked Jenny how she'd found her employer. Jenny had pointed out their advertisement in *Nursery World*.

> West End Nannies Agency: A bespoke agency, specialising in excellence and recruiting only the best people for private households, we can offer the dedicated nursery nurse the post of their dreams.

It sounded absolutely perfect so, as soon as she'd heard she'd passed her exam, Rita had made an appointment for an interview. She'd dressed with care, hoping to show that although she was a thoroughly modern girl, she was also well-mannered and respectable.

Rita had planned her every move meticulously. The girls in the nursery thought that she was going home on her days off just like everyone else, but she wasn't. When she wasn't visiting Gran, she used the small annuity the bank had awarded her after her mother's untimely death, and unbeknown to any of them, Rita had been investing in her own future by taking elocution lessons. She had also been attending the Miss Moorhouse School of Charm and Etiquette. Since taking her elocution lessons, Rita had mastered the art of communication and her diction was crystal clear. Miss Moorhouse had taught her how to sit in a modest way, how to get in and out of a car gracefully and she had helped to make Rita's social habits much more acceptable.

'An RSVP note is required if you are unable to attend a function,' Miss Moorhouse had explained, 'and if you do attend, a thank you note should be received within forty-eight hours of the event.'

She also learned that as a nanny she would be expected to be the sole carer for the children, but she could be asked to help out with her employer's engagements. That was why Rita had learned the correct way to serve at table: 'leave it at the left and remove it from the right', how to brew tea if hosting afternoon tea: 'make sure the water is cold and freshly drawn every time you fill the kettle and never over-boil'. She knew to use 'whole leaf tea for the finest flavour', and the dinner guest's golden rule – 'never discuss politics or religion'. She'd never realised before but there was even a dress code in the higher echelons of society. White gloves were required for formal occasions but coloured gloves could be worn for more social settings. Her ensemble should be colour matched and her hair always tidy.

By the time she had received her diploma, Rita was so well schooled, that she could have easily passed for a Norland Nanny. No one would ever guess that she'd had a public service training and had grown up in a tired seaside town with the dubious reputation of being full of newly-weds and nearly-deads.

All these acquired skills had given Rita the confidence that she would have no problem with her application for a nanny's post which was why she was so surprised not to receive a single communication from the agency.

Once everyone was settled down at the table, Bernie made a little speech about how much they were all going to miss Rita and handed her a signed card. On the front was a picture of a duck shepherding her seven ducklings towards a pond. Inside, under the card's *Sorry you're leaving…* everyone had signed their name and offered her their good wishes or best of luck. A couple of inscriptions made her laugh. 'We'll all miss your smiling boring face, ha, ha,' Sylvie had written. 'Best news we've had all year! But seriously I hope you get on well with your next post.' That was from Dora the girl who worked in the kitchen. They'd all clubbed together to give her a present and Rita was thrilled with the Coty L'aimant soap, bath cubes and hand cream set from Woolworth's.

As Rita bit back her tears, everyone thought it was because she was leaving. It was true that she'd miss her friends at the nursery but in truth she was mortified that the West End Nannies Agency hadn't thought she was good enough to go on their books. There was nothing else for it but to go back to Gran's cottage with her tail between her legs and look elsewhere.

Sylvie got up to pour herself a glass of water but as she did so she accidentally knocked the glass over. With Bernie jumping up to help her mop up the mess, she moved the table mat aside.

'Oh my goodness!' Bernie cried. 'There are two letters under this mat.'

They were both addressed to Rita and as she handed them over, Rita saw the WEN crest and logo in the left-hand corner. So they had written to her after all!

'I've been waiting for these all week,' Rita gasped.

'I can't think why they were under the mat,' said Sylvie.

'To make sure they were missed,' Bernie suggested.

Sylvie frowned. 'But who would do such a thing?'

Bernie raised her eyebrow and turned to look at her friend. Rita's face flushed angrily. 'Matron,' she spat.

Bernie nodded. 'And I bet if you asked her about it, she'd say she wasn't responsible and one of us must have put them there.'

'Well, go on then,' prompted Julie, 'open them.'

The first was postmarked four days ago. Rita read it aloud to everyone in the room. In it, Mrs Hunter had offered her a post with a diplomatic family travelling to the Middle East. 'I shall need to know by return of post if you would like an interview,' she had written.

Rita sat back in her chair with a bump. Well, that one was well and truly gone.

'She's lost me a job,' she said bitterly as she handed the letter to Bernie.

'Shame,' said Bernie after she'd read it.

'Cow,' Sylvie corrected.

Rita was cheesed off but on second thoughts, perhaps it was just as well. She wasn't sure if she was ready to go as far away as the Middle East, but, she told herself crossly, that wasn't the point, was it? Her letter had been deliberately hidden in plain sight.

'I can't believe that woman is so vindictive,' Rita spat. 'All because I reminded her about Maisie.'

'She did something like this once before didn't she?' said Sylvie. 'I remember Laura finding one of her letters in the table mat drawer.'

'And Dora got the blame for it,' Julie remembered.

'What about the other letter?' Bernie reminded Rita. 'What does that say?'

As she finished reading, Rita snatched up the envelope and stared at the post mark. 'This one only came today,' she gasped. 'It's to look after two children, the grandchildren of a novelist who lives in Belgravia.'

'Belgravia,' said Christine. 'Wowzer. That's proper posh, that is.'

'Will you take it?' someone said.

'You bet your life I will!' Rita declared stoutly.

Chapter 4

'You Really Got Me'
The Kinks

Rita spent the rest of the evening packing the last few things she had left in her wardrobe into a large holdall bag. The plan was that in the morning all she would have to do was strip the bed and grab her bag. She would go straight up to London and the West End Nannies Agency. If the post was suitable, she would ask Mrs Hunter to look after her things while she went for an interview. If everything worked out, she might even be starting her new life the same day.

When morning arrived and the night nurse came into her room for the very last time, Rita said her goodbyes to Bernie and Christine and waited until they were on their way to the nursery before she went into the bathroom. After a leisurely bath, she folded her blankets and put her sheets in the laundry box ready for collection. As she lifted it onto the bed, a piece of paper which had been stuck to the bottom fluttered to the floor. Rita's mouth gaped open as she saw what it was, and then she felt a rage well up within her. At first she was so angry she was tempted to rip it into a million pieces, but as she sat on the edge of the bed staring at the writing, some things began to fall into place.

When she had got back from visiting her mother's grave, she had been so sure someone had been in her room and moved her things. She remembered looking around to see if anything was missing but everything was there – maybe not in the right place but nothing had been stolen. Well, now she knew. She had been right. Someone *had* been in her room.

She knew who it was of course: Matron. What on earth was wrong with the woman? In her more charitable moments, Rita believed she behaved the way she did because she was war damaged. Everyone knew Matron had lost a brother at Dunkirk. Perhaps that loss had affected her more than they knew. Matron had few friends and they'd never seen her with a man. It was all very sad but did that excuse her vindictiveness, bitchiness and making other people's lives a misery? Rita guessed it was probably a power thing, but it was ugly and uncalled for.

Rita was holding an identical reference to the one she had initially been given by Matron, except for one difference. On the line where Matron had previously written, 'Rita Brownlow has been a diligent student, and I am pleased to say she has come away from the nursery a completely conscientious and trustworthy person,' she had added on this copy: 'I can only hope that she will learn to be more loyal to her employers and other members of staff.'

The bitch! So that's what she was doing. She must have been looking for the original reference so that she could swap it with this new one; one which would completely scupper Rita's chances of ever getting a decent job. But why was it stuck to the bottom of the laundry box? Somehow or other, Matron must have mislaid the piece of paper. It must have fallen under the bed – perhaps she was disturbed in the act? – and she'd accidentally pulled the laundry box over it. Thank the Lord the agency already had Rita's original reference. Who would want to employ a person who had yet to learn loyalty?

And all this because Rita had stood in between Matron and the birthday candles in order to prevent her from upsetting a fragile little girl who was terrified of fire. Anyone else would have admitted the blunder or at least been grateful, but not Matron. In her eyes, she had been humiliated and that was by far the greater sin.

Somebody called up the stairs. 'Rita, your taxi's here.'

Stuffing the doctored reference into her pocket, Rita pulled on her coat and grabbed her bag. With one last look around the room which had been her home for the past two years she closed the door and hurried downstairs.

Matron was waiting by the front door, all smiles and the epitome of a caring head of staff. Rita wondered why she had bothered to come and say goodbye but then through the open door, she spotted Miss Grimwold the nursery supervisor coming toward the house. Resplendent in her large blue hat, Miss Grimwold had obviously just parked her car and was about to begin her visit. Rita smiled to herself. *Oh good. Perfect timing.*

'Well, goodbye Rita,' Matron gushed. She held out her hand. 'I wish you all the best in your new situation. It's been a pleasure to have you here.'

Rita was sorely tempted to say she wished she could say the same, but something told her she didn't want to sink to Matron's level. So she took the proffered hand and shook it. It felt like shaking hands with an uncooked leg of lamb but she did her best to look pleased with the gesture.

'Goodbye Matron,' she said with dignity. 'I shall certainly never forget my time in Harefield House.'

They both knew what she meant. Matron took in a sharp breath probably in anticipation of a cutting remark.

'Are you leaving?' asked Miss Grimwold as she came closer.

'I am,' said Rita, enjoying the uncomfortable expression on Matron's face.

Miss Grimwold held out her hand and gave Rita a firm handshake. 'I wish all the best, my dear.'

'Thank you,' said Rita. She turned to go but then hesitated. 'Oh, I almost forgot. I think this is yours, Matron,' she said pulling the reference out from her pocket. 'I found it on the floor in my bedroom.'

Matron's eyes darted from Rita to Miss Grimwold and back again.

Rita smiled sweetly. 'You must have dropped it there while you were looking in my chest of drawers for the one you gave me last week.'

Matron's face flushed scarlet.

Rita placed her hand on the doorknob. 'You'll be pleased to know I didn't need it. I'd already sent the first one to an agency.' She smiled again as she headed for the taxi. 'In fact, they thought it was so wonderful that I'm off to my new post in Belgravia right now.'

—

If Mrs Hunter was slightly surprised to see her on the doorstep having not replied to either of her letters she didn't remark on it, but instead, she invited Rita into her office. She was an older woman, perhaps nudging her late forties or maybe slightly older. What could not be denied was her elegance. Tall and slim, Mrs Hunter was impeccably dressed. Today she wore a purple dress with a pencil skirt and a matching jacket. On the left lapel she wore a fairly large leaf-shaped brooch encrusted with small green stones. If they were, as Rita suspected, emeralds, it would be worth a small fortune. Jenny Lamar had told her that Mrs Hunter's glasses always matched her outfit and today was no exception. Her cat's eye shaped frames were dotted with green stones.

'I'm so sorry I didn't reply to your first letter, Mrs Hunter,' Rita explained politely, 'but I'm afraid it accidentally got mislaid for a couple of days. Having said that, sadly, I don't think that first post you were offering was quite right for me anyway.' Sitting herself down and remembering not to cross her legs but to sit elegantly, she went on to explain that going abroad at this moment would be a problem. 'You see, I'm trying to get a driving licence ,' Rita continued. 'I've already had some lessons and I am hoping to take my test in a few weeks' time.'

'That sounds like a wonderful idea, Miss Brownlow,' Mrs Hunter exclaimed. 'A driving licence will open up so many more opportunities.'

'I thought so too,' Rita hurried on, 'so I took the liberty of coming straight here because I would be very interested in looking after your client's grandchildren.'

Mrs Hunter went to her filing cabinet and pulled out a folder. 'The lady is called Mrs Plumb but you may know her as Cassandra Whitely. She's quite famous for her Regency novels.'

Rita blinked. Oh my goodness! Yes, she'd heard of Cassandra Whitely. She'd never read one of her books, but they always had pride of place in WHSmith's and the bookshops.

'The post is to care for her two grandchildren who have been living in Rhodesia. They are coming to this country to get an English education and she wants a nanny to help them settle in.'

Rita sat very still, trying to look as if she had offers like this every day. Cassandra Whitely… Belgravia… exotic foreign places… It felt like a dream.

'The salary is £316 per annum which works out at £8 a week. Your National Insurance stamp will be paid and of course you have free board and lodging in quite a select location. Will that suit?'

Rita was doing her best to appear casual but inside she was jumping up and down and cheering as if she'd scored the winning goal at Wembley. After existing on a mere £7 a *month*, this would be living a life of luxury. 'Yes, Mrs Hunter,' she said airily, 'I would be quite happy with that.'

'Now before I contact the client,' Mrs Hunter went on, 'I want you to know that if you have any problem with your post or you would simply like to meet other nannies, we have a coffee morning here every Thursday. It's only open for our nannies and although you can ask advice about anything, we are very careful not to allow any private details of our clients to be made public.'

Rita nodded. 'Of course, thank you,' she said although she had no intention of spending her days off with a load of crusty nannies who had nothing better to do.

Mrs Hunter smiled and leaned forward to pick up the telephone receiver.

When she climbed out of the taxi some twenty minutes later, Rita took in a deep breath. This had to be one of the most beautiful streets she'd ever seen. It might be the 1960s but she felt as if she had stepped back into a bygone era. She was faced by a long row of white stucco terraced townhouses which glistened in the summer sunlight. Each house had black cast iron spearhead railing surrounds and a white Doric porch with gleaming steps leading to the front door. The houses stood uniformly three floors in height, with attic rooms above. Each house was three sash windows wide and on the first floor there was a balustrade balcony some of which had potted plants and large shrubs. Even the rooftops were stunning, with tall chimneys stark against the azure blue sky and added to that, just a glance told her each chimney pot was unique with its own distinctive shape and pattern.

The street itself was unspoiled by litter, in fact, it was pristine with only a few parked cars at the kerbside. This was probably because of the newly created parking meters, which along with double yellow lines and traffic wardens had been introduced by Ernest Marples, the Minister of Transport. People grumbled about the expense, sixpence an hour and you could only stay for two hours or you risked a fine of two pounds. Rita's old room-mate Jenny Lamar lived in Mayfair where her employer had hired a young lad to constantly feed the meters outside their front door and move the car to a different bay every two hours. 'Bloody parking meters' were, according to Jenny's employer, the bane of her life, but it seemed that they were taking over all the streets in London, even those in Belgravia.

A maid answered the door. 'Are you the nanny?'

Rita nodded. 'Rita Brownlow.'

'Please wait here a minute, Miss Brownlow,' she said as they entered the hallway.

Rita glanced around. If the outside of the house was fabulous, the inside was something else. Gazing at the sweeping staircase, with the grandiose chandelier above it and the beautiful parquet flooring of the hallway, Rita had never seen such opulent, jaw-dropping splendour. Mrs Plumb must be seriously rich.

She was taken to an upstairs room which had been made into an office. Mrs Plumb was sitting at a large desk with a typewriter in front of her. Rita's first thought was that the author picture that appeared on the dust covers of her books must have been taken ages ago; on them she looked about thirty with short permed hair. In real life she seemed about fifty or fifty-five and wore a violet blouse with a string of pearls at her neck, a pleated skirt and sensible shoes.

Her interview went well and it was agreed by Mrs Plumb that when her two grandchildren, Hamish and Lauren arrived from Rhodesia in a couple of weeks' time, Rita would be engaged as their nanny. Their father was a government official and their mother had left them for some reason (undisclosed to Rita, who thought better of asking about what was clearly a sensitive topic), so their father had decided to send the children back to the UK to live with their grandmother (as Mrs Hunter had already explained) for an English education. The plan was that in January the two children would be attending prestigious schools, a boarding school for the boy and a day school for girl. Mrs Plumb explained that for her, the timing was all wrong as she was up against a strict deadline for her latest novel. Rita was to 'entertain' (Mrs Plumb's words) them and help settle them into what would be a very different way of life. Rita reflected that she was right; not only would their way of life be different but they would be coming from a hot country with temperatures in the high thirties when in London it would soon be more like the low single digits, especially as autumn would be on its way by the time they arrived. The post was hers until they went to their respective schools. After that, Rita would look after the girl for a month until she was settled into her day school and by which time Mrs Plumb was confident that she would have finished her book.

As she wasn't required until the second week of September, Rita decided to go back home and spend a few days with Gran.

Chapter 5

'The Runaway Train'
Michael Holliday
BBC Light Programme, *Children's Favourites*

Guinevere Cottage, Goring-by-Sea, didn't really live up to its beautiful name. The other houses on Jeffries Lane were larger, much more expensive and with manicured lawns and large flower beds. Guinevere Cottage was in a kind of time warp. Rita's grandmother had been left a small inheritance which she saved for years, so that by the time Rita was eleven her gran and mum had pooled their resources and bought the two-up two-down for the princely sum of two hundred pounds. Sadly, Valerie never got to live there. She was in the process of giving up her tenancy on Tarring Road when she was killed, with Gran just moved in. Gran didn't have the money to renovate the cottage, so although it wasn't in a state of disrepair, it had never been modernised.

The only toilet was outside the back door, which was a bane during the winter, especially when there was snow on the ground or it was pouring with rain and blowing a gale. The bath was under a board which doubled as a work surface in the lean-to kitchen which had been added in the 1930s. That meant that bath night was an upheaval as everything on top of the board had to be moved and the kitchen door firmly locked to visitors. The one advantage, as Rita had discovered, was that while she was soaking in the bath, she could watch the telly in the dining room through the crack in the half open door. Gran still had a coal fire which, it had to be said, made the dining room warm and cozy, but the rest of the house was unheated.

The walk from Goring-by-Sea station wasn't very far and fifteen minutes after her arrival, Rita was at the back door. 'Hello… I'm home.'

Winifred Brownlow wasn't by nature a demonstrative woman but she came hurrying to the door to meet her granddaughter. 'Oh good, you're here,' she said reaching to take Rita's small case. 'Come in, come on in, love.'

As she walked through the back door, Rita kissed her grandmother's cheek.

'How was your journey? Do you want something to eat? How are you?'

Gran's questions were predictable, but Rita patiently answered them all before adding, 'And what about you?'

Her grandmother, a small but determined woman in her early sixties who always wore a floral wrap-over apron, was sparing with her own news. As she got a Victoria sponge out of the cake tin, she told her granddaughter that she was fine; she'd got a nice piece of beef from the butcher to celebrate Rita's homecoming and a fox had got into the hen house and killed all the chickens bar one.

'Oh Gran, I'm sorry to hear that,' said Rita sipping her tea. Her grandmother was proud of her hens and later in the year at Christmas time she would give a couple away as Christmas dinner presents for needy families in the village. 'That's a bit of a bummer.'

'I wished I'd had a whatsit,' Gran said fiercely. 'I'd have blown his blooming 'ead off. I wouldn't mind if he took them for food but he chewed the 'eads off all seven of them and just left them there.'

'Couldn't you still eat them?'

''taint worth the risk, girl,' her grandmother said as she cut Rita a chunk of her home-made sponge. 'Those foxes have all sorts of 'orrible diseases and for all I know, them hens could have had been lying in the open all night.'

Rita took the plate and nodded sagely. 'This cake looks delicious.'

They spent a few more minutes catching up as they enjoyed the sponge and then Rita rose to her feet. 'I'd better take my things upstairs.'

It was good to see her old room again. It held so many memories both good and bad. The wallpaper was a bit dated now, she was well past faded ladies dressed in crinoline holding umbrellas, but she remembered the excitement she'd felt the day she'd chosen it. Gran had put it up herself. Rita had gone to school one morning and when she came back home, the room was almost done.

Rita sat on the bed with a sigh. It would have been wonderful if Mum had lived to be here. She recalled the tightness in her throat and the aching void in her chest she'd felt as she sat on this very bed the day of Mum's funeral. Only eleven years old and numb with grief, she'd listened to the murmur of voices downstairs as family, friends and neighbours squeezed into the tiny living room for the repast. That day, young as she was, she'd stared into the distance knowing that her life was changed forever.

And now, just seven years later, so much had happened already. She'd finished her training and she was about to have her first taste of working as a private nanny. The two experiences would be as different as chalk and cheese but she couldn't wait to start.

Having emptied her small case she was unpacking the last few bits when she heard her grandmother call her name. Rita hurried downstairs.

'I'm just popping round to Eddie's with a bit of hot soup,' said Gran patting her newly permed hair.

Rita was surprised. Eddie Wilson, Gran's widowed next-door neighbour was usually hale and hearty. 'Is he ill?' she asked anxiously.

'Got a nasty cold,' said Gran matter-of-factly. 'He was going to come over for dinner but I told him it was best to stay in bed.'

'Poor Eddie,' said Rita. He would have been gutted to miss out on Gran's cooking, especially when it was a roast like the one she could smell in the oven.

'A drop of my soup and he will soon be as right as ninepence,' Gran said cheerfully. 'Do you want to come or would you fancy a bit of a rest?'

'I think I'd like a walk,' said Rita. 'I'm dying to see the sea again.'

'Take a cardy, darlin',' her grandmother cautioned. 'There's a real bite in that wind.'

By the time she reached the little hut at the end of Sea Lane where you could get an ice cream and cup of tea until four o'clock, Rita knew her grandmother had been right: autumn was well on its way and the wind was chilly. It hadn't taken her long to reach the shore, ten minutes at the most, but she had to wrap her cardigan around herself tightly to ward off the cold. She stood for a few minutes looking out to sea and simply breathing in the salty sea air.

Apart from the time when her mum had been killed and she'd spent grieving, Rita had enjoyed a wonderful adolescence in this place. She and the other children – then, teenagers – in Goring-by-Sea had spent hours and hours down here by the water, whatever the weather. Her memories were of endless summer days which seemed to last a lifetime. There were no adults; they were trusted to keep each other safe. In the summer holidays she would say goodbye to Gran after breakfast and be home in time for tea. She smiled to herself, remembering. How on earth had she known it was teatime when she didn't even have a watch?

Shivering now, Rita only walked a short way along the seafront before turning back by the public toilets by the area called the Plantation and heading for home.

'Thanks for giving me that picture of Mum,' Rita said as she and Gran sat back from the table after their meal. Her grandmother had roasted a small beef joint, serving it with roast potatoes, carrots and gravy, making a delicious meal with the promise of an apple crumble to follow.

Winifred Brownlow plumped up her cushion as she sat in the cosy chair opposite Rita. 'Glad you liked it.'

'You said I could talk about my father,' Rita ventured cautiously.

'Course you can, luvvy.'

'I've never seen a picture of my father before,' Rita began. 'Mum told he was an American but she never showed me his picture.'

'She always said he was a nice man,' Gran said. She had a far-away look in her eye. 'He could have been, for all I know, but I never forgave him for what he did to her.'

Rita was surprised. 'You never met him?'

Gran shook her head. 'I was supposed to but then he got posted to France.'

Rita frowned.

'It was war time,' Gran reminded her.

'Yes, of course,' said Rita. She had been born in 1945. It followed that her parents were together during the years before when Adolf Hitler was doing his best to take over the world. She gazed into the empty fireplace. 'So, when did they meet?'

'February,' said Gran. 'Your mum fell for 'im 'ook line and sinker.' She sighed. 'Then of course, they was all gone by June.'

'The year of the big push,' said Rita, remembering her school history lessons.

'That's right,' said Gran. 'D-Day – and the fighting on the beaches in Normandy.'

'And that's where he died?' said Rita.

Her grandmother looked up sharply. 'Your father went to Normandy all right but he survived,' she said bitterly. 'He never died. Nah, not 'im. He went back 'ome to America, didn't he. Left your mum in the lurch and never came back.'

To say Rita was stunned to hear that her father was alive and somewhere in America would be an understatement. She was shocked – appalled even. Because her mother never talked about him, Rita had been utterly convinced that her father must have died a hero on the beach. For years she had imagined him as a sort of John Wayne, charging the enemy guns, pushing his comrades out of the line of fire, perhaps even killing the enemy, before he'd succumbed to his wounds. Now she knew all that had been a foolish romantic dream. In real life, her father had been the villain of the piece. He'd got an innocent Sussex girl into trouble then rather than marry her, he'd run off back home.

The minute Gran told her, Rita shut down. She didn't want to talk about this any more. She changed the topic.

'Have you got any plans for when I'm in London, Gran?'

'Not sure yet, but I expect Auntie Steph will come for a holiday,' said Gran. 'No point in two of us being lonely – her in Eastbourne and me down 'ere.'

'So she'll sleep in my room?' said Rita. Auntie Steph was Gran's sister.

'Dear Lord, no!' cried her grandmother. 'Your room is your room forever my girl. If you want to come home any time, your room will always be 'ere. No, I've been clearing out the front room and I bought a second-hand bed from on Tarring Road so Steph can sleep in there.'

'That's nice,' said Rita. 'How long will she stay?'

Her grandmother shrugged. 'Couple of days – a week? We'll 'ave to see how we gets on.'

Rita smiled to herself. Auntie Steph could be a bit feisty but then so could Gran. For that reason they sometimes fell out but they always made it up in the end – eventually.

'Last time you was 'ere, you was asking about Nat,' Gran began cautiously. 'Apparently he's in the merchant navy.'

'Is that cargo ships?'

Her grandmother nodded. 'The Union-Castle Line. He's on a brand-new ship called the *Southampton Castle* sailing to South Africa with mail and bringing back wine and chilled meat.'

Rita was impressed. 'Good for him. How do you know all this?'

'Mrs Humphries is in the Tarring branch of the WI.' There was a pause then her grandmother said, 'Rita, while I was clearing out the downstairs room for Steph, I found something.'

'Oh?'

'Some letters,' said Gran. 'They was taped underneath the top of that old cupboard we brought over from the house on Tarring Road.'

'Taped underneath? Why?'

'I'm guessing your mum didn't want to throw them away, but she didn't want nobody prying neither.'

Rita was intrigued. 'Whose letters?'

Win took a deep breath. 'Letters from your dad to your mum.'

Rita felt her stomach fall away.

'As soon as I realised what they were, I kept them for you,' said Gran rising to her feet. 'I didn't read them but be warned, they might upset you.'

She went to the dresser and pulled out a small bundle tied with a tired and frayed ribbon. Even bundled up, Rita could see they were old. The paper was foxed and stained with age and as Gran put them in her hands, they smelled musty. Rita's hand trembled. 'Why didn't you read them?'

'Like I said,' Gran said, her mouth tight, 'even after all this time, I'm angry with 'im. He hurt my girl and I shall never forgive 'im for that.'

Rita stared down at the letters. What secrets did they hold? What had gone wrong with their relationship? Why had her parents broken up? Her heartbeat had quickened but she didn't want to undo the little parcel now.

'I'll look at them later,' she said firmly.

Chapter 6

'When Santa Got Stuck up the Chimney'

Billy Cotton and His Band
BBC Light Programme, *Children's Favourites*

It was the middle of September when Rita arrived at the beautiful Victorian terraced house on Wilton Crescent, Belgravia. There was a communal green space just across the road and she was surprised that she could hear the birds singing. Imagine that, right in the middle of London! When she'd looked on the map she'd discovered that Buckingham Palace was not far from here. In fact, the back of the palace gardens were just across the main road, although of course you couldn't see inside as the grounds were behind a high wall.

'Of necessity you will have to be very much left to your own devices,' Mrs Plumb explained as she handed Rita a list of requirements once she had settled into her room. 'As I said, I am close to my deadline which has already been extended a couple of times and my publisher is getting jittery.'

And so it was that Rita spent the first week of her employment getting everything ready for Mrs Plumb's grandchildren. She was shown into a lovely suite of rooms and her own room was on the same floor as the children. Hamish was to have the larger room, which was furnished with a bed, table and chair, a sofa chair and a cupboard. In the centre of the room she saw several boxes and when she opened them she found the most amazing toys; a full set of Meccano, a football, cricket pads, ball and stumps, a Hornby train set complete with station concourse and people and an easel.

There were similar boxes in Lauren's room which turned out to contain masses of teddies and dolls, a doll's house, an Etch a Sketch and even a doll's pram. Everything was brand spanking new and when she saw the labels, some of the toys were breathtakingly expensive. Rita took everything out of their boxes and carefully filled the cupboards. As Mrs Plumb had told her to buy whatever else she felt the children would require, remembering the old adage 'the devil makes work for idle hands', when Rita went shopping she filled their cupboards with plasticine, Play-Doh, pens, pencils, paints, paper and glue.

There was also a small room behind a double glass door in between the children's bedrooms which she decided to make into a quiet space where the children could read or rest if they needed to. To that end, she asked permission to commandeer two small armchairs and a free-standing shelf which could contain books from other rooms in the house.

As for Rita's room, she had never seen anything like it, let alone been able to call it her own and sleep in it. She had a luxurious divan bed, a wardrobe, chest of drawers and bedside table with lamp. The room itself had a picture window which overlooked the backs of other houses and the courtyard garden below. It was decorated in a tasteful cream and pale blue with walls covered in what looked like a Sanderson's delicate flower wallpaper.

The only other staff in the house were Mrs Nikolopoulos, who went by the much more manageable name of Mrs Niko, and Gloria who worked as a maid. She had been the person who had opened the door to Rita the day she came for her interview. Both women were part time and lived in their own homes. Mrs Niko, who had lived in London all her life and married the son of a Greek Cypriot who had come to Britain during the 1930s, came in three mornings a week, Monday, Wednesday and Friday, when she cooked for Mrs Plumb. She also cooked in batches so that there was always something available to eat when she wasn't around. Gloria, who hailed from Battersea, came in to clean for the whole day on Monday and for two hours just to tidy up on Friday. Although they were both much older than her, Rita took a liking to both of them straight away.

Occasionally, Mrs Plumb had visitors but she wasn't always pleased to see them. Rita guessed it was because she'd rather be working. If she was upstairs when the doorbell rang, Rita would lean over the banister to see if she recognised the person calling. She was sure one of them was Richard Burton... well, if it wasn't, it was his twin. Gloria told her another person who had seemed vaguely familiar was the actor Robert Morley, who was apparently an old friend of Mrs Plumb's late husband. Rita remembered him then; she had seen him at the pictures in *Murder at the Gallop*, an Agatha Christie story starring Margaret Rutherford. Robert Morley, a rather portly middle-aged man, had also starred in the *Carry On* films. Rita had a scare when one visitor actually looked up and saw her peeping over the banister. She felt sure she was going to be in trouble when Mrs Plumb had asked to see her later that evening, but to Rita's surprise she handed her two VIP tickets for the Tottenham Royal.

'My friend Hugo is an agent,' she explained, 'and he thought you might like to have these.'

Because Mrs Plumb had left her to her own devices so long as she did her job, Rita took the opportunity to telephone Jenny Lamar who worked just over a mile away in Mayfair. Jenny had been her room-mate in Harefield House for a year until she qualified, and when she left the nursery the pair of them had kept in touch. Rita knew Jenny and her charge, Pixie, were in Hyde Park most days so the two of them agreed to meet at Hyde Park Corner.

When Rita saw her, Jenny looked amazing. She had a fantastic haircut, a bit like the new up-and-coming star Elkie Brooks. It was a long bob with a parted fringe and curled under with kiss curls just below her ears. Jenny's skin was flawless, her figure trim. The day was still fairly warm so she was wearing a smart nurse's style dress with a red cardigan. Pixie, whose proper name was Patricia but everyone called her Pixie, was a sweet child who was beautifully dressed in a pretty shift dress with long sleeves, white sandals and a short jacket.

'You look amazing,' cried Jenny.

'I was just thinking the same about you,' Rita laughed as she and her friend hugged each other.

Rita crouched in front of Pixie and held out her hand. 'And you must be Pixie. How do you do?' The two of them shook hands and as Pixie let go of Rita, she found Jenny's friend had left two Smarties in her hand. Pixie whispered a 'Thank you' and they became instant friends.

As the three of them strolled through the park towards the children's play area, Jenny and Rita chatted over old times and brought each other up-to-date. When Rita told her friend about Matron's petty behaviour the week she left the nursery, Jenny was sympathetic. After all, hadn't she been subjected to the same sort of behaviour herself?

'I think I shall enjoy this job,' Rita confided. 'Mrs Plumb seems very easy-going and generous too. How about you? Have you still got that dishy boyfriend?' Jenny nodded. 'We've been talking about getting engaged but it won't happen just yet. He wants to get as much training under his belt as he can and we're both saving like mad.'

'For your own place?'

'For a garage,' said Jenny. 'Simon wants to look after up-market cars so we'll have to find the right one in the right location.'

Rita pulled the corners of her mouth down. Impressed she remarked, 'He sounds ambitious.'

Jenny chuckled. 'He is. But in the nicest possible way.' She paused. 'What about you? Any one serious yet?'

Rita shook her head and quickly changed the subject. 'You know I said Mrs Plumb was generous, well she knows a lot of famous people and one of them is an agent. I sometimes look over the banister when visitors come and he spotted me and told her. I thought I'd be in trouble but lucky me, he's given me tickets for the Tottenham Royal next week. The Dave Clark Five are performing live. Fancy coming with me?'

Jenny took in her breath noisily. 'The Dave Clark Five? Do I ever!'

They'd both dressed to the nines and they met outside the tube station. There was no time for conversation as they hurried to get their train tickets. After that it was racing down the escalator and heading for the platform. Rita loved the loud noise as the Tube trains arrived and the whine as they left the platform, although she had to be careful that the rush of wind didn't disturb her hair. There was a good chance it wouldn't. It was rock hard with lacquer.

The Tottenham Royal was a Mecca ballroom as well as a venue for the stars. All the big groups had played there; The Migil Five, The Troggs, The Animals and The Who as well as some lesser-known groups who were up and coming. The Dave Clark Five, a local group from Tottenham, had just had a massive hit with 'Glad All Over' which had actually toppled The Beatles from the charts.

It didn't take long to get there from Hyde Park Corner along the Piccadilly line to Turnpike Lane. The Tottenham Royal was an iconic building with twin turrets and castellations on either side of the entrance. They knew they were getting close to the venue when they saw the neatly parked Lambretta scooters along the side of the road while the pavements were filled with teenagers, mostly girls. A large crowd waited outside the entrance but because they had VIP tickets, Rita and Jenny were able to go straight in. The place was packed mostly with young people like themselves and it was almost stiflingly hot.

A couple of warm-up groups came on first. One wasn't much good, but Rita really liked Kandy Krisp when they came on. They dressed a bit like The Beatles but their sound was really different. The lead singer Cameron Knight made her go weak at the knees, he was so good-looking.

When The Dave Clark Five came on stage everybody screamed and the noise in the auditorium became deafening. The boys looked very smart with cream-coloured trousers, cream polo neck T-shirts and dark blazers. Their hair was cut in an identical style which they called the Dave Clark Spike which according to her *Flair* magazine, was named after his dog! The vocalist Mike Smith was magic and in an instant the whole place was rocking as they sang 'Glad All Over'. In no time at all, the strong rhythmical beat seemed to fill the auditorium. Rita and Jenny took one look at each other and grinned. This had to be the most amazing experience of their lives.

Chapter 7

'I Get Around'
The Beach Boys

A couple of days before the children arrived, a van arrived from Harvey Nichols, a flagship store in Knightsbridge. Rita had never been there, but she knew it sold designer fashion and luxury goods. Gloria opened the front door and the delivery man staggered into the house with box after box of clothing. When she unpacked them, Rita found boy's trousers, shirts, jumpers, long socks and a winter coat. Other boxes contained girl's things of a similar ilk. She spent the rest of the day removing the shop tags and hanging everything in the children's wardrobes. It was only when she'd finished that it occurred to her that the clothes might not fit in which case they would have to be sent back. For a few seconds Rita suffered a mild panic attack but soon recovered. Too late now!

As this might be the last evening she had free for a while, Rita had arranged to meet Jenny again. Jenny couldn't meet until after seven, which made it too late for the pictures or anything else – apart from the seedy night clubs in Soho – so Rita caught the bus to Aldford Street just off Park Lane where Jenny worked. The house itself was just a few streets away from the Dorchester and Hilton hotels. Black railings flanked some stone steps leading to the front door. Rita mounted them and rang the doorbell. Jenny's employers went out to dinner every night, either to a friend's house or a posh restaurant so the girls knew they would be left alone to have a girly chat.

A moment later, Jenny opened the door and led her friend up the stairs towards a large sitting room. The whole house was carpeted in cream, including the sitting room. 'This is where my employers entertain,' said Jenny. 'Isn't it a lovely room?'

Rita nodded. A huge stone fireplace dominated the room and the walls were oak panelled. The room was dominated by two large sofas and more cushions, Rita thought, than pebbles on Goring beach! On a table in front of the only window stood a large bowl of cut flowers which had been beautifully arranged.

'Guess how much that lot cost?' Jenny whispered.

Remembering the seven and six bunch of flowers she had bought for her mother's grave, Rita shrugged and said, 'Fifteen bob?'

Jenny grinned. 'Try fifteen pounds a week,' she chuckled.

Rita gasped out loud. 'That's more than I flippin' get in a week!'

'Me too,' said Jenny. 'Some chap comes from Constance Spry every Friday and that's what it costs her.'

Jenny's charge Pixie, who was four, was asleep in bed so the pair of them sat in the small sitting room cum playroom downstairs. Liliana, the maid-chief cook-and-bottle washer had prepared Jenny a few nibbles like cheese on Ritz crackers and olives on sticks which were positioned either side of the biggest bunch of grapes Rita had ever seen. Jenny had splashed out on a bottle of Mateus Rosé and she had set up her record player so they were in for a good evening.

'We should do this more often,' Rita said helping herself to an olive.

That's when Jenny dropped a bombshell when she told her the family were shortly moving to Esher.

'Is that far from here?' Rita asked.

'Twenty miles or thereabouts,' Jenny said. 'I told them I wasn't too happy about the new location so I shall leave them after the move.'

'Shame. I thought you were happy here.'

Jenny shrugged. 'I am.'

'So when do you go?'

'I promised to stay long enough to help Pixie settle into her new home,' she said nibbling on a grape. 'Simon's even complaining about that, but I keep telling him it'll only be for a short while. I earn a good wage and we're saving like mad because he's finally found this garage and has put in an offer.'

'And then you'll get married?'

'Hopefully,' said Jenny. 'It's got living quarters over the top.'

'Would you be sad to give up working?' It might be 1964 but it was still accepted that when a girl got married she would have to give up any thoughts of a career.

'I shall enjoy making a home for us,' said Jenny, adding with a blush, 'and then I suppose my own babies will come along.' The two of them sipped their wine then Jenny added, 'Anyway, enough about me. What about you?'

Rita shrugged. 'Not much to tell. I still haven't actually met the children. Their father is some big wig in Africa and the children haven't even been to school yet.'

'And the boy is eight?' Jenny gasped.

'Ten,' said Rita. 'Apparently they've had a personal tutor but it sounds a bit doubtful that he was a qualified teacher, so I'm guessing they've led rather sheltered lives.'

Jenny chuckled. 'In that case, they're in for a shock.'

Rita nodded sagely. 'You might be right there.'

Sandy Shaw came to the end of her song so Jenny stood up to change the record. 'What shall I put on The Supremes "Baby Love" or Cliff Richard's "Twelfth of Never"?'

'Supremes,' said Rita.

'Anyway,' said Jenny as she dropped the needle onto the record, 'what about your love life?'

Rita reached for a couple of olives. 'I haven't even had a whiff of a man since I've been here,' she said casually. 'I've had the occasional evening off but where do I go? There's no way

I'm going to one of those sleazy nightclubs and you know very well no decent girl goes to a pub or a dance on her own.'

'Tell you what,' Jenny said eagerly, 'let's promise ourselves to go to the Lyceum for the New Year. Simon is bound to be working and we can have some fun.'

Rita frowned cautiously. 'It's not a nightclub is it? I mean you hear such things…'

'Of course not!' cried Jenny. 'It's a ballroom with perfectly respectable dancing and all that. You're bound to meet someone nice. What do you say?'

'All right,' said Rita. 'You're on,' adding jokingly, 'I'll put it in my appointments diary.'

—

The children arrived at Heathrow airport late at night, tired and hungry after a journey of over five thousand miles and lasting sixteen hours. Rita and Mrs Plumb were waiting for them as they came through customs each with a blanket over their shoulders. Their escort handed them over explaining that they'd arrived at the airport unsuitably dressed but she had done her best to keep them warm. When the blankets were removed to be returned to the airline, Rita was shocked to see that the children were in linen shorts and short sleeved cotton shirts. They wore sandals and their legs were bare. Neither of them had a coat. Lauren was shivering violently so Rita took her coat off to put it around the little girl's shoulders.

Their meeting with their grandmother was a little stilted, but then they had never actually met before. Mrs Plumb introduced Rita, but the children gave her scant attention.

Back at the house, Rita helped the exhausted children to get ready for bed and the pair of them were asleep before their heads had hardly touched the pillow. As she put their things out for the morning, Rita stood for a moment to watch them sleep. Hamish was ten. His blonde tousled hair was far too long and his skin was bronzed from the sun. He seemed a little short for his age but his legs were sturdy enough and he had a rather muscular look about him. Lauren was almost eight. A pretty girl with freckles across the bridge of her nose and she wore her hair in rather untidy plaits.

As she closed the door to their bedrooms, Rita smiled to herself. It was going to be fascinating to hear all about their African home and she couldn't wait to show them the sights of London.

When morning came, it didn't take Rita long to work out that they had come from a privileged family with a cartload of servants. The way they spoke to her showed her that they were used to making demands which had to be instantly obeyed rather than making pleasant and respectful requests. No pleases or thank yous; just a string of 'Get me this,' or 'Get it!' and more alarmingly, 'Come on woman. I shan't tell you again.'

In no time at all, Rita was in a state of mild shock. Coming into a well-ordered society which owed them nothing, one which would consider their behaviour crass and downright rude, Rita could see that she had her work cut out for her if she was to shape them into anything like a pair of decent human beings.

That first day was a nightmare. Mrs Plumb spent her time ensconced in her study so Rita was left very much to herself. The children refused to do anything they were asked and were extremely argumentative.

'Where are my shorts and sandals?' Hamish had demanded as soon as he woke up.

'It's really cold outside,' said Rita. 'You need warmer clothes. Look, your grandmother has got you some new trousers and a jumper.'

'I'm not putting those on. Get me my shorts.'

'Hamish, you cannot wear your shorts. These are the clothes your grandmother wants you to wear.'

Hamish's face darkened. 'Are you deaf or stupid, woman? Get. Me. My. Shorts and do it now!'

As soon as she saw her brother's reaction, Lauren followed suit, declaring that her stupid frock was absolutely ghastly and that she wasn't going to wear it. The dress was in fact beautiful and Rita had seen the price on the label before she'd put it into the wardrobe – it had cost a whopping £60. That was almost the same as two months wages for her!

As tempting as it was to get angry, Rita did her best to remain calm. She would merely observe them today and begin making changes tomorrow. She knew their grandmother had arranged for them to go on a sightseeing tour of all the London tourist attractions which would be followed by a trip to Hamley's, the exclusive toy shop, before they would meet up with Mrs Plumb for afternoon tea. Rita told them the plan in the hopes that it might help them change their minds about getting dressed. Sadly, it didn't. Instead, they got all the toys out of the cupboards and began playing with them. No amount of cajoling or persuasion would make them get dressed and in no time at all, they were carelessly walking all over their new toys.

'Let's pick up the toys and put them away,' Rita suggested.

Hamish gave her a look of disdain. 'You pick them up. That's your job.'

At the meal table downstairs they were rude and demanding. Gloria was horrified and Mrs Niko declared in a loud voice that she had never met such unruly and ill-mannered children.

'If you talk to people like that when you go to school,' she announced stoutly, 'the first thing they'll do is give you a damned good thrashing.'

The next day when the man called with the car which was supposed to take them all on the sightseeing tour, Rita had to send him away. There was no way she could escort two children around London in December while they were *still* in their nightclothes and refusing to wear suitable clothing. After a particularly fraught morning, Rita was beginning to think she'd made a ghastly mistake in taking this post.

At three o'clock, the children's grandmother heard them playing trains and came into the playroom.

'Oh,' she cried out in surprise, 'you're still here. Didn't the car come for you?'

Rita explained politely what had happened and then Hamish stood to his feet. 'She wouldn't let me have my clothes,' he snapped. 'She gave me some scratchy old trousers and a big coat and I won't wear it. I won't.'

His grandmother frowned. 'But Hamish… darling. It's far too cold for the things you wore in Africa.'

'When I say something,' he added pompously with his hand on his hip, 'I expect to be listened to. I don't like this woman, Granny. Send her away.'

'Hamish—' Mrs Plumb began again.

'Didn't you hear me?' her grandson demanded.

'Darling, please don't speak to me like that.'

'Or what?' he demanded. 'You'll smack me? Well, go on and smack me. I've had smacks from bigger people than you.'

Rita saw Mrs Plumb crumble before her eyes. She didn't answer him but with a shocked expression on her face, she turned and left the room.

Chapter 8

'Where did my Snowman Go'
Petula Clark
BBC Light Programme, *Children's Favourites*

The following Thursday should have been Rita's day off but there was no one to take over the care of the children and she wasn't willing to leave them unsupervised. She'd also done some serious thinking. Knowing that this chaotic household couldn't carry on like this and that things had to radically change, she'd come to the conclusion that she held the trump card. Having persuaded Hamish and Lauren to get dressed – under great protest – as soon as they were in the playroom with their toys, she took the opportunity to seek out her employer.

Rita had been instructed to only disturb Mrs Plumb in a dire emergency but ignoring that edict, she knocked on the study door. There was no answer, but Rita knew Mrs Plumb was in there. She could hear typing. Rita knocked a second time and walked in wearing her coat and pulling on her gloves.

Mrs Plumb turned to her with a scowl. 'Rita I thought I made it clear…' she began.

'Yes you did, ma'am,' said Rita, her voice calm but determined. 'I just came to tell you that I shall be off now.'

Mrs Plumb's jaw dropped. 'Off? Off where?'

'It's my day off, Mrs Plumb,' said Rita. 'I have managed to persuade Hamish and Lauren to get dressed and they are playing quite nicely in their room.'

Mrs Plumb rose to her feet, a strained and appealing look on her face. 'Oh Rita, you can't go now. I am so close to the finish. I realise you are perfectly entitled to your time off but couldn't you just this once…'

Rita raised her eyebrows. 'I'm so sorry Mrs Plumb but I'm afraid I can't. Not today. I have a pressing appointment.'

Her employer frowned. 'What appointment?' Her voice had dropped a couple of octaves and become sharp.

'If you'll excuse my saying so,' Rita went on sweetly, 'that is my business. But if you're really stuck, I can arrange to be back by mid-afternoon.'

Mrs Plumb gave her a look as if she'd been chewing a wasp. 'Well, I suppose that will have to do.'

Refusing to rise to the bait, Rita smiled. 'Thank you, Mrs Plumb. So, I'll see you later.' And with that she breezed out of the room.

Outside on the street, Rita blew out her cheeks. She hated playing mind games but what choice did she have? Of course she had no appointment, but she was heading to the offices of the West End Nannies Agency.

Up until now, she'd had no interest in their coffee mornings, but Jenny had reminded her that if she was ever stuck with a problem, there was always help to be had there. Mrs Hunter wearing a short-sleeved royal blue dress and a three-strand pearl necklace welcomed her with open arms. Rita was surprised to discover the room was heaving with other nannies who had come from several different training schools. Some were obviously Norland Nannies from the prestigious school of the same name, some were council trained as was she, and others wore uniforms she'd not seen before. They were of all ages too. Some were young like herself while others were evidently retired. Everybody was friendly and she was made to feel welcome. It was only as they were going to sit down for the talk that she spotted Jenny at the back of the room so the two friends sat together.

The talk was given by a nanny who had worked in America. Rita was fascinated to hear about the difference in the American way of life.

'Every American has a belief in the American dream,' she said, 'and they are firmly convinced that you can achieve anything through hard work.'

When the talk was over, Mrs Hunter invited any questions and most of them were centred around Hollywood and famous film stars. Rita was delighted to hear that the speaker had met the nannies of some very important people like Tony Curtis and the director Blake Edwards.

Towards the end of their time together, Mrs Hunter asked if anyone had a current problem with their post or their charges. Along with three other girls, Rita put up her hand.

'You are welcome to share your concerns,' Mrs Hunter said before they began. 'We are all family and we are here to help one another, but it would be best if you don't identify your employers. We must be careful about divulging personal details and we wouldn't want any embarrassment later on.'

Mary was worried about her charge biting other children.

Nanny Downey remarked that, 'Young children have very limited ways of communicating and a child who bites is often overwhelmed by their emotions.'

'But what do I do to stop it?' Mary said. 'I do my best to stay calm, but his mother goes mad, shouting and smacking his hand and even pretend biting him.'

'Well good for you staying calm,' said one of the older nannies. 'Take him to one side and tell him it's all right to be cross about something but he mustn't bite.'

'If the parent makes that amount of fuss,' someone else suggested, 'he's more than likely to do it again just to get her attention.'

'Then I would distract him with another activity,' said Nanny Downey.

A few other people made suggestions and by the time they'd finished, Mary looked a lot less anxious.

When it came to Rita's turn she told them that her charge was rude, belligerent and aggressive in his speech. 'I get the feeling that he's been left with servants who didn't really care about him and that he's got used to having everything his own way.'

'Tricky one,' said Nanny Frost. 'I think you're going to have to show him there are consequences for his actions. Does he have a favourite toy?'

'His train set.'

'Then I would explain that his behaviour is unacceptable and the next time he does whatever it is, I would tell him that I am going to take away some of his train track.'

Rita nodded and several other nannies murmured their approval.

'You may have a hard time for a while,' Nanny Frost cautioned, 'but if you remain steadfast, he will eventually get the message.'

'My employer gives in to him all the time,' Rita said uncertainly.

'Then have a word with your employer,' someone else chipped in. 'Get her on board. It's the only way.'

'Sounds like you've got your hands full,' said Jenny as she and Rita shared a light lunch in a small Italian bistro nearby.

'I think I'll quite enjoy the challenge,' said Rita. 'I just wanted to make sure I was on the right track.' She glanced at her watch. 'I'd better go. I've got a driving lesson at one thirty.'

'I meant to ask you how you were getting on with that,' said Jenny. 'When do you take your test?'

'Before Christmas, hopefully,' said Rita making for the door, 'or the beginning of January. Sorry, must fly. See you.'

—

Mrs Plumb was over the moon to see Rita when she got back. Her normally neat hair had fallen out of her bun and her face was flushed. She and the children were in her sitting room watching *Crackerjack* on the television.

'Ah there you are Rita,' she said rising to her feet. 'Perhaps you could take over now.'

'Could I have a word with you first, Mrs Plumb?'

'Of course,' she said.

'In private.'

Her employer's mouth set in a straight line as she sailed passed Rita and out of the room. They both walked a little way down the corridor then she turned to face Rita. 'I hope you're not going to tell me you're giving in your notice.'

'Oh no,' Rita said breezily, 'but I should like to talk to you about Hamish's behaviour.'

Visibly relaxed now Mrs Plumb shook her head. 'I know, I know,' she began, her hands up in surrender. 'The problem is things are so different where he's come from.'

'That may well be the case, Mrs Plumb,' Rita began, 'but as he is now, no school will take him. His behaviour is appalling.'

Mrs Plumb's mouth gaped. She hesitated then said, 'Come into my study. We can talk more freely there.'

It wasn't easy for Rita telling a much older woman that her child rearing skills were no help at all in the present circumstances, but by the time Rita came out of the study they had worked out a strategy to help Hamish and Lauren. At first her employer suggested that Hamish had a good smacked bottom whenever he was out of line, but as Rita explained, 'To punish violence with violence will only encourage his belief that the person who is physically stronger wins the argument.'

Mrs Plumb sighed. 'Oh dear…'

'There will come a day,' Rita continued, 'when he is bigger than you or I and already he's certainly more powerful than his sister.'

'Well, he'll certainly get a good hiding when he gets to boarding school.'

'Mrs Niko is of the same opinion,' said Rita, shaking her head. She went on to explain that if they could help him see the error of his ways they might avoid that very thing. Eventually, Mrs Plumb could see the sense of her argument. They both agreed that although it wouldn't be easy implementing a no smacking and no shouting policy, it was the only way. As she left her office, Mrs Plumb promised she would back Rita 100 per cent and do her very best.

The first big confrontation came the very next day. Hamish wanted a drawing pencil Lauren was using and when she refused to give it to him, he shouted at his sister and punched her arm. Lauren screamed and burst into tears.

Having made sure Lauren was all right, Rita asked Hamish to step outside the playroom. He refused. Rita didn't repeat her request but instead gave him a hard stare and for the first time since he'd arrived in England, she saw a look of uncertainty in his eyes.

'Hamish,' she said coldly, 'I said come outside. I wish to speak with you.'

To her amazement, he followed her into the corridor. Bending down to look him in the eye she said, 'Hamish, your behaviour is completely unacceptable. You are a big boy. Your sister is much younger than you and boys do not hit girls.'

He frowned defiantly. 'I wanted the blue pencil.'

'Then you should have asked for it. You should have said something like, "Please can I use that blue pencil, Lauren? I will give it back when I've finished."'

'Why should I?' he scowled.

'Because there is a right and a wrong way to behave.' Oh how hard it was not to shout for emphasis, but Rita forced herself to keep her voice level and calm.

He pushed his face towards hers. 'Well I don't see—'

'This is not open for negotiation, Hamish,' Rita said firmly. 'If you cannot behave in a decent and gentlemanly manor, there will be consequences.'

Hamish, still frowning, drew a circle on the floor with his foot.

'If you take something of Lauren's or treat her that shabbily again, I shall take one of your things.'

His head shot up. 'Then I shall tell my grandmother,' he challenged.

'Go ahead,' said Rita. 'I am sure she will agree with me.'

Once again that look of uncertainty was back.

'Now you can go back in the playroom.'

As he slouched his way in, Rita thought she should have made him say sorry but her gut instinct told her that this moment in time, that was probably a bridge too far. She had challenged his thinking and however reluctantly, he had been compliant. That, for now, had to be enough.

The rest of the day passed without incident but the day after, Hamish presented Rita with a new challenge. He flew into a rage when his sister took one of the little people standing on the platform alongside the railway track. Rita wasn't sure why she wanted it, but the model was eventually spotted inside her doll's house. Hamish was incensed.

'That man is mine,' he shouted. 'Girls aren't allowed to touch my train set.' Then he hit her so hard that she almost fell over.

'Hamish,' Rita said firmly as she rushed to comfort Lauren, 'go and stand over there.'

He obeyed her, albeit with a bad grace, and watched Rita comfort his sister with a sullen expression. Rita checked that Lauren had suffered no real injury, concluding that Hamish had probably caught her off-balance. Lauren was persuaded to dry her eyes and apologise for taking the model. Hamish didn't acknowledge her apology but as Rita put the figure back in place, he took the opportunity to rush forward and pinch his sister. Her scream was so loud and intense that Gloria came running.

'Oh, that boy!' Gloria exclaimed when she saw what was happening.

Rita took his arm and removed him to the quiet room next door.

'Hamish,' she said firmly, 'you will stay here in the quiet room until you have calmed down and then you will apologise to your sister. I told you yesterday, boys do not hit girls.'

'You can't tell me what to do,' he shouted defiantly. 'You're nothing in this house.'

'I am going to close the door now Hamish. You can't come back into the playroom until you are ready to say sorry.'

Gloria was still there, shaking her head with a frown. 'I don't know how you do it,' she said. 'You're so patient with him.' Then all at once she let out a startled cry.

Hamish had decided to wreck the room he was in. Rita pulled Gloria out of sight and the two of them stood together as he continued his angry tirade. They could hear books being thrown about then the shelf itself being pushed over.

'It's going to take me ages to clear up that lot,' Gloria remarked.

'You're not going to,' said Rita. 'I shall get him to do it, so please don't worry about it.'

The look of relief on Gloria's face was unmistakable. With a long-suffering sigh, she squeezed Rita's arm and went back to her other work in the house.

As for Rita, she left Hamish for a while before going back. Clearly they were going to have a long battle of wills but for his sake she had to win.

Chapter 9

'Where Did Our Love Go?'
The Supremes

Rita was exhausted but she could at last see the light at the end of the tunnel. In the month since she'd been here, Hamish had been extremely difficult at times but she and Mrs Plumb stood their ground. As a result, it was getting to the point when she could just give him a 'look' and he became a lot more manageable, albeit rather grudgingly. At long last Rita was beginning to feel as if things might be turning a corner although he was sometimes still violent towards his sister. The day he'd wrecked the quiet room had been the catalyst. After he'd exhausted himself, Rita had gone back into the room to talk quietly with him, but even though he had calmed down, he worked himself up into another confrontation fairly quickly.

'You have no right to talk to me like that,' he'd shouted. 'I shall tell my grandmother.' And breaking free from the room, he'd stormed downstairs to her study.

By the time Rita got there, he was standing by her desk screaming out his protests. 'Send her away. She is ruining my life. She won't let me play with my toys. Lauren doesn't like her either. I hate her, Granny. I hate her!'

Mrs Plumb was staring at him like a startled rabbit in the headlights.

Rita hovered in the doorway. She wanted her employer to know that she was there but she knew it wouldn't be right to interfere. It cut her to the quick to listen to the lies he was telling in his ranting but however tempting it might be to put her side of the story, Rita knew any input from her now would only fan the flames. This was the defining moment for all three of them.

'Darling, I don't understand why you're so cross. Rita is just trying to help you.'

'Help me? Of course she's not helping me.'

'Hamish, you really must stop being so angry. You're going to school soon and the teachers won't like it if you shout like this all the time.'

'It's because of her, Granny. That's why I'm angry. Shall I tell you what she does?'

As Hamish complained so bitterly about the way he'd been treated, Rita held her breath. If his grandmother caved in now, all her hard work would be undermined and they'd be back to square one.

'I am your family,' he was shrieking. 'I should have the right to do what I like in my own home. I will not be spoken to like that. Who does that woman think she is? She's a nothing, a worm... I am a man, she is just a woman.'

It was at that moment that Rita knew she was listening to something else entirely. Hamish was only ten years old. With his limited life experience, he couldn't possibly have formed those opinions of his own volition. Where could he have got these ideas and where did this jaundiced attitude about women come from? He demanded respect when he in turn gave none. He was without affection, cold, heartless and the centre of his own little universe. She shivered. This was learned behaviour and more chillingly, it had most likely come from his own father.

'Hamish,' his grandmother was saying, 'I really can't be dealing with this. I am very busy. You must do what nanny tells you. Now please go.'

The child was horrified. 'But, Granny—'

There followed a split second when Mrs Plumb glanced up at Rita. Rita gave her a slight nod of her head and she turned back to her grandson. 'But nothing, Hamish,' she said firmly. 'Now please go.' And with that, she swivelled her chair away from him and went back to her typing. Her grandson was left with his mouth gaping.

It was clear that Hamish had never encountered such a reaction before. After knocking some of her papers to the floor and kicking the leg of his grandmother's chair, he came away from her study in a surly mood, deliberately bumping into Rita in the doorway.

Back upstairs he folded his arms and slumped into a chair with a scowl. Rita decided to leave him for a bit rather than talk again. Right now, he needed time to lick his wounds more than another lecture. The funny thing was, although he refused to speak to her, he did make a start on tidying the quiet room. After a while, Rita went back into the room and in a soft voice she explained why she was asking him to do certain things. He listened in silence but with a murderous expression in his eyes. In the days that followed, they still had clashes, but they were nowhere near as violent as that last one.

It wasn't long before Rita encountered another problem. She was forced to miss a couple of her days off because Mrs Plumb had to go somewhere. Her employer had promised to give her another day in lieu but somehow that never materialised. In the end, Rita had to put her foot down and from then on she was determined to take her time off no matter what.

All in all, Rita was feeling a lot happier with how things were going. It felt like she was achieving something. Hamish was much more manageable and although they had the occasional skirmish, his behaviour was nothing like the way it had been. The two children slowly settled to their new routine and Rita managed to get Hamish enrolled with the local Scouts while Lauren went to Brownies. It meant a taxi ride each way, but Mrs Plumb was happy to pay and luckily they were scheduled on the same day, just half an hour apart. That meant Hamish had a burger in a new shop called Wimpy while Lauren went off to her Brownies, then while her brother was in Scouts, Lauren had six penny-worth in a small fish and chip shop just around the corner because by then the Wimpy bar was closed. Other than that, they went to the park most days or she would take them on the bus to the countryside to let off steam. The children seemed to be settling down and certainly the household was more relaxed and peaceful.

Since her first visit, the WEN coffee mornings became a godsend for Rita. She loved hearing all the useful advice the other nannies gave and she made friends with some of the girls, especially Celia who worked for a doctor.

'Madam is writing some sort of medical book,' Celia said and it was obvious by the rolling of her eyes that she less than impressed. Her charge, Alfie, three, was a mischievous little boy with pale blue eyes and a shock of yellow hair, which try as she may, Celia couldn't control. Rita's new friend said she had her work cut out when he was running around, but she was clearly very fond of him.

'When is your day off?' Rita asked eventually. 'Fancy meeting up?'

'Thursday,' said Celia, 'and yes I'd love to.'

So next Thursday it was and as soon as she could, Rita called out her goodbyes and left the house.

Celia, who worked in Kensington, had told Rita about an old chemist shop which had recently opened as a fashion boutique called Biba.

'It's amazing,' she said. 'You can get a dress for two quid and it's fab stuff. Not at all fuddy-duddy.'

Rita had seen something about Biba in *Vogue* magazine. She'd splashed out four bob for the magazine but then discovered that just about everything inside was way beyond her means. The model on the front cover was wearing a mink coat costing £1575!

When she was in the nursery she could only manage to buy magazines occasionally but now that she was earning good money, she was happy to buy them so long as she could relate to what was inside. In *Flair* they said people like Cilla Black, Diana Ross and Marianne Faithfull shopped in Biba. One of the nannies in Hyde Park had seen Cathy McGowan from *Ready Steady Go* in a Biba's dress too. Rita couldn't wait to get there.

When she and Celia met, Rita was in for a surprise. She knew her new friend was a fan of Twinkle, a fifteen-year-old pop star who had just had a massive hit with a gut-wrenching song called *Terry* which was about the tragic death of a teenage biker, but she wasn't expecting Celia to turn up looking just like her! Celia's normally neat hair, which she usually wore in a chignon bun at the nape of her neck to the WEN meetings, was loose and hung over her cheeks. The mascara on her eyes was thickly spread both above and below the eye giving her a 'panda' look. Her lipstick was ghostly pale. She wore a short dress, the hem just above the knee, which she had bought on the King's Road from another new shop owned by a fashion designer called Mary Quant. Rita stuck to clothes from shops like C&A and was quite proud of her outfit until she saw what Celia was wearing.

'Where shall we go?' Celia asked.

Rita shrugged. 'I'm not very au fait with the shops around here. I've been to Selfridges and along Oxford Street but that's about all.'

Celia's jaw dropped. 'You haven't been to the Kings Road or Carnaby Street?' she squeaked.

Shame-faced, Rita shook her head.

'Then today is the day you begin your education,' Celia declared stoutly. She set off for the bus stop and Rita hurried to catch her up. She had no idea where they were going and clearly she had a lot to learn.

They spent their day wandering around the shops before deciding that Carnaby Street was the place to be. A nondescript backstreet behind the London Palladium, it may have been small, but it had some thoroughly modern boutique shops.

The place was teeming with men because the most popular shop was John Stephen's *His Clothes*. Everybody knew the top stars of the day went there so Rita and Celia were hoping they might spot someone famous. They weren't disappointed. Somebody's bag banged against Rita's leg as she was gazing up at a nearby shop sign causing her to stumble.

'Whoops, sorry love,' said a man's voice.

A Rolls-Royce was drawing to a halt almost beside her and as she turned, it was only then that Rita realised the person who had bumped into her was none other than Mick Jagger from the Rolling Stones. For a split second, it felt like she'd died and gone to heaven. She and Celia stood gaping like a couple of goldfish as Mick climbed into the back of the Rolls and it sped off.

At the end of the afternoon, all shopped up and exhausted, the two girls came across another of the new Wimpy bars. They sat at one of the bright red and yellow Formica tables and stuffed themselves with a Wimpy and french fries followed by a Knickerbocker Glory.

A couple of good-looking lads sat at a table not far from them. Celia said she fancied one of them and flirted outrageously. Before long the boys came to join them at their table. The dark-haired boy was called Phil and the other one was Dennis. After a while, Phil offered to buy Celia a coke so they went up to the counter together. Rita stayed with Dennis. He seemed quite nice and they chatted together amiably. She discovered he worked in a bank in Woking. Today was his day off and he'd come up to town with his friend to do some serious shopping. Phil was getting married in a couple of weeks so they were looking for decent shirts and ties and things like that, which was why Rita was surprised when he and Celia came back holding hands.

'Can I get you anything?' Dennis asked Rita.

'I'll be lucky if my new dress still fits now that I've eaten that lot,' Rita quipped as she pointed to her empty Knickerbocker Glory glass and Celia chuckled.

'There's a record shop just up the road,' said Phil. 'Fancy going there and listening to some pop songs?'

They walked as a foursome to the shop, Rita and Dennis side by side while Celia and Phil were still holding hands. Rita felt a tad uncomfortable about it but what could she say? Once inside they browsed through the vinyl.

Celia picked Roy Orbison's 'Oh, Pretty Woman' which was at number one, but because Rita couldn't make up her mind, Dennis chose Herman's Hermits 'I'm Into Something Good'. They separated to go into the booths, Celia and Phil in number six. Rita and Dennis in number ten.

The booths were small so they stood in close proximity to one another but without making eye contact. When Rita looked across at her friend, Celia and Phil were kissing.

Rita blinked in surprise and turned her head away. They four of them stayed to listen to a couple more records and then Phil said it was time they made tracks. Outside the shop, they said their goodbyes and the lads hurried to the mainline train station.

'Dennis told me Phil is getting married in a couple of weeks,' Rita said.

'So what?' Celia challenged. 'It was just a snog. I fancied him and we had a snog, end of.'

They had already decided to round off their day out by going to the pictures. Celia had suggested The Beatles film *A Hard Day's Night* but when they saw the queue outside, they changed their minds. In the end they plumped for *Carry On Spying* the ninth in the series starring a new-comer called Barbara Winsor alongside the regulars like Kenneth Williams and Jim Dale.

'Did I tell you I'm leaving?' Celia said as they sat in the auditorium waiting for the show to begin.

'Leaving!' cried Rita. 'No, you didn't. Why? Where are you going?'

'Madam is going to some place I've never heard of called the Falkland Islands,' said Celia. 'She has a contract to be their doctor. It's only a small community so she says it will give her more time to devote to her writing. She wants me to come with her and look after Alfie.'

'Amazing opportunity,' said Rita impressed. 'Lucky you.'

'Yes,' said Celia. Her voice was flat. 'Lucky me.'

Rita was puzzled. 'You don't exactly sound thrilled.'

'Don't get me wrong,' said Celia. 'It is a fabbo chance to see the world, but she already takes advantage of me now. I can't help feeling it'll be ten times worse when I'm more than seven thousand miles and a thirty-day sea voyage away from home.'

Rita nodded sagely. 'My Gran told me that wherever I ended up, I should always make sure I had the return fare home.'

The lights dimmed and Celia relaxed into her chair. 'Which is why I told Madam I didn't want to go.'

Chapter 10

'I Saw Mommy Kissing Santa Claus'
Jimmy Boyd
BBC Light Programme, *Children's Favourites*

On Monday December 21, Lauren was invited to a party. She was very excited and Rita enjoyed dressing her in a party frock. Hamish was stunned that he hadn't been invited too, so Rita made light of it by telling him it was 'girls only' and when out of ear shot of his sister, she got him to agree that that he probably wouldn't enjoy their giggly games anyway.

Someone came to collect Lauren and then Rita went back upstairs for Hamish. He turned his back as she came into the room, clearly out of sorts with the whole world and everybody in it.

'I've asked your grandmother if I can take you out,' she said.

'I don't want to go out,' he said grumpily.

'I know you like trains,' Rita went on, ignoring his bad mood, 'so I wondered if you would like to do a little train spotting.'

Hamish sat up straight but didn't turn around.

'I haven't got a clue how you do it,' Rita admitted, 'but I've enlisted the help of some lads who do. They've told us to meet them at Waterloo station.'

Hamish turned around and blinked.

'Apparently there are twenty-four platforms at the station so it has more than its fair share of trains of all types.' Rita kept her voice casual as she reached into his wardrobe for his coat. 'They tell me you'll see electric trains and steam trains and even some of the new diesel trains.' She held the coat out. 'Do you want to come or not?'

And seven minutes later, they were in a taxi heading for the station.

Of course, Rita hadn't the faintest idea about trains except that there was an engine up front, or occasionally one at the rear, but once again the nannies of the West End Nannies Agency had come up trumps. According to his old nanny, Master Hugo Hall-Amberley was an enthusiast par excellence. He would be back home from boarding school for Christmas on Sunday December 20, so Nanny Compton, his new nanny, had arranged for them to meet the next day under the huge clock. She had assured Rita that from there the two boys, and a couple of Master Hugo's friends, could race from platform to platform taking down the numbers and details of any train. 'So long as they don't annoy the station staff,' she said, 'they'll be fine.'

It turned out to be a fabulous afternoon. Master Hugo gave Hamish a pencil and a train spotting book as he explained that each train could be identified by its class, subclass and number and at the same showing Hamish where to write the results. Nanny Compton gave both boys strict instructions that they should be back under the clock by four thirty and as soon as the other boys arrived with their nannies, Master Hugo, the oldest by far, had taken charge and they all raced off. Rita was a tad alarmed that they'd dashed off so quickly but there was no way she could have kept up with them anyway. However, as soon as they'd gone, Nanny Compton suggested having tea in a nearby tea room.

'I can't leave him,' Rita cried. 'Look at all the people milling about. He's only ten years old.'

But the other nannies assured her that he would be fine.

'Surely you played on your own when you were a child,' Nanny Compton said. 'Master Hugo is a school prefect, for goodness' sake. He won't tolerate any foolish behaviour.'

It was slightly nerve wracking, but Rita had to admit that they were right about one thing. She had played on her own for hours and hours on the beach at Goring-by-Sea when she was the same age as Master Hamish and never come to any harm. Allowing herself to be convinced, the four of them set off. The tea rooms were just across the road. They sat in the window seat at a table with a dainty embroidered tablecloth and drank from China cups and saucers. The cake stand was nothing special but they enjoyed a selection of coffee sponge, Victoria sponge and lemon drizzle and she was fascinated to hear their stories.

Nanny Compton must have been in her forties. She had looked after Master Hugo since he was a toddler, the last child of a city banker and his wife.

'His mother always says that he was an accident,' she said as she poured the tea for them, 'but a very happy one. He's a delightful child.'

Nanny West said she had been looking after Master Thomas for two years. 'I shall miss him when I go.'

'Go?' Rita enquired.

'I'm getting married in March,' said Nanny West.

'Congratulations.' Rita took a bite of her lemon drizzle cake. It was delicious.

Penny, who looked to be the same age as Rita, was relatively new to nannying. Her charge, Master Edward Bury, was her first posting and she had finished her training in July.

'Around the same time as me,' said Rita. 'Where did you train?'

'Cheshire,' said Penny. 'I was in a National Children's Home nursery in Frodsham. There's talk of closing it down now.'

'Was it something you did?' Rita teased and Penny laughed.

While Nanny Compton and Nanny West talked about more serious things, Rita and Penny got on to the subjects that interested them, like The Beatles and Cilla Black.

'I reckon The Beatles will be Christmas number one this year,' Penny said.

'Me too,' said Rita.

In no time at all, it was almost four o'clock and Nanny Compton said they should get back to the station. When they arrived on the concourse three of the boys were comparing numbers but there was no sign of Hamish. Rita's stomach fell away.

'Where's Hamish?' She did her best not to sound panicked, but she wasn't so sure she'd managed it.

'I'm here,' said a voice behind her. 'I went to the toilet.' And Rita felt a wave of relief.

'Well,' said Nanny Compton, 'I hope you boys have enjoyed yourselves?'

They all agreed they had and everyone began to wish each other a happy Christmas.

'I go back to school on January 7,' said Master Hugo. 'Could we meet again before that Nanny?'

'I don't see why not,' said Nanny Compton. 'If any of you boys are free the first week in January…?'

There were enthusiastic nods all round and a date was fixed for Wednesday January 5.

Penny gave Rita a nudge and slipped a piece of paper in her hand. Rita glanced down and saw that it was a phone number. She looked up a grinned. It would be nice to meet Penny again.

'Kensington Olympia would be better,' Master Hugo piped up just as they were all leaving. 'You get freight trains there.'

And so it was arranged.

—

On the Wednesday Rita, Hamish and Lauren boarded a red Routemaster bus and spent a very pleasant late afternoon and early evening on the top deck looking at the Christmas lights. The streets were very busy and the shops were crowded. Rita had thought she might take them to Harrods or Selfridges but in the end she decided against it. It was too big a responsibility with two excitable children. The day before, she had taken them to some local shops to buy a present for their grandmother and they had enjoyed the adventure, although Rita could tell that even in the less crowded areas, Lauren was a little disconcerted. She supposed that coming from a place like Rhodesia they were unused to being surrounded by so many people. In the evening, the children had wrapped their gifts and hidden them in a drawer.

Christmas 1964 was going to be unlike any other Christmas Rita had ever had. Until she went to the nursery, it was just Gran and herself with Auntie Steph. Since his wife died a couple of years before, Eddie from next door had joined them. In the nursery, she'd spent the day with twenty-four or more small children and she'd done her bit in present wrapping and making sure that somebody (usually herself) collected enough money for Matron's present. On Christmas Day, the nursery routine was suspended and the girls did their best to make sure the children had a good time.

This year, Mrs Plumb was expecting her relatives, so Mrs Niko, who would be at home with her own family, had put everything ready the day before. Someone came to put up the Christmas tree and the children helped with a few decorations. Then they laid their presents for their granny under the tree.

By late afternoon on Christmas Eve, they had been joined by three more people. Mrs Plumb's widowed sister, Elizabeth and her gentleman friend, Sir Arthur Hall QC who came with Royston, his nineteen-year old-son. Mrs Elizabeth who was obviously younger than Mrs Plumb but Rita could see the family resemblance, came from York. She was lodging in Bayswater and in the process of selling her house before her marriage to Sir Arthur. Mrs Plumb had invited all three of them to stay until Monday. Rita gathered from bits and pieces of conversation that Sir Arthur had been Mrs Elizabeth's bridge partner at their local club for some time before a friendship had blossomed into romance.

Rita was in the kitchen getting the children's tea when her employer and her sister came in to make themselves a pot of tea. After introductions, the two women apparently forgot Rita was there.

'He can be a little bombastic at times,' Mrs Elizabeth confided in her sister, 'but since his wife left him, he gets lonely.'

'So have you been seeing him long?'

'A while.'

'And you're really sure about this, darling?'

Rita saw Mrs Elizabeth blush. 'I'm not a giddy schoolgirl,' she chided.

'Of course not,' said Mrs Plumb. 'I'm happy for you to have found someone. You've been on your own for far too long.' But as the two sisters walked back to the sitting room with a tea tray, something in her employer's voice made Rita think that all was not well.

They began Christmas Day by going to church. St Mary Abbott was just along the high street and easy to get to. Sir Arthur and Mrs Elizabeth walked arm in arm, Rita held Lauren's hand and Hamish walked with his grandmother. Royston came up beside Rita. He was rather on the lanky side with a shock of black hair. He didn't say anything, but he kept looking at her and something about him made her feel slightly uncomfortable.

The service was the usual Church of England morning Eucharist and apart from a small nativity scene just inside the door as they entered, there was scant reference to the season.

'Sermon went on far too long,' Sir Arthur complained as they left. 'What was it Winston Churchill always used to say; "if the vicar can't say what is needed in twenty minutes, he's got nothing good to say."'

Back home in Kensington, the goose, which Mrs Niko had left with strict instructions, was already in the oven cooking nicely.

Everyone was asked to be in the sitting room for pre-dinner drinks. Lauren tugged at Rita's sleeve and whispered. 'Do you think my daddy is having a nice Christmas?'

'I expect he's missing you and Hamish,' Rita told her confidentially, 'but I'm sure he's having a lovely time.'

Lauren nodded gravely.

'I usually have Christmas with my granny,' said Rita. 'I miss her but she's with her sister in Eastbourne this year.' She squeezed Lauren's hand. 'And here I am, having a lovely time here with you.'

The little girl gave her a tight smile.

Once everyone had a drink, Mrs Plumb held up her glass. 'To absent friends and happy Christmas everybody.'

Everyone stood up and raised their glasses. 'To absent friends and happy Christmas.'

Lauren had raised her glass of orange juice and Rita leaned towards her and clinked their glasses together. 'I hope you have a very happy Christmas, Lauren.'

And the little girl giggled.

Chapter 11

'I Feel Fine'
The Beatles
Christmas No. 1

When Mrs Plumb had asked Rita to help her lay the table earlier on Christmas morning, she was confident she knew what she was doing. There were several glasses at each place, layers of cutlery, napkins and condiments to put within easy reach. Had Rita not been schooled in these things during her private lessons, it could have been embarrassing. When they'd finished laying the table, it looked good enough for the Dorchester Hotel.

The meal was amazing. First soup, followed by roast goose, roast potatoes, chestnut stuffing, red cabbage, greens, Brussels sprouts, carrots and cranberry sauce. Mrs Niko had prepared everything ahead of the day so all they had to do was cook or re-heat it. The men ate heartily and Rita served small portions for the children knowing full well that a massive plateful of vegetables was always a no-no for under-fifteens.

She, herself, had a small glass of wine but refused more. All the same, Royston kept topping up her glass even though Rita protested. In the end, she let him fill it to the brim but drank no more. The conversation at the table was lively until Sir Arthur asked Mrs Plumb what she was up to in her office all day.

'Don't you know that my sister is a world-famous author?' said Mrs Elizabeth. Mrs Plumb waved her hand, embarrassed, but her sister, clearly very proud of her added, 'She was shortlisted for the National Book Award this year.'

'But she didn't win,' he said pointedly.

'The winner was an American,' said Mrs Plumb. 'John Updike. His book is called *The Centaur*. Well worth a read.'

'It's still an accolade to be shortlisted, dear,' Mrs Elizabeth pointed out and turning to Sir Arthur she added, 'Have you ever read one of my sister's books?'

Sir Arthur looked down his nose. 'I have not,' he said, 'and I am sure that if I did there would be nothing of interest for me between its pages.'

Mrs Elizabeth gasped. 'Don't you think that a little presumptuous Arthur?'

'No offence intended,' he said. 'I firmly believe that even if you women have an education, the female brain is incapable of anything academically serious.'

'I beg to differ,' Mrs Plumb said tartly. 'Think of Madame Curie.'

'Great discovery, hers,' Sir Arthur scoffed. 'So good she died of radiation poisoning.'

Royston leaned towards Rita. 'Drink up,' he said nodding towards her overflowing wine glass. 'There's plenty more where that came from.'

Rita smiled and picking up the glass she took a tiny sip.

'All right,' Mrs Elizabeth continued, 'what about Rosalind Franklin. Her work on carbon and coal brought about the gas mask. How many lives did that save? A woman, working on her own—'

'Poppycock,' interrupted Sir Arthur. 'She had an army of men helping her, I'll be bound.'

'I think we ought to change the subject,' Mrs Plumb said mildly.

'Just a minute,' her sister insisted, 'what about Tilly Shilling; her thimble fitted over the Rolls-Royce fighter engine carburettor saved countless lives during the war.'

Sir Arthur poured himself another glass of wine. 'I think you have a romantic view my dear. Women are best suited to what they were created for – home building, looking after their husbands and raising the children.'

Incensed, Rita was dying to chip in with something, but she was conscious that although she was sharing a meal with them, she was only an employee.

'Oh Arthur…' cried Mrs Elizabeth.

'Please!' Mrs Plumb snapped. The table fell into an awkward silence. 'Let's changed the subject shall we. This is Christmas Day and I want the children to enjoy themselves.'

Sir Arthur poured himself more wine and turning towards Rita he boomed, 'You're very quiet nanny. Tell us about yourself. Where do you come from? Do you come from London?'

Slightly embarrassed by Royston's penetrating stare, Rita gave them a brief resume of her life.

'And your parents? What do they do?'

'Arthur, dear,' Mrs Elizabeth scolded, 'the poor girl isn't in your witness box.'

'For God's sake, Elizabeth,' Sir Arthur snapped. 'I'm just curious, that's all. We all are.'

'My mother is dead, sir,' said Rita, 'and I believe my father is living somewhere in America. He was an American GI.'

The room went quiet.

'Oh Rita, I'm so terribly sorry about your mother,' said Mrs Plumb. 'I had no idea.'

'What's a GI?' Hamish wanted to know.

Mrs Plumb rose to her feet. 'Rita would you help me with these plates and things and then we can bring in the Christmas pudding.'

Out in the kitchen Mrs Plumb apologised again. 'I hope Sir Arthur didn't embarrass you, my dear. I think being a QC must have made him rather insensitive.'

'Please don't worry, Mrs Plumb. I don't mind, really.'

Yet funnily enough, as they busied themselves with preparing the Christmas pudding, Rita discovered she did mind. For the first time since Gran had given them to her, she wanted to read her mother's letters. Why did her father desert her mum? Did he know she'd been killed? And if so, why had he never sent for his daughter?

They doused the pudding in brandy, then while Rita held the door, Mrs Plumb carried it into the room to the sound of cheers and clapping. Hamish and Lauren stared in wide-eyed wonder. Once the flames were out, everyone had small portions and agreed that the pudding was delicious. Everyone commented that Mrs Niko was a fantastic cook and Rita made a mental note to tell her so.

After the meal, all six of them went into the sitting room. Rita stayed behind in the kitchen to make some coffee. She could hear the exclamations of pleasure as the children spotted the Christmas tree groaning with presents. They were desperate to start opening their gifts but she heard their grandmother telling them they had to wait a while longer.

'We have to listen to the Queen's speech first.'

The family arranged themselves in front of the television and Mrs Plumb switched it on to warm it up. Rita put the tray of coffee down and perched on a hard back chair behind the sofa while they all waited for the picture of Buckingham Palace to come on the screen.

The television itself was no more than fifteen inches wide, so the picture was quite small. Her Majesty spoke mostly about the Commonwealth which everybody knew was a subject close to her heart. The rest of the Queen's speech was lost on her as Rita tried to imagine herself as a nanny extraordinaire traveling around the Commonwealth countries with her charges, visiting places like Australia, and Canada or even the more exotic places, like Fiji. Her mind drifted away until…

'Rita.'

She suddenly realised that Mrs Plumb was asking her to give out some of the presents. Rita stood up and handed a gift to Lauren.

'We shall all wait until everybody has something,' her employer announced, 'then we'll all open them together.'

Hamish and Lauren's piles quickly grew. Royston had quite a lot, too. The adults had mostly bottle shaped presents or long thin ones which were probably jewellery. Rita had wrapped a box of chocolates for Mrs Plumb, *The Boy's Own Annual* for Hamish and for Lauren she'd bought book called *Nordy Bank* by Sheena Porter. It looked as if it would be the kind of thing to grab her attention, an adventure book about some children camping in Shropshire.

They all opened their gifts to the sounds of tearing paper and 'Ooohs' and 'Aaaahs,' with the occasional 'Thank you' thrown in for good measure. Sir Arthur had a bottle of whiskey, presumably from Mrs Elizabeth and he had given her a fabulous necklace. To her great surprise, Rita had some presents too. Mrs Plumb had given her a lovely wristwatch. Lauren had wrapped some boxed handkerchiefs inside a sweet picture she had drawn herself and Hamish had made her a small box with a lid with some of his Meccano set. The lion's share of presents went to the children, of course. Among other things, they had a Mr Potato Head, a 3D View-Master, a walking robot and a school satchel.

When all the presents had been opened, Rita gathered the wrapping paper to throw in the bin. As she did so, she cast her mind back to her own childhood Christmases with her mum when all the wrapping paper was carefully smoothed out, folded and sometimes ironed to re-use next year. In the aftermath of the war, the 1950s were called the austerity years. Everything was tight and they didn't have much, and they were far less wasteful than people were now.

While the children played with their new toys, the adults dozed. Rita was reading the information about her watch when Royston came and sat next to her. 'Have you got a boyfriend?'

She shook her head. 'I don't get much time for one,' she said absentmindedly.

He was a bit intense and he sat a little too close to her, but she told herself he was all right really. It was rather unfortunate that he had such terrible acne on his face but he told her he liked rugger and sailing and that he was about to embark on a university course – banking or some such thing. Rita wasn't terribly interested but she did reflect on how different their lives were. She hadn't even had the opportunity to go to Sixth Form at school. As soon as she'd taken her end of term exams, she knew she had to go out and find a job. Gran couldn't be expected to carry on supporting her once she'd reached sixteen.

At around seven thirty, the children said their good nights and Rita took them off to bed. They were tired but happy. They'd had a wonderful day. After their baths, they'd jumped eagerly into bed. Lauren was almost asleep before her head hit the pillow. Rita brushed her curls from her forehead and kissed her. 'Night, Poppet.'

'Night…' Lauren said sleepily. 'Thank you for my present.'

Hamish was sitting on the top of his bed when she went to him. 'What's a GI?' he repeated.

'I'm not sure that it has an exact meaning, but it was what they called the American soldiers during the war,' said Rita.

'So your father was from America?'

Rita nodded.

'Did he know John Wayne?'

'I shouldn't think so,' Rita chuckled. She lifted his sheets and he clambered in. Tucking him up, she said 'Good night Hamish, and thank you for my lovely present.'

'S'all right,' he murmured. There was just a hint of a smile on his lips as he turned over. 'Night.'

What a difference in just a few weeks. Rita tidied up their clothes and switched off the lights. Back in the sitting room, Mrs Plumb and the others were relaxing in front of the television. They were watching a Whitehall farce with the actor and producer Brian Rix. Rita had seen one of them before and she knew they were always great fun. This one was about two buskers who were mistaken for British agents who were supposed to prevent the assassination of a prominent scientist. The play was full of misunderstandings and as usual, featured by a lot of people dodging one another and ducking and diving from MI5 and the KGB. The timing was skilled and very funny. Mrs Plumb invited Rita to join them and along with the others, she laughed out loud.

Rita said her good nights when it had finished, and after checking on the children, she had a bath and got ready for bed. She was about to switch off the light when she remembered her mother's letters. They were still in her suitcase, tucked away in a side pocket and all at once she was overwhelmed by a desire to read them. Having pulled the case from the top of the wardrobe, Rita took the bundle out and laid it on the bed.

She stared at them for a long time before she untied the ribbon. She had so many questions, but would they give her the answers? Did her father know he had a daughter? Had he perhaps refused to acknowledge that she was his child? Judging by the number of letters he had written, he must have known about her. Her birthday was in April and there was one letter postmarked May 1945. Her parents had corresponded for two years, but now that they were all spread out, there weren't that many. She counted out ten of them. That worked out at less than one every two months. Of course, it was possible that her mother had destroyed some, or maybe some had been lost in the post.

She fanned them out and put them in order according to the date on the franking over the stamp. The first had arrived in August 1944. Rita smelled it and turned it over in her hands before she opened it. It was musty. When she took the letter from its envelope, her father's handwriting had a distinct slope but it was very clear and easy to read.

> *My own dearest love,*
>
> *We have reached Le Mans. We are advancing against the Germans, but the fighting has been intense. The one thing that drives me on is you.*
>
> *Before I met you I never knew what love was. Remember the night we saw the film The Man in Grey? Well, I am your Stewart Granger and you my very own Phyllis Calvert, although you are far more beautiful. I never felt such a passion as I have right now for you, my darling. I want you to know you have made me complete.*
>
> *As soon as this damned war is over I want us to begin a new life together. I want to spend the rest of my days with you in my arms. I want to hold you and kiss you and love you as we did on that last night. Oh, my darling I burn for you. I used to think of you all the time but now it is every moment of every day. Sometimes my thoughts about you overwhelm me and I know that as time goes on, my love for you will grow and grow. It will never diminish. I shall never forget our last date. Fanny by Gaslight will be my favourite film forever. Funny how Stewart and Phyllis were starring together in that film, too. I can still taste your sweet kisses on my lips... tell me, my darling, what was that film about? I guess I was too busy kissing you to watch it.*
>
> *Sweetheart, I can't wait until the day when you will be mine for always. I have put in for permission for us to marry and as soon as it comes I want you to be ready. You may not get time to buy a wedding trousseau but honestly, honey, that doesn't matter. When we are in the States, I shall buy you all the gowns and beads and shoes you want. Don't forget me, my love. I love you so much.*
>
> *Forever and always, Dexter*

How beautiful. As she put the letter back into its envelope, she marked it 'Letter number one'. Rita was suddenly aware that she had tears on her cheeks. He had loved her mother so much, where had it all gone wrong? Why had they never married? Why didn't he send for her when he got back to the States? She put the letter back on the pile. She was feeling quite emotional so she told herself it was too late to read the others tonight, but even as she turned out the light, she had a feeling she wouldn't get much sleep.

Chapter 12

'I'm Gonna Be Strong'
Gene Pitney

Boxing Day was cold but sunny so everyone went for a walk in the park, Rita included. The obvious choice was Kensington Gardens which was only a short distance away. Rita was keen to be outside in the fresh air because it would be good for Hamish and Lauren to be able to let off a little steam.

Of course, being winter, the gardens were nowhere near as vibrant as in the summer, but wandering around part of such a massive parkland felt as if they were deep in the countryside. There were other strollers about but not that many. At the Peter Pan memorial Mrs Plumb took a picture of her grandchildren next to the boy who never grew up.

'We shall send it to Daddy,' she told them. 'I'm sure he misses you dreadfully.'

As they all stood around watching the children posing for the photograph, Rita felt a hand on her bottom. She spun round to see Royston right behind her. Glaring angrily at him, she moved away but he was quite unabashed, winking suggestively as he grinned.

'Where shall we go now?' asked Mrs Plumb when she'd finished.

Rita had brought some bread with them so she suggested that the children might like to feed to the ducks on the Long Water and everybody agreed it was a lovely idea.

'How long have you been a nanny?' Mrs Plumb's sister asked her.

'This is my first post,' said Rita. 'Before this I worked in a council-run Surrey children's nursery for two years.'

'And now you're enjoying the bright lights of London,' said Sir Arthur.

I wish, thought Rita. Sir Arthur and Mrs Elizabeth walked on just ahead of her.

'I know all about girls like her,' she heard Sir Arthur say. 'Not a care in the world. Parties and dances, that's all they think about. All on the bloody pill, don't you know.'

Rita bristled. Pompous ass. How dare he?

After an enjoyable time with the ducks, they all turned for home.

—

Lunch, which was served mid-afternoon, consisted of leftovers served with pickles and chutneys. Rita helped in the kitchen by preparing a salad and boiling some potatoes and when they were cooked, she tossed in onion, chopped bacon pieces and some parsley. Everyone agreed they were delicious.

In the afternoon, as the children played with their new toys and the adults dozed, Rita crept out of the room to clear up the kitchen. The family had helped with the washing up but many of the plates and dishes were in the incorrect place. Besides, she'd seen how diligent Mrs Niko was and she was positive the family's idea of clean and tidy wouldn't pass muster. She had just finished wiping out the oven when Royston appeared.

'Need any help?'

'All finished, thank you,' she said. 'Can I get you anything?'

He had something behind his back. 'You can give me a kiss,' he said and holding his hand up he added, 'I've got some mistletoe.'

Kissing him was the last thing Rita wanted to do. Ever since he'd been here he'd made her feel uncomfortable with his constant staring and intense personality, but what could she say? To refuse would probably be embarrassing for them both and she also wondered if he would make a scene.

'Oh, go on then,' but as his mouth came towards her, she turned her head at the last moment so that his rather wet-looking puffy lips landed close to her ear. That was when she realised that he'd pinned her against the closed door of the oven. Rita tried to push him aside in order to move away but he pressed his body even closer and put his hand on her breast. She could feel his arousal pressing on her stomach.

'Don't,' she said firmly.

He stared at her almost unseeing as he kneaded her breast. She tried to bat his hand away. 'I said, don't!' Her tone was far more authoritative but instead of removing his hand, he said, 'Go on, you know you like it,' then he pinched her nipple hard. Rita cried out in pain and rounded on him. 'How dare you,' she hissed. 'Get away from me.'

A voice behind them said, 'Ooh, lovers tiff?'

Royston sprang back and Rita saw Sir Arthur in the doorway. 'Don't mind me,' he said clearly the worse for drink. 'I just came for a glass of water. I remember what it is to be young.'

Rita threw her dishcloth into the sink and sailed past the two of them with as much dignity as she could muster. He was horrible… horrible, in fact they both were.

After she'd put the children to bed that evening, Rita decided to stay in her room. She didn't fancy conversation and she was tired anyway. Thank goodness Arthur Hall and his dreadful son were leaving first thing in the morning. From small overheard snippets of conversation she rather thought Mrs Plumb didn't seem very keen on him either, although Rita had overheard her telling her sister, 'If he makes you happy, that's all that matters.'

The business with Royston had shaken Rita up a bit and she felt a little tearful. She made up her mind to avoid him at all costs. He was vile and the sooner they all went home the better.

Maybe she was a bit naïve, she reflected, but it had honestly never occurred to her that she might be vulnerable in her place of work. Members of the household taking advantage of female staff had always seemed so Victorian and the stuff of romance novels, hardly a problem for the woman of today. This was the 1960s for goodness' sake.

Rita decided to distract herself by reading her brand new Agatha Christie novel, her Christmas present to herself. At sixteen shillings, it had cost an absolute fortune, but the story worked its magic from the very beginning and Rita decided it was worth it in spades. The main character, Miss Marple had been about to hear all about a man who got away with murder when her informant was found dead. Gripping stuff.

Too tired to read for long, and feeling much calmer, Rita turned out the light at about ten. She was just dozing off when something startled her. She heard a noise coming from the room next door to her, a sort of bump, and then Hamish cried out. Was he having a bad dream? As Rita sat up to go to him, she saw a shadow crossing her own room. Oh, poor boy. He was so frightened he'd come to her instead! Rita reached for the bedside lamp but as she switched it on and the room flooded with light, an adult hand came over her own and switched it off.

'No need for that,' said a gravelly voice.

She recognised him at once. Royston Hall! Rita's heartbeat quickened. She'd never been with a man but she knew what was coming. Batting his hand away, she tried to sit up but he seemed to have hands the size of spades and was pushing her in a direction she didn't want to go. In her desperation to make him stop, panic was setting in.

'Get off of me!' she shrieked, and as he pressed her back down into the bed, Rita began the fight of her life. As she tried desperately to push him away, she was unaware that she was still holding the light flex until the bedside light, her glass of water and her book crashed noisily to the floor. He was astride her now and she could hardly breathe under the weight of him but thank God she still had blankets and a sheet between them. However, the way he was tearing at them, it wouldn't be for much longer.

'Stop it, stop it,' she cried, her voice sounding more like a sob. His silence was more menacing than the first words he had spoken especially when he raised himself up and hit her. The blow on the side of her head made her see stars but something in her made her keep fighting. He pulled her body so that she rolled onto her side, but she wasn't going to give in yet. She continued to push and struggle and kick, anything to try to stop him but he seemed to have the strength of ten men.

Her pyjama top was open now, and the sheet was going further down the bed. He grabbed hold of her wrists and pulled both hands above her head. Now she was completely trapped. His hot and excited breath was loud in her ear as he fiddled with the buttons on her pyjamas bottoms. She was feeling more and more helpless and more and more terrified as his hand went inside her pyjamas and he stroked her bare skin. 'Don't,' she spat. 'Get off me!'

All at once, the room was suddenly flooded with light.

Royston turned just enough for Rita to see Mrs Plumb and Sir Arthur standing in the doorway with Hamish who appeared to be wiping his tear-filled eyes with the cuff of his pyjamas sleeve. Royston let go of her wrists and Rita grabbed at her clothing to make herself decent. She was crying; she hadn't realised that, and she was breathing hard. Her wrists hurt and so did her face where he'd slapped her.

'Just a bit of fun, Pa,' said Royston moving away from the bed and pulling up his pyjamas.

'Get him away from me,' Rita sobbed. 'Get him away!'

Royston let out a nervous laugh. 'She was all up for it downstairs.'

'I was not!' Rita shouted after him. Fear had given way to white hot anger. 'And certainly not with a creep like you.'

Mrs Plumb hustled her grandson back to bed.

'Sorry if we woke you up, Hamish old chap,' Royston called after him.

Rita became aware of someone else in the room. Through her tears she saw Mrs Plumb's sister walk in.

'I never really wanted her, Pa,' said Royston, 'but she egged me on. She even went to bed early so I could be with her. Made out it would be my Christmas present.'

'You bloody liar!' Rita spluttered.

Sir Arthur came towards the bed and glared down at her. 'You wanton hussy,' he snarled. 'Take advantage of my boy, would you?'

Rita pulled the sheet back up to her chin. 'Excuse me!' she snapped angrily. '*Your boy* came into my room uninvited and forced himself on me.'

Mrs Elizabeth took in her breath noisily.

'Don't believe a word she says, darling,' Sir Arthur said addressing her. Then turning back to Rita, he added contemptuously, 'I know your type. Lead a young lad on with your teasing and change your mind at the last minute.'

'Oh Arthur,' Mrs Elizabeth said uncertainly. 'You can't really believe that.'

Rita couldn't believe what he was saying. As she struggled to control her temper, Sir Arthur rounded on Mrs Elizabeth. 'Shut your trap, woman. What do you know about it? I told you, I know her type. I see tarts like her every day in my courtroom.'

Rita opened her mouth to defend herself yet again when Mrs Plumb came back into the room. 'You've made your point, Sir Arthur,' she said stiffly. 'I think it best if we all go back to our rooms now.'

'Trying to blame my boy,' Sir Arthur murmured as he and his son turned to go.

Mrs Plumb came to Rita and sat on the bed. 'Are you all right?' she said gently.

Rita nodded miserably. 'I didn't encourage him, ma'am, I promise,' she said.

'I don't think for one minute you did, my dear,' Mrs Elizabeth whispered as she patted Rita's arm.

'After all this I need a stiff drink,' Sir Arthur shouted from the doorway.

Mrs Elizabeth gave her sister an uncertain look. 'I'd better deal with this once and for all,' she said.

Mrs Plumb nodded her head and giving Rita a shaky smile, Mrs Elizabeth turned to go.

'I did not invite him to my room,' Rita said emphatically.

'Rita,' said Mrs Plumb. 'I saw the way he behaved towards you at dinner and at the park. He's a very unpleasant young man.'

Rita was trying to be professional but her kindness was the catalyst. She looked at her employer for a second or two then burst into tears. Mrs Plumb put her arm around her, gently rocking her until Rita stopped.

'Tell me exactly what happened, my dear,' Mrs Plumb whispered, as she handed Rita her own handkerchief, 'did he...?'

Rita wiped her nose and shook her head. 'I managed to keep the sheet between us and thank God I was wearing pyjamas.'

After a while she had calmed herself down, but it wasn't long before Rita and Mrs Plumb could hear heated and angry voices downstairs. A moment later there was a loud bang as someone slammed the front door and then they heard a car start. As it roared off into the night, Mrs Plumb's sister put her head around the door. 'They've gone.'

'Good,' said Mrs Plumb. 'If you hadn't done it, I would have. Honestly darling, you deserve better than that.'

Mrs Elizabeth came up to Rita. 'I'm so sorry.'

'You'll be safe now, Nanny,' said Mrs Plumb as she rose to her feet and reverted to employer/employee status, 'but when we've gone, feel free to put a chair under the door handle if you want to.'

Rita nodded and the two sisters linked arms as they left the room. Rita heard Mrs Elizabeth saying, 'I'm so sorry Philippa. I had no idea...'

'I'm just glad we all saw his true colours before it was too late,' said Mrs Plumb.

Rita climbed out of bed and went into the bathroom to wash her face. It was a shock to look in the mirror. She already had a large swelling on her cheek just under her eye, her wrists were bruised too. They should have called the police but even as the thought crossed her mind, she knew they wouldn't want the scandal. Anyway, the word of a eighteen-year-old nursery nurse against that of the son of a Queen's Counsel would count for nothing. She had another little cry then made her way back to bed.

She was just climbing into bed when her door opened slowly. Rita almost panicked but then she saw a tousle-haired little boy standing there.

'Hamish?'

'Don't worry if he comes back, Nanny,' he said raising his fist. 'Just give me a shout and I'll come and biff him one.'

Chapter 13

'Downtown'

Petula Clark

When she woke up the next morning, Rita was absolutely certain that she could put the events of that night behind her, but it didn't take long before she knew it had scarred her much more than she'd first thought. She certainly hadn't teased Royston, but had she inadvertently given him the wrong signal? She was jumpy, nervous and every now and then she kept going over the what-if's. What if Royston hadn't gone to the wrong room first? He must have given Hamish a scare because as soon as he blundered from his bedroom, the boy had raced downstairs to his grandmother. What if she hadn't knocked over her drink and the lamp – something which had brought Mrs Plumb running up the stairs? What if that blow to her head had been just a tad more serious and she'd been unable to resist him? She knew in her heart of hearts it was stupid going over everything like that, but her brain wouldn't stop churning up the same old ground.

She worried about something else too. Lauren had slept throughout the whole incident, but had it affected Hamish? He'd brought a tear to her eye when he'd promised to protect her if Royston came back, but what had this impressionable ten-year-old actually seen? He already had a rather warped idea of how to treat women. Would this cement his jaundiced view or maybe confuse him even more. To this end, Rita decided that she should talk to Mrs Plumb at her earliest convenience.

'Rita, come in, come in,' she said as Rita knocked on her door. 'Are the children all right?'

'Your sister is with them,' said Rita. 'They are all playing a board game – Mousetrap. They're having great fun.'

Mrs Plumb nodded her head. 'And what about you?' she said kindly. 'How are you feeling?'

'I'm not sure,' Rita admitted. 'A bit of a chump if I'm honest.'

Mrs Plumb frowned. 'I don't see why you should,' she said. 'It's funny how we women always look for a way to blame ourselves when something bad happens.' She gave Rita a serious stare. 'You must get it into your head that none of this was your fault. You behaved impeccably and at no time did you encourage that young man.'

Rita's knees begin to tremble.

'I can see you are still upset, Rita,' she went on, 'which is why I think you should take a couple of days off. Go home to your grandmother and enjoy some of her home cooking.'

'I don't want to let you down,' Rita said tearfully.

'You won't,' her employer said. 'Look, my sister needs a distraction, too. You take a break and she'll look after the children. That way you'll both have a moment to yourselves.'

'When do you want me back?'

'How about New Year's Eve,' said Mrs Plumb. 'Perhaps you would be good enough to look after the children so that my sister and I can go out.'

Rita didn't have the heart to tell her she had planned to go to the Lyceum with Jenny but as she turned to leave she had a sudden thought. 'I have arranged for Hamish to do some train spotting with his friends on January 5 just before he goes to school.'

'That's fine,' said Mrs Plumb. 'You be back here by Thursday and we'll all start afresh.'

'Thank you. You are very kind.'

'Not at all, Rita. You've done wonders with that grandson of mine. I don't want to lose you.'

—

Before she left London, Rita had to telephone Jenny to explain that she wouldn't be able to go with her to the Lyceum for the New Year celebrations after all. Rita had worried that she might annoy her friend and that the last-minute disappointment would damage their friendship but as they talked, Rita sensed a scintilla of relief in Jenny's voice.

'That's all right. Mrs Dawson has invited me and Simon to be with them for the countdown to 1965,' she said. 'They've booked a couple of nights in a hotel near Bath and Simon is to drive them there. I knew Simon wanted me to go but I felt a bit awkward about it because of our date. Well now I can say yes, so don't worry, it'll be fine.'

'What'll be happening with Pixie?' Rita asked.

'She's coming with us,' said Jenny adding with a chuckle. 'The car is as big as a bus. Pixie'll be in bed when we all celebrate the New Year of course. I just need to keep an eye on her that's all.'

Rita was relieved.

She heard her friend take in a breath. 'Is there any reason why you couldn't come to the dance?'

'I'm off to see my gran now, so I need to make up the time to work.'

'She's not ill, I hope,' Jenny said anxiously.

'No, no,' Rita assured her. 'Look, we'll chat next time I see you, okay?'

'Okay, if you're sure. Have a good time and I'll see you next year.'

'I am. I'm glad you're going somewhere nice. Have a great time and happy New Year.'

Rita put the telephone back onto the receiver. Happy New Year to me, she thought acidly. She took a deep breath. At least she could leave the memory of that night firmly in 1964 and there was every hope that 1965 would be a lot brighter.

—

Being back in Worthing at this time of year was strangely odd. From what she could gather, Gran and her sister had enjoyed their Christmas, although Rita was slightly sceptical that it was as wonderful as her gran made out. She and Auntie Steph had a prickly relationship at the best of times.

'We had a lovely chicken,' said Gran, 'and one of my Christmas puddings. What about you?'

Rita shared the bare facts and hopefully left her grandmother believing everything had been wonderful. On the train coming down she had decided she wouldn't tell her about Royston. If, for one minute, she thought Rita was in danger, Gran would be on the phone either to the WEN or Mrs Plumb – or both – immediately. She wasn't an openly demonstrative woman but she was a lioness if one of her cubs was hurt.

Evenings were quiet. Rita sat by the fireside with her book, the only sound in the room being the ticking of the clock. In times gone by, she'd hated the dullness, but now it was strangely comforting.

'Did you read your mum's letters?' Gran asked.

'I read one of them,' Rita admitted.

Her grandmother harrumphed.

Rita chewed on her bottom lip then said, 'Tell me about him, Gran. Tell me about my father. What was he like?'

Gran sat back and relaxed in her armchair. 'He weren't like a lot of them yanks,' she began. 'He didn't brag about what 'e had back home. He was gentle, kind. Your mother doted on 'im.'

'But you didn't like him, did you,' Rita said cautiously.

'I did,' said Gran, 'but then he went and done the dirty on her.'

Rita frowned. 'What does that mean?'

'He promised to send for 'er, but he never did. Kept her 'anging about for nigh on two year after he got back to America.' Her angry words were tumbling out. 'She had you all on 'er own and brought you up 'erself even though there was no money coming in. Cleaning people's houses she started with and I taught her bookkeeping. That's how she ended up in the bank. That girl saved every penny she could so's she could go to America. Never went out with nobody else. Never so much as looked at another feller. Oh no, she looked for the post every day and then all at once 'e writes to say he's very sorry but 'e's marrying somebody else!'

Rita blinked. 'In his letter, he said he was in France – Le Mans, I think it was.'

Gran nodded. 'They ended up marching through the streets in Paris,' she went on. 'Fifteen thousand of them, there were. We saw it, yer mum and I, on the *Pathé News* when they was liberated. All them Frenchies putting flowers on the tanks and kissing the GI's.'

Rita smiled. 'Did you see him on the screen?'

Gran shook her head, and glancing at the expression on her face, Rita sensed the time for talking about Dexter was over. 'Shame you won't be here to bring in the New Year,' she said changing the subject.

Rita shrugged. 'Can't be helped I'm afraid.'

Her gran was going to spend New Year's Eve with friends and neighbours in the scout hut across the road. It was always a low-key affair but very enjoyable. There would be bunting on the ceilings and lots of food. The women would drink punch and the men would have plenty of beer. Then they would play silly games and have a sing song. Rita would have liked to have met up with several of her old primary school friends, most of them married, and perhaps Nat Humphries the boy she use to play with when she lived in Tarring Road – who was now in the merchant navy, she remembered – but she had promised Mrs Plumb that she would be back in time to let her employer and her sister have their bit of fun. Gran said she had become the envy of everybody in Goring-by-Sea because she was 'living in London as a private nanny,' but Rita didn't respond to that. If only she knew. It wasn't always as glamorous as it sounded.

The short break gave Rita time to lick her wounds and come to terms with what had happened. She knew it would never truly go away but she was determined not to let it spoil her life. Surprisingly, the children were pleased to see her again. Lauren ran to her and hugged her waist. Hamish hung back with an embarrassed smile. When they were alone, she gave them both a present. Lauren received a small troll doll made out of hard vinyl with big brown eyes and a wisp of bright yellow hair. They were becoming hugely popular with some children making them a collector's item. Rita gave Hamish a railway porter's badge. It wasn't new, she told him. 'It belonged to my uncle who used to work at West Worthing station.' Hamish's eyes lit up and he couldn't wait to put the badge on his jumper.

'And don't forget,' she added, 'that we'll be meeting Hugo and his friends next week.'

Mrs Plumb and Mrs Elizabeth set off at around nine and by then Lauren was fast asleep. Hugo was allowed to stay up so they watched an interminably boring programme on the television then stood at the upstairs window to watch the fireworks.

'Happy New Year, Hamish,' she said.

'Happy New Year, Nanny.' And they shook hands.

—

A few days later, Hamish was very excited she took him to the station at Kensington Olympia to meet up with Masters Hugo, Thomas and Edward. He was proudly wearing the porter's badge on his coat, to the envy of his new friends.

Once again, while the boys raced around the station, Nanny West and Nanny Compton headed outside the station to the proper tea shop, but Rita and Penny opted for the station tea room where, from the window, they could see the boys on the bridge over the railway line. It was a much smaller station than Waterloo, so they were within plain sight all the time. Rita felt a lot more relaxed about the outing than she had done last time.

'You never got around to phoning,' Penny said as she brought their tea and a scone to the table.

'I'm so sorry about that,' said Rita. 'I never seemed to get a moment to myself.'

'Tell me about it,' Penny chuckled. 'How was your Christmas?'

Rita answered truthfully as she talked about the roast goose, presents under the tree and going for a walk on Boxing Day. 'How about you?'

'Amazing,' said Penny. 'I've never seen so much food and the house was heaving with people all day long. I was completely done in by six o'clock.'

'Did they work you hard?'

'I never stopped. It was all Nanny can you do this, and Nanny would you do that…'

Rita chuckled. '*Would you just…* jobs.'

Penny frowned, slightly puzzled.

'My friend Jenny told me about them. 'Oh, while you're ironing that shirt, *would you just* do mine?' 'Nanny, *would you just* go up to my bedroom and collect my cardigan…'.'

Penny laughed. 'I see what you mean and yes, I had plenty of *would you just* jobs. In fact, you could say I had them by the shedload!'

'But you enjoyed Christmas?'

Penny hesitated for a second then nodded, 'Yes, I think I did on the whole.'

'That makes me think you had a problem.'

'I just don't like my employer's familiarity,' said Penny. 'I don't think he means anything by it, but he comes up beside me and hugs me, or he whispers silly things in my ear when his wife is looking.'

'You mean when she isn't looking,' Rita corrected.

'Oh no,' said Penny. 'He makes sure she's watching us. He does it deliberately. The thing is, I don't know what to do about it.'

Rita took a bite into her scone. It was as hard as a rock and had probably been hanging around since a week ago last Tuesday. Should she confide in Penny about Royston? She didn't really want to talk about him. Even the thought of him made her shudder.

There was a deafening roar as a freight train thundered through the station. Hamish, Master Hugo and Master Thomas were scribbling down the engine number while Master Edward who was a lot shorter than the others kept appearing and disappearing as he jumped up and down to see over the barriers.

'They're having a whale of a time,' said Penny looking out of the window.

Rita abandoned her scone and watched. After a few minutes, she suggested going back onto the platform, so they did.

'Listen,' Rita said as they reached a seat on the platform, 'You've got my number but take the WEN telephone number as well.' She scribbled it down at the back of her diary and torn out the page. 'I'll tell Mrs Hunter about you. If you have any more trouble with your employer, something you can't handle, I know they will help you.'

Penny nodded grimly. 'Thanks Rita.'

'And if I was you,' Rita continued sagely, 'I'd get out of there as soon as you can.'

The other nannies came back about three quarters of an hour later after which everyone went their separate ways.

On the bus back to Kensington, Rita reflected that she wasn't the only one who had problems with her employer. Mr Royston had gone further than others perhaps, but just how did you deal with unwanted attention? Maybe it was time to ask the advice of the West End Nannies again.

Chapter 14

'You're a Pink Toothbrush'

Max Bygraves
BBC Light Programme, *Children's Favourites*

The next two days were hectic. Two very large parcels arrived from The Scarlet and the Grey, an upmarket clothing shop and when she opened them, Rita found two complete sets of school uniforms. The parcels contained everything you could think of from blazers right down to socks. All that remained was to sew labels into all of Hamish's school uniform as well as marking his shoes and other equipment with his name. When everything was done, she put them into the small trunk that he would be taking to his new school. Once Hamish's uniform was sorted out Rita had to do the same all over again for Lauren.

Hamish's boarding school, Dempster Vale, was in Slough, just inside the Berkshire border, twenty miles and a forty-minute car journey away. Mrs Plumb would not be able to accompany her grandson to the school on the day of his admission, as she had an appointment in York. Her sister preferred to stay in London, so she agreed to look after Lauren while Rita escorted him. Hamish was quiet in the days leading up to it, so Rita knew he was feeling nervous about it.

On the day, after eating an uncharacteristically small lunch, he changed into his new school uniform, an attractive grey with a fuchsia trim and tie. Mrs Elizabeth took some photographs in the courtyard garden and after saying goodbye to his sister, he and Rita set off in a taxi.

Dempster Vale, founded in the late seventeen hundreds, had a reputation for excellence not only academically but also in sport, music and drama. Pupils were encouraged to take part in the Duke of Edinburgh award and it had recently opened an Olympic-sized swimming pool. It sounded like the perfect place for Hamish, where he would have ample opportunities to discover where his expertise lay. When Hamish had first arrived from Rhodesia, he had been excited at the thought of going to a British school but now he seemed agitated. As they sat together on the back seat, Rita was aware that he was constantly kneading his hands together.

'Are you all right?' she asked quietly.

He nodded but his face was pale.

Rita laid her hand over his. 'What's wrong, Hamish?'

'Will they give me the thrashing as soon as I arrive?' he said anxiously.

'Give you a thrashing?' she spluttered. 'Whatever gave you that idea?'

'Cook said when I get to school they would give me a damned good thrashing.'

Rita squeezed his fingers. 'Nobody is going to give you a thrashing, Hamish,' she said. 'You will only get into trouble if you do something wrong.'

His sense of relief was palpable. 'But Cook…'

'Mrs Niko was angry because you were so rude,' Rita reminded him. 'You used to shout at me remember? Well, if you carry on the way you are now, you'll be fine. Just be a good boy and nobody will be cross with you, okay?'

Hamish nodded gravely.

Eventually they pulled into a sweeping driveway littered with expensive cars and their chauffeurs. The school itself was in a large country mansion. Several boys were greeting old friends and people were lugging trunks inside or kissing their sons goodbye. The vast and well-manicured grounds were stunning, and in the distance she could see tennis courts and a cricket pitch.

'I think you're going to like it here,' Rita said encouragingly.

She climbed out of the car and asked the driver to help them. He and Hamish got the trunk out of the boot while Rita carried his satchel. They made their way to the front door which was up a short flight of steps behind two simple Doric columns.

As they walked inside, a much older boy with a prefect's badge came up to them with a clipboard and pen. 'Good afternoon, ma'am,' he said politely. 'What name is it?'

'Master Hamish Plumb,' said Rita.

The prefect consulted his clipboard then having crossed off Hamish's name he turned towards several other boys standing by the wall and said sharply, 'Carruthers, Dorm 6.'

'Well, goodbye Hamish.' Rita was unsure what Hamish wanted to do so to spare his blushes, she held out her hand for him to shake but to her great surprise, he threw his arms around her waist and gave her a quick hug.

As Carruthers helped him with his luggage, Rita just had time to call, 'Good luck,' and then he was gone.

—

Back in Belgravia, Lauren missed her brother but she was excited about going to her new school on Tuesday. Her uniform was similar to that of her brother's; a blue blazer with the school badge, navy gymslip and white blouse and a navy cardigan. For games she was expected to wear an Aertex blouse and navy gym knickers. On the day itself, as the little girl got dressed, Rita felt a lump in her throat. Lauren looked very smart of course but seeing such a young child dressed in school uniform made her seem older than her tender years.

The school was within walking distance. They held hands all the way and at the gate, Rita promised to be there when Lauren came out at three.

When she had gone in, Rita glanced at her watch. She had asked Mrs Plumb if she could have a couple of hours off this morning because she was taking her driving test. The test centre itself was just over the river so she knew her timing would be tight, so Rita set off for the Tube. Twenty minutes later she was turning into the DVLA test centre where her instructor, Mr Fisher was waiting with the car.

'We've got twenty minutes before your test,' he said. 'Let's take a short drive just to help you warm up.'

Rita slid into the driving seat and a couple of minutes later, they had pulled onto the road. It was busy but not as manic as it could be in the rush hour. Rita did a right turn, a three-point turn and some backward entry parallel parking. Mr Fisher seemed happy enough as they made their way back to the centre. He came with her into the waiting room as Rita did her best to quell the butterflies in her stomach.

Three other candidates were called before an examiner, a smartly dressed man with a serious expression, before he returned with a clipboard and called her name. When she stood, she was asked to sign a form that he held on to and then he invited her to lead the way to her car.

'In a few moments, I shall ask you to pull away from the kerb,' he explained in a business-like fashion. 'I shall give you instructions in good time to manoeuvre the car. You may begin now.'

Rita switched on the engine, put the car in first gear, looked in her rear-view mirror, turned her head to the right to check that nothing was coming up beside the car and pulled onto the road. This was it. She took a deep breath and concentrated on what she was doing.

'Take the next left turn please.'

He was certainly polite as he asked her to do some parallel parking, an emergency stop, a right turn across a busy junction and to reverse around a corner and park some way from the crossroads. Every time she'd completed an instruction, he wrote something on the paper on the clipboard. After a while, he asked her to stop the car and she realised she was back outside the testing centre. The half an hour she'd been with him had flown.

'I am now going to ask you some questions about the Highway Code,' he continued. 'What do double white lines signify?'

'No overtaking,' she said clearly.

He asked her a couple more questions and then wanted her to read the number plate of the car parked just in front of them. Rita answered everything without hesitation.

'Well, I'm pleased to tell you that you have passed your driving test, Miss Brownlow. Now, would you sign your name at the bottom of this form and give me the number of your provisional licence.'

Rita was beaming from ear to ear as she did so. The examiner said, 'Congratulations,' and then he stepped out of the car. She punched the air and a second or two later, Mr Fisher opened the passenger door.

'I passed!' she cried.

He nodded contentedly. 'Well then, you'd better come back inside and collect your pink slip.'

A quarter of an hour later, she was holding her pink slip signifying Rita was no longer a learner – she was a qualified driver. *Brilliant... Brill...iiiant!*

As soon as she got back to the house, she told Mrs Niko and Gloria. They were thrilled for her but then Mrs Niko's expression changed as she told her that Mrs Plumb had asked to see her the minute she got back.

'Any idea what it's about?' Rita asked anxiously.

Mrs Niko shook her head. 'But you'd better go straight away. I'll have a nice cup of coffee waiting for you when you get back.'

Mrs Plumb was at her desk when Rita knocked on the door. 'Ah Rita,' she said. 'Come in. Sit down.'

Rita sat on the chair she indicated.

'Rita, this family is indebted to you beyond words,' she began. 'You agreed to stay with us until the children went to school and Lauren was settled, for which I am grateful, but as I'm sure you have realised, things have changed.'

Rita had a sinking feeling in her stomach about what was coming.

'As you've probably gathered, my sister is not going to marry Sir Arthur after all. What happened to you that night and his disgusting reaction finally opened her eyes to the sort of man he is. With the prospect of marriage, she had already sold her house. I went up to York in the hopes of being able to stop the sale, but everything has gone too far, the result being that she is now homeless.'

'So you'd rather I leave now?' said Rita.

'The short answer to that is yes,' Mrs Plumb added apologetically, 'but I'm not asking you to pack your bags right now. Could we say by the end of January? That would give you time to find another post.'

Rita nodded.

'Perhaps you would be kind enough to carry on as normal for the time being,' Mrs Plumb went on. 'My sister will move in next week and she has promised to help me with the children, which is why I no longer have need of your services.'

'Of course,' said Rita, fighting the urge to be emotional. What else could she say?

'I shall pay you regardless of whether you get a new post before the end of January or not, and I shall of course give you a marvellous reference,' Mrs Plumb went on. 'In fact, I have already sent one to the agency. Be assured, they know how grateful I am to them for sending you here.'

Rita turned to leave.

'Oh, by the way,' Mrs Plumb called as she reached the door, 'how did you get on with your driving test?'

'I passed.'

'Oh well done you,' said Mrs Plumb. 'That's sure to be a feather in your cap. It might help you with a new placement, too.'

As she left Mrs Plumb's office, Rita was very tempted to burst into tears but with gargantuan effort, she managed to hold it altogether. So 1965 had brought a rotten start after all. She had almost been raped by a lusty drip, then she'd had to take Hamish miles away from home and now, having parked Lauren in a strange school, in a strange country, far away from all that was familiar to her, she'd got the sack! Well, not exactly the sack – the push, the old heave-ho, but it all amounted to the same thing.

Mrs Niko was mortified when Rita came into the kitchen and told her. 'She did what?'

Rita dunked a biscuit in her coffee. 'I knew it was only a temporary post,' she admitted, 'but I hadn't expected it to end quite so quickly. I had thought I might still be here at Easter.'

'We shall miss you,' said Gloria who was on her break too. 'You did wonders with that boy.'

Rita gave her a sombre smile. *Good for him but a fat lot of good it did me*, she thought acerbically.

Chapter 15

'I Understand'
Freddie and the Dreamers

'So what will you do now?' Jenny blurted out.

Rita shrugged. 'Get another post I suppose. I've already told Mrs Hunter and she's looking through her records as we speak.'

The two friends were at the WEN coffee morning. As soon as she'd walked through the door, Rita had asked Mrs Hunter if she could have a quick word and brought her up to speed. Jenny wasn't far behind her, so as soon as she could, she caught up with Rita's devastating news.

'These people,' Jenny said cynically. 'They demand loyalty but they're only too quick to dump you when it suits.'

Rita frowned. 'You sound a little bitter. Has something happened?'

'You could say that,' said Jenny. 'My employer was supposed to move to Esher this month but it's all off.'

'Why?' Rita gasped.

'No idea,' said Jenny, 'but I can't say I'm upset that they're staying put. Their house in Aldford Street may be small but Simon is only just over the river and all this we're moving, we're not moving, is a bit unsettling.'

'I can imagine,' Rita said sympathetically.

They helped themselves to coffee and found a seat in anticipation of the talk. Rita was in a bit of a quandary. She had made up her mind to ask advice from the older nannies about how to handle unwanted attention but she wondered if she should have told Jenny about Royston first. In the end, the decision was taken from her. Almost as soon as they'd sat down, Mrs Hunter looking sensational in an ivory dress with a pleated skirt, announced the speaker.

Nanny Jones worked for a royal family in the Middle East. She began by saying that she could not divulge where her position was or the name of her employers, but she painted a vivid picture of the glamourous life they led.

'For almost two years, I cared for four children,' she began. 'Two boys aged seven and six, and two girls aged five and six months.'

She went on to describe royal palaces, luxury travel and fabulous hotels as well as divulging that she had been given an eye-watering salary. Everything sounded amazing until she came to the but... 'The downside,' she went on, 'if you could call it that, is that I was expected to work six or sometimes seven days a week, with only one day off a week when they remembered it. My working day included being on call at night as well and, being in a country with strict laws about women not being allowed out unaccompanied, my day off could only be spent in the palace itself.'

'Would you recommend such a job?' someone asked.

'I think you should be aware of what you're letting yourself in for,' she went on. 'Yes, I did see some amazing parts of the world and my days off in places like New York and Miami were much more enjoyable but quite honestly, it's not for the faint-hearted.'

As she listened, Rita made a mental note that somewhere in the desert wasn't for her.

She and Jenny planned to have lunch together, but first they parted at the door; Jenny would do some shopping while Rita went into Mrs Hunter's office for their chat.

'I must say,' Mrs Hunter said as she offered Rita a seat, 'Mrs Plumb has given you a glowing reference.'

Rita lowered her eyes modestly. 'I've also passed my driving test.'

'Brilliant.' Mrs Hunter scribbled a note in Rita's folder. 'Now I have a post which might suit you down to the ground. I wonder if you would be interested in taking part in a little experiment with me?'

Rita was intrigued.

'This agency doesn't simply place first-class nannies in top jobs,' Mrs Hunter went on. 'We also nurture a social obligation to help parents who may be going through difficult times.'

Rita grinned. 'Sounds interesting.'

'To that end,' said Mrs Hunter, 'I have two temporary posts which I think would suit you. They are rather unusual in that they are both part-time. The families live fairly close together and although the parties are unknown to each other, they are both single mothers, one divorced, the other widowed.'

'So, you're asking me to work for two families at the same time?'

Mrs Hunter nodded. 'Both ladies are trying to start their own business or career. Neither can afford a full-time nanny, but having one part-time will give them the freedom to kick-start their ambition.'

'Sounds amazing,' said Rita.

'I think the two jobs working in tandem would give you an exciting and fulfilling experience.'

Rita pulled a face. 'But how is that going to work?'

'Mrs Samson needs someone Monday, Tuesday, Wednesday,' said Mrs Hunter, 'whereas Mrs Boyd is in need of a nanny on Friday, Saturday and Sunday.'

'So my day off would be...'

'Thursday,' they both chorused.

Mrs Hunter obviously thought it a brilliant idea, but Rita could see at once that there was a problem. 'But I have nowhere to live in London,' she cried. 'My home is eighty miles away.'

'That's easily solved,' said Mrs Hunter. 'I suggest we find you a room in a single woman's hostel. There are a few dotted around Central London and I am confident that a room will become vacant between now and the end of the month when Mrs Plumb requires you to leave.'

Rita blinked. She didn't know what to say.

'I can see by your expression that this is a bit of a surprise,' said Mrs Hunter, 'so don't make a decision immediately. Go away and think about it. I shall tell the clients that I have someone in mind, so the offer will be open until, say, next Monday?'

Rita nodded in agreement. 'There's just one other thing,' she continued hesitantly. Her throat became tight and she paused. 'At Christmas I was attacked... by one of my employer's house guests.'

'Attacked?' Mrs Hunter gave her a startled look. 'Oh my goodness. Did you call the police?'

Rita shook her head and swallowed hard. Why was it always so hard to regain control of her emotions when she spoke about it?

'Take your time,' Mrs Hunter said kindly.

Rita told her everything. How she had become increasingly embarrassed and worried by Royston's behaviour, although none of the family seemed to notice. That she felt sure she had done nothing to encourage it and yet perhaps she had, because late at night, he had made his way into her room.

Mrs Hunter listened patiently and sympathetically.

'Mrs Plumb asked him and his father to leave,' Rita continued, 'and I believe the romantic relationship between his father and Mrs Plumb's sister is at an end because of what happened. Mrs Plumb's sister is in the process of moving in with her which is why she doesn't need me any more.'

Mrs Hunter took a deep breath. 'I'm glad you've told me Rita, but I can't help feeling none of this is your fault.' She paused then added, 'Rita, I don't excuse his behaviour for one minute but you don't seem to realise that you are a very attractive young woman. From what you've told me, I'm sure you didn't encourage him but I'm afraid some of these scoundrels think they can take advantage of innocence. From now on, be on your guard and make it clear, right from the start, that you will report any unseemly behaviour.'

'To the police?'

Mrs Hunter sighed and clutching at the beads around her neck, shook her head. 'Sadly we haven't yet reached the stage when the police take much notice of something like this. They may do one day, but the way things are going, probably not even in my lifetime. The prevalent attitude is that boys will be boys and when something happens, the girls were asking for it. Unpleasant and unfair but there it is.'

'So, if it happens again, you think I should have threatened to tell my employer?'

'If it looks like becoming a problem, that's exactly what you should do before it's too late,' said Mrs Hunter. 'And,' she added firmly, 'be brave enough to carry it through if necessary.' She gave her a wry smile and raised her eyebrows. 'Of course, if you were living in an all girls hostel rather than someone's home…'

Rita laughed. 'Thank you Mrs Hunter and I promise I will think about it.' Jenny had already ordered a pot of tea in the small back street café where she and Rita had agreed to meet. They both splashed out on bangers and mash and Rita ordered a Coca-Cola. As the waitress left them, Rita finally told her friend why she had gone home to her grandmother rather than go to the Lyceum for the New Year.

At first Jenny was appalled, then sympathetic. 'Rita that's awful! The pig. Are you all right? Oh Lord, he didn't hurt you did he? Did he…?'

Rita shook her head. 'No,' she said quietly. 'He hit me and my wrists hurt where he was holding on to me. He didn't manage to… you know, but I can't get it out of my mind.'

Their meals came as Rita dabbed her eyes with her handkerchief. When the waitress had gone, Jenny put her hand over her friend's. 'I'm so sorry.'

Rita nodded miserably then picked up her knife and fork. They ate in silence then, keen to lighten their mood she said, 'What are we going to do for the rest of the day?'

Jenny shrugged. 'We don't have a lot of choice do we. It's too cold to wander about and the tourist attractions aren't open until Easter. We could take a look around the sales or maybe go to the pictures?'

'What's on?' asked Rita.

'I quite fancy *Goodbye Charlie*. It's on at the Rialto on Coventry Street,' said Jenny. 'They say it's very funny.'

'Okay,' said Rita. 'I'm up for that.' Having finished her meal, she laid down her knife and fork. 'Mrs Hunter has offered me a new post, well, two really.' She went on to explain about the two part-time jobs. 'The only snag is,' she said wrinkling her nose, 'she wants me live in some sort of woman's hostel.'

'I know someone who lives in one of those,' Jenny said enthusiastically. 'My cousin. She works in Selfridges on the beauty counter.'

'I imagined it'll be full of old fossils eking out their time until retirement.'

'Far from it,' cried Jenny. 'Yes, you get all sorts but my cousin is only twenty and she has loads of friends. There's always something going on. In fact, she's never in!'

They paid for their meals and set off for the bus to Piccadilly. The film which starred Tony Curtis, Debbie Reynolds and Pat Boone, was quite funny even though the plot line was rather far-fetched. As they parted later, Jenny said, 'I think you should go for those part-time jobs. At least you wouldn't die of boredom.'

Rita chuckled. 'You might be right.'

Back in Kensington, Rita was just in time to kiss Lauren good night. Mrs Elizabeth was folding her school uniform on the chair when Rita walked into the bedroom. The little girl held out her arms and Rita sat on the edge of the bed to give her a cuddle.

'What did you do at school today?' she asked.

'We did lots and lots of things,' said Lauren.

'Lots and lots' was Lauren's new buzzword.

'And which thing did you like best?'

'I did a very big picture,' said Lauren. 'I drew lots and lots of testicles.'

Behind them, Rita heard Mrs Elizabeth splutter. 'What did she say?'

'Teacher said,' Lauren continued innocently, 'that we had to draw what you'd find at the bottom of the sea, so I drew an octopus with lots and lots of testicles.'

'I think you mean tentacles sweetheart,' Rita corrected gently, as she struggled not to grin.

—

By the time Monday came around, Rita had decided to take the posts Mrs Hunter was offering. In her heart of hearts she would have preferred a live-in post but every time she thought about it, her mind would go back to that night just after Christmas and she'd find herself either feeling sick or trembling. Perhaps having her own place, albeit one room, would help her get over the trauma and move on.

When she went back to WEN, Mrs Hunter told her to go to Warren Court which was close to Baker's Street and present herself to a Mr Dobson.

'He's the caretaker,' she explained. 'I shall telephone him to tell him you are coming. He will show you the room which has just been vacated. I have your references here so you can tell him a copy with be delivered by post first thing tomorrow morning, if you like it.'

Still a little unsure, Rita set off.

Warren Court turned out to be a solid looking building with no bomb damage nor seedy repairs, something which Rita had been expecting. She was surprised to find it looked smart and had probably been built during the 1930s with characteristic clean lines. She soon found the office and Mr Dobson couldn't have been nicer. He showed her to a room on the second floor. It was compact but not tiny. If she stayed here she would have a bed, a comfortable chair, a wardrobe, a small desk with hard-backed chair, a sink with draining board and a small refrigerator.

'We don't allow cooking in your room but there's a kitchen down the corridor,' Mr Dobson explained. 'You can use the pots and pans provided but we advise keeping all your food stuffs in your own room.'

Rita was impressed. It may be a little basic after her two previous positions, but the room was clean and the decor was liveable. 'Can I have a bath?'

'Three doors down the corridor.'

'What about washing?'

'There is a laundry on the ground floor for your personal things,' said Mr Dobson. 'Your bed sheets will be collected on Tuesday and clean bedlinen left outside your room.'

They left the bedroom and he led the way downstairs to show her the laundry room. It looked a lot like the one in Harefield House, with its dryers and heavy-duty sinks, so no surprises there. Back in the office she asked Mr Dobson about the rent.

'Ten and six for that room,' he told her. 'You get a rent book and pay every Friday.' When she hesitated, he added, 'It's a good price for round here you know. Don't forget, we are in Central London.'

'And when I want to leave?'

'Two weeks' notice, or two weeks' rent up front,' he said. 'So, what's it to be?'

'I'll take it,' she said.

Chapter 16

'Gilly, Gilly Ossenfeffer Katzenellenbogen by the Sea'
Max Bygraves
BBC Light Programme, *Children's Favourites*

Three weeks later, Rita was living in Warren Court and working for her new employers. She had gone back to Mrs Hunter on the following Monday and swallowing all her reservations, she had accepted the posts. Her contract was with the agency itself and was to last six weeks, so her employers would pay WEN and in turn they would pay her what she was owed. 'That way,' Mrs Hunter explained, 'it lessens the risk of one of them "forgetting" to pay your stamp.'

'And when the six weeks are up?' Rita asked anxiously.

'I shall look for a prestigious live-in post for you, Rita,' said Mrs Hunter. 'This is a kind of experiment; a new way of handling a modern phenomenon with little provision; helping the single mother on a limited budget.'

A short interview with each client had cemented the deal.

Her room in Warren Court was next door to a girl called Dorinda. She and Rita met just as Rita was moving in. She looked about twenty-five and was very friendly and welcoming. As Rita lugged her stuff upstairs she even offered to give her a hand. Having helped her dump everything on the floor and the bed, Dorinda invited Rita to her room for a cup of tea before she unpacked.

Dorinda's room was almost identical although she'd swapped the candlewick bedspread for one with red roses and foliage which brightened up the whole room. Rita made a mental note to look for ways to put her own personal stamp on her room as well. As they talked, Rita discovered that, surprisingly, Dorinda worked as a store detective.

'A store detective!' she exclaimed. 'What on earth does that mean?'

'I'm mainly on the lookout for shoplifters,' said Dorinda. 'Basically, I walk around the store all day long looking as if I'm going to buy something and if I see someone behaving in a suspicious way I keep an eye on them.'

'So do you have to arrest people?'

Dorinda chuckled. 'No, the police do that. If I spot someone, I alert security and then if the person doesn't pay, they nab them as soon as they leave the store.'

'What happens then?'

'We all go to the manager's office and the person is asked to open her handbag or shopping bag,' said Dorinda. 'Sometimes they hide things up their dress and pretend to be pregnant or they put stuff in the baby's pushchair and blame the kid for nicking it when mum wasn't looking!'

Rita laughed.

'What do you do?' Dorinda asked.

'I'm a private nanny,' she told her. 'I'm just about to start a part-time job near Regent's Park.'

'I always thought they were live-in posts,' Dorinda said as she reached up for the biscuit tin and offered Rita a Nice.

'They are usually,' said Rita nibbling the corner of her biscuit. 'This is a kind of experiment. I shall be looking after two lots of children and that's why I'll be living here rather than in their homes.'

'In that case, welcome,' said Dorinda.

Rita went to Mrs Samson's home on Monday. It was an early start as she was asked to be there by seven thirty. When she put the key in the back door, everyone in the house was still in bed. A few moments later, Mrs Samson, an attractive woman who was about thirty, with her fair hair caught up on the top of her head in a rather messy but attractive way and full of apologies, was still in her night clothes.

'Oh, it's you. Sorry, I'm usually up long before this but we had friends over last night.'

She'd said 'we' but there was no sign of a Mr Samson and Rita certainly didn't mention him. Rita was asked to accompany her upstairs to meet the children again and help them get dressed. She had two. Neil Samson was four and seemed to be a rather serious boy. Rita got the impression that he thought of himself as his mother's protector and head of the household. His sister Sophie, a bubbly little girl with a mass of golden curls, was two and a half.

Rita soon discovered where things were and by the time Mrs Samson had got dressed, the children were washed, dressed and had cleaned their teeth. Rita adored them straight away. They were delightful children, full of energy and fun to be with, making her confident that the three of them would have some good times together.

They went downstairs to the kitchen where Mrs Samson had put out breakfast cereals and a boiled egg. 'Have you eaten, Rita?'

Rita said that she had and sat Sophie in her booster chair.

After breakfast, while the children played in the sitting room, she and her employer sat together to talk about her duties. Rita knew from what Mrs Hunter had told her that Mrs Samson was trying to start a business, but she had no idea what it was. It didn't take long to discover that her employer made the most amazing celebration cakes to order. Judging by the incredible pictures she showed Rita from her album, it was obvious that Mrs Samson had a very special talent. The cakes had to be seen to be believed. There was so much variety; whales, houses, castles, snails, dogs, cars or cartoon characters, you name it, Mrs Samson made it.

'Once I've built up a firm client base,' she told Rita, 'my plan is to find some investors and then I can employ other people.'

'I can see that it won't take long before your cakes will be in demand,' Rita said admiringly.

'I bake on Monday and Tuesday, then deliver my orders on Wednesday,' she continued. 'If I can leave the children to you, I can concentrate on the business.'

Calling herself a thoroughly modern mother, Mrs Samson went on to explain that she wanted time to herself, without interruptions, while Rita was in the house. 'I wouldn't want you to think my children come second,' she added, 'but if I can be left to my own devices, I shall be able to devote myself wholly to the children for the rest of the week.'

'That sounds fair enough,' said Rita, 'and I can assure you that the children and I will keep well out of your way.'

Mrs Samson gave her a satisfied nod.

'What about the children's lunch and tea,' said Rita. 'If we can't use the kitchen, where shall we go?'

'I have put a small refrigerator in the dining room and the sideboard doubles as a kitchen cupboard. There's a Baby Belling in there, so you can heat milk or cook a simple meal without having to come to the kitchen.'

Rita was impressed. She'd thought of everything.

The day went well. They wrapped up warm and went for a walk in Regent's Park. Sophie was in the pushchair and when he was tired of walking, Neil stood on the back axle. When they got back, it was hard to ignore the delicious smells coming from the kitchen, but the children helped her lay the dining room table and serve their food (fish fingers, Smash mashed potato and salad). Rita ate with them. After lunch, Sophie had a nap while she and Neil had a quiet time reading books or doing puzzles. In the afternoon they played games and did some drawing. At teatime she let them help her butter the bread and make sandwiches and they found some of their mother's cakes in a tin on the sideboard.

At six she put them in the bath and while they were playing, Mrs Samson joined them. 'Oh, you have been good children,' she said.

Rita left them together while she put out clean clothes for the morning and took the children's dirty clothes downstairs. When she arrived back upstairs, Mrs Samson was drying the children.

'Rita has to go now,' she said pointedly, but the cries of disappointment from them both were very satisfying.

'I don't want you to go,' said Neil and his sister began to whinge.

'Can you come back tomorrow?' said Mrs Samson giving Rita a wink.

'I should love to,' said Rita.

The next morning, she was greeted by thunderous footsteps as the children raced each other down the stairs and her second day was just as fulfilling as the first.

On her day off, Rita went to Selfridges to buy a yard of ribbon in the haberdashery department. Dorinda had mentioned that she would be working in that particular store today so when she'd found what she wanted, Rita was on the lookout for her. It took a little while to spot her and of course she knew she couldn't make contact with her. It was quite exciting knowing a real store detective. They made eye contact then Rita saw just a hint of grin on her friend's face as she sailed off with her nose in the air.

The plan for the rest of the week was for Rita to work for Mrs Boyd. Her house in Ivor Place, was near Marylebone station and not far from the Planetarium. Rita turned the corner by the Gloucester public house and walked along the street. When she came to it, it was an impressive building, although the front door could have done with a lick of paint. She glanced at her watch to find that she had arrived at exactly eight o'clock as prearranged. Rita rang the bell and waited.

Mrs Boyd, Mrs Hunter had explained before Rita's interview, had been recently widowed. Her husband had been killed in a motor car accident just a few months before. She was also a dressmaker, but apparently 'one with a difference'.

Mrs Boyd's mother was able to pop in and look after the children at the beginning of the week if she needed to get out and about sourcing material or meeting with prospective clients, but Rita was needed at the weekend.

'My mother is getting on a bit now,' Mrs Boyd explained at her interview. 'A whole week with the children would be too much for her.'

Rita was to take over full time on Friday, Saturday and Sunday. In just the same way that Mrs Samson could do her baking uninterrupted, with Rita looking after the Boyd children, their mother would be able to get on with sewing her creations.

The door opened and Mrs Boyd cried, 'Come in, come in.' Rita was glad to step into the warmth of the house.

Having hung up her coat and familiarised herself with the layout of the house, Rita met the children at the breakfast table. Johnny Boyd was five, a rather serious child who according to his mother missed his father very much. Brian, his brother was a lively two-year-old, but not yet potty trained. Rita crouched down to greet them at eye level and they shook hands with her.

'Are you going to look after us?' Johnny asked.

'Yes, I am,' Rita said with a smile.

Brian offered her a piece of his toast.

'Oh, thank you, Brian,' she said. 'You're very kind but I have already eaten my breakfast. Why don't you finish it up.' The toast didn't last long.

'Well, I'll be going now,' said his mother.

Johnny jumped from his chair. 'No, no!' And running around the table, he grabbed his mother's arm.

'Don't be silly, darling,' said Mrs Boyd. 'I'm only going to my sewing room.'

Reassuring him that his mother would only be next door, Rita persuaded him to show her where to put the dirty dishes and the cupboard for the cornflakes and so, their day began with a shaky start.

Her first aim was to get the boys into some sort of routine. With that in mind, she found some little pants and took Brian's nappy off. He had a couple of 'accidents' but there were times when she took him to the toilet and he was still dry. It didn't take long for him to understand that praise and a clap when he used the potty was much better than walking around with wet trousers.

Johnny was a bit more of a challenge. It concerned Rita that he was constantly 'saving' this for Daddy or drawing a picture for Daddy. Every time the doorbell rang or someone knocked on the door (the postman, the boy from the corner shop bringing groceries, or the lady next door returning a borrowed alarm clock) he would race into the hall calling 'Daddy, Daddy.'

Johnny was also anxious about his mother. A couple of times a day he went to her sewing room door and listened until he heard the whir of her machine. Clearly, the child was disturbed. Rita had never really dealt with a child's perspective on death but this behaviour didn't seem healthy.

Rita had been there for a couple of weeks before Mrs Boyd invited her to see what she had been doing. As she stood in the sewing room Rita was surprised to see that she worked mainly with children's fashion, getting away from the frilly-flouncy styles of the 1950s and moving into more modern ideas of how to dress children. She made clothes with clean lines and simple shapes.

'These are amazing,' said Rita, loving the A-line dresses for girls and the cord trousers and dungarees for boys.

'I am desperate to get this business underway,' Mrs Boyd confided. 'This house belongs to my cousin and I shall have to leave when he gets back from America. I shall truly be on my own then.' She picked up a hanger with a delightful child's dress that had a sailor suit feel about it. It was cream with a wide blue collar on the shoulder and an embroidered anchor at the hem. 'I have to do something if I am to support my family.'

'I'm sure everybody is going to love them,' said Rita. 'They're so fashionable.'

Mrs Boyd chuckled. 'It's either sewing or getting married again. My mother keeps dredging up these so-called eligible specimens but I'm really not ready for another relationship yet.'

Their conversation was so relaxed, Rita decided to speak to her about her son. 'I hope you don't mind me asking, but does Johnny understand that his father is dead?' The word may have sounded rather blunt but Rita used it deliberately rather than the euphemistic expression of 'passed away'. She had a feeling Mrs Boyd, while realistic about her own situation in some respect, was fudging the issue when it came to her son.

'We wanted to spare him the grief,' she said. 'My own father died when Johnny was a baby, so my mother and I have told him Daddy has gone to be with Granddad.'

Rita chewed the side of her mouth. 'I think you need to tell him the truth, Mrs Boyd.'

'Oh no, I can't do that,' she said. 'He'd be desperately upset.'

'I'm sure he will,' Rita said gently, 'but isn't that part of the grieving process?'

'I don't think my mother would like that,' Mrs Boyd said coldly.

Rita ploughed on. 'But if he continues to think that his father is coming through the door at any moment, there will come a day when he realises everybody has lied to him. It will break down his trust in both of you.'

Mrs Boyd looked startled and for a minute, Rita thought she was going to shout at her.

'I think you'd better go now, Rita.' Mrs Boyd's eyes were brimming with tears.

'I'm sorry, Mrs Boyd,' Rita began again. 'I didn't mean…'
'Just go!'

Rita fetched her coat. When she reached the front door, she turned. 'Shall I come again next Friday?'

But Mrs Boyd didn't answer.

Chapter 17

'I Can't Explain'
The Who

Rita enjoyed her days with the Samsons but she was worried about Mrs Boyd. She felt she had been right to tell her about Johnny, but she realised now that perhaps her choice of words was a little unwise. She had told Mrs Boyd that she and her mother had *lied* to the boy – which was true enough, but maybe she could have phrased it a better way. Maybe if she'd said something like, 'There will come a day when he will realise that his daddy isn't ever coming home… Then he'll know what you've said isn't true.' She hadn't meant her words to sound harsh, but the more she thought about it the more obvious it was that she had unintentionally deeply offended her employer.

Rita kept it to herself, but Dorinda spotted her mood when she knocked on the door on Monday. She'd come to ask Rita if she would like to go with herself and some other girls to The Marquee Club on Wednesday night.

'You'll love it,' she said. 'All the best bands perform there. Manfred Mann will be on that night.'

Rita caught her breath. 'Manfred Mann! Oh, I love their records.'

Dorinda smiled. 'Okay. We're all meeting by the front door at seven. Can you be ready?'

Rita frowned. The timing would be tight. She didn't finish at Mrs Samson's until after six and she'd have to get back home and change. 'I'll do my best,' she said.

Dorinda who was already turning to go, hesitated. 'Are you all right? Only you seem a bit down.'

Rita felt a little awkward now. 'I'm fine.'

'I'm a good listener,' said Dorinda, then she waited a moment or two, so Rita invited her in.

Once she got going, it all poured out. The weird way Johnny was behaving and then her faux pas with the child's mother. 'I didn't mean to be critical,' Rita said, 'it's just that I've been there almost three weeks now and the child is constantly talking about his father. He makes him gifts, he saves him his toys and his whole day is centred on his father coming through the door at any minute, which of course, he never will. I'm really concerned about him.'

'Sounds to me like the mother is too preoccupied with her business to see what's going on,' Dorinda remarked.

Dorinda's comment seemed a little unfair so Rita made no comment. 'The point is,' she continued, 'what do I do now? Does she still want me to work for her or should I consider myself out of a job? And if she doesn't want me back, what am I going to do? I can't let Mrs Samson down, but I can't live here with just the money I get from her.'

'Umm,' Dorinda said thoughtfully. 'And since you had words, you've not heard from Mrs Boyd?'

'Not a dickybird,' said Rita.

'Then personally, I think if she didn't want you to work for her any more, she would have told you – sent a letter or told your agency. If it was down to me, I'd jack it in anyway, but then you're a much nicer person than I am.' She chuckled. 'I think you should just turn up on Friday as if nothing's happened,' she went on. 'She'll send you packing if she doesn't want you.'

Rita nodded.

'Come on, Rita. Cheer up.'

'It's all a bit unsettling, that's all.' She stood to her feet. 'Cup of coffee?'

'Go on then,' said Dorinda.

Come Wednesday evening, Rita was knackered and the last thing she wanted to do was jump on the tube to Tottenham Court Road, but she had promised Dorinda and the girls that she would come. She ran all the way home from Mrs Samson's place and got into Warren Court with about twenty minutes to spare. A quick wash and a change of clothes was all she could manage. There was no time for make-up but thank god she had kept her hair short since she'd had the geometric bob cut in a Baker Street training salon a while ago. She still went to the salon as it was the cheapest way to get a modern haircut and, quite often, she would be a Guinea pig for some student who was close to finishing his or her training. Once, she went on a Friday and the chap who cut her hair was going to be in an upmarket salon on the following Monday! Her hairstyle had evolved over the months and was now more like Vidal Sassoon's straight bob. Fuller and longer, it was easy to brush into place when cut well. Racing downstairs in her new above-the-knee dress, she had half a minute to spare.

There were four girls waiting with Dorinda. Her friend introduced them, but Rita didn't catch all their names. Everybody hurried to Baker Street Tube station and a few minutes later they were on their way.

They heard the club long before they reached the door. Inside it was packed, smoke-filled, hot and noisy... very noisy. The girls made their way to the back and bagged some seats. They turned a few heads. Women didn't as a rule frequent pubs on their own, but this was a club so the girls had taken a chance. They weren't on their own for long. Several young lads made it their business to look after them.

'What are you having to drink, love?'

Rita looked up into the face of a dark-haired man, fashionably dressed. The other girls were drinking coke so she asked for the same. He bought her one but as there was no room to sit next to her, he had to make do with shouting over the top of her head. Rita was polite, but even though so much time had passed since the Royston incident, she felt a little overwhelmed by his presence. *Don't be ridiculous*, she kept telling herself. *It's just a drink, he's only being friendly*, but all the same she wished he would go away.

The group, Manfred Mann, was amazing. They'd had a hit earlier in 1964 with '5-4-3-2-1' which reached number five in the charts. It was fun, boppy and had a catchy tune. Rita loved it and when they sang their new song 'Do Wah Diddy Diddy', everybody in the room joined in. Slowly but surely, Rita began to relax and enjoy herself. By the end of the evening, it was as if she'd found the real Rita again. She felt young and alive. She leaned forward to catch Dorinda's eye to thank her but she was snogging some feller. Rita sat back in her chair and a bubble of laughter filled her mouth.

The girls stayed in the Marquee Club until closing time and then rushed to catch the Tube back to Baker Street station. Rita and Dorinda linked arms as they walked back to Warren Court.

'Had a good time?'

Rita nodded. 'I had the best time. Thank you so much for inviting me.'

'You certainly look different,' said Dorinda. 'I get the feeling a load has been lifted from your shoulders.'

'I feel it. You looked as if you were enjoying yourself,' Rita teased.

Dorinda pulled the corners of her mouth down. 'He wasn't much of a kisser,' she said. 'I should have offered him lessons,' and they both laughed.

The one blessing from living in Warren Court was that Rita could have a lie-in on her day off. Working in the nursery she was always woken up by the night nurse coming in to give the others a cup of tea and at Mrs Plumb's there was Hamish and Lauren to see to. After her night out, Rita enjoyed the warmth of magnetic sheets until gone nine o'clock.

She planned to go to the WEN coffee morning and take the opportunity to speak to Mrs Hunter about Mrs Boyd. As it turned out, she did go to the coffee morning, but didn't speak to Mrs Hunter. Having listened to the advice of the speaker who highlighted the inconsistent and fickle behaviour of her employers, Rita decided to take Dorinda's advice and turn up on the Boyd doorstep the next day as if nothing had happened.

After she'd posted a letter to her grandmother, Rita spent the rest of her day looking around the National Portrait Gallery in St Martin's Place just off Trafalgar Square. The only time she had visited an art gallery was during a school trip six years ago, so it was fascinating to see the faces of history staring down at her from its walls. What must it have been like to meet Charlotte, Emily and Anne Brontë? And was Henry VIII really such a forbidding looking man? She was admiring the very first picture in the gallery's vast collection, the Chandos portrait of William Shakespeare by John Taylor when she stepped back and onto someone's toe. She heard a painful grunt behind her and when she turned around to apologise, she was faced with a pair of dark brown eyes on a very handsome face.

'I'm so sorry,' Rita spluttered.

'Please,' he winced. 'It is nothing.'

Rita felt herself blush.

The man smiled. 'It's a very good painting, no?'

Judging by his accent he was French. Probably a tourist, she told herself, but for the next few minutes he seemed to shadow her, making polite conversation about the various exhibits. Having gone through several rooms together, he asked her if she would like some 'refreshment' and they ended up in a small café behind the gallery. As he went to the counter for their cups of coffee, Rita smiled to herself. She's just been 'picked up' by a dishy looking bloke. Yes... the old Rita was back.

When she arrived on Mrs Boyd's doorstep the next day it was raining cats and dogs, she was soaking wet and a bundle of nerves. She rang the bell and waited. A little while later, the door opened.

'Oh, Rita. It's you,' said Mrs Boyd. 'Did you forget your key?'

The children were delighted to see her, Brian desperately wanting to show her his dry bed.

'Well done!' she cried. 'Good boy. Let me get my wet things off and then I'll come and look.'

The day began normally enough and as soon as the boys had their breakfast, Rita set up the playroom as an obstacle course. They were to climb over a chair, balance on a piece of cardboard without stepping on the carpet, run through a tunnel blanket between the sofa and the wall (she'd shut the other end of the blanket in the window) and put a hat on when they reached the chair and sit down. It was a riot of fun and it allowed the boys to let off a bit of steam.

After lunch, Brian had a nap and Johnny did a drawing. Once again, it was rather disturbing. He had his mother and brother next to him in the picture with his father right on the edge of the paper. It looked as if the man was on a kind of lead. Rita was left wondering what she could do to make Mrs Boyd see how disturbed her son was.

As she cleared everything away, Rita noticed Johnny fiddling around the back of the massive kitchen dresser. She pretended she wasn't looking but it appeared as if he was hiding something. It was only when he went to the toilet that she had an opportunity to look and see what it was. There were a few things pushed behind the dresser. Rita put her hand into the gap between the dresser and the wall and pulled out a dusty bundle. She could hear Johnny still in the toilet singing to himself, so she sifted through it. A man's dirty sock, a small notebook, a fountain pen, a scarf – whose things were these? It was only when she found an old birthday card that she realised they all must have belonged to Johnny's father. She pushed them back quickly as she heard Johnny close the toilet door. There was no time to deal with it now and besides she needed time to think.

A visitor, a rather austere looking man in a faded suit which had seen better days and carrying a briefcase, turned up to see Mrs Boyd in the afternoon.

'Mrs Boyd is expecting me,' he said curtly.

Rita knew the children's mother didn't like to be disturbed but the man was so insistent she felt she couldn't send him away without at least telling her employer that he was here. When Rita knocked on the sewing room door, all Mrs Boyd's creations were carefully laid out on the long table as if on display.

'Come in, Mr Dicks,' she called. The man went in and they closed the door.

The pair of them were ensconced in the room together for about an hour. Rita was getting the boys' tea and as he left, and she couldn't help noticing that Mrs Boyd seemed a little upset. Better not talk to her about Johnny today, Rita told herself.

As soon as the boys were ready for bed, Rita took them in to their mother. She fussed over them, but Rita could tell that she was preoccupied. Once they were tucked up in bed Rita knocked on the sewing room door once more.

'I'll be going now Mrs Boyd, if that's all right?' It was obvious by her puffy eyes that her employer had been crying. 'Is everything all right, ma'am? Can I do anything to help?'

'It seems I've been wasting my time,' she said bitterly. 'That man was from a firm of investors. I thought he would be willing to invest in the business, but he tells me nobody would want my designs.'

Rita frowned. 'Surely that can't be right,' she said. 'They're wonderful.'

Mrs Boyd gave her a weak smile. 'You're very kind, Rita.'

'I mean it, Mrs Boyd,' Rita said stoutly. 'They're bright, imaginative and more than that, highly fashionable.'

They stood in a moment of silence then Rita said, 'You're not going to give up are you? You can't throw in the towel yet.'

Mrs Boyd gave her a cold stare. 'The man says they're unsaleable, Rita.'

'Forgive me if I sound rude, Mrs Boyd, but what does a man like him know about fashion?'

'And what do you know about fashion?' she challenged.

Mrs Boyd's sarcasm bit, but Rita wasn't done yet. 'Not a lot,' she admitted, 'but I bet I know more than he does. Have you been to the King's Road and shopped in Biba? Take your dresses to the people down there and I bet you a shilling they'll be interested.'

Mrs Boyd's startled expression softened. 'You're quite a firebrand aren't you, Rita.'

Rita felt herself blushing. 'Only when I believe in something,' she said.

Chapter 18

'Somewhere'
P. J. Proby

Rita had tied her mother's letters all together with the blue ribbon she'd bought in Selfridges and put them in a blue box with a butterfly on the lid. Every now and then she would get them out and lovingly run her fingers over the envelopes. She desperately wanted to read them all but something always held her back. What if her father had said something awful? What possible reason could he have had for dumping her mother when his first was such a beautiful letter? She wrestled all the time wondering whether it was better to know the whole truth or to stick with her romantic imaginings, but up to now, she was too scared to take the plunge. The next letter in sequence was dated just after she'd been born. Was she the reason Dexter had changed his mind? Part of her thought she was but then he'd written several times after this letter. Rita took a deep breath and this time she lifted the flap and took the delicate paper out.

My precious sweetheart,
    You cannot imagine the joy your letter brought me. A baby. Our baby! Oh honey, this means everything to me. I promise I shall be the best father ever! Have you thought of any names yet? What about Leonard? My grandfather was called Leonard Clarence. Maybe Clarence is a bit old

fashioned now. Or maybe Russell. My best mate was called Russell. You remember him, the guy who danced with you at the Hop? He was killed when we landed. I miss that guy but if we named our baby after him it would kinda honor his name, wouldn't it?

I can't say where we are but we are close to the German border. It seems Gerry is gonna fight to the last man. I have some disappointing news I'm afraid. I spoke to the company commander about us getting married but the American government has decided not to issue any more permits. It seems too many dames are taking advantage of our boys just to get to the States. It's a bit of a bummer that a few bad apples spoil the barrel but at the moment I can't do anything about it. As soon as I get back to the States, I'll be demobbed and take it from there. If all else fails I'll come back to England to fetch you. I want to be with you and our baby, honey.

All my love,
Dexter

P.S. I just thought… our baby might be a girl. Can't think of any names for a girl. If we have a girl, I bet she'll be as beautiful as you, sugar. Keep loving me. I miss you so much.

The letter did a lot to restore her feeling of being loved and wanted. When her mother had died Rita knew her grandmother loved her, but she began to feel that perhaps she was a burden gran could have done without. Nothing was said, but during those first few miserable weeks, the feeling grew. Looking back she supposed it was that as much as anything which contributed to the decision to move away from home and make her life elsewhere. But now, Dexter's letter had made her realise that she was loved and she was wanted right from the start – albeit as a son first and foremost! She picked up her framed picture of her parents and ran her finger across her father's face. He had tried to get married to mum. He was excited about being a father, so why had he left mum in the lurch like Gran said?

She put the letter back inside its envelope with a sigh. She couldn't face another one, not now, and although she had been pleasantly surprised that Dexter had wanted his child, she still dreaded reading the letter telling mum he'd dumped her.

Back with the Boyds the next day, Mrs Boyd told Rita she was going shopping. As she kissed the boys and promised to bring back some sweeties, Rita noticed that she had some of her creations in her shopping bag.

'I'll be back early afternoon,' she announced as the front door closed.

Rita wrapped the boys up warm and took them for a walk. When they got back, they played on the floor while she got them dinner. She barely took any notice of what they were doing until she heard Johnny singing; it was a made-up song as he arranged his toy cars in the garage. She didn't catch all the words, but it was something like '*Daddy and me, we'll go in a car, car, car... We'll sit in the car... and they'll go broom, broom, bang crash and he won't come back.*'

So the boy knew more than everybody thought. Johnny's confusion must be because somehow he'd heard someone talking about the real reason why his father wasn't there but everybody was telling him something different. To some degree, Rita could relate to the way he was feeling. It had taken her a long time to comprehend the horror of her mother's death because everyone talked about her being with the angels and picking flowers in heaven and such like. She'd felt as if there was a story to tell but she couldn't put all the pieces together – a bit like having two completely different jigsaw puzzles and trying to fit them together as one. The boy needed help, but what could Rita do about it?

When she came back, Mrs Boyd seemed pensive. She had no shopping and she said nothing about where she had been, but she went straight back into her sewing room. She didn't seem to do any work though. For the rest of the afternoon, the machine was silent.

While Johnny and Brian watched *The Sooty Show* on TV, Rita got the boys' tea then gave them their bath. Usually, Mrs Boyd came upstairs to tell them a story, but this evening there was no sign of their mother. Rita kissed them goodnight and went downstairs. She knocked on the sewing room door and called, 'I'll be off now, Mrs Boyd.'

'Oh Rita,' said a muffled voice, 'is it that time already? Come in, come in.'

The room was in absolute chaos; materials, patterns and half-finished garments everywhere. Mrs Boyd was sifting through some papers.

'The boys are in bed and I've read them a story,' Rita began. 'Johnny is still awake and waiting for you.'

'Oh yes, Johnny,' she said absentmindedly and looking up she added, 'You were right, Rita.'

Rita's heart skipped a beat. So, she'd got it at last. She finally understood that her son needed to know the truth. 'I'm sure he'll be fine as soon as you tell him.'

'What?' Mrs Boyd was frowning.

'You said I was right, ma'am.'

'Yes,' said Mrs Boyd. 'I took some samples with me to the King's Road.' She bent to rub the calf of her left leg. 'I've walked miles and miles but I saw so many people. They were all positive Rita. They loved what I've done.'

Rita gasped. 'You sold some?'

Her employer shook her head. 'No, I didn't get any orders because all the people round there only make and sell adult clothing but look—' she held up a sheaf of papers '—I've got loads of contacts. They tell me all I have to do is get a portfolio together and then I'll find an investor.'

Rita smiled. It was good to see her so excited and positive about her future. Her passion for beautiful clothes shone through. Rita could only hope that one day she would find the same zeal when it came to understanding the needs of her own son.

—

It was still tipping it with rain when Rita came back the next morning. As she hung up her coat and went into the kitchen she was startled to see Mrs Boyd sitting at the kitchen table with her head in her hands. When she looked up, Rita could see that her employer had been crying. 'He's dead, Rita.'

Rita's eyes grew wide. She pulled out a chair and sat opposite in what she hoped was an expression of sympathy. What a bummer. Now on top of everything else, the poor woman had been bereaved. 'Who's dead?'

'Churchill,' said Mrs Boyd. 'Winston Churchill.'

For a split second Rita felt a sense of relief. It wasn't that she didn't care about Churchill, but he wasn't family. He was old. Ninety. Old people die.

Mrs Boyd blew her nose. 'I just heard it on the radio,' she said. 'The Prime Minister made the announcement a few minutes ago.'

'I'm sorry,' said Rita. Although she didn't feel the same sense of loss herself, she knew the high regard in which older people held him. Hadn't Gran said loads of times, 'If it hadn't have been for Churchill we would never have got through the war.' She caught her breath. And now he was dead. Gran would be devastated.

—

That next Monday, Mrs Samson could talk of nothing else. 'They say the Queen has ordered a state funeral and people will be able to walk past the coffin in Westminster Hall.'

'From today?' Rita asked.

'From Wednesday until Sunday,' said Mrs Samson. 'I think I'll take a moment or two to pop out on Wednesday while you're here.'

On her way home from Mrs Boyd's last week, Rita had posted a hastily scribbled note of condolence for her grandmother. Now that the arrangements had been announced, it occurred to her that Gran might like to file past the coffin herself. There was a strong possibility that her grandmother had never even been to London, and she certainly wouldn't know her way round, so Rita wrote another quick letter offering to meet at Waterloo station on Thursday which was her day off. If she posted it on the way home, it should get to Worthing by first post the next day which would give Gran plenty of time to organise the trip.

Rita had a reply waiting for her on Wednesday evening. 'I shan't be coming up on the train,' her grandmother wrote. 'Eddie is bringing me up by car. We hope to be there by nine o'clock so we'll meet you in the queue.'

Oh dear. Gran obviously thought it would be simple enough to get in but when Mrs Samson had set off early that morning to do the same thing, it was gone five before she got back home. 'The queue was easily a mile and a half long,' she said. 'It was good natured enough, but I've never seen so many people!'

On Thursday, Rita got up early and she was outside Westminster Hall by eight thirty. The queue was already very long but she joined the last people, glad that she would be in good time for Gran and Eddie. Her grandmother arrived at 9.10 and luckily the people behind her were happy to let her in.

'Where's Eddie?'

'Looking for somewhere to park the car.'

'I hope he finds somewhere that he can stay for a long time,' said Rita. 'I think we're going to need longer than the two hours you get on the parking meter.'

'I couldn't believe my eyes when I saw that,' Gran said in a loud voice. 'Sixpence for half an hour, that's two bob to park.

Day light robbery that is! Eddie reckons that Ernest Marples should have been locked up.'

Rita could hear a few titters from the people around them. There was no love lost when it came to the ex-Minister of Transport, even if he was the man who dreamt up the idea of premium bonds. Eddie arrived about fifteen minutes later and by then Gran and the people nearest them in the queue were getting on like a house on fire.

'Met him in person, I did,' said one old man with tears in his eyes. 'He came to Coventry when the old cathedral was bombed. Shook my hand.'

'I remember seeing him as a kid when they came to Droxford,' said another man. 'We was playing cops and robbers in the woods. Nobody believed me and my mate when we told them we saw him at the station.'

'Wasn't that the secret destination where the Allies met before D-Day?' somebody else piped up.

'The very same,' said the man. 'Course the soldiers sent us off with a flea in the ear, but we'd seen them all right.'

Then Gran said, 'None of us would be here if it weren't for 'im,' and there was a pregnant silence.

The queue moved slowly but when they arrived at the entrance they divided into two columns. The place was hushed, the only sound being the shuffle of feet as people walked forward in quiet reflection. Churchill's coffin was on a catafalque behind a huge ornate cross and draped with the union jack. There were six lighted candles on pedestals, one at each corner, one at his head and another at his feet. Four sailors with heads bowed, their hands resting on their swords, stood at each corner. As her grandmother reached the coffin, she suddenly stood to attention and bowed her head crisply and the man next to her crossed himself, before moving on again.

Outside, Gran trembled, her legs almost giving way. Eddie took her arm to steady her but she quickly pulled herself up. 'I'm all right.'

'So what do we do now?' Rita asked.

'I fancy a nice cup of tea,' said Gran.

Rita took them to one of the back street cafés she and Jenny frequented. It was already dinnertime, so Eddie ordered fish and chips. Rita and her grandmother fancied something lighter so they had a sandwich. The tea when it came was hot, dark and refreshing. Gran talked about the neighbours and the sad news that old Sam Haffenden's blacksmith forge and two thatched cottages were going to be pulled down.

'Somebody started a petition,' said Gran. 'I signed it. That forge has been on the edge of the village since Queen Victoria's time.'

Rita told them about her temporary posts and the prospect of a more permanent job on the horizon.

'Would you like to come back to my place,' said Rita. 'I'd like you to see where I'm living.'

'Eddie has a long drive back,' Gran cautioned.

'That's no trouble,' said Eddie. 'You show me the way and I'll drive us. We can go back to Worthing from there.'

Twenty minutes later, Rita was proudly showing her grandmother her room. She made them tea and when Dorinda came back from work, Rita introduced them.

'Dorinda is a store detective,' said Rita.

Eddie was curious to know what her job entailed.

'She catches shoplifters,' said Rita.

'Not just that,' said Dorinda, 'I have to have the proof that they've been stealing and if the store decides to prosecute, I have to have a solid case to take to court.'

'Sounds like a very responsible job,' Gran remarked.

They left soon after. Rita went downstairs with them and walked to the car. 'Thanks for bringing Gran,' she said to Eddie as he said his goodbyes.

Her grandmother waited until he'd climbed into the driver's seat then turned to Rita. Never one to show much affection,

Rita was surprised when her grandmother lifted her hand and gently stroked Rita's cheek.

'Bye then, love,' she said. 'Thanks for today. Your mother would have been really proud of you.'

Chapter 19

'Tired of Waiting for You'
The Kinks

Rita had a letter from WEN. She left for work early, so it was evening before she found it in her letter locker in the hallway.

Dear Rita,

I was hoping to see you on Thursday but I'm guessing you may have gone to Westminster Hall. I have had a communication with the personal secretary of a client who has been in Germany. It seems that he would like a fully trained nursery nurse to look after his two small children and a baby on its way. His wife will give birth in May. I had already told the client about you and his secretary is asking if you can come for an interview. I know you still have a week or two to fulfil your contract, but they want an immediate decision.

I am willing to be guided by your decision, but for obvious reasons I must have your answer by return of post. I am told that I can now divulge the name of the client. His name is Rupert Cavendish and he is a leading light in the oil industry. Once the new baby comes, the post may involve trips abroad including Germany and USA. You will need to get a passport and to be ready to go at a moment's notice.

> *I look forward to hearing from you asap.*
> *Yours sincerely,*
> *Muriel Hunter (Mrs)*

Rita re-read the letter a couple of times before the enormity of what was on offer finally sank in. Hadn't he been interviewed a couple of times on TV? He was both rich and unbelievably good looking. Wow, and now she had a chance to work for him. She'd had no idea that he was married, and of course any romantic ideas she may have had about him would never come to anything now. Rita enjoyed a flirt and she'd been sorely tempted to go all the way several times in her life but she had made up her mind a long time ago that stealing someone's husband was something she would never do.

As she got ready for bed she was already thinking about Germany – German boys to be exact, and possibly Americans. Wasn't the oil industry pretty big in America? What a fantastic opportunity. She wondered what lay ahead of her. Australia? The Far East? The world suddenly seemed a very small place. Thus her reply was written that night and she would post it in the morning.

—

The nation buried Winston Churchill on January 30. Over three hundred thousand people had lined the streets to say farewell. The armed forces marched in solemn procession to St Paul's Cathedral behind his coffin which was on a naval gun carriage pulled by ninety-eight sailors with forty more behind the carriage steadying it with drag ropes.

As Rita was busy looking after Brian and Johnny, she only managed to see snippets of the event on the BBC. Perhaps the most moving part of the occasion came when Churchill's body was moved onto a barge on the River Thames to take him to Waterloo station. All along the river, the massive cranes were dipped as he went by.

To make sure that the children were blissfully unaware of what was happening outside of their walls, Rita had mixed together water and flour so that they could make pastry animals and people. When the children were happy with their shapes, she arranged with Mrs Boyd to pop them in the bottom of a slow oven until they were cooked. The children knew they'd be inedible but to make it more fun, once they were cold, Rita got out the paint box and they enjoyed giving their creations eyes or ears and sometimes a blobby mouth.

Each evening Rita was eager to get back to her digs and open her post box but disappointingly, there was no letter from Mrs Hunter.

'I'm afraid I've heard nothing as yet,' Mrs Hunter told Rita when she accosted her in the hallway of the WEN offices on Thursday. 'All I can tell you is that they will check your background for themselves before they contact me again. They are ultra-cautious because Mr Cavendish's secretary tells me some people have pretended to be someone they are not just to be alone with him.'

Rita was a little frustrated but, she told herself sternly, *I'll just have to be patient.*

Back with Mrs Boyd again on Friday, her employer greeted her with some good news. An upmarket department store wanted her children's clothing. The buyer, a young woman with a keen eye for fashion, thought they were amazing. Mrs Boyd was to make two sizes of each of her designs. They were to be displayed in a shop where the assistant would take measurements from their customers. Mrs Boyd would then re-create the dress, dungarees or trousers in a material of the customer's choice. Rita vaguely remembered Jenny telling her about Pixie's dresses being made in a similar way.

'I can keep the boat afloat as it is for a while,' Mrs Boyd told her, 'but I shall soon need other dressmakers and a premises to work from.'

'Sounds amazing,' said Rita.

'Can you sew?' Mrs Boyd asked.

'Me? I can just about put a button on,' Rita chuckled.

In the morning, she took the boys out for some exercise in the park and they had an enjoyable time. Back at the house, when Brian was having his after-lunch nap, she noticed that Johnny's treasure box was overflowing and he was struggling to close the lid.

'Have you got enough room in there, Johnny?'

The little boy shook his head.

'Would you like me to look for another box so that you can have two treasure boxes?'

'Can I?' he asked eagerly.

'Of course you can,' cried Rita. 'You can have as many as you like. I'm not sure if I can find something today, but I can ask Mummy.'

Johnny nodded.

'May I see your treasures,' she asked, 'or are they secret?'

He hesitated for a moment, so she added, 'You don't have to show me if you don't want to. It's all right.'

When Johnny lifted the lid, Rita was surprised. Not only had he stuffed the fountain pen and notebook and the man's scarf and sock inside but he had other things too… like a pipe and a pair of gloves.

'You've got some lovely things in here,' she said doing her best to keep her voice casual.

'They're my daddy's,' he said. 'I'm looking after them for him until he comes back.'

When she got home from work, the long-awaited letter from WEN was in her post box in the hallway.

> *Dear Rita,*
>
> *I have arranged an interview for you on Thursday next week. It will be conducted in the WEN offices and I must ask you not to share this information with anybody. The client is anxious to avoid publicity. Please be here at ten thirty sharp.*

Yours sincerely
Muriel Hunter (Mrs)

Rita spent a restless night. She knew the other nanny job wasn't in the bag yet but she couldn't keep silent about Johnny's plight any more. However, she risked losing her job if she offended Mrs Boyd about the matter and that in itself would have a knock-on effect. Without the income from Mrs Boyd she couldn't stay in Warren Court for long. She had a little savings which was to go towards buying a car, yet she knew she couldn't live with herself if her silence left Johnny permanently damaged. Rita had no expertise in mental health but the child's obsession was disturbing. Johnny should be living a carefree life, exploring the natural world and taking childhood risks like climbing and other challenges, not storing his father's things for 'when he came back', doing peculiar drawings and longing for something which could never happen.

Having taken a couple of aspirin for her headache, she set off for work. It had snowed during the night so it took a little longer to get there. She got the boys up and as soon as they'd had breakfast, she wrapped them up warm and they set off for Regent's Park. The park itself was massive, but there was plenty of variety within its boundaries. At the far end were the Zoological Gardens and the London Zoo itself. Had she still been working for Mrs Boyd in the summer, it would have been nice to take a picnic and make a day of it. The boys would enjoy looking at all the animals and it would have been fun to introduce them to the famous Guy the Gorilla who had arrived at the zoo with great fanfare just after the war. Right now, Rita felt that her charges were too young for a lot of walking and the winter weather didn't make things easier though the flurry of snow had made their trip today more exciting. It didn't take long before they were making tracks and snow angels and of course they couldn't leave the park without having a snowball fight.

'Time to go now boys,' she said, glancing at her watch.

Johnny stooped to scoop up more snow.

'We have to get back for dinner, Johnny.'

'I want to put a snowball in my treasure box for my daddy.'

Rita took a deep breath. 'I'm afraid that won't work, Johnny,' she said sympathetically. 'As soon as we get into the warm house, it will melt. Snow is meant for outside only.'

He was clearly disappointed. 'But I want him to see it.'

'You could always do a picture.'

When it was time to go that evening, Rita made sure she and Mrs Boyd were alone when the boys were in bed. 'Can I show you what the boys have been doing?' she said, putting the two treasure chests onto the kitchen table and pushing Brian's towards her first.

The OXO tin she'd commandeered from the bin at her digs contained the sort of thing a two-year-old would class as treasure – a Dinky car with one tyre missing, a piece of ribbon which looked as if one end had been sucked, a piece of a jigsaw, two sweet wrappers, a nail and a glass eye, probably from his old bunny. Pushing her hand through the collection with an indulgent smile, his mother said, 'Aww. How sweet.'

When Rita pushed Johnny's box towards her, Mrs Boyd's expression changed as she lifted the lid. Pulling out the sock, she said, 'What's this?'

'The things Johnny treasures are a bit different,' Rita said quietly.

Mrs Boyd frowned as she saw the birthday card. 'But this was my husband's.' She paused then added crossly, 'Did you put him up to this?'

Rita felt herself bristle but forced herself to stay calm. 'No, I didn't,' she said. 'I started the treasure boxes because Johnny had squirrelled all these things around the house.' She picked up the pen. 'This was behind the kitchen dresser and the tie clip was at the back of his drawer. He was very secretive about them. I thought that rather than letting him get used to sneaking around, it would be better to have it all in the open.'

'I don't understand,' Mrs Boyd said plaintively. 'Why would he want all this stuff?'

'He tells me he's keeping it for his father,' said Rita. 'He thinks about him all the time, Mrs Boyd. Johnny doesn't understand that his father is never coming back. He's expecting him to reappear at any moment. I fear he's becoming obsessed about it. We went out in the snow today and he even wanted to bring back a snowball to show his father.'

'But we told him his father had gone to be with granddad.'

'I don't think Johnny understands that what you're telling him means his father is dead,' Rita continued. 'He needs to be told in words of one syllable. He needs to hear it plainly.'

Mrs Boyd's eyes filled with tears. 'But I can't tell him that,' she cried. 'He'll be upset.'

Rita nodded. 'That's true, but at least he'll stop fantasising that at any moment his father is going to come through that door. Right now, he's so confused. Why has the daddy he loved not come back home? Maybe he's thinking his father won't come back for him, but he might come back for his tie pin or his other sock.'

'You talk as if you're an expert in these things,' Mrs Boyd said huffily. 'You're just a chit of a girl. What would you know?'

Determined to stay the professional, Rita waited a moment before she answered. 'Actually, I do know a bit about these things Mrs Boyd. My mother was killed when I was eleven and although I was a lot older than Johnny, I do know how difficult it was to make sense of where she had gone and why.'

They stood in silence.

'I'm sorry to hear about your mother.' Her voice was small and she clearly didn't want to make eye contact with Rita. She replaced the lid on Johnny's box. 'But I can't do it.'

'Forgive me for saying so, ma'am, but for Johnny's sake, I think you must.'

Mrs Boyd looked up with a helpless expression. 'Will you do it with me, Rita?' Their eyes met and Rita nodded. 'We'll do it tomorrow.'

Chapter 20

'Sparky's Magic Piano'

Henry Blair

BBC Light Programme, *Children's Favourites*

'Fancy coming to the Club Noreik?'

Dorinda's cheery invitation when she got back to her digs was just what Rita needed. The chat with Mrs Boyd had left her feeling rather unsettled and the fact that her employer had pushed doing what was necessary onto Rita's shoulders was a little daunting to say the least. Funny how one minute she was just a chit of a girl over-stepping the mark and the next minute she was quite capable enough to tell a little boy his father was dead, she thought acidly. This was one thing she had never been taught in her training. Being honest, handling the truth without euphemisms, yes – but telling a five-year-old his father is dead, no.

'I won't be able to stay long,' Rita cautioned.

Club Noreik, which was in Tottenham, North London was an all-nighter. The best bands began at midnight and the club finished at six in the morning. Rita was to be back with Mrs Boyd in the morning and of course she was facing a difficult day, something she couldn't cope with if she was feeling jaded.

'That's okay,' Dorinda said cheerily. 'I'd rather not stay out all night anyway. Stay until two?'

Rita nodded. 'You're on.'

Half the fun was getting ready which they did together in Dorinda's room. Rita brought out her new camel and navy plaid skirt with wide pleats coming out from a dropped waistline, something that she had been dying to wear. She had topped it with a turtleneck navy sweater until Dorinda pointed out that while there may be snow on the ground, inside the club would be hot. Rita went back to her room and fished out the short-sleeved jumper which was part of an old twin set. It didn't look quite as fashionable, but Dorinda assured her that once they got there, she would be glad she was wearing it.

Dorinda had a lightweight pink and green blazer over a pale green blouse. Her oatmeal-coloured skirt was above the knee, and she wore her hair in a bouffant style with a big pink bow knotted at the front.

Rita was always keen to keep abreast with the fashion magazines to see the latest style for make-up. Hence, her flesh tone powder was complimented by light blue eye shadow and dark brown eyeliner on both her top and bottom lid. Her lipstick was pink. Dorinda had gone with much the same except that her eyeliner was black. Neither girl wore nail varnish. The department stores where Dorinda worked thought it unprofessional and Rita had been taught that if she was working with children, it was unhygienic. They set off for the bus just after ten.

When they got there it cost an eye-watering seven and sixpence to get in (most dance halls were three bob or so) but once again, Dorinda assured her it would be worth it. Inside, Rita was a tad disappointed. It looked very ordinary; a stage with a set of drums, a few posters at the back and a banner over the top saying, 'Club Noreik: Home of R&B', but by eleven, the place was packed and as soon as the groups came on, it was electric. The band was very loud and in no time at all, the place was heaving. A group called The Richmonds were playing. Dressed in collarless suits like The Beatles, they sang all the popular hits and they were good – but not that good.

The place erupted when The Yardbirds came on. They had just had a massive hit with 'For Your Love' which was currently at number three in the charts. Their guitarist, Eric Clapton, was amazing.

Rita and Dorinda danced together until a couple of nice-looking lads came between them. From that moment on, Rita didn't look back. Dorinda had been absolutely right. The only downside was that it was boiling hot and the drinks cost a fortune. Jack and Sandy bought some for them, but a couple of hours later, Rita saw Jack slip a pill into Dorinda's drink. Before her friend could take a sip, Rita had a 'nasty accident' when she bumped into the table. It ended up with the glass being tipped over and the drink was totally lost. Jack was none too pleased about it but while he was getting Dorinda another drink, and Sandy had gone to the toilet, Rita told her friend what he'd done. As it was already two thirty and Rita had to be at work in the morning, the two girls made their escape.

'What do you think he put in your drink?' Rita asked as they sat on the night bus.

'What colour was it?' Dorinda said sleepily.

Rita shrugged. 'Sort of clear but with shades of green perhaps?'

'Christmas tree,' said Dorinda. 'Some people call them uppers. They're cheap and easy to get hold of in a place like that, only trouble is, they give you one hell of a headache when they wear off.'

'That's awful,' Rita spluttered. 'Fancy doing it without telling you.'

'People do it all the time,' Dorinda said sagely. 'Slip a pill in your drink or onto a sugar knob so's you won't taste it.'

'You've had that happen to you before?' Rita spluttered.

'Once bitten,' Dorinda said with a grin. 'But thanks for telling me. You're a pal.'

To say she felt a bit jaded when she got up the next day was an understatement. Rita was shattered. She had only managed about three hours sleep so she struggled to get going but thankfully the walk to work woke her up. It was a cold morning and although they hadn't had any more snow, the pavement was icy in places. She decided to keep the boys inside today.

As she arrived at the house, Mrs Boyd was heading for her sewing room but before she managed to shut the door, Rita called out, 'What time shall we do you-know-what?'

Her employer gave her a tortured look. 'This afternoon.'

Rita and the boys enjoyed their morning. She let them play at the sink for a while. They poured water into measuring jugs and filled cups and a mug. Eventually bored with that, she had to change their jumpers for dry ones then they played games together. They loved the rhyming game *Who stole the cookie from the cookie pot?* even though it didn't quite work with only the three of them, but the card game Snap was always a firm favourite. After lunch, Johnny read a book while Brian had a nap. This was an ideal time, so Rita tapped on Mrs Boyd's door.

The three of them sat at the kitchen table, the two adults with a cup of tea. 'I've been telling your mummy about your lovely treasure box,' Rita said enthusiastically. 'Would you like to show it to her?'

Mrs Boyd sat with a pained expression as Johnny took out his treasures one by one. Rita noticed two more things had been added since she'd seen it the day before; a folded man's handkerchief and an old photograph taken years before Johnny was born.

'Did you take that photograph out of the picture frame in my bedroom?' his mother accused sharply.

Rita could have kicked her under the table. Johnny looked a little sheepish.

Mrs Boyd was just about to take a deep breath when Rita interrupted. 'I'm sure you had a good reason for taking the picture of Daddy, didn't you Johnny?' Her voice was much softer, quiet and gentle. Mrs Boyd seemed visibly deflated.

'I wanted to keep it safe,' said Johnny beginning to put the things back into the box.

'Why?' said Rita.

'For when Daddy comes back.'

Mrs Boyd took in a sharp breath and put her hand over her mouth.

'But Daddy can't come back,' Rita continued. 'It's very sad, but your daddy died in that car crash, Johnny. You do know that, don't you?'

The child carried on putting everything back in the box. 'But Mummy said Daddy had gone to be with Granddad.'

Rita was hoping that at this point Mrs Boyd would take over but instead she sat staring at her son with a look of surprised anguish on her face.

Rita leaned forward and took the boy's hands in hers. 'Mummy's right,' she said gently. 'But you see your granddad is dead too. And when you're dead, you can't come back.'

With a loud scrape of her chair, Mrs Boyd stood up from the table and left the room.

The boy had tears in his eyes. 'Is Mummy cross with me?'

'No, sweetheart,' said Rita. 'She just a bit upset. She misses your daddy very much, just like you do.' Rita squeezed his fingers gently. 'You do understand that even though your daddy loves you very, very much, he can't come back to see you?'

The little boy nodded his head miserably and Rita had an inkling that in his heart of hearts he had known that all along.

'Does this mean I can't keep my treasure box?'

'Of course it doesn't,' said Rita. 'When someone dies people often keep some of their things, not because the person will come back for them but because it helps them to remember them.'

Johnny put the lid on his box.

'Your box is very full now,' Rita continued, 'so I brought you a pretty box I had at home. Maybe you would like to put some of your things inside to make more room.'

She rose to her feet and went to her bag. When she came back to the table, she placed the blue box with the butterfly lid between them. 'My mummy died when I was just a bit older than you,' she said. 'I used to keep some of her letters in this box, but you can have it now.'

Johnny lifted the lid. 'I shall put the small things inside this box.'

She watched him putting the photograph, the pen and the sock in the butterfly box. 'What about your mummy's letters?' he said suddenly looking up with a concerned expression. 'Where will you put them now?'

'Don't worry,' she said with a smile. 'I have them in a very special place.'

Mrs Boyd came back into the room.

'Johnny would like to keep his treasure box,' Rita said firmly as she sat down. She didn't want Mrs Boyd snatching it away and telling him he couldn't keep it. 'He understands that his daddy isn't coming back.'

'I'm putting the things in my treasure box to help me remember him,' Johnny told her.

Mrs Boyd glanced at Rita. 'I think that's a wonderful idea, don't you, Rita?'

The rest of the day was a bit of a struggle. Every bone in Rita's body wanted her to sit down and have a snooze but with two lively boys to look after, that was impossible. When Brian got up, she taught them some finger plays. Five currant buns proved to be the favourite but they were quite good with Insy Wincy Spider and Wind the Bobbin Up. After that, Rita suggested a game of hide and seek which turned out to be hilarious.

After tea she found *Animal Magic* with Johnny Morris was on ITV so the boys sat in front of the television. They absolutely loved it, especially when Johnny Morris seemed to make the animals talk and their facial expressions fit so well with what they were saying. It was bath time after that and once they were in bed, Mrs Boyd came upstairs to read them a story. As Rita was clearing up the bathroom, she heard Mrs Boyd say, 'Johnny, I've got something you might like to put in your treasure box.'

Rita pricked up her ears and she heard him say, 'What is it?'

'It's a bow tie, darling. Your daddy used to like wearing them. He wore that one on the day we first met.'

'Can I have one?' Brian piped up.

'I've got a special tickle for you,' said his mother and the next moment, Brian was giggling fit to bust.

As Rita hurried downstairs with the washing she felt strangely content. It seemed that Johnny would be allowed to keep his treasure box and more importantly, his mother understood his need to keep the memory of his father alive. As she popped the dirty clothes into the washing machine, Rita smiled to herself. Now that the pressure was off the treasure box would probably be no more than a passing fad. Most likely it would be gone in a year or two, but for now, it allowed Johnny to grieve is loss, his way.

Chapter 21

'I'll Never Find Another You'
The Seekers

On Thursday when Rita arrived at WEN at ten fifteen, Mrs Hunter showed her into her office.

'Things have changed somewhat since I wrote to you, Rita. It seems that the client's personal assistant, Miss Marchant, will be conducting your interview,' she began, 'Will that be all right?'

Rita nodded. If she was nervous before she came, she was even more so now.

'I am fully confident that they will find none better than you, Rita,' said Mrs Hunter. 'You have extremely good references and you have gained a lot of experience in working with privileged people, who, let's be honest about it, are used to having their own way. However, if you feel you don't want to work for the client, I shall think none the less of you if you decline the offer. You must be absolutely sure that this is the right position for you.'

'I understand,' said Rita.

Miss Marchant was late. She arrived just before eleven and breezed into the office with no apology. In Rita's eyes this was a bad start, but Miss Marchant had done her homework; as they talked, Rita realised that her whole career was an open book.

'Could you tell me a bit about your client?' Rita asked.

The assistant was a little cagey with her replies. Apparently, the husband was away a lot, the house was in the country and she wasn't sure if there were any buses. When Rita asked about the children, she seemed unsure of their ages and she was rude enough to say that their mother was neurotic. Even though Rita was being offered a generous salary, Miss Marchant's vagueness about her off duty times, sounded warning bells.

'I believe your client's wife is expecting another baby?' Rita glanced at Mrs Hunter for affirmation.

Miss Marchant's face flushed. 'My client's wife is pregnant, yes.'

'So, I shall be caring for three children under five, in a house in the depths of the countryside, with possibly no bus connection and may or may not get one day off a week?'

'I'm sure—' Mrs Hunter flustered.

'So am I, Mrs Hunter,' Rita interrupted. Then turning to Miss Marchant, she added, 'Thank you Miss Marchant, but I'm afraid I must decline your offer.'

Miss Marchant's jaw dropped. 'But... I don't understand,' she spluttered. 'They really want you to come. You have impeccable references and it's a wonderful offer.'

Rita gave her a steady unflinching stare but said nothing. As far as she was concerned, the interview was at an end. Without another word, Miss Marchant gathered her papers and swept out of the room with her nose in the air. The door banged behind her.

'Oh dear,' said Mrs Hunter.

'I do apologise if I disappointed you,' said Rita, 'but that woman was insufferable. She was crass, rude and offensive. I still don't even know if the children are boys or girls or one of each.'

Mrs Hunter nodded. 'You're absolutely right, Rita. I think it is I who should apologise to you. I let the thought of a large fee come between myself and common sense.'

'Well,' Rita said with a grin, 'there goes my wonderful salary as well.'

They both laughed. 'How are you enjoying your present post Rita, or should I say posts?'

Rita gave her a quick update on both employers and their children. 'I have to say, I am enjoying living in Warren Court,' she confided. 'I've made friends with a store detective and we've been able to go out a few times.'

'Does that mean if another live-in position came up, you would rather not take it?'

'Actually, no,' said Rita. 'I think I am ready for something more permanent but not with the likes of Miss Marchant hanging around.'

'Point taken,' said Mrs Hunter opening the office door. The sound of laughter wafted towards them and suddenly Rita was glad she was here. Glad for Mrs Hunter and most of all, glad for WEN.

After the coffee morning and a light lunch, Rita took herself off to the Shaftesbury Theatre where she watched the matinee of *Our Man Crichton* starring Kenneth More and Millicent Martin. It was wonderful to relax in a comfortable seat and be whisked away to desert islands and romance. She came out to the grey early evening feeling so much better.

Back in her digs, she decided to read the rest of her mother's letters. They were now in an old biscuit box but still tied with the ribbon from Selfridges.

The first few after the baby announcement were much the same; Dexter declared his love for her mother time and again. Then came one dated May 1945 in which he declared, that he was 'cock-a-hoop' that he had a beautiful daughter, continuing:

> *Honey, you are the cleverest woman on God's earth. Please send me a picture of our beautiful daughter. Of course I'm not upset she's a girl. I can't wait to see her. Yes, I love the name Rita. It makes me think of Rita Hayworth. I remember us seeing her in the film Blood and Sand when we all came to England. It was a classic*

film even back then, but I was holding the hand of a wonderful English rose in the cinema, so it's a film I shall always remember – what was it all about again? I bet you don't remember either! I can't think why...

Oh honey, I'm working hard and saving every penny I can. I don't go out boozing with the guys any more. I reckon by the fall I should have enough to come to England and fetch you both. You will get on and get a passport, won't you?

All my love.

Your very own Cuddle bunny.

XXX

There was a knock on her door. When she opened it, Dorinda stood in the hallway with a couple of bags of hot chips. 'Fancy some?'

Rita invited her in and put the kettle on.

'How did you get on with the interview?' Dorinda asked as she pushed the letters up the bed so that she could sit down. 'What are these? Old love letters?'

'From my father to my mother.'

'Oh, how sweet,' cried Dorinda. 'I shouldn't think my parents ever wrote each other love letters. I only ever remember the constant bickering.'

Rita scooped Dexter's letters back into the biscuit tin. 'To answer your first question, the interview was a disaster.'

While they ate chips and drank tea, she went on to describe the dreadful Miss Marchant giving her friend a blow-by-blow account, with actions and drama which had the pair of them helpless with laughter.

Downstairs, somebody rang the doorbell.

'I'd better go,' said Dorinda standing up and looking for her handbag. 'I've got to be in court tomorrow.'

'One of your shoplifters?'

'One I've been trying to catch for ages,' said Dorinda.

'Ooh do tell,' said Rita.

'I first saw her in Bourne and Hollingsworth,' Dorinda began, 'and then she was hanging around in Debenhams. There was always something about her that aroused my suspicion; something I couldn't quite put my finger on.'

'So what did you do?'

'Nothing. Before I point the finger, I have to be absolutely certain or catch them in the act, but I never could,' said Dorinda fishing her handbag out from under the bed 'Then about three weeks ago, I spotted her in Selfridges.'

'And you finally caught her red-handed.'

'Not exactly, but I followed her and she went into the ladies'.'

Rita opened the door. 'And you nabbed her there?'

'No, but I did notice that when she came out, she was pregnant.'

'Pregnant!' Rita spluttered.

'Remarkable isn't it,' said Dorinda. 'She went to the toilet at three fifteen and when she came out ten minutes later, she was eight months pregnant.'

'Remind me not to go into the ladies' in Selfridges,' Rita laughed.

'Fortunately, she had a safe delivery,' Dorinda said dryly. 'A couple of nice coats and an expensive handbag.'

When her friend had gone, Rita was still in a buoyant mood. She got ready for bed then tidied up her mother's letters. Clambering under the covers, she realised she only had three more to read. Might as well finish reading them tonight.

In the letter which had reached her mother in Christmas 1945, the tone was much the same. Dexter had almost saved enough to come to England and pay for their wedding and fares back to America. He was still living with his parents and there was plenty of room for all of them until they could get a place of their own, probably in the 'fall' as he kept calling autumn. 1947 was going to be their year.

> *Honey, it's not long now and we can be together. I can't wait to hold you in my arms again. Kiss my baby for me and have a good Christmas.*
> *All my love now and eternally, Dexter.*

The next letter was dated the following year, April 1948. Rita could hardly believe her eyes as she read the pages.

> *They were travelling along the highway when this truck came out of nowhere. Eyewitnesses said the pieces were scattered all over the damn road. The driver was drunk – I mean pie-eyed drunk and he hit their car full on as it waited at the junction. My dad didn't stand a chance and my baby brother, Gene... Well, they pulled him out alive, but he was only hanging on by a thread. They took him to the hospital and called me down. The doc said he needed an operation and treatment, expensive treatment. We have healthcare but not nearly enough. I had a choice, either use the healthcare for the basics or shell out for proper treatment. Valerie, he's only twenty. He's got his whole life in front of him. What could I do? The only money I had in the world was what I'd saved to be with you, but honey, I couldn't leave my kid brother like that. I couldn't let him die.*

Rita stared down at the page. She would have dismissed everything he was saying as a con; a made-up excuse because he didn't have the money and probably had no intention of marrying her mum and bringing them back the States – it certainly sounded iffy, but then she read the neatly folded newspaper cutting he'd put in with the letter. Rita held up the flimsy paper, tarnished with age. On one side there was part of an advertisement for Kiwi shoe polish and on the other there was a picture of Dexter, his parents and his brother. Underneath the report there was another picture, this time it was of a crumpled car being towed away from the scene. She could feel tears in her eyes as she stared at the headlines.

> Local family in tragic accident. One man dead and another seriously injured.

Chapter 22

'A Little Bitty Tear'

Burl Ives

BBC Light Programme, *Children's Favourites*

Rita had arranged that Jenny and Pixie would come to Mrs Samson's to have tea. Both nursery nurses were aware that the winter months could be a little trying. It was too cold for walks in the park and most of the amenities were closed until Easter, so their charges often got bored with nothing much to do. Mrs Samson had been very accommodating with the idea and even made the children a little cake in the shape of a train. The wheels were Milk and Honey Biscuits, the engine barrel was a chocolate roll and the tender was a cake filled with Old English Spangles and Liquorice Allsorts on the top to represent coal.

They played some games and after that, Rita and Jenny let the children have some time to amuse themselves. They both agreed that it wasn't good for them to have adult-led and structured play all the time; they needed time to use their imagination and to learn to socialise together. The two girls did 'tea parties' and little Neil loved being spoiled.

'How's the new move coming on?' Rita asked Jenny when they had a moment to themselves. 'I hope it hasn't fallen through like the last one.'

'It's next Tuesday,' said Jenny.

'Gosh, so soon? And you're going with them?'

'Just for a month,' said Jenny. 'I leave on the tenth and then of course Simon and I get married on 27 March. You are still coming to the wedding?'

'Of course!' cried Rita. 'Wouldn't miss it for the world.'

'Good,' said Jenny. 'Bernie's coming and so is Carole.'

Bernie was still doing her training in Harefield House but Carole, who had been training as a nursery nurse, had left to have a baby. Bernie was the girl who had replaced her. Rita raised her eyebrows and smiled. 'Excited?'

'Yes and no,' said Jenny. 'Of course I can't wait to marry Simon, but I'm not so sure about the housewife bit. Yonks ago I went to a nursery school in Bermondsey as part of my training and one of the teachers said if ever I wanted to work there she would put in a good word for me.'

'Go for it, girl.'

'But do I tell Simon?'

Rita pulled a face. 'I think you should. You can't start your married life going behind his back.'

'But what if he says I can't?'

Rita gave her a playful nudge. 'I'm sure you'll find a way to persuade him to change his mind.'

Jenny giggled. 'You're right.' She paused. 'What about you? Anyone irresistible in your life?'

Rita smiled. 'Not yet, but that's not to say that I haven't met a few nice boys.'

'What about that new post you were telling me about?'

Rita rehearsed the tale once again.

'Flippin' Nora,' cried Jenny, 'she sounds an absolute cow. I think you're well out of that one.'

The door opened and Mrs Samson came into the room and Rita introduced her friend and Pixie. Pixie lisped, 'Thank you for having me,' with a small curtsy which left Rita's employer completely enchanted.

The children watched a little TV together and then Jenny asked to use the telephone to ring for a taxi. By now it was dark and besides, the walk back to Alford Street would be far too long for a tired little girl who was all partied out.

'Not looking forward to going back,' said Jenny fishing inside Pixie's coat sleeve to find her glove. It was joined to the other glove with a long tape but somehow it had got lost. 'Everybody is so stressed out with the move. I was packing up some of Pixie's toys yesterday and I needed to cheer myself up so I started singing.'

'Good idea,' said Rita. 'I always feel better if I sing.'

'Didn't quite work for me,' said Jenny finding the glove and putting Pixie's wriggling fingers inside. 'All of a sudden there was a loud knock on the door and Mr Dawson said, "Can you stop that racket, Jenny. I've got a terrific headache and it's really annoying me."'

'Bloomin' cheek!' Rita said with a chuckle. 'I hope you gave him short shrift.'

'Na,' said Jenny. 'I just said I didn't feel like singing anyway. There we are poppet, now let me tie your scarf.'

Mrs Samson appeared with some cake in a brown paper bag.

'Say thank you,' Jenny reminded her charge.

'Thank you. Can we come again?' Pixie asked.

'We'll be going to your new house next week,' Jenny reminded her.

'Bye, bye,' said Mrs Samson.

At the door, Rita and Jenny embraced. 'Good luck for next Tuesday,' Rita said, 'and keep in touch.'

'I will,' Jenny called from the taxi. 'And good luck with finding your new post.'

As she closed the door, Rita became aware that her employer was still standing just behind her. Her face was white. 'New post?' she said. 'You've never been here six weeks already, have you? Oh Rita, you can't leave me yet!'

It was an awkward moment. 'I'm not going just yet,' she said honestly, 'but we knew this was a temporary position, so I have to prepare for my future. That's why I'm actively looking for a live-in post.'

'Oh Rita,' she cried. 'What am I going to do? This arrangement works so perfectly for me.'

'Rest assured Mrs Samson. As I said, I'm not going just yet but if I do, I think I have an idea about that.'

—

Back in her digs, Rita sat on her bed with a cup of chocolate and opened the last of her father's letters once again. She'd read it last night but after the upset of reading about her American grandfather's death and her uncle's accident, it hadn't really registered. The letter had come three months after the previous one. Her mother had obviously sent him some sort of postal order or cheque because he began by thanking her for it. *'It was kind of you, my love,'* he wrote, *'but I am returning it.'* Her mother must have destroyed it or cashed it in because there was nothing in the envelope. Had she been offended that he'd refused her help? That was something Rita would never know. Val had taken all her feelings on this subject to the grave and even more frustratingly, although he had written his address on the back of every envelope, her mother had torn away every single one of them.

Rita's perception of her father had changed so much over the period of time that she'd taken to read his letters. She'd begun by thinking he must have been a bit of sod – deserting her mother and leaving her to bring up their child on her own, but now she could see that it wasn't like that. It wasn't like that at all.

He had told her mother that his brother had come through the operation and was making good progress. His rehabilitation was going to take a long time, but he was a 'tough cookie' and Dexter was sure he would make the most of all the help he was getting.

> *My very own darling, I have reached a point where I can see that our dreams are just dreams. Our marriage and*

> *setting up home together is not going to happen. Our whole family is in debt and will be for a long time. I must clear this debt and it's going to take me not just months but years. I cannot, will not, ask you to wait for me. You are young. You are beautiful and you deserve to be happy. I don't want us to part Val, but I must release you. Find yourself a man who will take good care of you and our baby. Find someone who can love you as you should be loved. This is my goodbye, honey. I pray to God that you have a good life.*
>
> *Thank you for loving me as you did. I shall never forget you.*
>
> *Dexter.*

It had made Rita cry last night and it did so again today. She was desperate to know what happened to them. Did Gene make a full recovery? Did her father eventually clear the hospital bill? Having grown up with the NHS she had a new respect for it. How wonderful it was to live in a country where, when faced with some terrible life tragedy, you didn't have to worry about how you were going to pay for it. Her father, all in the same moment, had to bury his own father and pay for expensive hospital treatment for his kid brother.

With a sigh, Rita put the envelope back in the pile. As she wrapped the ribbon around them all, the newspaper cutting fell out. Picking it up, she couldn't resist one more look at it and that's when she saw something. The reporter had written, 'Edgar McCloud' (her grandfather) 'worked as a longshoreman in New York harbor all his life and was a leading light in the war against labor racketeering.'

Now it occurred to her that if her grandfather had been a leading light, if he had made a name for himself, then surely people would still remember him. And if they remembered him, she could, possibly, find her father.

The newspaper cutting was very old and as luck would have it, on the back of the cutting above the advert was the daily almanac. Rita read about the weather, the temperatures, and she looked at the calendar. Running along the edge of the page it said —*ily News*, followed by the address —sey City, New Jersey. So, the newspaper had to be called *The Daily News*! Rita stared at the address, a plan forming in her mind. She would write to the editor and say she was trying to reconnect with someone who had been in England during the war. She wouldn't give away too much information in case some phony person got in contact, but she would try and think of something only her mother and Dexter could have known. She thumbed her way back through his letters until she stopped at the ones where he'd mentioned the films they'd watched, *The Man in Grey* and *Fanny by Gaslight*.

After much thought, Rita had written two letters. The first was a formal letter to the editor of *The Daily News*, New Jersey USA. In it she explained that having read an old article from the newspaper, she was looking for someone who had been in the Worthing area during World War Two...

> *I believe Edgar McCloud who worked as a longshoreman in New York harbor was my grandfather. He was instrumental in fighting the war against labour racketeering. I am hoping that some residents will remember him and put me in touch with any remaining relatives.*

She gave the editor her grandmother's address but used her own name. In the accompanying letter, she told Dexter she was a 'blast from the past' trying to make contact with someone who was important in her life. She said nothing about herself but wrote, '...*You may remember writing Valerie a letter from France. If Stewart Granger still wants make contact, I should love to see him.*' Was that too obscure? She hoped not. She sealed down the envelope with Dexter's letter and put it inside with the editor's letter.

She rested it next to the bedside lamp and as she lay in bed, she said a silent prayer before she switched out the light.

Chapter 23

'Nellie the Elephant'
Mandy Miller
BBC Light Programme, *Children's Favourites*

After the fiasco of that interview with Miss Marchant, Mrs Hunter had wasted no time. Rita found a letter waiting for her. In it she had the details of three live-in posts. Gillian Honeyfield an up-and-coming TV star, had just had her first baby and was looking to return to work in the next couple of weeks. Her baby was healthy and doing well. Her nanny would be expected to offer him round the clock care. No cleaning or cooking would be expected and she would be paid a handsome salary. The post offered one day off a week with a weekend every six weeks.

Mrs D'Silver had three children. She was a businesswoman running a company dealing in up-market cleaning products. Her son was six and attended a day school, her eldest daughter was three and had a part-time place in a nursery school while the baby was six months and at home. The nanny would be expected to get the children to school, she'd be the sole carer for the baby and she would be expected to clean the house and do the washing. Rita noted that Mrs D'Silver's salary was a lot less than Mrs Honeyfield's offer.

The third post was for a Mrs Knight. She had just had her second baby after a difficult pregnancy but was now at home, although not completely well as yet. Baby Daniel's sister Lucy was four. They lived in the country not far from Ewell in Surrey.

Of the three, Mrs Knight's offer had the greater appeal. Rita liked to think she could help in the mother's complete recovery from childbirth. It would be fun to do things with Lucy and as an added bonus, Ewell was not far from Harefield House where she had done her training which meant that she could catch up with Bernie and some of the other girls on her days off. The salary was on a par with what she had been earning with Mrs Plumb and Mrs Samson, but of course she would be in the home counties rather than Central London where everything was so much more expensive, and she would have her bed and board. Rita slept on it then put a letter in the post to Mrs Hunter first thing in the morning.

'They are asking you to sign a non-disclosure agreement on acceptance,' Mrs Hunter told Rita on the telephone.

Rita frowned, puzzled.

'Basically, that means when you leave their employment you will not be allowed to sell your story to *News of the World* and such like,' Mrs Hunter continued. 'I've not come across anything like this before, but apparently it's a new trend.'

Rita's thoughts went into overdrive. A non-disclosure agreement... that must mean the people must not only be rich but also famous. Who could it be? Cliff Richard wasn't married, and she knew from pop magazines that Tom Jones only had one son who, at eight was probably too old for a nanny. The suspense was killing. Doing her best not to let her excitement show, she said she was happy with that, so Mrs Hunter gave her the address and told her that she would set up an interview as soon as possible. She didn't have to wait long, on her next day off Rita was on the Greenline bus on her way to Ewell.

The house, at the end of a cul-de-sac, was almost hidden by a high wall and electronic gates. She had to press a button and say who she was before they opened. Once inside the grounds she saw the house itself. It was massive with white walls and a black Tudor style half-timbered frontage under the steeply pitched roof. Rita stood in the small secluded porchway and waited. She was surprised when a young woman no more than sixteen or seventeen opened the door.

'Mrs Knight? I'm Rita Brownlow.'

'Come in, come in,' she said stepping back. She was blonde with a pale face. Her lipstick was a ghostly pink and her eyes were lined top and bottom with black liner. In keeping with the new fashion, her liner extended beyond the corner of her eye in an upward sweep. 'My name is Tammy-Jane. I've just taken Mrs Knight up a cup of tea. She's been having a bit of a rest, but she'll be down in a jiffy.'

Rita blinked and followed her into the spacious hallway just as a nurse, a much older woman, walked down the stairs. She gave Rita a curt nod and walked through the kitchen door.

'Tell you what,' Tammy-Jane continued, 'why don't I show you round and by the time we've finished, Mrs Knight should be down.'

She took Rita into a spacious open-plan kitchen graced with all the modern conveniences. Through the wide windows, Rita could see a perfectly manicured garden with a large cabin or chalet at the far end.

'That's where they practice,' Tammy-Jane said. 'There's an underground room and it's well away from the neighbours you see.'

Rita didn't see but she didn't like to mention it. Who was Tammy-Jane anyway and how did she fit into the set-up? A much older child perhaps, or possibly a relative? She was certainly up-to-date with her fashion. Rita hazarded a guess that the dress she wore, a short, waist-hugging brown check A-line, with round neck and long sleeves, had come from Mary Quant's Bazaar or perhaps Biba.

As she leaned over the sink, Rita could see that a Silver Cross pram was parked under the window and she guessed the baby must be sleeping inside. A moment later, a nurse picked him up to bring him indoors.

From the kitchen, Tammy-Jane took Rita to a large sitting room which was beautifully furnished with carpets wall to wall.

'This is where Mr and Mrs Knight entertain,' she said. It was like a showroom with a cream three-piece suit and plain curtains.

A second sitting room nearby was slightly more homely than the first. The chintz curtains and luxuriously cosy chairs gave it a more farmhouse appeal. Rita guessed that this was where the family relaxed. She couldn't help noticing the framed pictures dotted around the room. Most of them were formal posed pictures of groups of musicians. The faces looked vaguely familiar but short of walking over to them and picking them up to peer more closely, she was left to wonder. A large portrait of a good-looking man holding a microphone in mid-performance on the stage hung over the fireplace. It was then that Rita realised who Mr Knight was. The picture was of none other than Cameron Knight, the lead singer of the group Kandy Krisp. As soon as it dawned on her, Rita instinctively took in her breath. Tammy-Jane saw Rita's moment of recognition and grinned. 'Dishy isn't he?'

A much smaller room on the ground floor, a sort of box room, had a comfortable looking armchair and a television, but little else. 'This is the nanny's sitting room,' said Tammy-Jane. Rita nodded approvingly. How lovely to have her own space.

Upstairs, she was shown into a spacious bedroom which was obviously for the children. It wasn't very tidy, but it was clear that the little girl lacked for nothing. There was a doll's house, a pram and a huge number of dolls, teddies, a Raggedy Ann, a Barbie and even the new British rival, Sindy. Next door was the bedroom which, should she get the job, would be hers. As expected, the baby's cot was in one corner. While he was so tiny, she would have to be on call twenty-four seven. Decorated in pale blue and cream, there was a divan bed, a wardrobe, a rather upright chair and a bedside table. The nurse was sitting in the chair with the baby on her lap giving him his feed. Rita smiled from the doorway and when the nurse looked up she said, 'May I?'

The nurse gave her a nod so Rita walked to her side and gazed down at an adorable baby. 'He's beautiful,' Rita said.

'Meet Daniel Peter Knight,' said the nurse.

The baby's eye fell on Rita but he didn't stop sucking his bottle.

'Nurse Watts is here temporarily,' Tammy-Jane cut in rather unnecessarily.

Rita admired Daniel Peter for a little longer, then they left. She would have liked to be able to ask the nurse what the family was like to work with but with Tammy-Jane slouching in the doorway it was rather awkward.

As they came back downstairs, Rita was breathless with excitement. The house was fantastic, as was the position. This was exactly the sort of post she had always dreamed of. Fabulously rich family, beautiful surroundings, a good wage and the added bonus of seeing the famous stars of today in the flesh should they come for a visit. Not to mention being in the very same house as Cameron Knight himself! It was every nursery nurse's dream. As soon as she got off the Greenline bus, she knew she was close both to Epsom and the village of Ewell. With any free time she had, she could take up where she left off with regards to clubs and old friends from training – provided they hadn't moved away of course. And she could still get into London on the train.

Mrs Knight, when she appeared, was quite pale. Dressed in a floor length red silk Japanese kimono with white crane birds, she floated into the room. 'I'm so sorry I wasn't here to greet you, Miss Brownlow,' she began as Tammy-Jane left the room. 'I'm afraid I haven't been too well since I gave birth to Daniel.' She pushed her lank hair away from her pale forehead. 'I just can't seem to regain my strength.'

'I'm sorry to hear that,' said Rita. 'He's a lovely baby.'

They sat together in the sitting room, drinking tea which a maid (not Tammy-Jane) had placed on the coffee table while Mrs Knight mulled over Rita's training, her references and her preferences. As the afternoon drew to a close, it had been decided that Rita would come after Jenny's wedding and a short break. Nurse Watts was contracted to stay for another month anyway, so Mrs Knight would not be left without help.

'Tammy-Jane? She's nobody important,' she said in answer to Rita's enquiry. 'Don't worry about her.' There was a note of contempt in her voice so Rita thought it best not to pursue the matter.

As their time together continued, it was obvious that both women were comfortable in each other's company. The atmosphere became less formal, more relaxed and a couple of times, they laughed together. Rita would have a day off every week, two evenings off each week and a weekend every two months. Her salary would be nine pounds a week and Mrs Knight would pay her stamp.

After a while Rita said hesitantly, 'And your little girl...?'

'Oh yes, of course,' said Mrs Knight. 'Forgive me, I should have explained. Lucy is at my friend's house at the moment. We had a few problems when Daniel was born.' She took in her breath as if embarrassed. 'I'm afraid she's a bit jealous and right now I don't feel I can cope with it. I don't know why but there are times when my head is all over the place.'

'That's understandable,' said Rita, 'and she's not the only child to find it hard to accept a new sibling.'

'I appreciate your sensitivity,' said Mrs Knight. 'A lot of girls have had no experience of working with such children.'

'I have to confess that I haven't either, Mrs Knight, but I shall make it my business to do the best I can.' As soon as the words were out of her mouth, Rita panicked that she'd been too frank but Mrs Knight seemed content.

The afternoon sped by and after a cordial handshake, Rita agreed to take the post. On the Greenline bus back to London she could hardly contain her excitement and she decided to read up all she could about jealous siblings and sibling rivalry.

It seemed odd to have Mrs Samson and Mrs Boyd together in the same room, but here they were. All the children were playing nicely as Rita put three cups of coffee onto the table. The two women had been sharing their business dreams with each other and looking at photographs of their achievements thus far.

'We shall be lost without you, Rita,' said Mrs Boyd.

'We couldn't have got as far as we have if you hadn't come to look after our children,' Mrs Samson agreed. 'We are pleased that you've got a new post but for us it's a shame that you're going.'

Mrs Boyd sighed. 'Yes, it does have its problems.'

'It doesn't have to,' said Rita. She stirred a spoon of brown sugar into her coffee. 'That's why I asked if we could all meet together.'

'You've changed your mind?' Mrs Samson squeaked.

'No.'

'To say goodbye,' said Mrs Boyd.

'To see if there is another way forward,' said Rita. 'I was doing two jobs. Monday, Tuesday and Wednesday with you Mrs Samson; Thursday was my day off and then Friday, Saturday and Sunday with Mrs Boyd. You each fitted your business into those three days.'

'The agency gave us a special rate,' said Mrs Boyd, 'I can't see how I can do anything different.'

'We knew it was a bit of an experiment,' said Mrs Samson, 'but Mrs Hunter made it clear it was a one off. To be absolutely honest, I'm not in a good enough position financially to pay the normal rate. Understandably, most girls want a full-time job.'

'But what if you help each other?' said Rita.

The two women stared at her in amazement.

'I realise that I've put both of you on the spot and that you might hate the idea, but what if on Monday, Tuesday and Wednesday, Mrs Boyd has the children and on Friday, Saturday and Sunday, Mrs Samson has them.' Rita put up her finger. 'Listen.'

The whole house was silent.

'I shall go and check up on them in a minute,' she continued, 'but it sounds as if your children are playing together very nicely.'

The two women looked at each other.

'On Thursday,' Rita continued, 'which was my day off, you could both have your own children to yourselves.' She paused for a moment, 'Or change the day off to Sunday which will mean you'll both be doing a full week's work, but you won't have to pay anyone.' She rose to her feet. 'I'll go and check on the children and leave you to think it over.'

As she suspected, the children were enjoying themselves. Neil and Johnny were laying on the floor with a car mat and the two girls, one with a nurse's cap and the other with a stethoscope around her neck were looking after their dollies. 'We're playing hostibles,' said Sophie.

Chapter 24

'It's Not Unusual'
Tom Jones

It was very disappointing when Jenny's wedding day turned out to be wet. Thankfully it wasn't pouring, but it was enough to need an umbrella. Rita set out from her digs and caught the bus to Newgate where the church was. She was wearing a beautiful outfit which had thrilled her no end when she'd bought it – an A-line short sleeved dress in a vibrant pink with a box jacket. The skirt had box pleats with four cream buttons along each seam at the front. At the neck there was a back-to-front cream collar and to complete the ensemble she had cream gloves and a small cream handbag. Her umbrella was a peaked pagoda design in cream with a black pencil line along the struts. Rita's hat was the fashionable bow clip whimsy with cream netting.

The wedding which was in the Holy Sepulchre church in Newgate was packed. It seemed as if most of the traders from the market had come and as she walked in, the whole place buzzed with anticipation and excitement.

'Are you a friend of the bride or the groom?' The usher had walked silently to her side.

'Bride.'

He indicated the left-hand side and as she walked down the aisle, Rita heard a theatrical whisper as someone called her name. She turned her head to see that Carole and Bernie from the nursery were beckoning her so she went into the same pew. Carole's husband Martin swapped places so that she could sit next to her and Rita laid her wet umbrella on the floor under the pew in front. Carole had her baby on her lap although he wasn't so tiny now. Peter was almost twenty months old.

'He's gorgeous,' Rita whispered as she took the little boy's hand. He looked very handsome in a white suit with a blue jacket and white button shoes. He was cuddling his teddy and was well behaved.

Carole positively glowed and Rita could see she was expecting again. Martin, dressed in a navy suit, was smartness itself and Bernie looked really elegant in a dusty pink shift dress with its own matching coat. Her pillbox hat had a bow and her navy shoes and handbag gave her the air and poise of a catwalk model.

They exchanged a few niceties. 'You look lovely.' 'I adore that hat.' 'The bridegroom looks nervous.' 'Which one is Jenny's mum?' until the Vicar came to the front and said, 'Would you all please stand,' and the bride came down the aisle on her father's arm.

Jenny looked radiant. She wore a fashionable knee-length dress in the swing style. She didn't have a veil but instead she wore a daisy scarf on her head. Her dress was scattered with daisies and the bouquet she carried contained daisies as well. On her feet she wore T-strap heeled shoes. As the bride and her father sailed past, Rita could hear the gasps of pleasure and admiration from the assembled congregation.

The service was traditional and Jenny made her responses in a clear and confident voice. Rita wondered vaguely if she had sorted out her differences with Simon. Was he going to let her take a job after their marriage or was he expecting her to stay at home?

After they'd signed the register, the wedding party made its way outside. There were few photographs – the weather put paid to that – so everyone hurried to the reception. They were all good-natured enough about the rain although there was a lot of sympathy for the bride and groom. Once everyone was in the hall, waitresses came round with wine and the photographer organised the poses.

The wedding breakfast itself was served on trestle tables which had been covered with a white cloth or a sheet, and they sat on tubular steel chairs with canvas seats. The food was home-made with everybody in the market and the local pub coming together to make it a meal fit for a king. They began with prawn cocktail served in a glass (all sorts of sizes, borrowed from just about everyone on this side of the Thames), this was followed by either fish and chips or sausage and chips (Don's Plaice came up trumps for that) and to round it off everybody had an exciting new pudding called an Arctic roll (ice cream surrounded by sponge cake – how did they do that?) which came from the local Safeway supermarket.

The girls were able to catch up with news during the meal. Carole told them she was five months pregnant and that she hoped it might be another boy and a companion for Peter.

'He's such a placid baby,' Bernie remarked as Peter sat on her lap, banging a spoon against the table. 'He's been as good as gold even though there are loads of people here.'

'I think he might be a bit tired by now,' Carole confessed. 'I'm not sure where I'm going to put him if he falls asleep.'

'Didn't you bring a pram?' said Rita.

'No room in the van,' Carole said shaking her head.

'Don't worry,' said Bernie, 'we'll figure something out.' And they did. Having commandeered a cardboard box from the deliveries, they broke down one end because Peter was longer than the box and the guests offered their jackets or coats as bedding. Some had to be refused because they were too damp, some were too expensive looking to put under a risky baby who might make them wet, but others had survived the showers and were robust enough to provide a soft bed. With the box close to his mother, Peter lay down quite happily, put his thumb in his mouth and despite the racket all around him, he quickly fell asleep.

'How are you liking marriage and motherhood?' Rita asked.

'Love it,' said Carole. 'My plans didn't quite work out as I had expected but I don't regret anything. Martin is a good dad and he's so loving and caring.'

'And now you have another one on the way,' said Bernie.

Carole nodded. 'I'm thinking that once I've had the baby and everything has settled down again, I might take up child-minding.'

'That's a brilliant idea,' said Rita.

Carole nodded. 'There aren't enough nursery school places and most people I know couldn't afford the fees anyway. I could earn a few pennies myself and be helping others too.'

'What about you, Rita?' said Bernie. 'Are you still working for the same people?'

Rita shook her head and told them about Mrs Samson and Mrs Boyd. 'I've finished working there now,' she continued. 'After today, I'm having a few days with my gran in Worthing and then I shall take up my new live-in post. Did I mention I'm going to work for someone famous?'

Her friends knew she was teasing them. 'Ooh,' cried Carole. 'Who for? And where? Do tell.'

They were all agog as Rita told them about Cameron Knight and his beautiful house in Ewell.

'Quite near the nursery!' cried Bernie. 'Perhaps we could meet up sometime.'

'I was rather hoping you might say that,' said Rita. 'That would be lovely, and you must be getting near to your mock exams by now.'

'I took them last week,' said Bernie.

'And?' Carole asked eagerly.

'I think I've done fairly well.'

'Has your mother come round to it all yet?' Rita asked. She remembered how the last time she saw Bernie she had said that her mother wasn't speaking to her.

'Sort of,' said Bernie.

'I remember when you first came to the nursery,' Rita said with a nod of her head, 'that she used to make you sit in the car with her in your two hours off duty every day.'

'She found it difficult to let me go,' Bernie said sagely. 'She's not ill but she wants life to be the same as it was when they were in the diplomatic service. Back then, everybody waited on her all the time and she had loads of parties and stuff. She thinks a woman working for a living is vulgar. I think she'd sooner have me at home looking after her.'

'But you're her daughter!' Rita exclaimed.

'Well I've made it perfectly clear I won't be doing that,' said Bernie, 'but I can't abandon her altogether, can I? She is my mother.' And the others nodded sagely.

The bride came to their table. 'Thanks for coming.'

'You look amazing,' said Rita standing to give her a kiss on her cheek.

The others agreed.

'Where's Peter?' Jenny asked. His mother pointed between their chairs to her sleeping child and everyone laughed. Someone called Jenny and she turned to leave. 'Better go.'

'We wish you all the best,' Rita called. 'But before you go, what's it to be? Housework or job?'

Jenny grinned. 'I start at the nursery school in Bermondsey as soon as I get back from honeymoon.'

'Good man, your Simon,' said Rita sticking up her thumb as she sat back down.

The others were all ears, so Rita told them about the discussion she'd had with Jenny a few weeks back.

'Good for her,' said Bernie. 'Shame to let all that training go to waste.'

'And how is Matron Evans?' asked Rita, adding sarcastically, 'still as loving and caring as she always was?'

Bernie chuckled. 'Just the same. It beggars belief what she does.'

'What's she done now?' Carole asked.

'Umm, well she asked one of the new students to clean the outside of her bedroom windows,' Bernie began. 'As you know, there's a small balcony out there, though how safe it is I have no idea.'

'I remember it only too well,' said Rita. 'The window cleaner refused to go up there.'

'Well, poor old Gillian was left standing on the balcony cleaning the glass at one end when Matron forgot she was out there and closed the window.'

'Oh my goodness!' cried Carole clutching her chest. 'Whatever did she do?'

'She banged on the glass but Matron had left the room. She had to wait until the girls in the toddler room downstairs took the children into the garden, then she shouted like mad until somebody looked up and saw her.'

'If you wrote that in a book, nobody would ever believe you,' said Rita.

'Well, it happened as true as I'm sitting here,' said Bernie tucking into her Arctic roll.

After the meal came the speeches and then there was dancing.

Rita expected someone to produce a gramophone but to her surprise a band took the stage at the end of the hall. They weren't famous but they were quite good. At the same time, Jenny and her new husband left the reception to get ready to go on their honeymoon. Everything paused while their guests waved them goodbye.

'Anybody know where they're going?' asked Bernie as the band started up again.

Rita shrugged her shoulders but Carole said, 'Somewhere in Devon, I believe. One of his clients has lent him his second home for a week.'

'Lucky them,' said Rita.

Just then Peter woke up so his mother took him to the ladies' to change his nappy. Bernie was talking to somebody at the other end of the table when a voice behind her said, 'May I have this dance?' and turning, Rita looked up into the most captivating blue eyes.

He said his name was Travis and when she looked a little sceptical he said, 'Travis Roberts.'

'Pleased to meet you Travis,' Rita chuckled. 'I'm Rita Brownlow.'

He reminded her of that singer she'd seen on *Ready Steady Go!*, the one who sang 'Catch the Wind'... Donovan? Of course, she couldn't say no; not when his slightly turned up nose and long sideburns looked so perfect with his mop of dark hair. As she stood, she wondered if he was going to waltz her off into the sunset but the music didn't really lend itself to that. The band was playing 'Twist and Shout' which had to be the most played track on Rita's *Please Please Me* LP by The Beatles, so they moved alongside the other dancers doing the Twist. It was a magic moment.

They stayed together for the next dance, Chubby Checker's 'Let's Twist Again' and the one after that, 'Twistin' the Night Away' made famous by Sam Cooke. Travis was a good mover and every time she glanced up at him, her heart did a little flutter.

The band paused and he leaned towards her. 'Fancy a drink?'

They didn't make it to the drinks hatch because the bride and groom had arrived back at the hall to say their goodbyes. Jenny looked stunning in a blue swing coat over an equally pretty blue flowered dress. Simon looked dapper in a skinny grey suit with a two-inch skinny tie in aqua blue. There were lots of photographs and eventually Simon's father said, 'You two better get a move on or you'll miss the bloody train!' and then they were gone.

'About that drink?' said Travis.

'Now I'm gasping,' Rita said so he took her arm, gently guiding her towards the food hatch where they were serving drinks. She had a fruit punch and he opted for a beer.

'Are you a friend of the family?' he asked as they moved away from the hatch to lean on the wall.

'I did my nursery nurse training with Jenny,' she said. 'You?'

'I went to the same school as Simon. We've been pals ever since.'

Rita sipped her drink. 'What do you do?'

'I work in advertising,' he said. 'I have to put together everything from people like the copywriters and typographers and make sure the ads get to the newspapers before their deadline.'

'Sounds complicated.'

'Not really,' he grinned, 'and I work in some pretty fab places like Park Lane.' He paused, 'That's where Jenny used to work.'

'I know,' said Rita. 'I was just up the road in Belgravia.'

'Was?' he queried.

'I'm just about to take up a new post in Ewell.'

He moved a little closer until she could feel his breath on her cheek. 'Just my luck,' he said. 'Do you have to move so far away?' And his lips closed tenderly over hers.

Chapter 25

'Come and Stay with Me'

Marianne Faithfull

Her grandmother wasn't in the house when Rita arrived home the next day. As she called out her hello in the garden, Eddie put his head over the hedge.

'She's gone to her sister's,' he said. 'Steph hasn't been too well lately so I took her over to Eastbourne on Friday.'

'Oh!' cried Rita. 'Is it serious?'

'I don't think so,' said Eddie, 'but your gran was worried about her.'

'Any idea when she'll be back?'

'I'm collecting her about four,' said Eddie. He paused and pointed back towards his house adding, 'I've just put the kettle on. Fancy a cuppa?'

Rita was about to say no but changed her mind in an instant. Even though he'd lived next door for ages, she didn't know that much about Eddie but he seemed to have taken her grandmother under his wing. They were much the same age and she knew Eddie was a widower, but Gran was a bit cagey about saying anything else. Now might a good time to get to know him better. 'Thanks, that would be lovely.'

Being semi-detached, his house had the same layout as Gran's but in reverse. She went in round the back and was pleasantly surprised to see it was what Gran would call 'as shiny as a new pin'.

'Tea or coffee?'

'Coffee please.'

He invited her to sit at the kitchen table while he took the Nescafé Gold Blend from the shelf and busied himself with making their drinks. 'How long are you home for?'

'A week,' she said. 'I start a new job on Monday.'

'Looking after someone's baby?'

'Two children,' said Rita. 'The little girl is four and the baby is a few weeks old.'

He put the cups on the table. 'Biscuit?'

'No thanks,' said Rita patting her stomach.

He chuckled. 'Got to watch the figure, eh?'

She nodded and Eddie sat opposite. 'She don't say much but your gran is right proud of you.'

For some reason, his remark made Rita feel quite emotional. He was right about one thing, Gran never showed her emotions. Rita supposed it was because of the war. Back then people learned to hold everything in – after all, everyone was in the same boat and if you bleated on about your own troubles, you might be talking to someone who had suffered a good deal worse.

'You've been very good to her,' Rita remarked.

'My pleasure,' he said. 'She was a brick to me when my Maureen was ill. Helped me with the washing and she cooked us a meal now and again. You don't forget something like that.'

'No, I don't suppose you do,' said Rita. So that was it. When he brought Gran up to London to file past Churchill's coffin and when he taken her to Eastbourne, he was simply repaying a kindness.

'My wife's been dead four years now,' he said before continuing on with a few stories of their life together and Gran's kindnesses. Rita let him talk. It was probably doing him good to let it all out. She nodded and smiled at the appropriate places even though she was hardly listening to him. Her mind was full of what she was going to do in the next few days, old friends she would visit, taking a walk around the shops and of course strolling along the beach. It would be grand to see the sea once more and breathe in all that fresh sea air.

It went quiet and Rita looked up sharply. Eddie had stopped talking. Slightly embarrassed, Rita smiled into her coffee cup. 'How long have you lived next door to Gran now?'

'Nearly three years,' he said. 'I managed to buy the place at the beginning of sixty-three. Course I had no idea Win lived next door then. That was quite a surprise.'

Rita frowned. 'But you said Gran helped you out when your wife was ill.'

'So she did,' said Eddie, 'but she was just the lady from the WI back then. We lived in Lansdowne Road and she'd come on her bicycle with a meal or some shopping in her basket. Sometimes she'd stop and talk to Maureen, sometimes she had other folks to visit.'

Rita nodded sagely.

He sighed. 'Of course I think the world of her now,' he went on. 'Last Christmas, I asked her to marry me but she wouldn't have it.'

Rita blinked. Blimey that was a surprise. Her grandmother hadn't breathed a word about that! 'You asked her to marry you?'

He nodded.

'I don't understand. Why wouldn't she do it?'

He looked her straight in the eye. 'Because of you my lovely.'

—

A few hours later, Rita stepped back from the kitchen table to admire her handiwork. It looked perfect. She'd laid the table with the better China set (not the best – Gran kept that for the vicar or somebody important!) and she'd put a vase of early daffodils in the centre. She'd made a few sandwiches and she'd found some cake in the tin.

Rita could have opted to go with Eddie to pick her grandmother up but had chosen to do this instead, knowing they would need something to eat when they got back.

He'd given her a bit of a surprise when he'd told her that Gran had refused his offer of marriage because of her. 'But I don't understand!' she'd cried. 'Why on earth would she do that?'

'Your dad rejected you and your mum, and then your mum died,' said Eddie. 'She was worried it might upset you if we got wed.'

Rita had frowned. 'Why? Sorry, I still don't get it.'

'She doesn't want you to feel pushed out.'

Rita could feel the tears coming unbidden into her eyes. 'Oh Eddie, I'm sorry.'

'Don't upset yourself, my lovely. It's fine.'

'No it's not,' she cried. 'I had no idea Gran felt like that. She should have said. I want her to be happy. I want you both to be happy.'

He grasped her hands in his and they'd stared at each other for a second or two before Rita rose up. Then he stood to his feet and they'd hugged.

She glanced up at the clock. Ten past six. If he'd picked gran up at four as arranged, they should be here at any minute. She lowered herself onto a chair. Funny how you can live with someone all your life and not really know them. She had worked out how to help Hamish out of his temper tantrums and into a better frame of mind and she'd guided Mrs Boyd with her grieving son, but she hadn't noticed that her grandmother was willing to sacrifice her own happiness rather than upset her grandchild. The awful irony was that the feelings her grandmother worried about didn't even exist!

It was a bit like Dexter, wasn't it? Gran was convinced that he'd deserted mum, but the final letter he'd written proved that was the last thing on his mind. He had only wanted to set her free – free to love someone else while she was still young. As far as Rita knew, though, Valerie had never even gone out with anyone else. How tragic that Dexter had set her free and he had no idea that her mother had held a torch for him for all those years.

She heard a footfall outside and turned to switch the gas on under the kettle. 'Hello,' she said in a sing-song voice. 'Good journey?'

Her grandmother slept in late on Monday. Normally she was up at six thirty to open up the hen house and let the chickens out, but Rita had done it that morning. She'd fed them and changed the water in the shallow dish which served as their supply. When she'd lived at home, every chicken had a name but Rita didn't know any of these ones. Having vowed to give up having chickens after the last time the fox got them, her grandmother had soon caved in. Rita was used to seeing Leghorns which were white, but these were Rhode Island Reds, birds with luxurious deep red feathers. They were a hardy breed and didn't need the services of a rooster to lay eggs. Of course, without a rooster the eggs would be infertile and incapable of producing chicks, but the hen would still lay anything close to two hundred or more eggs a year. The Leghorn laid slightly more at three hundred a year.

Back up at the house, Rita made the tea and got a couple of eggs ready for their breakfast. Gran emerged at seven thirty.

'Sit down Gran,' said Rita. 'One egg or two?'

'You're spoiling me,' she mumbled.

The week turned out to be a memorable one. She and Gran talked as they had never talked before. In fact, at one point, Rita felt the urge to apologise for the times when she had been less than willing to share her plans about what she was doing with her life. Gran brushed it off good-naturedly but it was clear that she was enjoying this new phase in their lives.

On Thursday, they took the train to Brighton and spent a happy day wandering around the shops. Rita wanted them to do something different, something which would be memorable, so as a special treat, she took her grandmother to Hanningtons for an afternoon tea. Although there was talk of a takeover, the department store which was known as the Harrod's of Brighton had been a feature of the town for as long as Rita could remember. Established in 1808, it had, for the whole of that time, been run by the same family and with no less than seventy departments, it offered its customers everything from clothing to funeral plans. Afternoon tea was expensive and normally way beyond Rita's pocket, but now that she was earning good money, although still pricey, it was doable. She knew this would be something her grandmother would talk about for a long time.

They walked up the Edwardian staircase gazing up at the stained glass ceiling on the first floor. The tea rooms were beautifully furnished and a maître d' showed them to a table for two near the window. Rita ordered a full cream tea. Looking around the room where matronly women wearing Elizabeth Arden perfume made whispered conversation, Gran seemed a little overawed.

'Did you ever read Mum's letters?' Rita asked as she shook out her serviette and put it in her lap.

Her grandmother shook her head. 'I have no interest in what that man had to say.'

'I think you should,' Rita said cautiously. 'It took me a while to do it, but I'm glad I did.'

Her grandmother gave her an stern look and Rita began to question the wisdom of bringing up such an emotive subject in here.

'Honest, Gran,' she said quietly, 'He wasn't the villain we all thought he was.'

'He hurt your mother,' her grandmother said savagely. 'I can't forgive him for that.'

A waitress brought a tea tray with China cups and saucers and laid them out in front of them.

As she left, Rita leaned forward again. 'I'm sorry. I don't want to spoil this afternoon.' She covered her grandmother's hand with her own. 'Sorry.'

'We'll talk about it later,' Gran said stiffly.

The waitress was back with a plate which included one of Hannington's famous salmon and cream open sandwiches. Gran poured them tea and as they tucked in, it all felt deliciously decadent.

They were on their second cup of tea when Gran craned her head up high. 'Don't turn around now,' she said out of the corner of her mouth, 'but that actress, you know, what's-'er-name is over there.'

'Who?'

'You know, thingamajig. That actress,' Gran said crossly. 'Oh, what's she called?'

Rita began to turn her head.

'For goodness' sake don't draw attention to yourself! She'll see you.' Gran hissed loudly. 'Who the Dickens is she?'

'Gran if I don't turn around, I can't tell you who she is, can I.'

When the waitress returned to the table with scones and cake, Rita looked back over her shoulder. As her grandmother helped herself to some cream to put on her scone, she leaned forward again. 'It's Dora Bryan.'

'Eh?' said Gran.

'The actress,' Rita whispered. 'It's Dora Bryan.'

'Laura who?'

Rita shook her head. 'Don't worry. I'll tell you later.'

Her grandmother stared past Rita's shoulder. 'Oh!' she cried in a voice loud enough to awaken the dead. 'I remember her name now. It's Dora Bryan.'

Chapter 26

'The Last Time'

The Rolling Stones

Rita set off for Jenny's house the following Sunday to start work in Ewell on Monday morning. Unusually, her grandmother came to Goring-by-Sea station to see her off. If she were to be asked what they had done during this week, Rita would have said that they had spent a good deal of time together talking over old times and resetting their boundaries. That would have been the expert jargon for the comprehensive notes on their relationship, but for Rita and her grandmother it simply meant they had grown closer together. She hadn't been able to persuade her grandmother to read her mother's letters, but Gran had agreed to 'look at them sometime', which was a marked improvement on her categorical refusal to have anything to do with them.

As they waited on the platform, Rita finally broached the subject of Eddie.

'Eddie tells me he wants to marry you.'

'Stuff and nonsense. I'm far too old for all that malarkey.'

'You're not even sixty yet Gran.'

'I'm sixty-two.'

'I stand corrected, but you know sixty-two isn't old these days.'

Her grandmother harrumphed.

'And Eddie is a nice man,' Rita insisted. 'You'd be daft to let him go.'

'An expert on marriage now, are you?'

Rita could see the hint of a twinkle in her eye as she said, 'Yes Gran, I am. Just do it. You deserve a little happiness.'

She punched Rita's arm playfully. 'Go on with you.'

'I mean it, Gran. Snap him up before someone else does.'

The train appeared in the distance and Rita gathered her bags. 'Thanks Gran.'

'What for?'

'For the wonderful time I've had and for all that you've done for me.' The train drew to a halt and after a hug, Rita walked towards the nearest door. She opened it and climbed aboard. Putting her cases in behind her she closed the door and pulled the leather strap to open the window. 'I should have told you this all those years ago. I love you, Gran.'

She saw her grandmother's chin tremble as she said, 'Go on with you, you daft apeth.'

The train began to move. 'Tell Eddie yes and don't forget to invite me to the wedding.'

Gran lifted her arm to wave. 'Bye, love. And all the best.'

'I love you, Gran.'

'I love you too, darlin'.'

The train had a corridor so Rita wandered along to find an empty compartment. The Ladies-Only carriage had one rather sleepy old woman in it. Rita bundled her stuff inside and sat down. This was it. Once again, she'd left home for another adventure.

It was late morning when Rita arrived at the black Tudor-fronted house. Having spent Sunday night south of the river with Jenny and Simon back from their honeymoon, she'd caught the Greenline bus for Ewell on Monday morning.

There was a van parked on the driveway, white with *Basil Du Bois – Photographer* written in copper plate on the side. Rita felt a shiver of excitement. She really was hob-knobbing with the rich and famous now. Basil Du Bois was an up-and-coming photographer, becoming almost as famous as David Bailey and he got to photograph all the well-known people like the Stones and Jean Shrimpton and even gangsters like Ronnie and Reggie Kray.

Once again, Tammy-Jane opened the door to her and pointed the way to her room. When she walked into her bedroom with her suitcase, the nurse was packing the last of her things. 'Oh good,' she said, 'you're here. I've got a taxi coming within the hour.'

'I think I saw it pulling into the gate as they opened the door for me,' said Rita.

At the same moment, the doorbell rang. The nurse crammed her hat on her head and picked up her case. 'Well, good luck with this one,' she said in a bleak voice. 'Believe me, you're going to need it.'

Rita stepped aside to let her pass. 'Why do you say that?'

The nurse sighed. 'They're all mad,' she announced. 'I give you a month.' And she hurried down the stairs calling, 'If you manage more than that it'll be a miracle.'

Rita put her own suitcase onto the bed and opened it. By now she was feeling more than a little concerned. What did she mean they're all mad?

She was busy putting her clothes in the drawers when there was a light tap on the door. A maid with an apologetic expression on her face said, 'Ma'am says can you come as quickly as possible.'

'I'll be right down,' said Rita.

She had treated herself to a new uniform for this job. It was a button-through dress with side pockets and a skirt which was a bit shorter than Rita had been used to for work. In pale blue cotton with navy piping, it was in the A-line style, with a Peter Pan collar. Her face now devoid of make-up, she pushed her hair back under a blue jersey bandana. Her sturdy lace-up shoes with a Cuban heel completed the new look and when she turned to face the full-length mirror, Rita liked what she saw.

As she hurried down the stairs she could hear the baby crying. Rita knocked on the sitting room door and walked in.

At one end of the room the photographer had rigged up a pale background behind a wingbacked chair. Her employer was sitting in the chair with Daniel in her arms. Judging by the empty bottle on the table she hadn't long fed him, but Mrs Knight was struggling to control the baby who was clearly upset and grizzling. A little girl, whom Rita presumed was Lucy, stood at the side of the chair looking very pretty in a flouncy pink dress but the expression on her face was rather cross and she had her arms folded. Standing behind the chair was Cameron Knight himself and Rita's heart skipped a beat. He looked amazing in a pale brown suit with black piping, yellow shirt with button down collar and a black tie. On one wrist a fancy, most likely very expensive watch peeped from under his sleeve and on the other, he wore the thick black plaited leather bracelet which was his trademark symbol. Rita could feel her face heating up.

As she closed the door behind her, Rita became aware of Tammy-Jane standing almost out of sight by the French windows. She had a faraway look, but she was smiling indulgently at the family scene before her.

Mrs Knight leaned towards a side table and picked up what Rita imagined was a cup of tea. She took a few sips but then all at once, Lucy leaned over the arm of the chair and with a grimace on her face, she pinched her brother's arm. The reaction was instantaneous. The baby screamed and her mother, dropping the teacup lopsidedly into its saucer, shouted, 'Lucy! You mustn't do that.'

Cameron's eyes flashed as he hit her on the shoulder. 'You little devil!'

By now Lucy was howling too. Tammy-Jane disappeared. Basil stood frozen to the spot, camera in hand with his mouth open.

'Are you the new nanny?' yelled Cameron as Rita came forward.

Rita nodded.

'Then get her out of here.' He pushed his daughter roughly towards Rita and turned his attention to the baby. Mrs Knight had put Daniel onto her shoulder and was rubbing his back in an effort to comfort him.

By now Lucy was standing in the middle of the room, crying her heart out. Rita came towards her with her hand outstretched, but Lucy snatched her arm away. Rita bent and crouched in front of the child so that they were eye to eye.

'It's all right, sweetie,' she said quietly. 'I know you're feeling cross. It's okay to be upset.' Whispering conspiratorially she added, 'Shall we go outside for a bit?'

With everybody else's attention on the baby, Rita, with a little more cajoling, managed to persuade his sister to leave the room. They sat together on the stairs and as the little girl sobbed, Rita put her arm around Lucy's shoulders.

'That was hard for you wasn't it,' she said gently. 'Your brother wouldn't stop crying and it was making mummy and daddy upset.'

Lucy's body juddered as she nodded.

'It made you feel bad, didn't it.'

Lucy sniffed. Rita got a clean handkerchief out of her pocket and wiped her nose. 'Tell me about it.'

Lucy shook her head.

'That's okay,' Rita reassured the child. 'We haven't been introduced, have we? My name is Nanny Rita and I have come to live in your house for a while.'

Lucy looked up at her.

'Have you got a name?' said Rita.

'Lucy.'

'Lucy!' cried Rita. She smiled. 'What a pretty name.'

Having calmed the child and distracted her by taking her upstairs to show her where Rita's things were, they had become sort-of friends. Lucy was wary, probably because when this sort of thing had happened before, any adult dealing with it would have lulled her into a false sense of security before coming out with all guns blazing. Lucy wasn't to know that Rita had no intention of doing that. The little girl's problem was clearly deep-rooted. Of course she shouldn't have pinched her brother, but she was only four and was trying to deal with some big and scary feelings. Jealousy, sibling rivalry, the feeling of being usurped in the pecking order, maybe afraid that with a new baby, Mummy and Daddy wouldn't love her any more; Rita knew this was going to take time and there would probably be more incidents like the one she'd just witnessed. Her biggest challenge would be the attitude of the parents. She couldn't deny that she was more than a little disappointed that her idol had been so harsh with his little girl. But, Rita thought to herself as she tried to be generous, he didn't really mean it. He was just stressed. Famous stars like him have a lot to think about.

When they came back downstairs about twenty minutes later, Lucy had promised to say sorry to Daniel and Mummy, but when they walked into the room, her father was still angry.

'Take her away,' he shouted. 'We don't want people who hurt babies in here.'

Rita felt Lucy trying to take her hand away from hers, probably to run, but she held on firmly, not tightly. 'Daddy, Lucy has something to say to you. It's very important. Please can she say it?'

Rita manoeuvred the child so that she was in front of her, but she kept her hands on the top of Lucy's shoulders in an effort to give her encouragement and support. 'What do you say, sweetie?' Rita whispered in her ear.

'Sorry,' Lucy murmured.

Ignoring her, Cameron went to the drinks cabinet and poured himself a whiskey. Mrs Knight, who was still sitting in the chair with a now sleeping Daniel, held out her hand to her daughter. Lucy crossed the room hesitantly, with a wary eye on her father.

'What do you say to Daniel?' Rita encouraged.

'Sorry, Daniel.'

'Can we get another shot now?' the photographer suggested.

'No, we can't,' Cameron said tetchily. 'We're done.'

The photographer clicked the shutter anyway.

'I said we're done,' Cameron said churlishly, his voice raised.

'Darling, she has apologised,' his wife said.

'What's the matter with you people,' Cameron snapped. 'I said *we're done*.' He turned to the photographer. 'That's it. Clear out of here.'

Basil turned to pack up his things. Cameron poured himself another drink and having downed it in one gulp, he opened the French windows. 'I'll be in the den if you want me.' And with that, he was gone.

'You'll have to excuse my husband, Nanny,' Mrs Knight said, holding out the baby for Rita to take. 'He's a little preoccupied at the moment. He's working on a new single and there's a possibility of the band going to America.'

'Wow,' said Rita. 'Let's hope it comes off.' The baby's nappy obviously needed changing. 'I'd better take Daniel back upstairs to change him. Shall I put him in his pram afterwards? What's his routine?'

Mrs Knight put her hand to her forehead. 'I've no idea, Nanny. I leave all that stuff to you.' She sank back into the chair. 'And take Lucy with you, will you?'

Upstairs in the small bathroom, Rita let Lucy 'help her' change Daniel's nappy. After he'd been washed and patted dry, Lucy sprinkled talc over his bottom – a little too much, but Rita made it an object of fun rather than scolding, so Lucy remained happy.

Judging by the bucket of Napisan beside the changing mat, Mrs Knight didn't use a nappy service. Rita disposed of the excess in Daniel's nappy then pushed it under the water in the bucket.

While Rita carried the baby downstairs, Lucy followed behind with Daniel's blue rabbit. They put him in the pram and Lucy put the rabbit near his head where he could see it when he woke up. After that, Rita played hide and seek with Lucy in the garden. When it was Lucy's turn to count up to ten, Rita was easily caught, but reversing their roles proved to be a bit more tricky. The little girl hadn't quite mastered the object of the game because she thought standing near a tree with her eyes tightly shut and covering them with her hands was a brilliant way to hide.

Actually, she may have been right.

It took Rita ages to find her.

Chapter 27

'Big Rock Candy Mountain'
Burl Ives
BBC Light Programme, *Children's Favourites*

For the first few days, Rita did her best to cement a good relationship with Lucy. Despite their terrible introduction, Rita liked her. She was clearly struggling with the changes in her family life and her mother seemed at times to be rather vague.

'I don't know what's the matter with me,' she complained. 'My head is all over the place and I can't seem to think straight.'

'Shall I ring for the doctor?' Rita suggested, but her employer was always of the opinion that if she had 'a little lie down' she would feel better.

Once Rita had established a routine, she and the children settled into a comfortable and companionable time. She would get them up and dressed, then while Lucy ate her breakfast, Daniel would enjoy his bottle. To begin with, breakfast was always upstairs in the nursery, but Rita decided it would be better to have all their meals downstairs in the kitchen. That way, Lucy would be able to socialise with other people working in the house and occasionally with her parents.

There were two other members of staff. Mrs Fordham, who had worked for the previous owners of the house for more than twenty years, and Sally, the maid Rita met on that first day.

'It was different when the colonel and his wife lived here,' she would say wistfully. 'A lot quieter for a start!'

Mrs Fordham was a widow but she didn't live in. 'I've got a nice little cottage the other side of the village.' She put her hand to the side of her mouth and whispered conspiratorially, 'The colonel left it to me in his will.'

Rita smiled. 'He must have thought an awful lot of you.'

Mrs Fordham ignored the compliment. 'When the Knights came here I promised I'd stay on until they got straight.'

'Which was months ago,' Sally chuckled.

'I always keep my promises,' Mrs Fordham said pointedly.

'How long have Mr and Mrs Knight lived here?' Rita asked.

'Eight months,' said Sally, looking towards Mrs Fordham for confirmation. 'That's when I came. They wanted me to live in, but I couldn't do it. I've still got my Stan to look after.'

'Stan?'

'My hubby,' said Sally. 'That's why I can only do part time.'

'Do you have children?' asked Rita.

Sally shook her head. 'Ain't never been blessed.' There was a note of regret in her voice and Rita felt sorry she'd asked. Sally was about forty so she probably never would have children now. Maybe that was why the pair of them always made such a fuss of Lucy and they adored the baby.

Apart from the times when she was resting, Mrs Knight saw her children fairly regularly, but Cameron spent most of his time in the garden. Tammy-Jane had said there was a room underneath and when she asked Mrs Fordham about it she had quite a surprise.

'It was an old air-raid bunker,' she said. 'It's quite big; almost as big as the lawn and it's well ventilated.' She pointed to two posts at either end of the garden which she said were ventilation shafts. 'I reckon that's why they bought this house. He's down there all day and half the night sometimes with his music.'

Tammy-Jane seemed to spend most of her time with Cameron. Rita had no idea where she lived but she was either down in the den or hanging around the musicians. Rita wondered if she had a job of some sort. Or did Cameron pay her? And if he did, what did she do? It was a bit of a mystery.

There was a park near the village. It had a small children's area with swings, a roundabout and a slide. Rita got into the habit of taking the children down there most mornings. Lucy enjoyed the freedom of being able to run around and the fresh air and the movement of the pram helped Daniel to sleep soundly. When she came back to the house, if she came in the back way, Rita would gaze longingly at the door of the den. What was it like down there? Should she ask if she could go inside to listen to the music sometime?

The group were working on a new album. The only problem was they stayed up so late that they couldn't get up in the morning. That meant they were even later going into the den the next day. Nighttime often began with a party with the rich and famous dropping in at all hours. The music was always loud, so Rita, unable to sleep, spent a good deal of time at her window 'talent spotting'. She saw some big names of both screen and stage going down the concrete steps and into the bunker. Some stayed, while others popped in and out again. Weird.

Rita was downstairs in the laundry room rinsing the nappies before putting them into the washing machine when Tammy-Jane came in. 'Hello, I haven't seen you for ages.'

Tammy-Jane gave her a superior look. 'I've been busy,' she said.

'Do you work here then?' Rita asked.

'I don't work,' Tammy-Jane said indignantly. 'I look after Cameron.' She put a strong emphasis on the word 'I'.

Rita frowned. 'In what way?'

'Every way,' said Tammy-Jane pulling down her clean underwear from the overhead pulley.

Rita scoffed. She couldn't help it. 'But surely his wife...?'

'His wife doesn't look after him the way I do,' she said dismissively.

Rita blinked. 'So are you down in the den when they're practising.'

'Of course,' she said. 'Cam relies on me. He loves me.'

Feeling slightly uncomfortable, Rita turned back to the sink. She could hear Tammy-Jane hauling the pulley back up.

'I've seen you looking out of the window at night,' she said. 'Do you want me to ask Cam if you can come down and watch a rehearsal?'

Rita turned to face her. 'Could I?'

Again, that superior look. 'Leave it with me,' she said as she left the room.

Back in the kitchen, Rita asked Mrs Fordham if she could have some potatoes. 'I'd like to do some potato cut pictures with Lucy,' she said. 'Can we use the small table in the kitchen? We won't get in your way.'

'It'll be a pleasure to watch you both.' Mrs Fordham found two potatoes which were a decent size so Rita set about making shapes after she'd cut them in half – a triangle, square, circle and heart.

'She'll love doing that,' said Mrs Fordham.

And she was right. Lucy's creative juices flowed for the rest of the morning and the pictures piled up.

As Rita cleaned up the mess, Sally came downstairs with an empty tea tray. As she put the cup into the sink Rita heard her say, 'Ugh, what's that?'

Rita and Mrs Fordham looked over her shoulder. The cup had a grey sludge in the bottom.

'Looks iffy,' said Mrs Fordham.

'She must have put her medicine in the drink and it didn't quite melt,' said Rita.

Sally shrugged and plunged the cup under the water.

—

A few days later, Cameron accosted Rita in the hallway. 'Tammy-Jane says you want to come down to the den.'

'I'd love to. I've been a fan of yours forever,' Rita said, her chest already tightening with the nearness of him.

He nodded. 'See you then.'

Rita had to wait until the children were asleep and as she wasn't going to be in the house, she felt obliged to tell Mrs Knight where she was going. She didn't want Lucy waking up and finding she wasn't there.

'I don't think you'll like it,' Mrs Knight said mysteriously.

'I won't stay long,' Rita promised.

'If you'll take my advice, you won't drink anything,' she said which made Rita feel slightly miffed.

'I never drink on duty, ma'am.'

Rita dressed with care and she spent some time doing her make-up. At ten thirty, she crept downstairs and walked across the lawn. The door was wide open, the music spilling out into the still night air. There was nobody about so she walked to the concrete steps and made her way down. It was a study, robust building and Rita was sure Mrs Fordham was right. It had been an underground bunker.

Once inside, the first thing that struck her was the smell. As she emerged into the large space, the atmosphere was earthy, a bit like a damp day in the woods. There were quite a lot of people sitting on the floor, maybe a dozen or more. No one she recognised, although one man looked familiar. The music was much louder down here of course, and Cameron was performing on the small stage at the other end of the room. The band was playing one of his greatest hits and Cameron was giving the song everything he'd got, bending backwards as he hit a high note. Perspiration dripped from his forehead and he looked like a man possessed. Rita stood for a moment as if hypnotised. Here she was in the same room as Kandy Krisp, one of the music scene's leading groups. She would be the envy of every girl in Harefield House when she told them. The drummer went wild as the song came to a close and Cameron, pushing the mic back onto its stand, gave her a mock salute.

'You came then.'

'Just for a while,' she said. 'I can't stay long because of the children.'

Behind her, a sultry voice said, 'Of course I did.'

Rita turned to see Tammy-Jane behind her. Uncomfortable, Rita turned back and for the first time, she became aware of even more people in the room. They lined the room, some sitting with their backs to the wall, some leaning on one another. Someone was smoking and a white cloud of musky smoke hung in the air. The smoker didn't keep the cigarette to himself, he passed it on then they all seemed to share it. Some took a few short puffs, others rotated the cigarette in their mouth as they inhaled while others took a long, slow deep breath and held it for a couple of seconds. The white smoke with its pungent musky smell hung everywhere. It was only as the smoke cleared and she saw the sleepy expressions on people's faces that she realised they were taking drugs.

Just then, Cameron jumped down from the stage and coming over, he put his arm around Tammy-Jane's shoulder before asking Rita, 'How's my boy?'

'Fine, sir,' Rita said politely.

'Sir,' Tammy-Jane sniggered. 'She actually called you sir.'

Something in Cameron's eye flashed and Tammy-Jane suddenly cried out in pain. Rita was horrified to see that he'd grabbed the side of her neck and was squeezing it hard. 'Nobody laughs at me,' he snarled.

'I wasn't laughing at you, Cam,' she protested.

'Nobody,' he repeated as he shook her like a dog.

'Don't Cam. It hurts. Please.'

He pushed her violently and Tammy-Jane fell forwards like a rag doll. For a second or two, Rita just stared in disbelief. Cameron didn't say a word but as the drummer began a new rhythm on the skins, he went back to the stage.

Tammy-Jane was still in a heap on the floor. Rita bent to help her up, but she snatched her arm away and swore. As she rose to her feet, her nose was bloodied and she was crying.

'Here, let me help you,' said Rita. 'You're bleeding.'

But Tammy-Jane batted her hand away and staggered towards the stage crying, 'I didn't mean it, Cam. I'm sorry. I promise I wasn't laughing at you.'

Someone nudged Rita's arm and the cigarette, or what remained of it, was passed in front of her. 'No, thank you.' She didn't even look at the person who handed it to her as she blocked the gift with her hand and went back to the steps to leave the room.

Outside in the fresh air, Rita realised that she was trembling. The way her employer had treated Tammy-Jane would stay with her for a long time. She wasn't sure she liked the girl much, but nobody deserved that kind of treatment. And Tammy-Jane's overwhelming need for his approval was sickening. Didn't she realise that the man was using her? Probably not, Rita thought darkly as she walked back to the house.

As she undressed for bed, Rita stripped everything off and put it into the laundry basket. It reeked of that evil smelling thing they were all smoking. It was a bit late to run a bath so she had to settle for a thorough strip wash. By the time she lay in her bed, Rita realised she was on the horns of a dilemma. She'd seen a side of Cameron Knight she didn't like. For two pins she'd jack the job in, but Lucy and Daniel were too young and vulnerable to be exposed to that party lifestyle, especially with a mother who spent all her time in bed. What could she do about it? Under normal circumstances she would have notified social services, but then she remembered that she'd signed that wretched confidentiality agreement.

Chapter 28

'Catch the Wind'
Donovan

At the end of her second week, Rita had a date with Travis on her night off. He had left a note with Jenny and Simon which she had picked up the night she had stayed with them. When she made the call someone else answered the phone, and when she asked to speak to Travis she could hear them yelling his name.

'Thanks for ringing,' he'd said when he finally came to the phone. He sounded out of breath.

'Who was that who answered the phone?'

'One of the other guys. I live in digs during the week. Home at weekends.'

Rita chuckled. 'The way he yelled for you sounded as if you were a mile away.'

'Third floor,' he said. 'Listen, I'd like to take you out. Have you heard of The Swan in Kingston? Bobby Angelo and the Tuxedos used to play there and Castor and Pollux.'

'I've heard of Bobby Angelo,' she said. 'I remember his record "Baby sittin'".'

'It's a pretty swinging place,' Travis continued. 'Fancy coming?'

'Okay. How do I get there?'

'Don't worry about that. Just give me your address and I'll pick you up.'

Ewell was only fourteen miles from Central London so although he had been disappointed that she no longer lived in Belgravia, she wasn't that far away from him. Travis had warned her that he was coming on a motorbike which turned out to be a BSA A65 Lightning Rocket no less. Rita knew nothing about bikes, but she was impressed by the colour (red and black) and the fact that he said it was almost brand new.

She sat as pillion (thank goodness that she'd worn slacks) and they rode to The Swan public house on Mill Street, Kingston upon Thames. Close to the Hogsmill river, The Swan was a two-story building on the corner. Even as they approached the pub, they could hear loud music.

'You'll love it here,' he said killing the engine and getting off. 'Great music, great bands.'

Rita had never been to the place before but it was obviously a bikers pub. There were bikes everywhere, along the street, some parked round the corner and a few more were in the back area. Travis struggled to find a space for his bike but eventually found a place behind a huge oak tree in the overgrown garden.

If the music was loud in the street, inside it was deafening. The place was hot and crowded. Once they'd managed to find somewhere to sit, Travis went off to buy some beer. The band, Sid and the Boozers who were at the far end of the room, were good. With three guitars and a set of drums, they bashed out all the latest pop songs. A few people were dancing on what little of the floor they could find while all around her rockers with tattoos and masses of rings on their fingers drank their beers. Almost everyone was dressed in leather. Only a few people, like herself, were more soberly dressed but they all had the same thing in common: they loved the music.

Travis put two pints onto the table and sat down. 'You'll have to watch your drink,' he said as the band finished a song. 'The tables aren't flat and the vibration makes the glass slide along the top.'

Rita laughed but it didn't take long to realise that he wasn't joking. Once the music started up again, it was impossible to make conversation. They had to resort to sign language.

There was a short interval at nine which gave them an opportunity to chat. She discovered that he had two brothers and a sister, all older than him. One brother was in the army, the second worked in a garage. 'Handy when I need something done on the motor and it meant I got a good deal with the bike,' he chuckled.

'What about your sister?'

'She's still at school.' He pulled out his wallet and produced a photograph of two older people and a young girl aged about fifteen.

'She's very pretty.' Rita smiled as she handed the picture back adding, 'I'd like to meet her someday.'

By now, The King's Trailblazers had squeezed themselves onto the small stage and struck up a song as Travis grinned and said something.

'What?' Rita yelled but she couldn't catch what he was saying. The music was too loud. He nudged her arm and pointed to her beer glass. It had reached the edge of the table and she grabbed it just in time. As she sipped the warm beer, she decided this was her first and last pint. Next time – if there was a next time – she would ask for a coke. All at once, Travis reached for her other hand and caressed it so deliciously that it sent shivers down her spine. Pulling her closer, he kissed her tenderly, once, then twice, then once again. Rita's heartbeat quickened. They could talk when they got outside. Right now, she was living for the moment.

Rita had been in the Knight's household for almost a month before she found the courage to say something about Lucy. The child still struggled with her conflicting feelings about her baby brother. One minute she was kissing and caressing him but the next she was wound up, angry and hitting out. The torrent of fury and criticism she got from her parents, particularly her father, didn't help. He resorted to calling her names like 'stupid', 'moron', 'bloody vicious cat' and worst of all she'd heard him tell Lucy, 'Nobody likes you. Do you hear me? Nobody wants you around.' Once again, Rita was put in an unenviable position, but she couldn't ignore it. This little person's life depended on her getting some sort of positive feedback from her family. When she was with Rita and the baby, Lucy's feelings, although still there, were more under control but when she was with her parents it was much harder. They made it so obvious they doted on Daniel that Lucy felt left out in the cold.

It was going to be doubly difficult to tackle this situation because Rita struggled with her relationship with Cameron Knight. She had gone from thinking of him as a legendary icon of pop music to seeing that he was bad-tempered and self-absorbed, so much so, it looked as if his marriage was already on the rocks. He drank too much and she guessed that he was taking drugs, too. His pupils were often dilated and his clothes smelled funny and just lately there were times when he seemed rather vacant.

Rita had hoped to befriend Tammy-Jane but their paths didn't seem to cross very often. Since Rita had been in the house, she had noticed a couple of other young Cameron worshippers hanging around. They never did any work although they would pose for photographs whenever people from the press turned up. Mrs Knight made no secret that she resented them, so Rita guessed they must all be her husband's temporary girlfriends.

It was a real eye-opener for Rita, and she didn't like it. She didn't consider herself in any way a prude, but the way Cameron flaunted his affections towards young girls barely out of school in front of his wife just to annoy her seemed particularly cruel. Tammy-Jane still came up to house. She'd do a bit of own her washing or make Mrs Knight some tea, but since the incident in the den that night she didn't really talk to Rita. It was slowly becoming a fact that the only reason Rita remained in her post was because of Lucy. Someone had to try and alter the status quo for her sake.

Eventually, Rita got to see both parents one evening when the children were in bed. As soon as she entered the sitting room, Rita sensed an air of hostility. Because of her odd behaviour she wondered if Mrs Knight had been drinking and Cameron made it obvious that he was eager to be back in the den.

'Better make this quick, Nanny,' he snapped when she asked to speak to them. 'I have an important gig next week. I can't be hanging around in here for long.'

'And we all know why,' Mrs Knight slurred.

'I wanted to talk to you about Lucy,' Rita cut in, ignoring Mrs Knight's barbed remark before it descended into another row. 'As you know, she has been struggling a bit since Daniel came along.'

'She's a vicious little toad,' Cameron mumbled.

'I don't see what we can do about it,' Mrs Knight complained.

'Actually, I think that we can help her,' said Rita. She paused and for a glorious second she realised she'd got their full attention. 'I've been trying to put myself in Lucy's shoes. She's been the only child for almost five years. This is her territory and up 'til now, she's had your full attention. Then, all of a sudden, someone else has taken her place.'

'So what?' Cameron challenged. 'That's life.'

'Forgive me for saying so Mr Knight, but you and I are adults. We understand that. Lucy is a small child with little or no experience of life. Right now she feels pushed away, left out, second best. She's obviously jealous and frustrated and the people she loves the most are cross with her all the time and she doesn't understand why.'

Cameron lowered himself onto a chair. 'Because she's a bloody danger to my son.'

'I try to make sure she's never alone with him,' Rita went on, 'and whenever possible, I let her "help" me look after him.' As she used the word 'help' Rita drew imaginary quotation marks in the air. 'For instance, when I change his nappy, Lucy powders his bottom. We bathe him together and she chooses which toys he gets to have in his pram. I ask her opinion about his clothes simply to make her feel she is the important one who is grown enough to make decisions. She's not there yet, but she is less tense than she was.'

Mrs Knight sat up straight. 'So what do we do?'

'I know it's sometimes difficult to find a reason to do so,' said Rita, 'but Lucy has had little praise just lately.'

'How can we praise her when she hits a baby!' Cameron challenged.

Rita turned to him. 'You can't, sir. Of course you can't,' she agreed. 'But you can tell her she's got a pretty dress on, or that she's been a good girl or that you love her.'

'I can't be doing with all this mumbo-jumbo,' said Cameron rising to his feet. 'You deal with it,' he told his wife. 'This is women's work.' And with that, he strode from the room.

Rita was gutted. She had really thought she was getting somewhere, but once again Cameron had shut down. She rose to her feet. As she reached the sitting room door, Mrs Knight, her voice thick with emotion, said, 'Thank you, Nanny. You've certainly given me something to think about.'

Rita nodded and left the room. A taxi was drawing up outside and she saw Tammy-Jane with a suitcase. As she climbed into the back seat and the driver put her suitcase into the boot, Rita smiled. Perhaps the girl had come to her senses at last.

It wasn't until later when Rita was mulling over what she'd said to Mr and Mrs Knight and wondering if she could have worded it better, that something occurred to her. Cameron had referred to Daniel as 'my son'. He'd said, 'She's a bloody danger to *my son*.' She frowned. Did that mean that Lucy wasn't his child? If that were the case, it went a long way to explain why he was so hostile towards her.

The funny thing was, although Rita worried she had spoken too soon, or that she'd overstepped the mark, Mrs Knight suddenly made more of an effort to be with her children. She seemed much clearer headed when she came to the nursery, and taking her cue from Rita, she would encourage her daughter to share her pleasure with the baby. Lucy wasn't relaxed yet, but she was certainly much happier. One morning, Rita suggested that the two of them take Daniel into the village together.

'There's a pretty little tea room near the end of the street,' said Rita, 'and I happen to know they have a small courtyard garden round the back. You could park the pram there and maybe have an ice cream?'

Lucy's eyes lit up. 'Oh could we Mummy, please, please?'

'All right,' said Mrs Knight. 'Are you sure you wouldn't like to come too, Rita?'

Rita smiled. 'I think this should be your special time together, you and Lucy, don't you ma'am?'

The three of them set off shortly after. Rita had plenty to do anyway. She did some washing and cleaned the nursery in the way she wanted it. Sally was good, but Rita preferred everything Harefield House standard.

Downstairs in the laundry room she was emptying the bucket of Napisan when Cameron walked past the door. He leaned back as he spotted her then came in. 'Hello gorgeous. What are you up to?'

Embarrassed, Rita felt the colour rise on her cheeks. What gave him the right to be so familiar? She was his child's nanny and he was married.

He came towards the sink, but when he saw that she was wringing out nappies ready to put in the washing machine, he let some air out of his mouth and retched. 'Bloody hell, how can you do that?' he mumbled as he walked away and for the first time in her life, Rita was glad to be dealing with a pile of dirty nappies.

When they came back, it was obvious that Mrs Knight and Lucy had enjoyed their morning out. Lucy was tired after the walk to the village and back, so as soon as she'd had her lunch, Rita suggested she lay on her bed with a book. A quarter of an hour later, the child was fast asleep and Mrs Knight was resting in her room. Rita had just finished feeding Daniel and was rubbing his back to wind him when Mr Knight came into the nursery. His hair was wet and he looked as if he'd just had a shower. He was wearing an expensive looking pair of jeans and a plain white T-shirt. His feet were bare. At first Rita's heart sank, but then as he came over towards them she was pleased to see that he was taking more of an interest in his son.

'Would you like to hold your son?'

Mr Knight shook his head. 'You carry on, Rita.'

He made no attempt to come closer to the baby but instead he lounged in the chair opposite her. Daniel burped. 'Good boy,' she told him. His father said nothing.

Cameron was making her feel uncomfortable. He was staring at her as he leaned back and put one leg over the side of the chair. Every now and then, he would touch himself. Rita tried to ignore it, looking everywhere but at him but he was scaring her. He didn't saying a word. Just stared.

Daniel finished his bottle and Rita sat him up to burp him again.

'Where's he going now?'

'I'm going to put him in his cot,' she said, willing her voice not to quaver.

He rose to his feet and came closer. She felt even more uncertain now.

She turned to put the baby in his cot but then realised he was standing really, really close. If she bent over the cot sides to lay Daniel down, there was every possibility that they would be touching each other. What should she do? She didn't want this. Should she say something? Now she was holding her breath. She knew how quickly his mood could change, especially after the way he had treated Tammy-Jane that night in the den.

'Why don't you put the baby down, love?' His breath fell softly on the back of her neck as he spoke.

Their bodies weren't actually touching... yet. Rita's heart was beating wildly. She glanced down and saw that his foot was right next to hers. Shuffling slightly to the right, she put her sensible lace-up working shoe with a Cuban heel right onto the centre of his bare foot and transferred all her weight.

He shrieked and cursed loudly as he pushed her forward and got out of the way. Daniel cried, startled.

Rita blinked. 'Oh, I am so sorry, sir,' she said innocently. 'Was that your foot?'

He glared at her. 'You cow,' he growled as he turned to limp from the room.

Ignoring him, Rita comforted Daniel.

Cameron stopped by the door and looked back. 'You did that on purpose didn't you, you bloody bitch. You'll pay for this!'

Chapter 29

'The King's New Clothes'
Danny Kaye
BBC Light Programme, *Children's Favourites*

For the next few days, Rita was on edge. After she'd snubbed Cameron's advances she had quite expected to be instantaneously sacked, but fortunately for her, he was preoccupied with something else entirely. His manager had booked a session for a new album in the EMI recording studios in St John's Wood. When they told her, Rita caught her breath because that was the very studio where Cliff Richard and his previous group, the Drifters, had recorded 'Move It', their first ever single.

The work would take a few days, so it was agreed that Cameron would stay at a mate's house nearby until the recording sessions were done. His new single would be out shortly and because his previous record hadn't even made the top forty, Mrs Knight told her that he was anxious to keep the ball rolling. Rita was beginning to realise that being a pop star was a cut-throat business and that you were only as good as your last chart topper.

With Cameron and all the hangers-on away, they had the house to themselves and Mrs Knight seemed like a different person. She was alert, funny and she spent time with her children which meant that the bond between them grew stronger.

There was time for outings too. A couple of days after he'd gone, Mrs Knight took Rita and the children to Chessington

Zoo. The day was exhausting but such fun. They took turns to push Daniel around in his pushchair while they took Lucy to see the zebras, tigers and watch the penguins being fed. They stopped for a Punch and Judy show and to admire an amazing wooden clock complete with a man with a bell, rotating arms and doors which opened and closed on the hour. Rita sat next to Lucy while Mrs Knight held Daniel as they had a ride on a small train around the perimeter of the zoo and she looked after Daniel while Mrs Knight and Lucy had an elephant ride sitting sideways on a box-like contraption strapped to its back. They took photos and it was a day to remember.

On Sunday, Mrs Knight drove Rita and the children to Richmond Park where they had a picnic. For Rita it was just like being in the middle of the country with only the distant views of St Paul's Cathedral to remind her how close she was to Central London. Lucy was fascinated when Rita pointed out the fallow deer and they spotted some red deer in the distance as they ate their picnic. Lucy tried desperately to catch one of the meadow butterflies which made everybody laugh, including Lucy herself.

Back at the house, Rita put the children to bed. Mrs Knight was on the telephone so Rita sat in front of the telly with a bacon sandwich in her sitting room. She sighed contentedly. If only all her days could be like this one.

Cameron came back at the end of the week. He was so delighted with the way things had gone that he decided to throw a party and before long, all the old hangers-on reappeared including Tammy-Jane.

Slightly disappointed to see her back again, Rita tried to be friendly but Tammy-Jane was a little stand-offish. Wearing some fabulous clothes and with a new hairstyle, it seemed to Rita that she thought of herself as a cut above the children's nanny. She was reluctant to talk and her answers to Rita's questions were frugal to say the least.

'How did the recording go?'

'Perfectly. What else would you expect?'

'Love the outfit,' said Rita. She was wearing a black skinny rib sweater with tight sleeves under a shiny bright red sleeveless shift with three large black blobs on the front. It was made of PVC, probably an imitation of one of the new 'space age' dresses by Pierre Cardin. Her tights were black and lacy and she had black kitten heeled shoes.

'My boyfriend bought it for me,' Tammy-Jane said before sticking her nose in the air and swanning off.

Rita blinked. She had no idea Tammy-Jane had a boyfriend, but that was good wasn't it? Until now Rita had only ever seen her with Cameron.

Rita kept out of everybody's way as much as she could, but the household was back to loud music and people turning up at all hours. After a couple of days, Mrs Knight went back to her usual vacant self and stopped coming into the nursery, taking to her bed much of the time.

On the following Saturday a whole troop of caterers came to the house. They took over the kitchen – thank goodness Mrs Fordham didn't work at the weekends – and before long some amazing food was making its way down to the den. In the afternoon, a van from the local off-licence turned up with crates and crates of drink.

Of course, Rita wasn't invited. Her job was to look after the children but once they were tucked up in bed, she stood behind the curtain in her own room to watch the guests arrive. There were a lot of people she didn't recognise but then she took in a breath when she spotted the fair-haired mop belonging to Adam D'John of the Olive Branch. Gosh, he was even better looking in real life. Her pop magazine had told her the Olive Branch were about to embark on a tour of Germany in September and that Adam himself had just moved into a house – or was it a flat? – in Chelsea. Rita thought she was in seventh heaven. Surprisingly, at the same time, Mrs Knight looking very attractive in a white mini dress, came out of the kitchen door and began to walk towards the den. Rita hadn't expected her to go to the party, and from what she could gather, she certainly wasn't looking forward to it. After giving Mrs Knight a kiss on both cheeks, Adam tagged alongside as she made her way to join her husband.

Rita stayed by the window for a while but didn't recognise any more stars after Ray Baxter the lead guitarist of Mac's People joined the party.

Rita went to bed at the usual time, but it seemed that the party was only just starting. The night was warm, but the music was loud and so, in the interest of getting some sleep, she decided to close the window. As she did so, she saw Mrs Knight making her way back to the house while a few people outside were sitting on the grass in a small group. They appeared to be swapping a pipe, taking a couple of puffs then passing it on. It was obvious that they were getting high.

As she lay in her bed staring at the ceiling, Rita's conviction to leave grew, but so did her nursery nursing instincts to protect the children. She wondered vaguely if she was an oddball to care so much about Lucy and Daniel. Perhaps she was being ridiculous. After all, they weren't *her* children. What happened to the siblings was the responsibility of their parents. If she hadn't signed that legal paper, she would have whispered something in the ear of social services long ago. Young children being exposed to drug taking could only spell trouble. But then again, were they exposed to it? She'd checked up on them not more than ten minutes ago and they were sleeping peacefully.

She must have drifted off to sleep because Rita suddenly woke with a start. She became aware of a grunting noise outside. As she tried to make sense of it, she realised it was rhythmical and regular. Pulling back her sheet, Rita crossed to the window and pulled back the curtain. The lights were still on in the den but it was not nearly as noisy as it had been earlier. She could still hear the music, but it was much quieter and then the song finished. There was no sound of laughter or chatter, just an eerie stillness apart from the sound which had woken her up. She thought the lawn was empty until she looked at the area directly under her window. Tammy-Jane and some man were having sex. Another man stood close by holding a cine camera. All at once, Tammy-Jane's eyes opened and as she cried out in ecstasy, she looked straight up at Rita. More in shock than surprise, Rita stepped back and let the curtain go. She felt sick with embarrassment. With the cameraman already watching her, the girl must have thought Rita was a voyeur as well. How on earth was she going to face Tammy-Jane in the morning?

The next day, it took some while before the debris from the party could be cleared up. Several people were still hanging around, hungover or still spaced out, and the lawn was littered with dog ends, empty bottles and glasses and drug paraphernalia. Mrs Knight had taken to her bed and Cameron was nowhere to be seen. The caterers came back to collect their dishes but no cleaning could be done until Monday when Sally was due to come. To avoid any awkward questions, Rita took the children to Sunday school in the morning and she planned to go out with them again for another walk in the afternoon. Sunday school was good option because she knew from her own experience as a child that they would play games and sing songs. It would be something of a social occasion for Lucy. Daniel, of course, was far too young to appreciate it, but his big sister loved every minute.

For Rita, the church served coffee after the service and it gave her a chance to talk about something other than Cameron Knight. She didn't exactly make new friends but it had been a pleasant morning.

In the afternoon, with neither Cameron nor Mrs Knight having appeared, Rita took the children to the park. She and the children had an enjoyable time and Lucy played with another little girl on the slide. Back in the house, there was still no sign of her employers, but Tammy-Jane was laying a tray in the kitchen.

'Hi,' said Rita. 'You look busy. Who's that for?'

'Mrs Knight wants a cup of coffee.' While Rita laid Daniel in the playpen and started to get Lucy's tea, Tammy-Jane busied herself with the Italian stovetop percolator. Eventually she turned around and glared at Rita darkly. 'Enjoy watching me last night?'

'I'm sorry about that,' Rita protested. 'I heard a funny noise and happened to look out of the window just at that moment.'

'Yeah, right.'

Rita felt embarrassed. She thought about protesting but the mood Tammy-Jane was in she didn't think it would do much good. She tried changing the subject. 'Are you going out tonight?'

Rita was putting an apron around Lucy's waist.

'What's with the inquisition?' Tammy-Jane snapped.

'Oh, Sorreee,' said Rita tetchily. 'I was only trying to be friendly.'

Lucy climbed onto a chair and washed her hands under the running tap. Rita had told her she could help with 'making the tea' and she was very excited.

Tammy-Jane picked up the tray and stalked out of the kitchen. Rita followed her to the kitchen door to take an apron for herself from the hook on the back. As she took it down, she could see Tammy-Jane in the hallway. She had put the tray down on the hall table and she was taking something out of her pocket. Tammy-Jane had her back to the kitchen door and she didn't seem to realise that she was standing in front of the mirror so Rita could see most of what she was doing. She was holding something wrapped in foil. She unwrapped what looked like a sugar lump and placed onto the top of the sugar bowl. Then, stuffing the empty foil back in her pocket, she picked up the tray and mounted the stairs.

Puzzled, Rita went back. Lucy was drying her hands on the towel and Rita washed her own hands. Then the pair of them set to work making their sandwiches.

It was only as Lucy was sprinkling hundreds and thousands onto a burnt bit on one of the small cakes Mrs Fordham had left for them that a thought came to Rita's mind: the icing and the jam underneath the hundreds and thousands would mask the taste of the over-cooked cake; that sugar knob Tammy put in the bowl had something in it. Once in the coffee, the taste would be masked. She suddenly remembered what Dorinda had told her when they went to that night club yonks ago. *'They slip a pill in your drink or onto a sugar knob so's you won't taste it.'*

Had Tammy-Jane given Mrs Knight a drug?

Just at that moment, there was a loud thump on the floor of Mrs Knight's bedroom which was immediately above the kitchen.

Swinging Lucy towards the sink, Rita gave her the job of washing up the dish and spatula to keep her busy. 'You do that,' she said. 'I need to quickly go up and see mummy.'

Rita flew up the stairs. Mrs Knight's bedroom door was open. Their eyes met as Rita tumbled onto the landing. 'Are you all right?'

'Yes,' said Mrs Knight. 'Sorry. I didn't mean to alarm you. I was sorting out some picture frames and I dropped them.'

Rita went into the room and sure enough there was a sizable wooden frame halfway under the bed and several smaller ones scattered on the floor. Rita bent to pick one up and put it on the bed. Mrs Knight was on her knees picking up the big one. Rita glanced at the tray of coffee. It looked untouched. As her employer had her back to her, Rita scanned the sugar bowl but couldn't see anything untoward. As Mrs Knight rose up, Rita flipped the bowl and the sugar knobs went everywhere.

'Oh no!' she cried. 'Clumsy me. I'm so sorry.' She was on her hands and knees grabbing the scattered sugar lumps. 'You can't have these,' she went on. 'I'll bring you up some fresh.'

'Don't worry,' Mrs Knight said casually. 'The coffee's cold by now.'

'Lucy and I are making tea,' said Rita, willing her voice not to sound as panicked as she had felt a second ago. 'Perhaps you would like to join us.'

Mrs Knight smiled. 'I'd love to.'

'Must go,' Rita said. 'I've left Lucy doing the washing up.'

Downstairs again, her charge was singing to herself as she dunked the bowl under the soapy water once again. Behind her back, Rita sifted through the sugar knobs. There was one with a pink blob on one of the sides. She slipped it into her apron pocket and lobbed the rest into the bin.

Chapter 30

'Looking Through the Eyes of Love'
Gene Pitney

Bernie had written to say that Matron was on holiday and she had Friday off, so now seemed a good time to meet up with the girls in the nursery. Rita hadn't been back to Harefield House since she'd said goodbye on the last day of her training the year before. She hadn't missed the place, but she had missed the people she worked with and she'd missed the children. Bernie kept her abreast of what was going on within the nursery walls but it wasn't the same as actually going back. Rita had wanted Carole and Jenny to come as well but Carole was within weeks or even days of giving birth to her second child and although Jenny had started her job at the nursery school in Bermondsey, it turned out she would be able to come too.

Rita felt a tad disappointed that Jenny wasn't with her when she walked up the drive to fetch Bernie in Harefield House, but she had arranged that all three of them would meet for lunch at London Bridge station. She and Jenny had been in the same bedroom for ages and so many of Rita's memories of life in Harefield House were inextricably interlinked with her friend. She recalled the day the fire engine turned up by mistake after a fire drill and how much she'd enjoyed working with Jenny in the tweenie room. Then there were the stressful days when parents came to see their children in the toddler room, and that awful winter of 1962–63 when she couldn't get back to Worthing to see Gran. Jenny had been the mate who had kept her going; the one who encouraged her when Matron was being her usual toxic self and the person with whom she could be sure to have a laugh.

It was Liz who opened the door. 'Rita! You came. How lovely to see you.'

'You too,' said Rita as they embraced. 'I'm surprised you're still here.'

'I decided to stay on after I passed my exam,' Liz said. 'I've only got three weeks left before I move to London.'

'What's in London?'

'I'm going to Guy's hospital,' said Liz closing the front door behind them.

'Oh!' cried Rita. 'I'm so sorry. Nothing serious I hope.'

Liz chuckled. 'I'm going there to train as a nurse.'

'Wow,' said Rita. 'That's amazing.'

'It's something I've been thinking about for a long time,' said Liz.

'Was it hard to get in?' Rita squeaked. She had memories of the stories her grandmother used to tell of girls being accepted for nursing school only because they had been recommended by their doctor or because they knew somebody who knew somebody else.

'It's all changed now,' said Liz. 'You have to have five O Levels. That's why I had to stay on. I needed to get one more because I only had four, so I went to night school.'

'And Matron gave you the time off?' Rita gasped.

'It was either that or I'd have to leave and she's short-staffed.' Liz giggled. 'Come on down to the dining room. You're just in time for coffee and Bernie's waiting for you in there.'

As soon as she walked in, the people she knew jumped to their feet and welcomed Rita with beaming smiles and hugs. She was delighted to see Belinda, the girl who had been in the baby room with her and Sylvie who went on protest marches and held up 'Ban the Bomb' banners in Trafalgar Square. And of course, there was Monica. Everyone was talking at once but from what she gathered, Belinda, who had always struggled with college work, was halfway through her training now and would be taking her exam next June. Bernie was only weeks away from her final exams and Sylvie would be taking hers at the same time. Monica, who had passed her exam at the same time as Rita, was engaged to Humph, so she had opted to stay on until they got married.

'Have you set a date yet?' Rita asked.

Monica shook her head. 'Humph's parents are being awkward,' she said as she gathered her things to go back to work. 'Sorry, I'd better go or I'll be late. See you soon.'

'What does that mean?' Rita mouthed to Bernie.

Bernie tapped her nose. 'Tell you later.'

There were a couple of other girls there that Rita hadn't met before. 'I'm Judy,' said one. 'I hear you're a nanny in Belgravia.'

'I was,' said Rita. 'I'm with a different family now. I'm a bit closer, my new family live in Ewell.'

'Come on,' said the girl who had been sitting next to Judy. 'We'll be late.'

Judy stood up and edged towards the door. 'How did you get the job?' Judy was eager to know.

'Through the West End Nannies Agency. I'll give Bernie the address and you can apply as soon as you know you've got your NNEB.'

'Come on Judy,' her friend insisted, so with an apologetic shrug, the girl turned to go.

Bernie smiled. 'Do you want to see some of the children or shall we go straight out?'

'I'm not sure if any of the ones I knew are still here.'

'A few are: Vera, Porter, Fola, Sam,' said Bernie.

'I don't remember Sam,' said Rita, 'but I do remember Vera and her sister.' She frowned, puzzled. 'I thought they went to be fostered.'

'They did,' said Bernie, 'but it didn't work out for Vera. She was brought back and then the people decided to adopt her sister.'

Rita was horrified. 'But that's not fair!' she cried. 'How could they separate two sisters?'

Bernie shrugged. 'If I was in charge I wouldn't have allowed it to happen, but I guess the council decided to let her go because they'd have one less child in care.'

'Can you imagine the damage that will do to Vera?'

'I know, I know.'

Rita's stomach was churned up. Poor Vera. Her sister was young enough that she might not remember having a sibling, but Vera would never forget. It was appalling.

They strolled towards the nursery. Most children were outside today. Bernie led the way through the double door to the big playroom and out into the spring sunshine. Rita smiled. A couple of boys, one in a peddle car, the other pushing him from behind, rattled past at speed. Another child sat on the steps leading to the lawn with his thumb in his mouth. Two little girls were sitting in the sand pit 'making tea'. Others were running around willy-nilly. Her heart went out to all of them. True, they were well looked after, well fed and wore good clothes but what a rubbish start they'd all had in life. And for some, like poor Vera, the nightmare went on. Rita was scanning the garden to spot Vera when she felt a hand slip into hers. Looking down, a pretty little face looked back at her. 'Fola!' she cried crouching down. 'How lovely to see you. My how you've grown!'

Rita and Bernie caught the train about twenty minutes later. It was fantastic having someone to talk to and Bernie had blossomed since that shy girl with her overbearing mother had appeared in Rita and Jenny's room all that time ago. Now an attractive well-dressed young woman, she seemed self-assured and confident.

'Have you got any plans for when you finish your exams?'

Bernie nodded. 'I think I shall do what you've done,' she said. 'A private nanny job will give me a lot of opportunities. I'm used to travelling and I enjoy seeing other parts of the world.'

'So will you try WEN?'

'Possibly, but there is one thing I should like to do,' Bernie continued. 'Have you heard of the Travelling with Aunty Agency?'

Rita shook her head.

'They employ fully trained nursery nurses to accompany children abroad. Sometimes you take children to join their parents for the school holiday or sometimes it's the other way round and you escort the children from their parents to their boarding school in this country.'

'Golly, that's a big responsibility,' said Rita.

'I think I'd be all right,' Bernie said confidently. 'My parents once paid someone to bring me out to Hong Kong, so I know first-hand how it works. The only trouble is you have to be twenty-five before they will accept you.'

'There's always a snag somewhere,' Rita joked.

When they got to the station, Jenny was waiting for them outside in the street. She looked amazing and chattered nineteen to the dozen about the Bermondsey nursery. She was also very happy in her marriage. As she listened, Rita reflected that while her friend might have her own children before long (or perhaps not, if she was on the pill), until then she was doing the only sensible thing. Rather than sitting at home doing nothing, she was using her training to further her own career and that in turn was a real benefit to the community.

When the three friends crossed London Bridge, they found a lovely little café on the other side of the river. Having ordered their meals, Bernie asked Rita how her job was going.

'You're with the lead singer of Kandy Krisp aren't you?' said Jenny. 'You jammy thing! He looks really dishy.'

'He does have a wife and children,' Bernie scolded.

'Oh, I didn't mean it like that,' Jenny cried, 'but it must be really fabbo living in the same house as somebody that famous.'

'It's okay,' said Rita adding darkly, 'he may be good looking but looks aren't everything.'

'Oooh. You make it sound as if you know a dark secret,' said Jenny wriggling in her seat. Her eyes were bright with excitement. 'Do tell.'

Rita sighed. She wanted to talk about it but she couldn't, could she. 'That's just it,' she said. 'I'm not allowed to say anything. They made me sign a legal document which means I could be in serious trouble if I talk about the family to anyone.'

Bernie frowned. 'But I can tell from the look on your face that you are worried about something.'

'We won't tell a soul,' Jenny encouraged eagerly.

Their meals arrived at the table. As soon as the waitress was gone, her two friends looked eagerly at Rita who said, 'Pass me the salt please.'

They began to eat, their conversation dead in the water until Jenny changed the subject. 'Simon is going into another business. He and a friend are renting a lock up under the railway arches.'

'For cars?' asked Rita.

'Storage,' said Jenny. 'Mostly for the people at the market but other people as well.'

Bernie raised an eyebrow. 'Aren't you scared they might use it for things they shouldn't?'

'We're not all gangsters south of the river, you know,' Jenny teased.

Her friend immediately apologised. 'You know,' Bernie said looking at Rita, 'we may be able to help you. It's what we're all thinking about, isn't it.'

Rita shook her head. 'I just told you I can't say anything.'

'That's fine,' continued Bernie, 'but let me tell you about a children's book I'm going to write.'

'I didn't know—' Jenny blurted out.

Bernie put her hand up. 'Perhaps you could help me with the plot.'

Rita looked sceptical.

'It's about a bunny rabbit who married a fox.' She glanced up at Rita. 'Am I on the right track so far?'

Rita suddenly understood what she was doing. She nodded.

'They have two bunny-foxes, a boy and a girl,' Bernie went on. 'Then the fox becomes famous. Everybody loves him.'

'I think your story might be more interesting if the first child is a girl bunny,' said Rita. 'The second child is a little boy bunny-fox.'

Her friends frowned, puzzled.

'The girl bunny belongs to the mummy, but the bunny-fox is Mr Fox's child,' said Rita. 'Mr Fox is not nice to the little girl bunny because she is jealous of the new baby bunny-fox.'

'Ah,' said Bernie. 'So what are mummy bunny and daddy fox going to do about that?'

'They should get help,' Jenny suggested.

'They could,' said Rita, 'but Mr fox is not a good fox. He doesn't really care about the little girl or his wife. He's more interested in chasing other rabbits.'

Bernie looked concerned. 'And am I right in thinking that Mr Fox wants to have Nurse Rabbit as well?'

Rita nodded. 'He's already tried.' Her two friends looked up at her, their faces full of concern. Jenny reached for her hand and gave it a squeeze.

'Then I think Nurse Rabbit should get out of there as soon as possible,' Bernie said stoutly.

Rita's eyes were filling with tears. 'But Nurse Rabbit is terribly worried about Mrs Bunny and the children.'

'Bernie's right,' said Jenny. 'If Nurse Rabbit isn't safe, she should leave.'

'I don't want my book to have a sad ending,' said Bernie.

Rita nodded. She couldn't tell them about the drugs either, but she did wonder if she should tell them about the sugar knob she'd re-wrapped in foil and squirreled away. In the end she decided not to. 'Neither do I,' she told Bernie. 'I'll certainly think about the ending.'

The conversation stopped for a while as everyone turned their attention back to their food. Rita blew her nose. 'So, what shall we do for the rest of the day?' she asked eventually. When neither of them had a better idea, she added, 'Have either of you ever been to the Tower of London?'

It turned out that nobody had, so they set off about twenty minutes later. It cost them two bob each to get in but once inside it was worth the expense in spades. They followed a guide (one of the Beefeaters) who told them about the places they'd only read about in school history books. They paused at Tower Hill where two of Henry VIII's wives were executed, and lingered by Traitor's Gate to look down at the now dry moat which had been converted into allotments during the war. The crown jewels which cost an extra shilling to see, were fantastic and all in all they had a wonderful time.

Travelling on to the West End, they went to the pictures for the early evening show. *The Sound of Music* had been released in March and was still showing to big audiences. It was a bit long, so they ended up watching the end of the film and stayed for the beginning until they recognised the point where they'd come in.

As they went their separate ways, Bernie caught Rita's arm, 'Don't waste time, Rita. Take the book back to the library. There are plenty more baby bunnies out there who need someone like you.'

Rita gave her a hug. 'Thanks Bernie.'

'And don't forget,' her friend called as she walked away, 'if ever you're in trouble you know where we are.'

Chapter 31

'Hole in the Ground'
Bernard Cribbins
BBC Light Programme, *Children's Favourites*

Rita certainly felt more like her old self when she got up the next morning. She had slept surprisingly well considering how uptight she had been the day before. Bernie's way of addressing the problem had been helpful and even if it was not what she wanted to hear, she knew they were right. Rita felt comfortable that she hadn't betrayed a trust and yet her friends had understood her predicament only too well. It wasn't going to be easy to tell Mrs Knight that she was going to leave, and Rita had decided she wouldn't – she couldn't – tell her employer the real reason why.

That meant telling a lie which was watertight, something Rita was never very good at. Her Auntie Steph was ill – that was true – and she needed to go to Eastbourne. That sounded feasible enough. No, it couldn't wait and she didn't know how long she was going to be there, so it wouldn't be fair on Mrs Knight and the children if the post was left open for her. Better to get a new nanny. Preferably a much older woman with a wart on her top lip. She wouldn't say that last bit of course, even if it would be a good idea.

Having got the children up, Rita took them downstairs. She planned to supervise Lucy's breakfast and feed the baby at the same time, but the whole place was in chaos. The hallway was cluttered up with bags and guitars. Mr Knight was in a state of mild panic as he demanded somebody find the mic stand while Mrs Knight was running up and down the stairs with costumes and other props ready to pack.

'What on earth is going on?' Rita asked Mrs Fordham when she went into the kitchen.

'Apparently Mr Knight's agent has just telephoned to say that Kandy Krisp is to be a supporting act starting tonight.'

Rita had put Daniel in the little playpen near the table and was helping Lucy sit in a chair. 'That's a bit short notice isn't it?'

Mrs Fordham nodded. 'Somebody had a serious accident last night,' she said.

'Oh no,' said Rita. 'Not one of the members of the family, I hope?'

'I can't remember his name,' Mrs Fordham went on, 'but he's the singer of another pop group. Quite famous so I'm told. He's been taken to Intensive Care.'

'Oh dear.'

Rita put a Weetabix into a bowl and poured some milk on the top. Placing it in front of Lucy, she said, 'There you are, sweetie. Eat up.'

'Two other members of the same group are in hospital with minor injuries,' Mrs Fordham continued.

Rita took a baby's feeding bottle out of the fridge and put it into a Pyrex jug. 'When you say accident,' she went on, 'what sort of accident?' She poured some water from the kettle into the jug to warm the feed.

'Car,' said Mrs Fordham. 'Crossed the central reservation, so I believe.'

'How terrible.'

'How long will Mr Knight be gone?'

'A couple of months,' said Mrs Fordham.

It took every ounce of Rita's will power not to whoop for joy. Two months. That meant she needn't give her notice until the middle of July. As she sat beside Lucy she ruffled her hair. 'Nice?'

Lucy, her mouth full and traces of milk seeping from the sides, nodded.

Daniel drank his bottle greedily while Mrs Fordham got on with what she was doing. Rita could see people walking past the kitchen window with all the gear ready to pack it into the Bedford van, and then Mrs Knight burst into the kitchen.

'Oh Rita, isn't it wonderful,' she cried. 'Cameron and his group will be playing on the same tour as B.G.Scoby and Sandy Harry.'

'Sounds great,' said Rita. Even better that he'd be gone for two months, she thought to herself. 'Is he going far?'

'Liverpool tonight,' she said, 'which is why we're in such a rush. Then he'll be touring with Gene Vincent and Lulu the month after. Cam is super excited because it'll be a brilliant opportunity to plug his latest record.'

'Can I get down?' Lucy asked.

'Yes, you can,' said Rita, 'but don't get in anybody's way, okay?'

Lucy went to watch what was going on, standing in the doorway.

Having fed the children and snatched a little breakfast herself, Rita decided it would be a good idea to make all of them scarce, so she got the pram ready and told Mrs Knight they were going to the park.

'Say goodbye to daddy, darling,' her mother told Lucy.

But Cameron paid scant attention as his daughter called, 'Bye-bye, daddy.' They hung around for a bit to see if there was the chance of a real goodbye for the little girl until Rita could see there was a very real possibility of Lucy being shouted at, so they set off. Once away from the house, Rita felt a huge sense of relief. With the husband gone for two whole months she could concentrate on helping Mrs Knight regain her confidence so that by the time she had to leave, the children's mother would more able to stand up to her husband and his shenanigans.

Lucy wasn't her usual self.

'Tell you what,' Rita said as they walked to the park, 'why don't we write a letter to daddy every day?'

'I can't write,' Lucy said bleakly.

'But you can draw beautiful pictures, and we can tell him what we've done. We'll put it in a journal.'

'What's a bernal?' Lucy asked.

'A journal is big book,' said Rita. 'A big very special book.'

The baby slept while Rita and Lucy had an enjoyable morning. They fed the ducks and played in the children's play area. There wasn't a lot of equipment, but with a little imagination they danced with princes and hid behind the trees from the Sheriff of Nottingham. Lucy picked a tulip (which Rita didn't notice until it was too late) and a dandelion.

'We can put them in your journal,' Rita said and the little girl beamed.

When they arrived back home, they were just in time to see Cameron set off with all his gear in the Bedford van. He kissed his wife and his son but forgot Lucy until Rita rather pointedly mentioned it. He did condescend to bend down to her and kissed the top of her head.

'We're going to make you a bernal,' she said proudly.

He gave her a quizzical look and said dismissively, 'Yeah, right.'

That was the moment Rita realised how much she disliked him.

As everyone ate their mid-day meal it was as if the house itself relaxed and became more peaceful. After lunch, Mrs Knight rested as did Lucy, while Rita scoured the pages of *Nursery World* to see if anything took her fancy. In the late afternoon, while Daniel kicked his legs on a mat on the floor, she and Mrs Knight taught Lucy how to play Snakes and Ladders. Like all children her age, Lucy struggled a little when she was losing but loved it when she was on a winning streak.

'Did you bump your cheek, ma'am?' Rita asked as Mrs Knight turned her head. Her employer had a red mark just below her eye which Rita could see was becoming more puffy by the minute.

Mrs Knight put her fingers to her face and let out a nervous laugh. 'Oh dear, does it show? Silly me, I walked into the open toy cupboard door.'

The two women looked at each other. Nothing was said, but they both knew it was a lie.

'Shall I kiss it better, Mummy?'

'Would you darling? That would be lovely. Thank you.'

Life was so different in the house without Cameron. He didn't bother to telephone his wife and family so the only news they had of him was from the newspapers. Mrs Knight bought the *Daily Mirror*, a paper that had a sprinkling of news about the music scene which was taking the world by storm. They called it The Swinging Sixties now. The biggest groups like The Beatles, the Rolling Stones and The Animals were touring almost non-stop, not only in this country but all around the world. Right now, the Stones were in Sweden and The Beatles, who had just released their first film, *Help!* were going back for a second tour of the USA beginning in New York in the autumn. Kandy Krisp had a new release in the spring, but in all honesty it hadn't done very well and everyone knew Cameron was desperately looking for a new hit song.

Travis came over on his bike quite regularly to take Rita to some gig or other. She quite liked him and she enjoyed most of the bands they'd watched, but he was becoming a little more persistent when they were alone. She was confident enough to believe that he would never force himself on her, but she realised that he was growing weary of her constant nos.

'All the girls I know are on the pill,' he said dejectedly. 'You'll be quite safe on the pill.'

'You have to be married to go on the pill,' Rita told him. They had been snogging which had become much more intense lately. She enjoyed it but he always wanted to go further. She might have been tempted if she had loved him but the passion just wasn't there. Travis was not what she wanted in a boyfriend – or a husband, for that matter – let alone the fact that she had vowed to be older before she settled down. It was becoming a bore to keep pushing his hand away from her crotch and keeping her bra in its proper place meant she had to keep her arms moving more quickly than she did when practicing semaphore in the Girl Guides!

'Oh, come on Reet,' he groaned for the umpteenth time. 'You know you want to.'

No, you're the one that wants to, she thought acidly as she pushed his hand away yet again.

When Rita met Althea, one of the girls from WEN on her afternoon off, Althea was much more pragmatic as they discussed their boyfriends over a coffee.

Althea's boyfriend, Jack, had apparently had his wicked way with her and now sex was all he thought about. 'He used to take me to the pictures or the pub,' she complained good-naturedly, 'but now I spend just about every evening laddering my tights in the back of his van.'

'Oh dear,' Rita chuckled. 'But why did you do it, if you didn't want it?'

'I got to thinking my virginity felt like a massive ball and chain. Everybody else said they were doing it, so I thought I might as well get it over and done with.'

Rita stirred some sugar into her coffee. 'Does that mean you regret it?'

'Do you know what?' said Althea. 'I think I do. He's not even much good at it.'

Rita grinned.

Her friend took a deep breath. 'I think you're absolutely right. I shall dump him.'

'I never said a thing!' Rita protested.

'Bloody men,' Althea suddenly snapped. 'They've only got one brain cell and it's centred between their legs.'

Rita might not have put it so crudely, but she was beginning to feel that she didn't want to go down the same route. When she made love with someone, even if she wasn't engaged to them or married, she wanted that first time to be special.

'D'you know what,' Rita said as she sipped her coffee, 'After what you've just said, I don't want to go out with Travis anymore.'

'Good for you!' said Althea and they both laughed.

'Now that we've both got our love life sorted,' said Rita said brightly and changing the subject, 'what shall we do today?'

Her friend's face lit up. 'Fancy having a go in the Hampton Court maze?'

-

As soon as she got back to Ewell, Rita wrote a letter to her grandmother telling her she would be coming the following Friday for a weekend and then she wrote to Travis. She did her best to let him down gently and finally, pleased with her effort, she put both letters on her dressing table ready to post in the morning.

When Rita and the children came downstairs the next day, there was a letter waiting for her on the hall stand. Once Daniel was fed and Lucy was standing on a chair at the sink with Mrs Fordham 'helping' with the washing up, Rita opened her letter. It was from Travis.

> *Although I could keep on seeing you, it would never work out between us. You see, that little bit of 'magic' between you and me is missing. Since our last date, I have met a girl who is already very dear to me. I told her all about you and she suggested I write this letter. She doesn't hold back. She wants all of me because she is in love! Thanks for all the fun we've had together. Travis.*

At first Rita was indignant but when she re-read his letter she felt differently. Their last date had been only four nights before, so if he'd met this new girl three days ago... She began to giggle. Lucky Travis. It seemed that his one brain cell had hit the jackpot first date!

Chapter 32

'Ticket to Ride'
The Beatles

The back door was locked when Rita arrived home. It was unusual – Gran seldom bothered to turn the key even when she was going into Worthing on the bus. Rita fumbled in her bag for her own key and went inside. It was lovely to breathe in the familiar smell of home once more and already she was feeling relaxed and contented. Everything was neat and tidy. She had expected to find a note on the kitchen table but there was nothing. Gran knew she was coming, so why wasn't she here? A shiver of apprehension ran through her body. Was Gran all right?

She heard a foot fall outside and a soft knock on the back door. When she opened it, Eddie was standing on the step. 'Oh!'

'I thought I heard you come in,' he said. 'The walls are as thin as paper and I was listening out for you.'

'I came on the eleven twenty,' she said. 'Come in.'

'Your gran's gone to Eastbourne,' he said stepping over the threshold.

'Auntie Steph?'

He nodded. 'She's been in hospital.'

'Hospital!'

'She had her gall bladder out,' said Eddie. 'Win wanted to bring her back here but Steph was having none of it. She's been there two weeks and I'm picking her up tomorrow.'

Rita was wrestling with a little guilt that all she could feel was relief that it wasn't her grandmother who was poorly. 'Shall I put the kettle on?'

'That would be grand,' he said, lowering himself into a chair.

While Rita boiled the kettle and made the tea, they made small talk. His tomato plants were doing well and Rita told him how much she loved a home-grown tomato. She told him about her job and the fact that she would be leaving before long and he said if she wasn't happy, that was probably a wise decision.

Eddie put his cup silently into his saucer. 'I got something to tell you.'

The gravity in his voice and his tense body language made Rita give him her full attention.

'Someone came here yesterday asking for your mother. A man.'

'A man?' she said. 'What man?'

'An American.'

Her stomach fell away. Dexter? Her father was here, in this country? In Worthing? 'Did he have a name, this American?' Rita was doing her best to sound nonchalant.

'Stewart,' said Eddie. 'Stewart Granger. Funny, I thought he was a film star.'

Rita's heart leapt. 'He is,' she said with a chuckle. Her thoughts were in overdrive. Was this really Dexter? It had to be, didn't it? He must have read her letter. It was the only way he'd know about Stewart Granger. 'Did he say what he wanted?'

'Just to speak with Val,' said Eddie.

'To speak with her!' Rita squeaked. 'What did he look like?'

Eddie pulled a face as he tried to recall the stranger. 'Wrong end of forty, hair going grey at the sides, nice suit,' he said. 'If you don't mind me saying so, he looked a bit shifty.'

Rita frowned, puzzled. That didn't sound at all like the picture she had of Dexter, so who was it? 'Did he leave a message?'

Eddie shook his head. 'Only that he was staying at the Beach hotel.'

Rita frowned, puzzled. 'And he had no idea my mother was dead?'

'Didn't seem to,' said Eddie then he added, 'Come to think of it, he also asked for you by name. "Can I speak to Miss Rita Brownlow," he says.'

'Did you tell him I was coming home today?'

'I thought it best not to,' said Eddie.

Rita picked up the cups and put them in the sink. She was hoping that Eddie couldn't see her hand was shaking. 'Well, I'm sure I don't know anyone like that,' she said brightly. 'Bit of a mystery, isn't it.'

Eddie went back home soon after. Rita sat at the kitchen table trying to think. She had written the letter to Dexter shortly after she'd read the last of his letters to her mother. She'd been cagey about what she'd said but she was sure that all she had told him was that she was doing well and working as a nursery nurse. She hadn't mentioned her mother because she presumed that he already knew that Val was dead. But now that she thought about it, that was stupid wasn't it? How could he possibly know? They had split up way back when Rita was a toddler, years before Val had died. As far as she knew, her mother had never written to him again, and Gran was probably too angry with him to write and tell him that Val was gone.

When Eddie had described the American, he didn't match what she had imagined, but of course she was thinking of that handsome young fellow her mother had fallen in love with, when twenty or more years had passed since he'd posed for that photograph. He was probably twenty or twenty-one when it was taken so he'd be anything between forty and forty-five now. That meant the man Eddie had described could well be her father. Now she was agitated. Why was he here? And why now? Eddie had said he had a nice suit – travel from America wasn't exactly cheap so perhaps he was doing well in business? But was it just a coincidence that he was in Worthing at the same time as she was?

With her grandmother out of town, Rita went to the shed and got out her old bike. She hadn't ridden it for ages but after pumping up the tyres and with a bit of grease on the chain and a wipe of the saddle with a damp cloth, it was ready to go.

The Beach Hotel was along the seafront, close to the gardens at the sea end of Heene Road. She parked her bike against the wall and went inside.

The receptionist looked up. 'Can I help you?'

Rita's heart was racing. 'I believe you have a Mr Granger staying here,' she said.

The woman ran her finger down the registration book. 'No, I'm sorry,' she said. 'There's no one of that name here.'

Puzzled, Rita turned to go. At the door, she paused. Stewart Granger was just a code name. If Dexter thought mum was still alive, he might have used their special name to remind her of the past. For a moment or two, Rita chewed her bottom lip before going back to the desk. 'Would you happen to have a Mr Dexter McCloud staying here?'

'Yes,' she said, 'we have a guest of that name.'

Rita's heart almost stopped. 'Could I speak with him please?'

The receptionist glanced at the board behind her where rows of keys hung from brass hooks. 'Mr McCloud appears to be out at the moment.'

Rita willed herself to sound business-like rather than give away the fact that she felt like she was on a roller-coaster; one minute high up, the next plummeting down to earth. 'Do you know when he'll be back?'

'I'm afraid I don't,' she said, 'but dinner is served from six.'

Rita nodded and left. Back outside, she looked at her watch. It was four thirty. Perhaps she should go for a bike ride along the seafront or something and come back later. After all, it wasn't as if she had to be back home in time for a meal. With Gran in Eastbourne, she was her own person. When she was hungry, fish and chips from the parade of shops near Gran's house would be perfectly acceptable and she knew that the chippy didn't close until ten o'clock. She pulled the bike away from the wall. A bike ride it was then.

Worthing was in the grip of change. Some thought it was about time, but others resented the town's history being wiped out. There were rumours that the shops in Ann Street, the little theatre and even the old Town Hall were earmarked for demolition. The council was keen to drag Worthing into the twentieth century and create a modern seaside town with a large shopping mall where the big department stores could trade alongside smaller retail outlets. Rita biked as far as Lancing before deciding to turn around and from there she went inland along Brougham Road and past the hospital in Lyndhurst Road, then down Little High Street onto Steyne Gardens before returning to the seafront. Parking her bike outside the Beach Hotel once again, she walked back inside.

'Ah, yes,' said the receptionist. 'I told Mr McCloud about you.' And pointing a finger behind Rita, she added. 'He's waiting over there.'

As she walked towards him, he rose from his seat gasping, 'My God, you're the spitting image of your beautiful mother.'

His hair was flecked with grey and he had lines on his face, but she recognised him instantly. He was the same as the man in her mother's photograph.

She was nervous as she sat opposite him but the moment he leaned forwards and took both of her hands in his, all that fell away. *This is my father*, she thought. *My Dad. It's 1965, I'm almost twenty years old and I'm here talking to my dad for the first time ever.*

There was so much to catch up on. He had no idea that her mother was dead, let alone that she had been killed in a bank raid. As soon as she told him, Rita could tell at once that it had come as an awful shock.

'After my brother's accident, she wrote and told me she had married someone else,' he said. 'I've always imagined her with other children, a wife and mom.' His eyes grew moist and at one point a lone tear travelled the length of his cheek. 'I am so sorry. We were young, but she was the love of my life.'

Mum had told him she'd married someone else. But why?

'She never married again,' said Rita.

His face clouded. 'She said it was better to have a clean break,' he went on. 'She told me her new husband wouldn't want me interfering.' He shook his head. 'That's why I was so excited to get your letter. I thought it was from Val. I never knew she had died,' he said brokenly.

Rita wished she'd been more specific in her letter. So now, gently, she told him everything about the shooting and how her mother's funeral had been attended by all the bigwigs from the bank and half of Worthing's police force. 'Children don't usually go to funerals in this country,' she explained, 'but my grandmother let me. People criticised her for it but I'm glad she did. As horrible as it was, it made it real. When it was all over, I knew for sure my mother wasn't coming back.'

He squeezed her hands again. 'I'm so sorry.'

When Rita changed the subject and asked him about his life, Dexter surprised her. He told her that he and his family had spent many years in relative penury because of the huge bills incurred by his brother's accident. Then he told her he was married and had three children. It didn't come as a shock, Rita had guessed that he might be.

'You have three half-siblings,' he told her as he drew a photograph from his wallet. 'Scott, he's fifteen in a couple of weeks, then there's Darlene, she's eleven and Bonnie who is nine.' In the picture he was showing her, his three children, her half-brother and sisters, stood with their arms around each other. Judging by what they were wearing, Scott was an American baseball player and Darlene liked tennis. Bonnie was dressed in a short skirt and carried a pair of bright red pom-poms, so she was probably the school cheerleader.

'They're all into sport,' Dexter said proudly. He glanced at Rita. 'Are you sporty?'

Rita shook her head. 'If you ask me to go onto the sports field, I have to have to lie down in a darkened room for two hours first,' she quipped.

Dexter chuckled. 'I see you have your mother's sense of humour too.'

'So why are you here?' she asked.

'Business,' he said. 'I've come over here to look at the British health service. I work in insurance for SWC which is Senior year Welfare and Care and we're trying to find new ways to help older people.'

'Is SWC like the National Health Service then?'

'Not exactly,' he said. 'Your health service is for everybody – from the cradle to the grave, don't they say? SWC is only for over sixty-fives, but we're interested to learn how your system works.'

'How long have you been doing that?'

'Since my brother's accident,' he said. 'The bills nearly crippled us and although younger people can get their own insurance cover, it's not so easy for older people.'

Rita gave him an anxious look. 'And how is your brother?'

'He lost sight in one eye and he still struggles to walk but we managed to get him a job and he's independent now.'

Time passed quickly and it was only when the dinner gong sounded that they were brought back to the here and now.

'Would you care to join me in a meal, Rita?'

Rita shook her head. Much as she wanted to be with him, their meeting had been so overwhelming that she was too emotional to eat.

He walked with her to the entrance. 'I know this hasn't been easy for you,' he said, 'but promise me that we'll see each other again before I go back home to the States at the end of the week.'

Too choked up to say anything, Rita simply nodded. A second or two later, he crushed her to him in a bear hug.

She knew he was watching her as she turned the bike towards Goring and mounted it, but she didn't look back. She couldn't. Rita needed time and she needed a good cry. And after that, she would face the daunting task of telling her grandmother what she had done.

Chapter 33

'King of the Road'

Roger Miller

Gran, bless her heart, listened to what Rita was saying even though she could see it was uncomfortable for her. They were sitting at the kitchen table after a lovely meal. Rita's culinary skills weren't exactly Fanny Craddock, but she had produced a delicious shepherd's pie with tinned carrots and peas (too early to come from the garden yet) followed by rice pudding.

Apparently Auntie Steph was doing well, which meant Gran was happy to come back home. As they sat in the quiet sipping a cup of tea, Rita took a deep breath. 'Gran, I need to talk to you about something.'

'And I need to talk to you,' said Gran.

She had her 'this is very important' look on her face. Rita hadn't seen that look for simply ages. In fact, the last time might have even been when Gran told Rita that her mother had died. Rita blinked nervously. 'You go first.'

'No, no,' said Gran waving her hand. 'You go first.'

If this wasn't awkward enough, now Rita was worried about what her grandmother was going to say.

'It's a long story,' she began, 'but I've met my dad.'

Gran blinked. 'Dexter? He's here in this country?'

Rita nodded. 'It wasn't what we both thought, Gran. He did love Mum.'

'But he never came back for you, did he.'

'There was a reason for that,' Rita said gently.

'Tell me then,' Gran challenged.

Rita chewed at her bottom lip. 'I think it best if you read the letters and form your own opinion.'

They made eye contact for a second then Gran said, 'So what's he like?' There was challenge in her voice.

Rita spent the next few minutes telling her about her father's insurance company. 'He married—'

'Huh,' Gran scoffed.

'In 1950,' Rita added pointedly, 'and he has three children.'

Her grandmother rose abruptly to her feet. 'So I suppose you'll be off to America now. Rich man, better life.'

'Oh, Gran please don't be like that,' cried Rita. 'It's not a question of leaving you, I love you. You mean the world to me. I was just curious, that's all.'

Her grandmother threw the dirty dishes into the washing up bowl and turned on the tap. 'When do you go?'

'I'm not going anywhere, Gran. Please don't be cross with me.'

Win's stiff body language relaxed. 'I ain't,' she protested mildly. 'It's just a shock, that's all.'

Rita came up behind her and threw her arms around her gran. They stood together by the sink in a tender cuddle. 'I'm not going to leave you, Gran,' Rita said gently. 'You're the best.'

'Ah go on with you, you daft apeth,' said Gran as they parted and she fussed with the washing up bowl.

'Anyway, why should I want to go,' said Rita as she picked up the tea towel. 'Your fruit cake is the best in the world.'

Her grandmother chuckled contentedly.

'Now, what was it you wanted to tell me?' said Rita.

'Don't worry about that now,' said Gran but Rita noticed that her cheeks had gone pink.

'Come on, tell me.'

'Eddie has asked me to marry him.'

Rita took in a big breath. 'I hope you've said yes?'

Her grandmother smiled sheepishly. 'I've said yes.'

Rita shrieked with excitement and the next minute the pair of them were dancing around the kitchen with Gran's soapy hands shedding bubbles all over the place.

—

Back in Ewell, Lucy was so excited to see Rita that as she walked into the house, she ran to her and hugged her waist. Rita put down her case and bent to hug her too.

'Mummy and me went swimming,' she announced. 'I did the crawl and I splashed everywhere.'

'Did you now?' Rita was aware of Mrs Knight listening to them as she stood in the doorway to the sitting room.

'And then we put Daniel in the water,' Lucy went on breathlessly, 'and Mummy let me hold him while he was swimming.'

Rita raised her eyebrows. 'You helped Daniel to swim?'

Lucy nodded proudly.

'Well done,' said Rita. 'Daniel must think you're the best big sister ever.'

When she looked up, Mrs Knight wore a benevolent smile. 'Let nanny take her suitcase up to her room first, Lucy, and then we'll tell her all about it.'

Reluctantly the little girl stood aside and Rita mounted the stairs. As she unpacked, she felt really chuffed. A fabulous weekend had been had by all. It was obvious that Mrs Knight and her children had enjoyed some quality time together, Rita's grandmother was engaged to be married and Rita herself had met her father for the first time. What could be more perfect?

Back downstairs, she knocked on the sitting room door.

Lucy was playing with her dolly. Daniel was outside in his pram and Mrs Knight was glowing with health although she did look a little anxious.

'Lucy, darling,' said her mother. 'Mummy has left her cardigan on the end of her bed. My arms are a bit chilly. Would you run up and fetch it for me please.'

Rita felt sure Lucy's chest stuck out a mile as she hurried out of the room and thundered up the stairs.

'I hope you had a nice time, Rita.'

'I did, thank you ma'am and from what I hear, you had a good time too.'

Mrs Knight nodded. 'But,' she added with a sigh, 'I'm afraid my poor husband hasn't been so fortunate.'

Rita's heart sank. Don't say he was coming back early. There was at least another two and a half weeks left of his tour. 'Oh dear.'

'Before Lucy comes back I must tell you that there was a drugs bust,' Mrs Knight said matter-of-factly. 'Cameron got arrested.'

Rita lowered herself into a chair. She was well aware that Cameron did drugs, even though he didn't do it in the house. They could hear Lucy running across the landing.

'So what happens now?'

Mrs Knight shrugged. 'No idea. His manager is handling all that. Hopefully the police will let him off with a caution.'

The door burst open and Lucy, complete with cardigan, ran to her mother. 'Thank you, darling.'

'What a helpful girl,' Rita said encouragingly.

'Isn't she just,' said Mrs Knight pushing her arms into the cardigan.

They heard the sound of car tyres on the gravel outside and to her horror, Rita saw two police cars pulling up on the driveway. Mrs Knight clutched at her chest.

'Shall I take the children out for a walk?' Rita asked.

Mrs Knight nodded as someone began banging on the front door. As Sally opened the door, Mrs Knight went into the hallway. Rita hustled Lucy into the kitchen. 'Come on, sweetie,' she said, as her charge picked up her dolly. 'Mummy's got visitors. We'll go to the park and feed the ducks.'

No time to grab a coat or a ball to play with, Rita snatched up the half a loaf from the bread bin and they hurried to the pram outside in the garden. Lucy held onto the handle while Rita took off the brake.

'Just a minute,' said a man's voice behind her.

Rita turned sharply to see a policeman standing by the garden gate. She froze as he came towards her. Rita could feel Lucy's hand tremble as she held onto her leg and moved behind her.

The policeman stood over the pram. 'Where are you off to in such a hurry?'

'With all those cars outside, I thought it best the children weren't upset,' she said. 'Please don't wake the baby.'

'What have you got underneath that pram?' he said coldly.

'Nothing,' cried Rita. 'I was just taking the children away from the house. Like I said, I didn't want them frightened.'

He seemed reasonable enough and he was of an age that she wondered if he had children of his own. 'I'm afraid I've got to check there's nothing in the bottom of that pram,' he said, his voice softening.

'The baby is asleep,' Rita said rather unnecessarily.

The policeman pulled a 'don't let me have to tell you again' face.

Rita reached in and picked the sleeping baby up. The policeman felt along the bottom and the sides of the pram before removing the bedding and the tray. Having satisfied himself that there was indeed nothing in the pit of the pram, he gave her a nod. Daniel was squirming now and Lucy was hiding behind Rita. She laid the baby down and straightened the covers.

'I am afraid I have to search you, Miss,' he said. 'Empty your pockets please.'

Rita did so but they only yielded a used handkerchief, two sweet papers, an old shopping list and some fluff. The policeman looked down at Lucy.

'Oh no,' Rita said firmly. 'She's only a child. I'm a fully trained nursery nurse. Do you really think I would give my charge drugs just to avoid the police?'

'I need to look at the doll,' he said making to grab it.

Rita put her hand up to stop him, then knelt in front of Lucy. 'Listen, sweetie,' she said, 'the policeman is looking for something. He's looked in my pockets and he's looked in Daniel's pram but he hasn't found it. Now he's wondering if dolly might have it.'

Lucy clutched her doll closer.

'I'm sure dolly hasn't got it,' said Rita, 'but shall we let the policeman have a look? I'm sure he won't hurt her. Just to look.'

Lucy glanced up at him with an anxious expression.

'He was very gentle with Daniel, wasn't he,' Rita insisted. 'I'm sure dolly will be all right.'

Reluctantly Lucy handed Rita her doll and Rita stood to her feet. The policeman took it from her and squeezed the doll from top to bottom. He lifted her dress and shook her.

'Nooo,' cried Lucy. 'Dolly doesn't like that.'

The policeman handed the doll back to Rita and giving her a jerk of his head, he indicated that they could go.

'Dolly doesn't like that man,' Lucy said as they reached the pavement.

'I'm sure he didn't mean to upset dolly,' Rita said diplomatically. 'You give her a nice cuddle and she'll feel better in no time.'

By the time they had walked to the park, the baby was asleep again but as they reached the swings, Rita could tell by her anxious looks over her shoulder that Lucy was afraid the policeman might be following them. She was quiet; not at all her usual chatty self. It was obvious that she'd been disturbed by their experience.

'Let's put dolly in the pram with Daniel while you have a swing, shall we? I'm sure your brother will take good care of her.'

Lucy let her do it, but she was clearly apprehensive. They played for a while on the swings and the slide then Rita walked the pram to the duck pond. By that time, Lucy was back to her usual self and they fed the ducks.

Eventually Rita decided that the police had probably left the house by now but even if they hadn't found anything, there was a real cause for concern. The children would have to be protected from not only the drugs themselves but also the press wanting a story – and just how Mrs Knight would react to all this was an unknown quantity as well. And what of Cameron? Would this damage his already fragile career? And if he was no longer a success, what would that do to his mood? It was a worrying time all round.

When they got back, the police had indeed gone but the whole house was in uproar. They had pulled open drawers and spilled the contents, lifted carpets, stripped beds, including Rita's and Lucy's, and emptied every pot, storage jar and cupboard in the kitchen. Cameron's den was in chaos, as was the shed and garage. Sally, Mrs Fordham and Rita herself would have their work cut out for them getting the place back into some semblance of order. The good news was, they had found nothing.

As she made a start in the children's playroom, Rita did her best to try and make a game of it, but Lucy stood close by with her thumb in her mouth and a bewildered expression on her face. Mrs Knight was tearful and Mrs Fordham was furious that her kitchen had been wrecked. Sally had gone back home to her Stan.

It was at times like this when routine was a godsend. Nobody else felt like eating but the baby still had to be fed and so did Lucy. By the time seven o'clock came around that evening, Rita and Mrs Knight were exhausted. Mrs Fordham had long since gone home and the children were in bed.

'Can I get you anything, ma'am?'

'Has Mrs Fordham left a meal?'

Rita shook her head. 'I'm afraid there was such chaos in the kitchen, ma'am.'

Mrs Knight picked up the telephone receiver. 'We'll get the Chinese shop to bring something over.'

Half an hour later they were sitting in front of two plates of fried rice with Peking duck and a glass of wine. Rita had never eaten Chinese before and although she had no idea what was in the meal she was eating, it was delicious.

Chapter 34

'I'm Alive'

The Hollies

The next day, Rita busied herself with the children as Mrs Knight received a steady stream of visitors. Cameron's manager, Billy, came, as did someone from the record company and a couple of members of the band. Judging by the raised voices in the sitting room, they were not best pleased.

'Keep the children in the house today, Rita,' Mrs Knight said after the manager had gone. 'Billy has arranged for a bodyguard to stand outside the front door but the press are lurking in the lane behind the house and at the entrance to the Close.'

She looked upset and tearful but it wasn't until later in the day that Rita heard that Cameron had been remanded in custody and was to appear before the Magistrates court on Wednesday. A couple of other people had been arrested alongside him. One of them was Tammy-Jane. Rita was surprised to hear her name mentioned in connection with Cameron's arrest. It was hard to get to the truth of what had actually happened, but the tabloids were awash with lurid details of sex orgies and drug-filled parties.

On Wednesday, Mrs Knight went to the Magistrates court and because all the attention would be centred there, Rita took the opportunity to take Lucy and Daniel out for a breath of fresh air. Desperate to talk to someone about normal things, she decided to go to Rosebury Park on the off chance that she might bump into some of the girls from the nursery. It was a bit of a trek so she put the seat on the end of the pram so that Lucy could have a ride when her legs got tired. She was a bit big for it now but that couldn't be helped.

As luck would have it, Bernie was by the playground with some of the Harefield House children. 'Oh blast,' she teased after she'd given Rita a hug, 'I should have brought my autograph book. I'm in the presence of a celebrity now.' And Rita gave her a playful bump on the arm.

Once all the children were playing, Bernie turned to her friend. 'Are you all right? Things sound a bit hairy for you right now.'

'It gets worse,' said Rita. 'Mrs Fordham and Sally have both given notice.'

'Why?'

'I'm guessing they've been troubled at home by members of the press,' said Rita. 'I know it'll turn out to be a five-minute wonder, but it is a bit upsetting. I'm only here today because I know they'll all be at the court.'

'Do you think he's guilty?'

'Oh yes,' said Rita.

'You're not scared to talk about it now?' said Bernie.

'That bit is public knowledge,' Rita reminded her.

Bernie hurried over to one of the nursery children who had fallen off the turnstile. He wasn't hurt and after brushing down his hands, she put him back on. 'Now hold tight this time,' she cautioned.

Lucy was playing with Fola. As she watched them, Rita reflected that the two girls couldn't look more different but neither of them had noticed. Children never notice colour. They were playing together like old friends and having a wonderful time.

'What about Mrs Knight's family?' Bernie asked as she came back.

'You know,' said Rita, 'that's the funny thing. She never mentions her family. I not even sure she has any.'

Bernie shook her head. 'Sad.'

Daniel woke up and Rita changed his nappy and sat him on her lap to feed him. Some of the children came to watch but Daniel hardly noticed his audience. His mind was on one thing – his bottle as he stroked it with his hand and made contented swallowing sounds.

'We'd better be off now,' said Bernie glancing at her watch.

Rita nodded. 'Thanks,' she said.

'What for?'

'For being a friend,' said Rita.

Bernie gave her a quick hug. 'It'll all blow over,' she said as she called the children and got ready to go. 'Take care.'

Rita nodded. 'It's your exam soon, isn't it?'

Bernie pulled a face. 'Two weeks.'

'You'll be fine,' said Rita. 'I'll be keeping my fingers crossed for you.'

—

'They've remanded him in custody.'

Mrs Knight had thrown herself into her chair and Rita could tell that she was fighting back her tears. 'He's pleaded not guilty so it has to go to trial.'

'Do you know when?' Rita asked.

'A couple of weeks, I think,' said Mrs Knight. 'Billy has got him a good solicitor.'

'What about the tour?' said Rita.

Mrs Knight shook her head. 'That's not going to happen. Cameron doesn't know it yet but Kandy Krisp is being disbanded.'

Rita gasped in shocked surprise. 'I'm so sorry, ma'am. Really, I am.'

Out in the kitchen Sally shrugged when Rita told her and Mrs Fordham. 'I can't say I'm surprised,' she said. 'Their last record was a flop and he puts more energy into chasing girls than singing.'

'Do you know if Mrs Knight has any family?' asked Rita. 'Maybe she should get in contact with them.'

'They cut her off when she married him,' Mrs Fordham said bleakly. 'Someone in the village told me they live abroad somewhere. No chance of them popping over.'

Rita was shocked but she said no more. Perhaps the family had seen what a waste of space Cameron was from the word go. Sally was right. He'd been a fool. When she'd first seen him all that long time ago, she would have tipped Cameron for the top. He was easily as good as Eric Burdon of The Animals or Ray Davies of The Kinks but the booze had already altered his voice and now it looked as if he was into drugs big time.

As soon as it seemed appropriate to do so, Rita asked to see Mrs Knight on a private matter.

'You're not going to leave me as well, are you?' she asked as Rita sat opposite her.

Mrs Knight looked so concerned Rita didn't have the heart to tell her she was indeed considering it, so she shook her head. 'I came to tell you that my grandmother is getting married again.'

'Your grandmother?' Mrs Knight squeaked. 'But that's amazing. When?'

'The end of next week and I should very much like to go to her wedding.'

'But of course you must go, Rita,' said Mrs Knight. 'How lovely. She brought you up, didn't she? Yes, yes, I remember you telling me. Oh, absolutely you must go.'

Rita had been right about the story of Cameron's arrest and police custody being a five-minute wonder. The press melted away and set off in pursuit of their next big story and the family settled down. Lucy was to go to school in September, so Mrs

Knight was trying to decide where to send her. She should have thought about it ages ago but with everything else going on in her life, she had dithered. Rita had no idea about private schools so she kept quiet when her employer talked about them. In the end, Lucy and her mother visited three local schools and one evening she announced that her daughter would be going to The Priory.

'Can you take Lucy to the uniform shop,' she said handing Rita a type-written list. 'You'll find it on the lower ground floor of Bentall's department store. Get her everything she needs and charge it to my account.'

Without Daniel in tow, Rita decided to make it an outing. They spent ages in the shop trying on this and that, making sure that Lucy would have all she needed, then Rita arranged for everything to be boxed up and delivered to the house. The problem came when Rita said everything should be put onto Mrs Knight's account.

A few minutes later, just as she and Lucy were leaving, the assistant who had served her came back. 'I'm sorry Miss Brownlow, but would you mind waiting a moment?'

Rita frowned. 'Why? Is there a problem?'

A man in a pinstriped suit had joined them. 'If I could have a word, Miss,' he began. 'Miss Rogers will look after Miss Lucy.'

'Would you like to feed the fishes in the fish tank Lucy?' Miss Rogers held out her hand and Lucy went willingly.

Rita followed the man through a door and into a rather untidy office. Having invited Rita to sit down, he moved to the other side of the desk. 'I'm afraid this is rather embarrassing,' he said. 'There is a large sum of money outstanding on Mrs Knight's account so we are unable to let you take the school uniform. We will, however, hold the items until such time as your employer has settled the account and then we shall of course release your purchases. I have asked my secretary to draw up another bill, although I'm afraid the past four have been ignored.'

'I'm so sorry,' Rita blurted out. 'I had no idea.'

'Of course not,' he said. 'And I am sorry to have to embarrass you this way but perhaps if we could use your services to deliver a letter by hand, I'm sure this can be quickly resolved.'

'Perhaps I could settle the previous invoice,' Rita suggested. She hadn't been paid for a couple of weeks, but she did have a bit of savings in her post office book. It might be less embarrassing for Mrs Knight to pay her back rather than suffer the indignity of having her purchases refused.

'The outstanding invoice is for £189/7/6,' he said. 'Are you able to settle that?'

Rita felt her legs wobble. Blimey, that was almost a year's wages when she worked in the nursery. 'No, I'm afraid I can't.'

He smiled benevolently. 'I didn't think you could Miss, but I appreciate your kind offer.'

A woman came into the office and handed him a letter. He in turn, handed it to Rita and she left the room. Lucy had enjoyed feeding the fish and was keen to begin her 'treat'. Rita had promised to take her to a special ice cream shop which was run by an Italian family. Had she known their shopping trip would end in this way she never would have suggested it, but for Rita, a promise was a promise and she couldn't let the little girl down.

Gelato was a small ice cream parlour run by Salvatore and Liliana. They were dotty about children and so Rita knew they would make a fuss of Lucy. Almost as soon as they arrived in the small café Rita and her charge were being tempted by the most delicious looking ice cream. With everything positioned in large trays at the front of the counter, it was exceedingly hard trying to make up their minds what to have. In the end, Rita plumped for one scoop of lemon and another of chocolate ice cream while Lucy had raspberry and chocolate chip with hundreds and thousands sprinkled over them. They sat at a table covered with a red checkered tablecloth.

Halfway through their ice cream, Liliana came out to talk to them. She made Lucy feel very special, asking her questions about herself and teaching her an Italian word – *prego*. 'It means "you're welcome",' she said. Lucy practiced it over and over, much to the delight of Salvatore who roared with laughter. The two ice creams were an eye watering ten and six but Rita thought them worth every penny.

Back home, Lucy couldn't wait to tell her mother what they had been doing, and Mrs Knight gave Rita a grateful smile.

'When will the delivery be arriving?' she asked.

Rita asked Lucy to go upstairs and put on her play shoes and while she was gone, she tackled the moment she was dreading the most. 'As we left, the manager gave me a letter for you, ma'am,' said Rita fumbling in her handbag.

As Mrs Knight took it from her, she said, 'And you must let me know how much the ice creams were, Rita. It was very kind of you to take Lucy for a treat.'

Rita hesitated. Should she stay while her employer opened the envelope? In the end she decided it would be embarrassing for both of them, but it was too late. As Rita turned to go she heard Mrs Knight gasp. 'Who did you say gave you this?'

'The manager, ma'am. He called me into his office.'

'So where is Lucy's uniform?'

Rita stared at the floor. 'They are holding it in store until…'

Mrs Knight rose to her feet. 'But I don't understand,' she said crossly. 'We have a monthly account with Bentall's. The bank should have covered this.' As she sat by the telephone and thumbed through the address book to look for the number, Rita slipped quietly from the room.

Chapter 35

'Mr Tambourine Man'
The Byrds

Later that day when she saw Mrs Knight, it was obvious that she had been crying. Her eyes were red and puffy and her complexion, usually flawless, was grey. Rita had just put the children to bed and was walking downstairs to her own little sitting room. She had her Basildon Bond writing pad and fountain pen in her hand and planned to reply to her father's letter which had come by second post. Mrs Knight's bedroom door was open and as Rita went by, she called her in.

The room was in chaos. The safe, which was behind a painting on the back wall, was open and an array of jewellery boxes were scattered on the bed. Most were empty. Mrs Knight had also been looking through official papers; letters with a bank logo on the top, a folded document which looked a lot like the deeds document she and Gran had for the cottage in Worthing, and a small pile of bills. The one of the top of the pile was stamped 'Final Demand'.

Rita did her best to avert her gaze. If Mrs Knight wasn't forthcoming with what was going on, she didn't want to embarrass her by asking questions.

'I have to go out tomorrow, Nanny,' she began. 'Lucy had been invited to a tea party so I should like you to take her in the car. Sally will look after Daniel until I get back. I've put your name on the insurance, and the party is in Banstead.'

'Yes, ma'am.' Rita did her best to contain her excitement. Drive the car? Wow! She hadn't driven since she'd taken her driving test. How far was Banstead?

'There's a map downstairs in the cupboard,' said Mrs Knight as if reading her mind. 'You can read a map?'

Tongue-tied Rita gave her a nod and made a quick exit. What on earth was going on? Why had she got all her jewellery boxes out? And why were some of them empty? Mrs Knight hadn't said she'd had a robbery, and she hadn't telephoned the police. By the time she reached the bottom of the stairs, Rita had a very unsettling feeling in her stomach. It had to be something to do with Cameron, didn't it? The police had searched every inch of the place, so Mrs Fordham had said. Surely they wouldn't have taken any of Mrs Knight's stuff without her permission, yet judging by her employer's tearful face, she'd obviously had a shock when she'd opened those boxes. Rita thought back to the purchases she'd made at Bentall's, it didn't take a rocket scientist to work out that Cameron hadn't been paying the bills. The only person who had access to the master bedroom, apart from Sally when she cleaned, was Cameron, so it had to have been Cameron who had emptied those jewellery boxes. Rita could only imagine the state of their bank account, and it wasn't good.

Once Rita had familiarised herself with where Banstead was (four miles away), and how to get there, she sat deep in thought in her sitting room. Through no fault of her own, she was at a crossroads in her life. If Mrs Knight had no money, she would have to leave her job immediately. She was already owed two week's pay and much as she wanted to help and support her employer, she couldn't afford to work for nothing – especially now that she was in contact with her father.

Dexter had been thrilled to find her, but he had to consider his wife's feelings before he invited his firstborn daughter to the States. He never said as much, but Rita understood that could be a bit of a problem. And if she did get an invitation, the plane fare would be very expensive. She needed to save every bean she could. So, much as she wanted to, she couldn't afford to stay here. With her grandmother's wedding at the weekend, Rita decided that she didn't want gran to face the upheaval of her turning up on the doorstep of the cottage, suitcase in hand, the day before their marriage. It would only spoil things. Rita had no other option but to carry on as if nothing was amiss until after the wedding.

Lucy was very excited to be going to a party. At two, the pair of them set off in Mrs Knight's car. Lucy was on the back seat holding her gift. Rita was surprised to find that after a couple of kangaroo starts, she remembered how to drive. The journey wasn't far, but far enough to give her a small challenge.

The house on Chalmers Road was huge. Probably dating from the 1930s, it too had a mock Tudor front and the pair of them walked through a lovely rose garden to reach the front door. They rang the bell and a maid opened the door. As they stepped into the hall, a voice cried, 'Lucy, darling. Come in, come in.'

Lucy ran to a well-dressed woman in an expensive looking blouson dress with a pleated skirt and embraced her. On the other side of the open sitting room door a conjurer was getting ready to begin his act. At least ten children sat on the floor in front of him. Rita settled Lucy among them and stepped back.

The woman who was just about to close the door glanced up at Rita. 'Perhaps you would like to go into the kitchen with the other nannies, dear,' she said.

Rita followed the direction of her pointed finger and to her delight, found one of her friends, Althea, from WEN among them. There were three of them, all sitting at the huge kitchen table each with a cup of tea in front them.

'They don't seem to need us in there,' Rita said as she settled herself at the table.

'They've hired a troupe,' said one girl. 'They do the whole thing: party games, prizes, food, the lot.'

'Nice to see you again,' said Althea quietly. 'I haven't seen you in yonks.'

'Now you're making me feel guilty,' said Rita, her voice in the same low tone. 'I just haven't got around to coming to the coffee mornings lately.'

'If you feel guilty,' said Althea, 'imagine how I feel. I never really thanked you for helping me dump Jack.'

Rita shook her head as if it was of no consequence. 'It was nothing.'

'Nothing!' Althea exclaimed in a whisper. 'If you hadn't showed me the light, I could have been horribly married by now.' She nudged Rita's side playfully. 'Spoilsport.'

They laughed.

'Jam scone, Nanny?' someone said.

'Umm, yes please,' said Rita.

The four of them spent a very pleasant hour chatting among themselves. She knew Althea of course, but the other nannies were strangers to both of them. Nanny Sue looked after three children all under five, they lived in a large house nearby and knew the party girl through dancing class. 'I've been with the family since their first was born,' she said. 'I keep thinking I ought to spread my wings a little, but I like being with them. They're easy-going and I get to have holidays in Switzerland in winter and Spain in the summer.'

'What's not to like,' Althea said jokingly.

Sue turned her head. 'Who do you work for Rita?'

Rita became the source of envy when she told them about Kandy Krisp. She shared the good times but didn't bring them up to date and luckily nobody asked about Cameron's arrest. Perhaps they hadn't heard about it yet. Althea told them about Master Andrew who, since the age of three, was dinosaur mad. 'We've got them everywhere now,' she said. 'Wallpaper, pyjamas, pencil cases, you name it he's got it.' Everyone chuckled.

The last to speak was the older nanny. She had apparently been looking after members of the same aristocratic family for years and years. 'I came to the Hall more years ago than I care to remember to look after Lord Darcy's children and then their children and now I'm caring for the first great-grandchild,' she said. 'Good job I'm hale and hearty. Master Georgie is a live wire and no mistake.'

The other three smiled admiringly. She was the epitome of everybody's idea of a nanny; grey haired, gentle, with an open smiley face and an air of peace and tranquillity. Rita imagined that her whole life had been one smooth pond with little to ripple the waters. 'I expect you've seen a lot of changes in childcare since you started, Nanny,' she said.

'Oh my goodness, yes!' she exclaimed. 'Children stayed in the nursery when I started. There was little change from nursery routine.'

'So tell us the biggest change,' said Althea.

Nanny Singleton thought for a moment then she said, 'I think the way in which children are told absolutely everything these days,' she said. 'There's no mystery in life any more.'

Sue pulled a face. 'What do you mean?'

'I think milady has read just about every book on childcare, especially Doctor Spock,' Nanny Singleton continued. 'I remember her telling me once that she didn't want Master Georgie to be told fairy stories or untruths. So, one day when milady and I were in the garden, he came up to us and said, "Mama, where did I come from?"'

'What did you say?' Rita wanted to know.

'I didn't say anything,' said Nanny. 'Milady took him to one side and started telling him how she and daddy had loved each other very much...' Rita was aware that Althea and Sue were beginning to look a bit uncomfortable. 'She told him everything,' Nanny went on. 'How they got married and how daddy put his seed into mummy's love pouch and after a few months, the seed grew and grew until Georgie was ready to come down the love pouch and into the world.'

Rita's eyes were wide open.

'Crumbs,' said Sue. 'I'm not sure I'd have told him all that. How old was he?'

'Four,' said Nanny, 'and I agree with you, even if it is the modern way of doing things.'

'Was he all right about it?' asked Althea.

'Well,' said Nanny, 'I did think he looked a little confused at the time, so when I had the opportunity, I said to him, "Master Georgie, why did you ask Mama where you came from?" And he said, "Johnny—" that's the son of the gardener and they play together a lot "—Johnny said he came from London, so I asked Mama were I came from."'

They sat staring at her for a moment in stunned silence then everyone, including Nanny Singleton, burst out laughing.

The kitchen door opened and a member of staff came into the room. 'We've finished,' she said. 'The children can all go home now.'

The three younger nannies hugged each other and shook hands with Nanny Singleton – all except Rita. Giving the older woman a gentle embrace, she said, 'Thank you, Nanny. You're an inspiration. If I could be a nanny half as good as you, I should be really pleased.'

'How sweet of you to say so my dear,' said Nanny Singleton, 'but your reputation goes before you. What you have done for little Lucy is nothing short of remarkable.'

Rita blinked. How did she know about Lucy? And what had she been told? But she would never know, because with a benevolent smile, Nanny Singleton gently patted her cheek and set off to find Master Georgie.

Back home, Lucy babbled away to her mother about the party and the wonderful time she had had. Although Mrs Knight appeared to give her daughter her full attention, it was obvious to Rita that her mind was elsewhere.

Chapter 36

'To Know You is to Love You'
Peter and Gordon

The house was quiet when Rita arrived back in Worthing on Friday evening for the wedding the next day. Her grandmother was sitting at the table with the photograph of her first husband on her lap and a faraway look on her face.

'Gran?'

Win turned her head. 'Oh, there you are darlin',' she said.

Rita was startled to her eyes were glassy with tears. 'Are you all right?' Her grandmother never cried.

Win nodded. 'Just remembering,' she said, her voice thick with emotion. Gently, she brushed the glass over her long-dead husband's face with her forefinger. 'I said I'd stay true to him all my life.'

Rita slid onto the chair next to her. 'And you have, Gran. Your marriage vow was "until death us do part", remember? You've been his widow long enough.'

Win sucked in her lips.

'I never knew granddad,' Rita ploughed on, 'but from what you've told me about him, he would want you to be happy.'

Win nodded grimly.

'And Eddie is a lovely man. He'll look after you in your old age.'

Win's body stiffened and the old Gran came back. 'I don't need looking after,' she said tetchily.

'All right, then,' Rita said with a smile. 'You can look after him.'

Her grandmother patted Rita's hands. 'I'll put the kettle on.'

There wasn't a lot left to do to prepare for the wedding. All week, Gran had baked for England and the larder was stuffed to the gunnels with cake tins. Apparently, some of the WI ladies were going to make sandwiches in the morning, and the reception was to be in St Mary's church hall which was in the grounds of the church itself. Gran's friends from the village were setting up and decorating the hall that evening and she had been strictly banned from going to help. Everyone saw this as their opportunity to give something back to the woman who had been there for so many in sickness and bereavements.

'So, tell me what you've been doing?' said Gran as they settled back to relax after their evening meal.

Rita hadn't wanted to go into a lot of detail about her situation with Mrs Knight so she didn't, but she did say that she was most likely going to look for a new post. 'Little Lucy will be going to school next term,' she said making this her excuse, 'and I should like a post with more money. I may go to America to see Dexter and I need to save up for the fare.'

'Won't he pay for you to go?' Gran said indignantly.

'I'm your granddaughter, Gran,' she teased. 'I pay my own way.'

Win smiled contentedly. 'I read his letters,' she admitted. 'And you were right, I had him all wrong.'

'We both did,' said Rita.

'It's not going to be easy,' Gran cautioned, 'meeting his new wife and family.'

'Maybe not,' said Rita, 'but it's something I want to do.'

Her grandmother looked thoughtful. 'We must make another decision, you and I. What are we going to do with this place?'

Rita blinked in surprise. Oh yes, of course, tomorrow was the wedding and then the honeymoon, after which Gran would be living next door with Eddie. This house, her old home, would be empty.

'You don't have to decide now,' said Gran, 'but do we sell up, do we leave it empty as a bolt hole for you to come back to whenever you need to, or do we rent it out?'

Rita's mind went blank.

'Don't worry about it now, love,' her grandmother repeated. 'Think about it.'

They spent a quiet evening together watching *Emergency Ward 10* followed by an episode of *Armchair Theatre* on TV and then they went to bed early.

The weather for Win and Eddie's wedding day was a little cooler than of late. The sun was hazy rather than bright and there was a gentle breeze which had come up from the sea. Gran was up with the lark of course, and by the time Rita appeared she'd done her morning jobs like feeding the chickens and watering the sweet peas, after which they ate a light breakfast.

As soon as Rita had cleared the table, a steady stream of visitors began to come to the house. Nobody needed to be told what to do. Whatever role they had was done with precision like a well-rehearsed, well-oiled machine. Two ladies emptied the larder of cakes and put the tins into an old pram before wheeling them away. Someone else came for some sheets which Gran had left at the bottom of the stairs and they raided her dresser drawers for tablecloths. Elsie Warren, who lived in one of the malthouses further up the lane, turned up with her hairdressing equipment. She had a salon in the village but as an old friend of Gran's she'd come in person to wash and set her hair. Rita became chief tea maker and errand runner.

Still only in their petticoats at twelve, Rita and Gran had a quick bowl of soup before getting ready. Gran looked slightly ridiculous with her hair done and her hat on, but Elsie had fixed it so firmly it was best not to take it off again, and of course one look at each other started them off in a fit of the giggles.

Just after one o'clock, Rita helped her grandmother to step into her wedding dress. It was absolutely perfect. An ivory coloured short sleeved, knee-length sheath dress with a lace bodice and plain skirt together with a plain jacket with three quarter length sleeves and lace on the shoulders. It was elegant and stylish and showed off Gran's slim figure. She had chosen wisely as well; both the dress and the jacket could be worn with other outfits for other occasions.

'Oh, Gran,' Rita whispered. 'You look beautiful.'

Rita, her only bridesmaid, had a simple dress in peacock blue with a tight-fitting bodice and a chiffon knee-length skirt. She added a small bolero jacket with rhinestones along the neckline. Once again, her grandmother had erred on the side of practical. Rita would be able to dress it up for a party or dress it down for a more informal occasion.

The bride and groom were each going to walk to the church and, in keeping with the tradition that the groom should not see his bride before the wedding ceremony, Rita went into the front room to check when Eddie came out of his house. At one forty-five, she gave Win the all-clear.

'Ready?' she said.

Her grandmother took a deep breath and nodded. They came out of the back door together. Rita locked the door and put the key behind the water butt. The lane was clear as they walked out of the gate. It was no more than two hundred yards to the road, but Rita hurried ahead to check that Eddie and his best man – his son – were out of sight.

As they emerged onto Sea Lane a few villagers were standing on the pavement calling out things like 'Good luck, Win,' and 'All the best, love.'

The man giving her away was waiting by the church door. Win had given that privilege to the winner of a raffle which had been held in the Conservative Club on Mulberry Lane. It was a bit of a risk, but Win didn't care. The raffle had raised nearly twenty pounds for the children's ward in Worthing Hospital. The winner turned out to be the local newsagent who was beaming like a Cheshire cat.

Rita led the way as the organist struck up 'Here Comes the Bride' and everybody rose to their feet as her grandmother followed her down the aisle.

After the ceremony and the photographs were taken, Win and Eddie went into the churchyard. She laid her bouquet on Cyril's grave and Eddie put his buttonhole on Maureen's. That done, they walked hand in hand to the hall and as they came through the door, a loud cheer went up and everybody clapped.

The reception itself was very enjoyable; Rita caught up with people she hadn't seen in years – her old primary school teacher, someone who had worked in the bank the same time as her mum did, a couple of old school chums and a lad she had gone out with for a while. He was now married with two rather snotty-nosed children.

'Somebody told me you were a nanny.' Rita turned but didn't recognise the face.

'Nathaniel Humphries,' he said. 'Nat. We used to play together.'

'Yes, yes of course,' she said. She could see it now, but only because he had reminded her. She would have passed him on the street and not realised. He'd grown into a tall and very handsome man. Rita hesitated. 'Nice to see you again. Yes, I am a nanny – I work for a family in Ewell.'

'Where's that?'

'Near Epsom in Surrey,' she said. 'Do you still live in Tarring?'

Nat shook his head. 'Mum moved to Teville Gate. I joined the merchant navy when I was sixteen.'

'Wow,' said Rita, although she already knew that. 'Do you enjoy it?'

'I do,' he said cautiously, 'but I'd prefer to be on a cruise ship.'

'I'd quite fancy that, too,' she chuckled. 'So why don't you go?'

'You have to be twenty-five,' he said, and lifting up his hand he counted his fingers.

'Four years to go.' Rita chuckled.

Nat's face suddenly went serious. 'I never saw you again after what happened to your mum. They never told me it was her that got shot and you simply vanished.'

'People tried to protect children from horrible things back then,' she said sagely and he nodded. 'I'm sorry.'

'I know.'

He hesitated then said, 'Can I get you some punch?'

'Yes please, Nat,' she said. 'And then you must sit beside me and tell me everything about the merchant navy.'

They ate sandwiches and cake and then came the speeches. Win and Eddie were clearly popular people and everybody wished them well. They cut the cake and at four thirty, Eddie took his bride back home to change into their going away outfits. He'd booked a hotel near Bournemouth for a week and they were to drive down that evening.

Rita and Nat had enjoyed the afternoon together. They'd reminisced about the games they'd played as children and especially the time he'd got into trouble for taking aim at Rita with a catapult.

'When I look back,' he said, 'I can't believe I did that. It was so dangerous.'

'We were only kids,' she said. 'Anyway, don't take all the blame. I was a chump agreeing to stand there while you played William Tell with your catapult.'

'Don't,' he shuddered. 'When she found out, the look your mum gave me could have made hell freeze over.' He stared at Rita in an almost perfect imitation glare.

She laughed. 'She could stop me in my tracks with that look too. I just remember that when you hit me in the face with that fir cone all you could say was, "don't tell your mum, don't tell your mum". The bruise on my cheek lasted a whole week!'

He looked horrified. 'I could have taken your eye out.'

'But you didn't,' she said comfortingly. 'Look it's still there.'

'And very pretty it is too,' he said, making her blush.

The happy couple reappeared just before six; Eddie in a new suit and Win wearing a silky blouse under a lightweight blue two-piece. Her hat had a wide brim which she had pulled rakishly over to one side.

'Your Gran looks amazing,' Nat whispered in Rita's ear and she nodded proudly.

As the cameraman took more photos, Nat said, 'Let's not lose touch again, Rita. I'm not home very often, but I'd like to see you again.'

Rita smiled shyly. 'Me too.'

Having posed for a few more photographs, the happy couple said their goodbyes.

'Thank you for a wonderful day darlin',' Gran said as she gave Rita a proper hug.

'It has been wonderful hasn't it,' said Rita. 'Now off you go and enjoy the rest of your life with Eddie.' Rita kissed her cheek. 'No looking back.'

Her grandmother chuckled. 'No looking back.'

Chapter 37

'Almost There'
Andy Williams

Rita arrived back in Ewell by late morning on Monday. As she walked onto the close with her suitcase, Mrs Fordham and Sally were coming out of the front gate. Sally seemed visibly upset and Mrs Fordham had a face as black as thunder.

'Hello,' Rita said. 'Is something the matter?'

'If you'll take my advice you'll turn around and go straight back home,' Mrs Fordham snapped. 'They should have locked that man up and thrown away the key.'

Rita frowned. 'What man?'

'Mr Knight,' said Sally, her voice brittle.

'Mr Knight!' Rita exclaimed, 'but he's on remand until the trial, isn't he?' Looking at their expressions, her heart sank. 'Don't tell me they've let him out. Why?'

Sally shrugged. Mrs Fordham's lip curled. 'Oh, come on,' she said viciously. 'You know very well why. Rich people, clever lawyers; that lot get away with blue bloody murder.'

Rita blinked. She'd never seen Mrs Fordham like this before.

'I'm sorry, love,' said Mrs Fordham immediately repentant. 'I shouldn't have taken it out on you. It's just that I feel so bloody angry.'

'So, what happened?' Rita asked. 'Was he rude to you or something?'

'He found out that Mrs Knight had paid us what we was owed,' said Sally. 'They had a big bust up about it and then he told us to give him the money back or get out and never come back.'

Now Rita was even more confused. 'I'm sorry, I don't understand.'

Mrs Fordham came closer. 'She sold her jewellery to pay us,' she said confidentially.

'And he didn't like it,' Sally added.

'He's as mad as a box of frogs,' said Mrs Fordham. 'Get out while you can, girl.'

Rita looked up at the house. They could all hear shrill voices and then there was the sound of a crash. 'The children...' she murmured as she stepped onto the path.

Mrs Fordham snatched at her arm. 'Let me give you my phone number,' she said, hurriedly opening her handbag. 'Phone me this evening to let me know you're all right.' She was scribbling a number on a page from her diary. 'If you don't ring, I shall go to the police.' She tore out the page and handed it to Rita.

Rita stuffed it into her pocket and hurried towards the door.

'Good luck,' Sally called after her.

Rita rang the doorbell but nobody came, so she went round the back. Luckily the kitchen door was ajar so she went in calling, 'Hello, hello. Is anyone at home?'

There was a sign of a struggle in the hallway. The coat stand had been knocked over and the coats were strewn all over the floor. Rita's heart began to thump. Putting her suitcase down, she looked in the sitting room. The French doors were wide open and she caught a glimpse of Cameron striding across the lawn to his music den. She breathed a sigh of relief. Well at least he was out of the way for a bit. Calling as she went, Rita mounted the stairs. She could hear Daniel crying in the nursery. The door was firmly shut, something which never happened. Rita opened the door and the baby's desperate cries speared her heart. He was more upset than she'd ever seen him before. Hurrying to the cot, she found him kicking his legs and waving his arms. 'It's all right, poppet,' she soothed. 'It's okay.'

At the sound of her voice, he quietened a little but he was still upset. As Rita leaned in and picked him up, she could hear someone else sobbing in the room. With the baby in her arms, she turned. The voice was Lucy's but where was she? 'Lucy? Lucy, where are you?'

She heard a rustling sound and Lucy's foot appeared from the small gap between the cupboard and the wardrobe. Rita hurried over to her.

She had pushed herself right against the wall. Her face was pink and wet with tears. Rita got down on the floor and with Daniel, calmer now as he lay in the crook of her right arm, she held out her left arm to his sister. Wriggling on her bottom, Lucy came out from her hiding place and Rita cuddled her close until she managed to stop crying.

'It's okay, sweetie,' she said gently. 'It's all right now.'

As soon as she stopped crying, Lucy put her arm around her brother. 'It's all right,' she said repeating Rita's words. 'Rita is here now.' Daniel reacted with a small lopsided smile.

Rita sat quietly with them for a few minutes. She knew it was important to fully restore their sense of safety, but where was Mrs Knight? She had made no attempt to comfort her children, which as far as Rita was concerned was completely out of character for her. Rita was also a little afraid of what she might find when she eventually had to go and look for her. Mrs Fordham had said Cameron was as mad as a box of frogs. Had he done something to his wife?

The sound of music drifted through the open window and Rita relaxed a little. He was obviously practising his songs and with a bit of luck he would be in there for hours.

'Can you tell me what happened?' Rita asked casually. It was important that Lucy didn't feel panicked again.

'I was giving Daniel a cuddle,' she said, 'and Daddy got really cross with me.' Her eyes began to fill again. Rita pulled her close. What could she say to that? *Oh I'm sure he didn't mean it* – he most likely did. *Are you sure you were only cuddling Daniel?* Rita might have asked that question a few weeks ago, but not now. Lucy and Daniel had a good relationship. *Daddy was scared you were going to hurt Daniel.* That would only confuse the child. 'Well,' she said, 'I know how much you love Daniel and how much he loves you, too.'

Lucy reached out and rubbed her little brother's leg.

After a minute or two, Rita started to get up. 'Listen, sweetie,' she said, keeping her voice light, 'I must go and look for Mummy. She's probably having a little lie-down but I should tell her I'm back now. Can you look after Daniel for me while I go and find her?'

Lucy puffed her chest as she nodded. Rita laid the baby on the floor and he kicked his legs as Lucy waggled a toy teddy in front of him.

'Shan't be a minute,' Rita assured her.

As it turned out, she didn't have to look for her employer. As Rita opened the door of the nursery wide, Mrs Knight was coming towards it. She looked an absolute mess. She was still in her dressing gown, her hair was wild and she was unsteady on her feet. She was holding her head.

'Mrs Knight!' Rita exclaimed. 'Are you all right?'

'The children,' she said shakily.

'Are fine,' said Rita. 'They were a bit upset but they're okay now.'

Her employer had an ugly red weal across her cheek. Rita wondered whether to say something but she would most likely get the same old 'walked into the cupboard door' explanation. 'Can I get you something, ma'am? A cup of tea; a cup of coffee?'

Mrs Knight shook her head. 'No thank you, nanny.' She hesitated. 'I think I'd better go and get dressed.' And with that she turned and wobbled away.

Rita spent the rest of the morning seeing to the children then clearing the mess downstairs before raiding the larder to find something for Lucy's lunch. A little later Mrs Knight reappeared, fully dressed but without make-up.

While she'd been on her own with the children, Rita had done a lot of thinking. There was no way she wanted to stay in this house with Cameron. There were happy drunks and belligerent drunks and presumably it was the same with drug addicts. The only problem was that she still felt a sense of loyalty towards Mrs Knight and the children. She was also concerned about Lucy. The child had already suffered mental abuse and now she could be in danger of physical abuse as well, especially if her father was back to attacking her mother.

The two women focused on the children until Daniel was upstairs in his cot and Rita had settled Lucy in a corner of the sitting room with a book. It was only then that Mrs Knight and Rita addressed the elephant in the room.

'I don't think I can stay here under the circumstances,' Rita began apologetically. She spoke in low tones so that Lucy couldn't hear.

Mrs Knight nodded. 'I think I have to make a serious sea change as well, Nanny.' She sighed. 'I have tried, by God I have tried, but I have to think of my children now.'

'I will do all I can to help, ma'am,' said Rita.

'And you've done wonders with Lucy,' said Mrs Knight. 'She's a completely different child.' There was a small silence then she added, 'When I leave him, I won't be able to afford to keep you on.'

Rita had already guessed that. If her employer had already sold her possessions to pay Mrs Fordham and Sally, it was obvious there was nothing in the bank.

'It's not going to be easy to leave him.' Mrs Knight gave her a long hard look. 'I had Lucy before we married and she isn't his daughter,' she said. 'I don't think my husband gives a fig about her or me, but he will fight to the death to keep his son.'

'If you don't mind me saying so,' Rita said cautiously, 'I don't think you need to worry about that. The authorities wouldn't allow it. He's in no fit state to look after him.'

Mrs Knight laughed sardonically. 'That won't stop him.'

'So what will you do? Where will you go?'

Mrs Knight shrugged.

'Do you have family? Can they help?'

'My family cut me off when I married Cameron,' she said.

'But surely now...' Rita hinted.

'That would be a pretty big slice of humble pie,' Mrs Knight said bitterly.

The room suddenly went dark. They looked up and Cameron was standing by the French windows. 'What are you two witches cooking up?' His voice was slurred and Rita guessed he was on something.

Lucy got up and disappeared behind the armchair.

'If you want something to eat,' his wife said coldly, 'we've left it on a plate in the kitchen.'

Without another word, her husband headed towards the kitchen.

'I'll go and check on Daniel,' said Rita rising to her feet. 'Lucy.' A small face peered around the chair and Rita held out her hand as the child ran to her.

They went upstairs and even before they reached the nursery, Rita could hear raised voices. It seemed best to take the children out, so having changed Daniel's nappy, they set off for the village. It was a glorious day and everybody needed cheering up so a couple of Country Maid wafer ice creams did the trick. Rita and Lucy let Daniel have a bit of theirs, 'But only a bit,' Rita cautioned. 'We don't want an upset tummy,' and the time they all spent together was fun.

Back at the house, things were obviously no better, so Rita had an awkward evening. She really needed to talk to Mrs Knight again about the next step but with Cameron hanging around there was no chance of a private discussion. She was also scared that if Mrs Knight told Cameron she was leaving him, he was just as likely to attack her again. And what then? Daniel was probably safe but what of Lucy? It was all very frustrating.

When she put the children to bed, Cameron came into the nursery. He was wearing a pair of tight jeans and a white T-shirt but no shoes. Lucy, who was in her bed, pulled her covers over her head. Rita was just about to lay Daniel down in his cot.

He came towards her with a leery grin. 'Did anyone ever tell you you've got a lovely sexy bum,' he began.

Rita straightened up and looked at him coldly, noticing that his pupils were dilated. 'I'll thank you not to address me in that way... sir.' As she said 'sir' she hoped her sarcasm wasn't wasted. She was trembling and her heart was thumping in her chest – not from excitement as it might have been when she first took this job – but with indignation and anger. This man was despicable. His wife was just down the hall and what sort of a father was he? His son may be very young but Lucy was nearby and this was no way to behave.

'Ooh,' he said in a sing-song voice. 'Listen to you. Proper ice maiden aren't you?' He reached his hand out towards her and Rita noticed that he was trembling. 'I can soon change all that,' he said in a lecherous voice.

Rita stood her ground and said coldly, 'Touch me again and I'll be on that phone quicker than you can blink.' And remembering what Nat had said about her mother's 'look', she gave him her stoniest glare.

His hand went down. 'Nah, don't think I'll bother,' he said. His lip curled and his voice was full of contempt. 'Who'd want to kiss you anyway, you frigid cow? You've got a mouth like a cat's bum.'

And turning on his heel, he left the room.

Rita's legs had gone to jelly and she had to grab the cot side to steady herself. Like any good nursery nurse, she smiled and behaved as if everything was fine in front of the children. It wasn't until she left the room that she allowed her tears to fall.

Alone in her bedroom, she stared at herself in the mirror and touched her lips. Cameron Knight was a pig, there was no doubt about that. She had stood her ground, but his nasty remark would stay with her for a long time.

And oh, how it hurt.

Chapter 38

'The Little Engine that Could'
Burl Ives
BBC Light Programme, *Children's Favourites*

As soon as she felt up to it, Rita snuck downstairs to the sitting room to use the telephone. She had to be quick. Having reassured Mrs Fordham that she was all right, Rita hurried back upstairs to her room.

There had been little opportunity to talk to Mrs Knight. Now, Rita could hear that her employers were having another row and after what sounded like yet more verbal abuse from Cameron, everything went quiet. Something made Rita put the chair against the doorknob. About twenty minutes later, she was glad that she had done so; the doorknob turned but whoever was on the other side couldn't get in.

It was late when she heard Cameron's heavy tread going downstairs. A few minutes afterwards, she heard the back door slam. She looked out of the window and saw him walking unsteadily towards the den. He was in no hurry and wore no coat despite the fact that it had been raining steadily all evening.

Rita grabbed her washbag and hurried to the bathroom to wash and clean her teeth. Outside, the sound of pounding music filled the air; inside, the telephone was ringing.

On the way back to her room, she looked in on the children. Daniel was awake but quiet. He rolled slightly as she walked up to the cot and made a cooing sound.

'What are you doing awake young man?' she whispered.

He bumped his feet on the mattress and smiled.

Rita glanced towards Lucy's bed and her heart nearly stopped. It was empty.

'Where's your big sister gone?' She looked around the room and there she was again; stuffed in the tiny space between the cupboard and wardrobe.

'What are you doing out of bed, sweetie?' said Rita. She crouched down to Lucy's level and was alarmed by the expression on her face. 'Lucy? Are you all right?'

As Rita encouraged the little girl to come out of her hiding place, she wondered why both her hands were tightly fisted. 'What have you got there?' She had to coax the child to open her hands and when she did, Rita started to panic. There was a small blue tablet in each hand.

'Where did you get these, Lucy?' Rita was doing her best to sound casual even though she could feel the anxiety inside rising. She didn't want Lucy to clam up. These were some sort of pill but what was she doing with them? And how had she got them?

'Daddy gave me his sweeties,' she said, 'but I didn't like it.'

Rita reached up to the drawer and took out a clean handkerchief. 'If you don't like them, put them on here,' she said unfolding it. Elsewhere in the house, the telephone was ringing again.

Lucy put one tablet onto the handkerchief but the one in her right hand was reluctant to move. It remained stuck to her palm. It was then that Rita could see it was slightly darker than the first one, most likely because it had been made wet. 'Open your mouth,' said Rita. 'Have you got one in your mouth?'

Lucy opened her mouth. It was empty but there was a telltale blue stain in the middle of her tongue. 'Stick your tongue out, sweetie.' The child did as she was told and Rita quickly wiped it with the refolded handkerchief. Lucy retched but she wasn't sick. 'There now,' said Rita, 'has the nasty taste gone?'

The child nodded.

Rita cuddled her close. What was she going to do? That pill was most likely some sort of drug. She knew there was a new drug from America called LSD and someone had once told her that it tasted metallic which could be the reason Lucy didn't like it. Surely it had to be dangerous to give such a thing to a child? She suddenly shivered. What if Lucy had already swallowed a tablet? She seemed all right but Rita couldn't be sure. She couldn't leave it, could she? Somehow or other she had to get her to a doctor.

'Jump into bed,' said Rita. She didn't want the child panicked any more than she already had been, and she didn't want to take her with her when she went to look for her mum, but she couldn't leave her on her own very long.

As she was tucking the bedclothes around her, Rita's mind was working overtime. If Mrs Knight wouldn't do it, she would have to get the police involved herself. Having settled them both, she looked out of the window. The door to the den was wide open and the light spilled onto the darkened garden. With the door open, the music was blaring out, but Mr Knight might not stay outside for long – if she was to get help and the wheels in motion, Rita had to be quick. Checking that Lucy still seemed okay, Rita kissed her forehead. 'I'll be back in a minute.'

It went against everything she knew to leave the child, even for a minute. As Rita knocked on Mrs Knight's door, the telephone was ringing for a third time. Her employer was sitting up in bed. She looked awful. Her forehead was bloodied and her lip swollen. 'Mrs Knight!' Rita exclaimed as she hurried to her side. 'What on earth has happened?'

'The neighbours keep ringing to complain about the noise,' she said weakly.

'I don't give a hang about the noise,' Rita said fiercely. 'I mean what happened to you!'

Mrs Knight's eyes filled with tears.

'Listen,' said Rita. 'I'm going to ring for an ambulance.'

'No, no,' she cried as she snatched at Rita's arm. 'For God's sake don't do that. He'll go ballistic.'

'We've got to get you to a doctor,' said Rita.

Her employer patted her arm. 'I'll be all right in the morning.'

Having seen the state she was in, Rita hadn't wanted to worry Mrs Knight about her suspicions in the children's room, but it was obvious that her employer needed help as much as Lucy. The child seemed okay for now, but if Cameron had given her LSD or some other weird drug, who knew what might happen to Lucy during the night?

'We've got to go to the hospital Mrs Knight,' Rita repeated. 'I don't want to alarm you, but I think your husband has given Lucy something.'

Mrs Knight was tidying the bedclothes and didn't seem to comprehend what she was saying.

'I think your husband has given Lucy some sort of pill.'

The telephone began to ring again.

Suddenly, her employer's eyes grew wide. 'What?'

'I found her clutching two odd looking pills she called her daddy's sweeties,' Rita continued. 'I don't think she swallowed any because she didn't like the taste, but I can't be sure.'

Whoever was on the telephone rang off abruptly.

Mrs Knight was already out of bed but judging by her unsteady movements, it was obvious she was either drugged herself or concussed. Rita knew then that *she* had to telephone the police. She reached for the telephone beside the bed first but when she put it to her ear, there was no sound. 'He's cut the wire,' she said quietly.

'Oh God,' Mrs Knight's voice wobbled.

'I'll take you in the car,' Rita said firmly.

They heard a footfall on the stairs. 'He's coming,' Mrs Knight squeaked. 'Quick, hide in my dressing room.'

Rita only just had time to push herself between the rows of Mrs Knight's dresses before the bedroom door began to open.

'Oh Cam, darling,' she heard her say. 'Look at the state of you. You're soaked to the skin.'

'It's raining,' he slurred.

'No, no,' cried Mrs Knight. 'Don't sit on the bed. Let's get you out of those wet things and I'll run you a bath.'

'I don't want a bloody bath.'

'Then have a shower darling. You must get out of those wet things or you'll catch your death of cold.'

Through the crack of the open door, Rita saw his wife trying to take his sweater off but he pushed her roughly away. *Come on, come on*, she thought desperately. *We've got to get Lucy to a doctor.*

Now someone was banging on the front door. 'Turn that blasted row off, Knight,' whoever it was yelled through the letter box. 'It's one in the morning and you've got half the neighbourhood wide awake.'

Lucy began to scream and Rita could hear the baby's reedy cry. The next second, the music suddenly stopped and the lights went off.

'What's he done?' Cameron shouted angrily. 'He's turned off my music. He's touched my stuff.'

She heard him cursing and swearing as he thundered down the stairs and then she came out of the closet. Mrs Knight was motionless in the middle of the room. Rita heard Cameron yanking the front door open and then there was a lot of angry shouting. It sounded as if the neighbours were out in force. There was definitely more than one person on the doorstep. Mrs Knight was still standing there as if frozen to the spot.

'Quick,' said Rita taking charge. 'Get dressed. We must get the children to the hospital.'

Her employer started as if she'd only just heard her distressed children for the first time. Rita hurried to their bedroom. Both children were obviously terrified of the noise and the dark. Fortunately, it was a moonlit night so although all the lights seemed to be off and not working, when Rita pulled the curtains, they could see each other fairly clearly. Bundling Lucy into her dressing gown, Rita said gently, 'Shh, shh. We're playing a special game. We have to be as quiet as mice and creep downstairs. Mummy is coming too. Okay?'

Lucy choked back her tears and nodded. Mrs Knight appeared in the room fully dressed. The row downstairs hadn't abated but it had moved outside and towards the den.

Cameron was furious. 'If you've damaged any of my stuff, I'll sue.'

'I've only thrown the switch,' someone said.

'You've no right to come in here and turn the electricity off. Who the hell do you think you are?'

'I wouldn't have to if you weren't such a bloody lunatic,' somebody told him. 'My wife is a nurse and she has to be on duty at seven tomorrow morning.'

The two women hurried down the stairs. Mrs Knight held Lucy's hand and Rita carried the baby. On their way through the kitchen, Rita grabbed Daniel's morning bottle from the fridge. He was very upset and although it would be ice cold, she was fairly confident that someone would warm it for them at the hospital. They had to go out via the back door because the car keys were kept in the laundry room. As she grabbed Mrs Knight's car keys, Rita's fingers touched the keys to Cameron's Alpha Romeo. It gave her a frightening thought. What if he grabbed his car keys and came after them? He drove like a madman at the best of times but now that he was angry, who knows what he might do. That's when she got an idea. Lifting the lid of the Napisan bucket, she pushed the keys inside. She was confident that he wouldn't look for them in there and if he did, the way he had been revolted by the soiled nappies when she was wringing them out in the laundry room, convinced her he wouldn't want to plunge his hand in the bucket to get the keys.

Through the window in the back door, they could see Cameron and the neighbours on the lawn. There was a lot of pushing and shoving going on but eventually Cameron reached the den and a second later the lights were back on and the music started up again. The angry shouting grew louder.

As Rita and her employer came out of the house, they saw one neighbour take a swing at Mr Knight. All at once, he seemed to have the strength of ten men. Three of their neighbours were punched, kicked and manhandled back onto the lawn.

By now, Rita and Mrs Knight had reached and opened the garage door. Rita unlocked the car and Mrs Knight slid onto the back seat. Lucy was next to her and Rita handed her the baby before climbing into the driver's seat. She started the engine and the sound of it roared into the night.

'Hey!' They heard Cameron yell. 'Where the hell do you think you're going?' He began to run towards them shouting. 'Come back here, bitch!'

Her heart racing, Rita put her foot down and the car kangaroo jumped onto the driveway. Mrs Knight locked her door and leaned over to do the same on the other side. She pulled Lucy down to the floor and crouched down herself so that they couldn't be seen. Lucy began to cry again and Daniel, still in his mother's arms, was beside himself. With Cameron coming ever closer, Rita was in panic mode. He reached the car's front passenger door and pulled it open. Rita squealed and lurched forward, stalling the engine. The jerk of the car had made him stumble. He recovered himself quickly, but the car door had slammed back shut. Rita leaned over and locked it.

'Go on, go on,' Mrs Knight hissed from the back.

Rita started the engine again and just as Cameron reached out for the door again, she jerked the car onto the road. *Thank God, thank God*, she thought, but at exactly the same moment, a police car, siren blaring, came flying onto the close and pulled up sharply in front of the bonnet, in effect trapping them where they were.

Cameron began hammering on the passenger door window. 'Open this door,' he shrieked. 'Open this door now.'

A policeman got out of the patrol car. 'What's going on here?'

'That woman is my child's nanny,' Cameron bellowed, 'and she's kidnapping my son.'

Chapter 39

'You've Got Your Troubles'
The Fortunes

The policeman knocked on the driver's window and said coldly, 'Open the door, Miss.'

'I can't,' said Rita. He didn't understand. If Cameron made a grab for Daniel, they'd never get to the hospital.

By now the policeman was surrounded by at least four angry men. Most of what they were saying was incoherent because they were all shouting at once, but Rita caught a few sentences.

'Why don't you arrest him? That bloody row has been going full blast half the night.'

'Harry pulled the plug, but he put it back on again and kicked him in the goolies.'

'Look at him. He's as high as a kite. Get the bloody cuffs on.'

Eventually, the policeman threw his hands into the air. 'That's enough. Be quiet!'

'What are we going to do?' Rita asked Mrs Knight anxiously. She was still crouched on the floor with the children. 'If I get out he'll go for me for sure.'

Cameron began banging the roof of the car with his fist. 'I want my son.'

The second policeman climbed out of the patrol car and sauntered over.

One of the angry neighbours ran up to the group. 'Listen mate,' he said, 'we need an ambulance. Harry Hawksworth is lying on the grass over there unconscious. That lunatic—' he pointed at Cameron '—kicked him where the sun don't shine and he went out like a light.'

'Go and have a look will you, Tom,' said the first policeman. Then, turning to Cameron he said, 'Stop thumping that car will you, sir. It's getting us nowhere.'

They all looked around as another police car, sirens wailing, pulled into the close and two more officers came over. After a short conversation between them, another policeman came up to the car and gesticulated that Rita should wind down the window.

'I have to get these children to hospital,' she began but just then Cameron rushed around the car and pushed the officer away.

'You bloody bitch,' he spat. 'Give me my boy.' He made a grab at Rita's hair and she screamed as her head went through the narrow gap between the window and the door frame. It took all three officers to pull him away.

Once they'd got him off her, Rita wound up the window. Her head really hurt. When she ran her fingers around, everything seemed to be there, but the pain felt like half her hair had been pulled out by the roots. She watched through the windscreen as they handcuffed Cameron and manhandled him into the back of the second police car. One of the officers came back.

'He says you're taking his kid without his permission.'

'I am,' Rita began, 'but…'

'Then I won't tell you again, Miss. Get out of the car.'

It was at that moment that Mrs Knight sat up. 'I'm the children's mother. Rita has my permission and we really need to go.'

Rita fished in her pocket and took out the folded handkerchief. 'I found Lucy with these pills in her hand. She had blue stains on her tongue as well. She's only four. I think he's given her some sort of illegal drug so we need to get the children medical help.'

The policeman shone his torch onto the handkerchief. 'Right,' he said, his attitude and demeanour immediately changed. 'Follow me.'

They reached Epsom Hospital on the Dorking Road in double quick time, the Winkworth bell on the black Wolseley police car carving a path through what little traffic was still on the road at almost two in the morning. The children were rushed to Accident and Emergency and Mrs Knight explained what had happened, while Rita showed the doctor the blue tablets Lucy had been holding. She gave a nurse Daniel's bottle and both children were whisked away with only their mother allowed to stay with them.

Exhausted and with her head still throbbing, Rita sat in the corner of the empty waiting room for twenty minutes without moving. A policeman came up to ask her some questions. Who gave Lucy the pill? Her father. Why? Rita didn't know. She fished for the sugar cube wrapped in foil which was now in her pocket. Then she told him about Mrs Knight and her suspicions that her husband's girlfriend had tried to drug her and how she'd hidden the lump in the backseat ash tray of Mrs Knight's car. 'I was pretty sure no one would think of looking in there,' she told him. 'It has a secret button which you can't see unless someone shows you.'

As he put it into an evidence bag, he said, 'It may not be much use after all this time. It may have degraded.'

When he finally left her, all the what if's were going round and round in her head. *What if* she hadn't looked in on the children before she went to bed? *What if* with all this delay it was already too late. *What if* she hadn't managed to get Mrs Knight on her side? The poor woman was obviously not functioning properly – but why? It was obvious that Cameron had hit her, but was there another reason for her aloofness? Rita could only hope that the doctors would examine her as well.

As she sat in the dimly lit waiting area, she came to the firm decision that there was absolutely no way she could stay in this job a minute longer. She loved Lucy and Daniel but their family set-up was truly awful. Then, another disturbing thought crossed her mind. She'd signed that non-disclosure thing and now she had told the police about those pills and the sugar lump. What if Cameron found out? Maybe when she was in the car he'd even heard her telling them. No, he couldn't have done. He was already handcuffed in the police car. All she had said was that she needed to get the children to hospital. Oh Lord, that was as good as spilling the beans, wasn't it. If they took her to court, her career would be finished.

Despite her churning anxiety, it was a struggle to keep her eyes open. The clock on the wall told her it was three fifteen. She pulled a couple of chairs closer and lay on the seats of all three. They were as hard as a brick but it was a relief just to lie down. Her head where he'd pulled her hair was still throbbing. As she closed her eyes another disturbing thought came to mind. *What if* she really was in trouble with the law? It would certainly put paid to ever getting to America. Oh, the irony of it. After all this time, she had just found her father and now she might never get to be with him. Who would have thought working in private nursing could be such a minefield!

She felt a tear roll over the side of her nose. One of her tutors at college used to say, 'A good nursery nurse never shows her feelings when on duty.' Angrily wiping her tear away, Rita had never felt more miserable.

She hadn't meant to sleep but what seemed like five minutes later, Rita felt someone shaking her shoulder. When she opened her eyes, Rita was shocked to see that it was daylight and the clock on the wall said five to six.

'Rita, are you awake?' It was Mrs Knight.

Rita sat up and willed her brain to focus. 'How are the children?'

'They're fine. The doctors examined them thoroughly and it seems that Lucy did put one of those pills in her mouth but thankfully she didn't keep it in there long enough to do any harm.'

'Have they any idea what it was?'

'Diazepam. Cam takes it for his anxiety.'

Rita gasped. 'And he gave Lucy two tablets? If she'd swallowed them both they could have killed her.'

Mrs Knight nodded. 'I could say he didn't know what he was doing but he's never liked my daughter.' She squeezed Rita's hands. 'Good job you found them when you did.'

'Thank God,' said Rita, her voice thick with emotion and her tears threatening to return.

'We owe you a great deal, Rita,' Mrs Knight continued. 'If you hadn't…'

She looked up at her employer and waved her hand in a gesture as she sat up. It was only then that she noticed that Mrs Knight had a plaster on the side of her head. 'What about you?'

'They said I had a slight concussion. I'm all patched up now and ready to go.'

Rita yawned. 'So what now?'

Mrs Knight sat beside her. 'The police tell me my husband will be released at eight thirty. They say he'll probably be charged with something else but they have to get the evidence first.' She took a deep breath. 'I'm leaving him, Rita,' she continued. 'I've finally come to my senses.'

Rita nodded. If she had been a friend, she would have given her a hug.

'I want to ask you one last favour.'

'Of course,' said Rita. 'What do you want me to do?'

'Take me back home. The children are still sleeping and the nurses have promised to give them some breakfast. They tell me not to drive because my head is still all over the place. If we go now, I could pack a bag for me and the children before he's let out.'

'Where will you go?'

Mrs Knight shrugged. 'A hotel somewhere until I can get things sorted.'

Rita smiled. 'You won't need a hotel, ma'am. I know just the place and he'll never find you there.'

Back at the house in Ewell, Rita had grabbed all of her things and then helped Mrs Knight to take only what was necessary for the time being. They made sure they had Lucy's favourite toy and the little piece of blanket Daniel had grown to love. By eight o'clock they were back in the hospital to collect the children, and by the time Cameron was due to be released, they were already on the road.

They arrived in Worthing in the early afternoon. The cottage had that cosy, love-filled feeling as they walk in. 'Oh Rita, it's charming,' Mrs Knight exclaimed.

'It's much smaller than you're used to,' Rita said, though why she felt the urge to be apologetic she wasn't sure.

'It's perfect.'

Rita resisted the urge to tell her she might not think so when she knew about the bath under the boards in the kitchen and the outside lavvy. Still, she'd find out soon enough and even if it might not seem so perfect then, it was a place of safety.

Lucy loved it. She thundered upstairs and then down the garden. Seeing the chickens was an absolute revelation to her and when Rita told her they laid the eggs she loved to have at breakfast, she was fascinated.

Their surprise visit was not without its problems. There was no cot for Daniel so they decided to make do with using the deep bottom drawer from the chest of drawers for his bed. This worked as a temporary solution but couldn't be a permanent one. Daniel was becoming active now and it wouldn't be long before he'd be rolling out over the side. Mrs Knight and Lucy could sleep in the same room in Gran's old double bed, meaning that Rita could use her old room.

Of course, when Elsie Warren from the malthouses turned up to shut up the chickens, everything changed again. In no time at all, she had rallied help from just about everywhere; a cot for Daniel which her husband put up for them, an old pram which would be useful, even though the wheels squeaked a little and it was a tad lopsided, some toys for Lucy and a home-made pie and some cake for their tea. Rita was used to this sort of thing because her grandmother would have done just the same, but Mrs Knight was quite overcome with people's kindness.

Once the children were in bed and the two of them sat together at the kitchen table, Mrs Knight reached into her handbag and pulled out a long envelope. 'I keep meaning to give you this,' she said handing it to Rita. 'It's a bit grubby and I'm so sorry you've had to wait for it. I had no idea my husband had instructed the bank to stop all outgoings.'

Taking the creased and foxed envelope, Rita realised by the weight of it that it was her wage including back pay. 'Thank you. But how did you keep it from him?'

'It was in the bin in the kitchen,' she said sheepishly. 'You know how fussy Cam is about cleanliness.'

Rita nodded, remembering his car keys in the nappy bucket.

'I'm very grateful to you,' Mrs Knight added. 'You've gone above and beyond in every way.'

Rita demurred.

'I mean it,' Mrs Knight insisted.

'I'm afraid I've made a decision,' Rita began.

'There's no need to say it,' Mrs Knight interrupted. 'You want to go now and that's fine. Things must change for me as well.'

'Forgive me for saying so,' Rita began, 'but can't you contact your family for help?'

'I think I must,' she replied, 'although it won't be easy. My father can be rather overbearing. He never wanted me to marry Cameron in the first place and he refused to come to our wedding. He always thought he was a wastrel and he was right.' She sighed. 'It looks like I'm going to have to eat that large slice of humble pie after all.'

'Better that than trying to soldier on, on your own,' Rita said sagely.

'I shall telephone them tonight.'

'My grandmother doesn't have a phone,' Rita said apologetically.

'Oh!' It was clear that Mrs Knight had never heard of such a thing. 'So what do you do in an emergency?'

'There's a telephone box near the parade of shops,' said Rita. 'If you don't have enough cash, you can always ask the operator to reverse the charges.'

The next day felt almost like a holiday. Mrs Knight had finally telephoned her family later that evening. She had left the cottage at seven and returned an hour and a half later. All she would say was that they would come to fetch her sometime, so Rita suggested that, just for today, they made the most of the beach just down the road.

The early morning post had brought Rita a letter with a London postmark. When she opened it, it was from her father.

> *Just spoken to my wife by transatlantic telephone. She is so excited to meet you. Can you come to New York for Thanksgiving? All my love, Dexter.*

Worthing Borough Council were in the process of tidying up the seafront. When Rita was a girl, the now-pristine green had been a rough patch of wild grass, a haven for insects. A little further along Marine Crescent, between St John's Avenue and Alinora Avenue there had been a pond where she had lifted tadpoles in the spring and watched the pond skaters and dragonflies in the summer. All that had been cleared and it had been recreated as an area for ball games and picnics, a little sterile perhaps, but family friendly. The small hut at the end of Sea Lane where you could buy ice creams and tea was open, so Mrs Knight and the children sat on the beach close by. Lucy had a wonderful time filling up a bucket and making sandcastles when the tide was out. The pebbles on Goring-by-Sea made life a little challenging, but the weather made up for any inconveniences.

'There's something I have to tell you, ma'am,' Rita began. 'Only I hardly know where to start.'

Her employer gave her a quizzical look. 'Go on.'

So, Rita told her about her suspicions about Tammy-Jane. Mrs Knight was shocked but she confessed that now some things finally made sense. Her nausea, her unsteadiness, her terrible dreams and the fact that sometimes she would wake up with her heart racing. 'Did the policeman say what was in the sugar lump?'

Rita shook her head. 'He took it away for testing.'

They sat for a while in silence. Lucy came back up the stones to present her mother with a long strand of seaweed.

'What will you do now, Rita?' Mrs Knight asked when her daughter had gone again. 'Do you have a long-term plan for your life?'

Rita told her about Dexter which led to explaining what had happened to her mother. Then she told her about his invitation to spend Thanksgiving with his family.

'Thanksgiving is bigger than Christmas over there,' said Mrs Knight. 'Of course you must go to America.'

'I do worry a bit that my father's new wife might not be as keen as he thinks to have me in her home. After all, I am the result of a wartime dalliance.'

Mrs Knight shook her head sympathetically. 'It may not be as difficult as you imagine.'

But Rita wasn't so sure.

Chapter 40

'The Price of Love'

The Everly Brothers

The four of them, tired but happy, made their way back to the cottage at four. As she rounded the corner onto Jefferies Lane, Rita stopped dead.

'What?' said Mrs Knight. 'What is it?'

'There's a big car parked outside the house.'

Mrs Knight pushed Lucy behind her and came slowly towards Rita. Peering round the hedge, she took in a noisy breath.

'Do you recognise it?' Rita asked as she stepped back onto Sea Lane.

Mrs Knight shook her head.

'Could it belong to one of your husband's friends?'

All the colour had drained from her face. 'I don't know,' she whispered. 'How did he find us, Rita? Did you ever tell him your home address?'

'No,' Rita said earnestly. 'That's why I thought you'd be safe here.' She put her head around the hedge again. 'There's someone by the car now. A man in uniform. A chauffeur.'

Mrs Knight frowned. 'Cam wouldn't bother with a chauffeur,' she said. 'He likes to drive himself. What does he look like?'

Cautious, Rita looked again. 'Older man. Bald. Glasses. Got a bit of a paunch but very tall – like a bean pole.'

Mrs Knight joined her. 'That's Finnegan,' she cried. 'He's my father's chauffeur.' She began walking quickly towards the cottage but soon broke into a run. Rita put Lucy on the end of the rickety pram and hurried after her.

Finnegan looked up as Mrs Knight came towards him and shouted out, 'Sir, sir, she here.'

A small white-haired man appeared from the gate and froze. Then, calling out her name, the man opened his arms and Mrs Knight ran to him. As they hugged and the old man wept, Rita slowed down to give them a minute to themselves. Finnegan tactfully bent around the opposite side of the car as if to examine one of the tyres, and a second later, a woman came into the lane. Now all three of them were hugging each other, laughing and crying.

Lucy looked up at Rita with a bewildered expression. 'Those people are your mummy's mummy and daddy,' she said. 'Your granddad and grandma.'

Although she'd never met them and hadn't for that matter even seen a picture of them, Rita hoped what she was saying was right. Judging by the heartfelt and tearful reunion, they had to be somebody special. All at once the woman saw Rita and the children and broke free. As she strode towards them, Lucy went behind Rita's skirts.

The woman stopped and smiled. 'You must be Lucy,' she said. 'We've heard so much about you.'

Rita glanced down at Lucy then back at Mrs Knight's mother. 'She's just a bit shy, that's all.'

By now, Mrs Knight, her arm around her father's waist, was coming back. As they reached the children, Mrs Knight bent to pick Lucy up.

'Lucy, darling, this is your granny and granddad.' The child turned her head away shyly as they all started back towards the cottage. Rita followed with the pram. As they reached the car,

Rita heard Mrs Knight saying to Lucy, 'Granny and Granddad are Daniel's Granny and Granddad, too. Can we show them your baby brother?'

Lucy nodded gravely and Mrs Knight put her down. She and Lucy came up to the pram and after a signal to her mother, she said, 'Would you like to tell Granny and Granddad your brother's name?'

Lucy looked over the edge of the pram. 'He's called Daniel,' she said, 'and I'm his big sister.'

Mrs Knight's mother bent to Lucy's level and peered over the side. Daniel gave Lucy a gummy smile. 'Oh Lucy,' said her granny. 'He's lovely.'

'He's my brother,' Lucy told her proudly.

'Mummy tells me you help Rita to look after him,' she said.

Lucy nodded and as her grandfather came up to admire the baby, Lucy slipped her hand in her granny's. Above her head, Mrs Knight and Rita exchanged an emotional smile.

—

Mrs Knight's parents and their chauffeur had arrived earlier that afternoon. Having knocked the door to no avail, they were about to leave when Eddie and Win arrived back home. Of course, they had no idea Rita, Mrs Knight and the children were staying in the cottage but as soon as she saw the nappies blowing on the line and opened the door to find Rita's case and things in the house, the four of them worked out that they must all be on the beach. Win, hospitable as ever, offered everyone tea and wedding cake in her new home. Finnegan had just been sent to the car to bring his lordship's reading glasses so that he could look at the wedding cards and that's when he'd spotted Mrs Knight coming up the lane.

Rita suggested the family go into Guinevere Cottage to talk things over. Finnegan was happy to take a walk to the sea with Eddie while she stayed with her grandmother.

'Did you know he was a lord?' Gran asked.

Rita shook her head.

'Lord Brockenhurst no less,' said Gran. 'Apparently one of the oldest landed gentry in the country. Lives in... oh, what d'you call it? Trafford Hall.'

Rita stood and curtsied. 'And you entertained him in your cottage,' she teased.

Gran gave her a playful push. 'Anyway, what have you been up to? Why are you all here?'

Over the inevitable cup of tea, Rita brought her gran up to speed.

'You should have told me last week,' Gran complained when she'd finished.

'You wouldn't have enjoyed your honeymoon if you'd been worrying about me,' said Rita.

'So what happens to you now?'

Rita shrugged. 'I'm out of a job because she's got no money and I've told the police about the pills Cameron gave Lucy.'

'What's wrong with that?' Gran wanted to know.

Rita told her about the non-disclosure document she'd signed.

Gran squeezed her hand. 'You've done the right thing,' she said firmly. 'If you'd kept quiet, that little girl's life would have been in danger.'

Rita nodded. All at once she felt teary. Her grandmother walked around the table and putting her arm around Rita's shoulder, crushed her to her bosom. For the first time since her mother died, Rita wept and wept. It was probably relief, but for too long she'd been juggling with circumstances and trying to do the right thing for the children – now, someone else could deal with the problem. She had no idea what would happen to Lucy and Daniel but it seemed that Mrs Knight was reconciled to her family and most likely, as they had come down to Worthing in such a hurry, they would offer them a home.

Her cuddle with Gran was interrupted as Eddie came back with Finnegan. They had enjoyed a long walk along the seafront as far as George V Avenue. Gran set about getting some tea and Rita helped her.

—

Sometime later, there was a knock on Eddie's door. When her grandmother opened it, Mrs Knight's father stood on the doorstep. Win invited him in and he asked to speak to Rita. Gran and Eddie made themselves scarce and Rita sat facing the old man.

He began by thanking her for all that she had done and then he offered her a position. 'I'm taking my daughter and her children back to Yorkshire. She will make her home with us until her divorce is finalised after which she can make her own decision as to whether she stays or goes.'

Rita could tell by the way he spoke that Mrs Knight had obviously taken up his offer of protection and a home but reserved her right to move on when she felt safe.

'The point is,' Lord Brockenhurst continued, 'we should very much like you to continue to look after the children for a while. Mrs Knight thinks a lot of you and we all feel that having you around would help the children, particularly Lucy, to settle down.'

Rita chewed the side of her mouth. 'I'm not sure if you realise, sir, that Mrs Knight had to sell all her jewellery to pay Mrs Fordham, Sally and my wages.'

'I know,' he said. 'You will be employed by me.'

Again, Rita hesitated. 'I may be in trouble with the law, sir.'

He sat back in his chair and frowned. 'How so?'

Taking a deep breath, Rita told him about the non-disclosure agreement and the fact that she'd told the police about the diazepam and the unknown substance on the sugar knob meant for Mrs Knight which was being tested.

'Is that it?'

Rita looked down at her hands and nodded miserably.

Lord Brockenhurst leaned forward and smiled. 'My dear, that agreement becomes null and void if the law has been broken, and in this case, it most assuredly has. Cameron Knight will be charged with giving a dangerous drug to a minor with intent to harm. That little minx of his will be charged with unlawful possession of drugs and attempting to administer a substance to a person without her knowledge.'

'Do you think there will be enough evidence?'

'Assuredly – with your testimony and the others.'

A wave of relief hit Rita. 'So, I won't have to go to the police?'

'Only to give your statement,' he said. He patted her hands. 'Without your quick action my dear, we could have been talking about murder.'

Rita looked up with red rimmed eyes and gave him a wobbly smile.

'So,' he went on, 'what's it to be?'

'My father has invited me to go to America for Thanksgiving,' she said.

'Right,' he boomed. 'That's the end of November, isn't it? Can you give us until then?'

Rita smiled. 'Yes, I think I could.'

311

Chapter 41

'The Hippopotamus Song'

Flanders and Swann

It had taken virtually all day to get to Yorkshire and everyone was feeling jaded, but as soon as the car slid onto the long driveway leading to Trafford Hall, Rita was transfixed. The manicured landscape was beauty itself with what seemed like miles of English oaks, Beech trees and mature Limes dotted within the lush green grassland. The deer lifted their heads as the Rolls-Royce glided passed them and here and there a rabbit bolted for its burrow. Lucy stood with her nose pressed against the window as her mother pointed out pheasants hurrying across the road, sometimes stupidly endangering their own lives in an effort to get away. Rita was imagining some Regency lord and lady traveling this very route in their carriage. It was like stepping back in time.

Trafford Hall itself had to be seen to be believed. As it burst out in front of them, Rita took in a breath. A large castle-like mansion built in pale stone, its windows glistened in the early evening sun as it faded. Mrs Knight had told her the house had a fascinating history, its predecessors entertaining royalty such as Henry VIII and some three hundred years later, Queen Victoria. Below stairs, in its dungeons – now a wine cellar – it also had been the resting place for ne'er-do-wells on their way to the gallows or, in some cases, transportation for what in this day and age would seem to be minor misdemeanours.

Several servants greeted them when they walked into the great hall and before she could gather her wits, Rita's case was whisked off to her room.

Mrs Knight went with Lord and Lady Brockenhurst into their sitting room where they were served refreshments while a maid escorted Rita and the children to the nursery rooms. As she walked into the children's bedroom, Rita guessed that their mother had once occupied this space. Although scrupulously clean, it was a tad old-fashioned but there was a cot, a small divan bed and behind a screen, an adult-size bed. Rita laid Daniel in the cot and turned to Lucy first. There were some toys in a large box but Lucy was very sleepy and too tired to take much notice, so Rita asked the maid if she could have some milk and biscuits before she set about getting her charge ready for bed. After a quick bath and Rita's fumble through the case for her nightie, Lucy managed to drink half a glass of milk before she crawled into bed. For a moment or two she lay there watching Rita seeing to her brother but within minutes she was fast asleep. Daniel needed his nappy changed and then, having found a tiny milk kitchen next door, Rita boiled up some water, made up his formula and gave him his bottle early. When she laid him in the cot, he wasn't far behind his sister in falling asleep.

Rita had thought she was to sleep on the divan behind the screen but then she found her suitcase on the bed in an adjoining room. Rita unpacked a few things and had a wash. Hungry but mostly exhausted by the strain of their drive, she couldn't wait to crawl into her own bed, but when Rita came back into the room, she discovered a tray with a pot of tea, some sandwiches and some home-made cake on a small table. Sitting in the comfortable chair, Rita ate a sandwich and poured herself some tea.

There was a light tap on the door and Mrs Knight walked in.

'Are they looking after you, Rita?'

'Yes, thank you,' Rita said putting down her sandwich and rising to her feet.

'No, no, don't get up,' said Mrs Knight. 'I came to say dinner is at eight.'

'Thank you, ma'am,' said Rita, 'but this will be enough for me. It's kind of you to offer but quite frankly, I'm too tired to do anything else. I'd prefer to have an early night.'

'So do I,' her employer chuckled. She looked around. 'The children?'

'Fast asleep.'

After going into her old nursery, Mrs Knight kissed her sleeping children and left her to it.

As she climbed into her bed, Rita wondered what lay ahead of her now. Being in private certainly brought its surprises, and living in a stately home was one experience she would never have dreamt would happen to her, not even in her wildest dreams.

—

It took Rita several days to discover all the rooms in the house. She made a bit of a game of it with Lucy, hiding behind tall chairs or behind the huge drapes at the windows as they progressed. The house was well-furnished and cared for and the family rooms were beautifully and tastefully decorated. From the front door, she walked through the wide hallway with its huge fireplace guarded by two massive stone dogs. A large Chesterfield sofa faced the hearth. A door led to a corridor and a suite of rooms; a sitting room, writing room, library and finally a sunroom with an Edwardian conservatory leading out into the garden. On the opposite side of the hall, she found other rooms which, although they were clean and tidy, were not in frequent use. A curved stairway took her to the rooms above. She and the children were on one side of the balustrade while Mrs Knight and Lord and Lady Brockenhurst were on the other. At the top of the stairs a massive chandelier dominated the whole place. Outside, the gardens were just as sumptuous. An orangery on the south side of the hall, kitchen gardens and rolling lawns completed the picture.

It didn't take long for the children to thrive and be happy. Rita played with Lucy in the vast grounds, organised picnics (pretend and real) or socialised with other local families who called in at Mrs Knight's behest. As for Mrs Knight herself, they'd only been in the Hall for a week before she looked so much better. Gone were the dark circles under her eyes and the vacant looks. Her bruises had faded from blue to green then they vanished. Her hair, once lank and dull, became glossy and well-groomed. Before long she was meeting old friends and going on shopping trips for a brand-new wardrobe.

Rita had been in Trafford Hall for eight days when the postman brought a letter from her grandmother. It wasn't very newsy, but it was obvious that she and Eddie had settled happily into married life. The envelope contained a letter which had been addressed to Guinevere Cottage. When Rita opened it, she realised that Nat had written as he'd promised. He was enjoying the warm South African sun and was about to begin the round trip back the docklands and Canary Warf.

> *This time the ship is having a quick turn-around, so after a couple of days in London I shall be on my way back to South Africa. When I get back to England at the end of October, I have a couple of weeks leave. If you're around, perhaps we could meet up again, maybe do a show or go to the pictures? Arriving October 16.*

Funny, she hadn't thought of Nat for years until he'd come to mind when she was putting flowers on mum's grave all those months ago. Then she'd bumped into him at Gran's wedding and now the thought of seeing him again gave her a warm glow. Nat and a show... As soon as she could, she searched Lord Brockenhurst's old copy of *The Times*. Nothing much took her fancy until she saw that Flanders and Swann were coming to the

Globe Theatre with their show *At the Drop of Another Hat* the day before he arrived. Flanders was in a wheelchair, a victim it was said of polio, and Swann played the piano. Rita loved their humorous songs and the one about the hippopotamus was a particular favourite. Unable to pop to the Globe in person for obvious reasons, she asked Mrs Knight how she could get tickets and to her absolute delight, a couple of days later, Lord Brockenhurst himself gave her two tickets for October 19 using his personal box stating, 'Take the week off, Rita. You deserve it.'

The first thing Rita did was to write to Jenny and ask if she could put her up for the week. When Jenny's reply came back, Rita couldn't wait to tell Nat. She wrote to him straightaway but just in case he would be at sea and unable to get her letter, she also sent a telegram.

> Tickets for Flanders and Swann Stop October 19
> 7.30 Stop The Globe Theatre Stop See you there
> Stop Rita

Dexter had kept in touch, too. He sent his letters to Guinevere Cottage and Gran forwarded them on. Rita replied and, having accepted his invitation to visit him and his new family, she made plans to go to America. However, when she discovered that the plane fare was an eye-watering £107/3/5 it was obvious it was going to take her a while to save up for it. Rita was determined not to ask her father for money so she explained in her letter that it would have to wait at least until next year. Something in her psyche made her want to pay her own way.

The staff in the Hall were very nice. The night she'd arrived, Rita felt as if there were loads of them, but there were just two maids, Mrs Possit the housekeeper and Cook. Outside there were two gardeners to keep the grounds looking good. They were friendly enough but there was little time for socialising during the day, and they went home at night.

Rita hadn't seen Cameron since that last day but she'd read in the paper that he'd been found guilty of possession of drugs and common assault involving a neighbour. After a brief prison sentence, he'd launched an attempt to get custody of his son which put Mrs Knight in panic mode for a while. However, Lord Brockenhurst took charge and got some high-powered solicitor to handle the case who reassured her that everything would be all right. And it was. Apparently, someone sent her husband something to calm his nerves and when the case came to court, Cameron was so high on drugs he couldn't even remember the boy's name. Because he kept calling the baby Lionel, the judge deemed him an unsuitable parent. Everyone at the Hall was visibly relieved but it did cross Rita's mind to wonder who could have given him the 'medication' in the first place, but she thought it better not to ask. As for Tammy-Jane, what became of her, Rita had no idea.

At the beginning of September, Lucy went to the small village school. Mrs Knight and Rita took her the first day, but after that, it was Rita's job. She was given the use of a car and her days settled into a new routine. Lucy loved school and before long had made a firm friend in Suzanna Morton-Burke, the daughter of the Master of the Hunt and an old friend of her grandfather. Suzanna's mother suggested that Lucy enrolled in her ballet class and the two friends joined a Brownie pack as well.

As for Daniel, he was crawling and Rita had to have eyes in the back of her head once he was on the loose. He moved like a rocket!

Lucy was an adorable child. Funny, articulate and very loving towards her baby brother, Rita's days were busy and sometimes tiring, but never dull. Lucy was also curious about life as well. One evening after her bath, Rita was drying her in a luxuriously fluffy white towel. As she put it down and picked up Lucy's nightdress to put it on, her charge stared at her reflection in the long mirror.

'When I grow up,' she said sagely, 'I shall have boobies like mummy.'

'I'm sure you will,' said Rita.

Lucy poked one nipple then the other before adding with a puzzled frown, 'I wonder which one will grow first.'

Chapter 42

'Ticket To Ride'
The Beatles

By the time October came along, Rita couldn't wait to see Jenny and Nat. At long last she had the whole week off and planned to travel down south by train. Jenny had invited her to stay at her place and would be waiting to meet her when she arrived at King's Cross. Rita was looking forward to a long natter and plenty of girly time with her old friend. Best of all, she had arranged to see Nat again. He would be coming over on Saturday, and his suggestion of a wander through Hyde Park, a meal at a proper restaurant followed by Flanders and Swann at the Globe Theatre had all the promise of a very special time.

Rita loved Yorkshire but as time went on she was becoming more unsettled. When she'd first arrived, its peace and quiet and its people were just what she had needed to make her feel whole again. The gardener had told her there was an old bike in his shed, so having spruced it up a bit, she spent her days off biking in the countryside and exploring the villages and hamlets. While the weather was good, she enjoyed herself immensely but as time went on, and the season changed she had to spend more time indoors and it felt as if something was missing... something just out of reach... something she couldn't quite put her finger on. Her employers were kindness itself and seeing Mrs Knight and the children beginning to enjoy their lives together was worth its weight in gold. Lucy was relaxed and happy. She and Daniel absolutely adored one another and even though Mrs Knight had a wide circle of friends, she always had time to play a game of hide and seek or to read them a story. The whole family had a great deal of respect for Rita and the story of how she had rescued them was told over and over again.

'It wasn't just me,' Rita would protest but nobody believed that. She had become more than just the nanny. In fact Rita was included in everything as if she was part of the family.

All the same, Rita had looked forward to this break but by the time the train was pulling into King's Cross station, she was feeling a tad nervous. London, with its crowded streets and noisy traffic was so different from the quiet solitude of Yorkshire where all too often all she could hear was the bleating of sheep. Would she be able to cope with the change?

When she opened the carriage door, it was all there and she felt a rush of excitement. Everything from the woolly announcements from the Tannoy, the sound of slamming carriage doors, the railway staff at the gate calling out, 'Tickets please', the smell of diesel, the thunderous roar of the few steam engines which were still around, the pong by the overflowing litter bin mixed in with the aroma of hot sausage rolls from a stall she was walking passed, the dust and the shabbiness it all made Rita spirit soared. Now she knew why she had been so restless. She'd missed the hustle and bustle of London. She missed the bright lights. She missed her friends and the WEN coffee mornings. This was where she belonged. The place where she could put down roots.

Then she heard someone calling her name. 'Rita, Rita! Over here!' And there was Jenny, waving like mad. Rita took a deep breath. She'd arrived. She was home at last in wonderful, wonderful London.

A Letter from Pam

Dear Reader,

Once again in creating this story I have been reminded of so many of the children I once looked after. I hasten to add that the story you have just read is just a story but it crosses my mind to wonder what became of the babies and under-fives who were once in my care. I had the pleasure of living in some beautiful surroundings and occasionally meeting the rich and famous, but it was hard work with long hours and tons of 'would-you-just-jobs'. 'Oh Nanny, while you're there, would you just iron that basket of laundry which has been there so long it's a mile high…, and while you're doing that would you just…' Well, you get the picture!

I hope that within the pages of this book, dear reader, you have found laughter and, yes, a few tears. If you have enjoyed it, I would love to hear your comments.

As for me? Onwards and upwards to write the next in the series of West End Nannies.

Pam

Acknowledgements

Once again my heartfelt thanks goes to Jennie Ayres, the commissioning editor of Hera Books, and the team and to my agent Megan Carroll of Watson Little without whom this book would still be on the computer!